Nov. 12, 2012

To Gail,

Best Wishes

Praise for *Hitler's Priest*

"*Hitler's Priest*, a captivating novel, offers its readers more than an eye-opening and potent story: this book contains profound observations and unforgettable life lessons. Thank you, S. J. Tagliareni, for giving us this important novel."

—ARTHUR KURZWEIL
American author, educator, editor, writer, publisher, and illusionist

"*Hitler's Priest* is a stunning novel with many fascinating twists and turns."

—JOSEPH J. PITTELLI, MD
Former executive VP, Wyeth Pharmaceutical

"A gripping story of treachery, heroism, and life-altering choices."

—AARON T. BECK, MD
Institute for Cognitive Therapy

"A powerful read that will stay with you long after you finish it."

—SUSAN SHERMAN
President and CEO, Independence Foundation

"This is a real page-turner. From the gritty coal mines of Pennsylvania to the majestic fountains of Rome, Dr. Tagliareni weaves a story that combines his insider knowledge of the Vatican with his instinct for love, family, and morality to give us insight into the nightmare that was the Holocaust. Through the misery of some comes redemption for many. You won't forget this story."

—GEORGIA MURRAY
CEO, MMI Investments

"Tagliareni has given life to the monsters and the heroes in this astounding story."

—**ROBERT AND PATRICIA GUSSIN**
Author of *Trash Talk*
Author of *And Then There Was One*

"Extraordinary and powerful. A must-read."

—**RABBI CHARLES A. KROLOFF**
VP for special projects, Hebrew Union College

"A brilliant portrayal of the Catholic Church's struggles during World War II."

—**LINDA HAHN**
Executive director, Metropolitan Career Center

"There's forty years of friendship between us. This novel is so worth the wait! *Fantastico!*"

—**BO GLOSTER, MD**
Swedish Hospital Medical Center, Seattle

"From his priesthood and academic experiences, to his personal relationship with Holocaust survivor Viktor Frankl, Sal's writing of *Hitler's Priest* calls forth a strong emotional response that continues throughout a very powerful read."

—**DENNIS K. MCCORMACK, PHD**
Former US Navy SEAL, expert in leadership
training with the US Army, and studied with Viktor Frankl

Hitler's Priest

S. J. TAGLIARENI

Brown Books Publishing Group
Dallas, Texas

Hitler's Priest

Brown Books Publishing Group
16250 Knoll Trail Drive, Suite 205
Dallas, Texas 75248
www.BrownBooks.com
(972) 381-0009

A New Era in Publishing™

ISBN 978-1-61254-055-9
Library of Congress Control Number 2012932553

Printing in the United States
10 9 8 7 6 5 4 3 2 1

For more information or to contact the author,
please go to: www.HitlersPriest.com.

This novel is dedicated to:

Stefano and Severio Pittelli, whose courage changed lives on both sides of the Atlantic

Dr. Viktor Frankl, my friend and mentor, who altered my life through his wisdom and guidance

Rabbi Sanford Hahn, who taught me the beauty of finding ways to reach out to those who are marginalized by society

Rabbi Charles Kroloff, who imbued me with the spirit to speak out against war and to dialogue with those who are different

Judy Cohen, my guide and friend, who taught me to revere the process of writing this book

Acknowledgments

I am grateful to friends and family who supported me in the writing of this book. I would particularly like to thank Joseph Pittelli for sharing the history of the Pittelli family and for his constant encouragement. I wish also to thank Evelyn Anderson, Lisa Contini, Mark Maloney, Maryvelma Smith O'Neil, Judy Quinn, Sarah Rosenberg, and Colleen Welsh for their invaluable insights and editorial suggestions.

Thanks to Milli Brown for her tireless leadership. To Nina Romberg for her marvelous ability to enhance the vitality of the plot and characters. To David Leach for his enthusiasm and support of my work. To Cathy Williams for her exceptional marketing strategies. To Cindy Birne for her outstanding publicity and exceptional ability to gather significant endorsements. To Jessica Burnham and Omar Mediano for their remarkable cover design and web page. To Rayven Williams for her superb organizational ability to keep the project focused. And to Jerry Coburn for his financial acumen and guidance.

Most of all, I would like to thank Elaine for her love and total support in this and every other adventure of the last thirty-eight years.

Chapter One

Calabria, 1916

A panorama of silver Calabrian pines rose a hundred meters above the sea with their branches extending out on both sides in distinctive wide, gnarled shapes. The lower slopes of the crystalline granite mountain were filled with oaks whose brown tinted leaves resembled lilies. Cascading olive groves with their rugged topography covered the mountainous terrain. The area was filled with vibrant flowers in colors as varied as pale pink delicately edged in crimson and pristine white with broad bands of purple.

The richness of this natural beauty masked the realities of hunger, illiteracy, and economic privation in the tiny village of Esca. Its few inhabitants were imprisoned by a deep poverty that was belied by the breathtaking views from their mud abodes.

In this impoverished village lived the Pittelli family. Despite the lack of a father figure, Stefano and Severio, sixteen and eleven, had matured far beyond their years. Stefano, the elder son, had assumed the responsibilities that his father had ignored. He despised his father's weakness and was proud that his mother had mustered the courage to remove him from their home. She could no longer tolerate his drinking and the ongoing shame of his carousing with other women.

Fortunately, Stefano had been able to spend time with his mother's first cousin Benjamin, a teacher in Soverato. Benjamin had taught Stefano to read and had opened his mind to the wonders of learning. He had always said that few—if any—of his students had the leadership instincts of Stefano. Benjamin had also told his cousins that he saw great promise in Stefano, but he worried that Stefano's abilities would be thwarted by the lack of educational opportunities.

Under the guidance of Benjamin and the local priest, Stefano had accepted responsibility for the economic survival of his mother, brother, and sister. Assuming the role of provider in an economically backward community would have been impossible for the average boy of sixteen, but Stefano was anything but average and always found ways to feed his hungry family.

The odd jobs available to Stefano were so limited that his initial plans centered on hunting in the neighboring woods. The only legacy that his father had left the family was two shotguns that could be used for killing wild boar. The area at the top of the mountain was filled with boar and other animals, and one large boar could provide food for up to a month.

Stefano had learned to hunt with Benjamin, and he believed that he could teach his younger brother Severio well enough to secure food. He practiced with Severio for days before their first attempt at hunting a wild boar.

As they climbed the rugged terrain early one morning, Severio revealed excitement about his new venture. He chatted incessantly and strutted with a young boy's bravado. Stefano smiled at the exuberance of his younger brother and mouthed a silent prayer that the hunt would be successful.

When they had walked deeply into the woods, Stefano scouted the area and selected a rocky ridge that overlooked a deep, verdant path where he had seen boar tracks. He climbed the rocky slope and helped up Severio. They lay down in the grass with a clear view of the opening in the dense brush. Dew covered the grass. Morning sunlight glistened on the silver pines. In the complete stillness, the brothers lay prostrate, barely breathing as they waited for their prey.

Stefano looked at the innocent face of his brother and felt a wave of sadness pass over him. The challenges of their future seemed almost overwhelming, but they couldn't give up. A rustle in the bushes broke his thoughts and he glanced at his brother. Severio's hands trembled as he aimed the shotgun at the place where the boar would most likely appear.

Stefano could tell that it was an extremely large animal from the loud growling and squealing sounds. He knew that it would require two shots to immobilize and kill it. He raised and aimed his shotgun with steady hands. Suddenly a shotgun blast rang in his ears even though the boar had not yet appeared.

He turned and saw his brother lying in a pool of blood with his left arm shattered. Despite his shock, Stefano immediately acted. He tore off his shirt and tied a tourniquet around what was left of his brother's arm. He could not fathom what had happened. Had Severio slipped on the wet grass? Had the gun misfired?

Severio was turning ashen from loss of blood. Stefano must hurry if he was to save his brother. He lifted his brother into his arms and then struggled down the mountain as fast as he could go. The terrain was difficult for one person. He fell to his knees, tearing his trousers and scraping his flesh. Yet he never let go of the limp form of his brother.

When Stefano finally reached home and entered the doorway, his mother fainted at the sight of her younger son. While his sister Calista helped his mother, Stefano gently laid Severio down on a straw bed. After his mother and sister brought ripped pieces of sheet boiled in water, he cleaned Severio's bloody wound. Although the shattered arm looked ghastly, he was determined to save his brother's life.

For days Stefano sat beside Severio's straw mattress. He changed the dressing frequently, applying heated olive oil, the only remedy he had to ward off infection. He blamed himself for the accident because he thought that he should have better prepared Severio in the use of a shotgun. His mother continuously reassured him that it was not his fault, but nothing she said could comfort him as he watched fever consume the body of his beloved brother. Without medical help, it appeared that Severio would die, but Stefano refused to accept this outcome. He changed the dressings every four hours without fail.

After three exhausting days and nights, Stefano could barely stay awake. When he heard Severio call his name in a weak voice, he was overjoyed. His brother's fever had broken. In some miraculous way, it appeared that Severio would live.

Yet the Pittelli family still faced other great challenges. They had no money, no source of income, and what little work existed was already taken by others in the village. A young boy with no trade, impaired for life with the use of only one arm, compounded the situation.

The family's plight fell directly on the shoulders of Stefano. He vowed he would find a way to save his family. For days he worked without respite, hunting for food and performing any menial chore that would bring small amounts of money. His mother and Calista tended a large garden, gathered wild fruit and nuts, and put much of it up for winter. Still, there were no long-term prospects for survival in the town of Esca.

The only feasible alternative was for Stefano to find work elsewhere and send money home. He knew that some of the townspeople had ventured to America with the hope of finding a new life. His cousin Benjamin had immigrated to America five years earlier and had written often, telling about his new life in a place called Kulpmont, Pennsylvania. He had become a teacher of Italian immigrant children. If Benjamin could send money, maybe Stefano could join him in America. He would hate to leave home, but he had strong resolve and a commitment to his family.

Benjamin was generous, sending money and inviting Stefano to join him in Pennsylvania. As quickly as possible, the Pittelli family prepared him to go. On his last night in Esca, his mother could only afford to cook a meager dinner. He felt pained that her last memory of him would be tainted by such paltry food. He knew she was devastated by the thought that she might never see him again. The family ate in silence; the only sound during the meal was that of the soup spoons clanking against the earthen dishes.

Finally Severio broke the silence, tears streaming down his face. "When I woke up, I was so weak and confused. I didn't know what had happened. Mother told me I would not be alive without your carrying me down the mountain. The first thing I remember was that I was so hot and you put a cool towel on my head. I will never forget all that you did for me."

Stefano felt his brother's words pierce his heart. He was filled with so many emotions that speech was impossible. He merely nodded to acknowledge Severio's gratitude.

After sharing family stories so he could better remember his loved ones on the far shores of another land, Stefano bade them good night and prepared for the future.

As dawn flickered through the house, Stefano gathered his few belongings and quietly slipped out the door. As he walked away from his home, he gazed at the familiar countryside. This small world was all he had known for his seventeen years. Now he was embarking on a trip that was totally outside the scope of his imagination. His only link to America was a cousin who lived in a strange-sounding place called Kulpmont. He tried to dismiss his anxiety as he began the steep trek down the mountain. The sun shone in all its brilliance and the temperature steadily rose to lift his spirits.

He descended, layer by layer, until he reached the road that ran parallel to the sea. The lapping waves caressing the empty white beaches created a magnificent early morning vista, but he paid little attention. He was gripped with the fear that his family could not sustain their marginal existence without him. He knew that his choice was the right one, but that did little to alleviate his pain and guilt.

As he walked the dusty road for six hours in the steaming hot sun, the sounds of the valley filled his ears. Parched from the heat, he stopped at a farm and requested a cup of water. The farmer pointed him to the well and went back to tending his sheep. He thanked the kind man and continued on his journey. The rest of his trip to the train station was without human contact.

Stefano bought a third-class train ticket to Naples, regretting that he had to part with the money. He found a bench in the shade where he could sit and wait. Hungry, thirsty, and tired, he held on to the hope that he had made the right choice. Nodding in and out of slumber, he was awakened by the sound of a whistle as a train made its way through the Calabrian countryside, spewing black smoke into the pure azure sky.

When he mounted the steps to the nearly full train, he found an empty place on the floor near the doorway. He learned that the train was packed with families bound for the docks of Naples where they hoped to gain steerage to the new world. The chatter of excitement and fear filled the compartment.

Swaying back and forth for hours, Stefano became aware that he was the only one on the train who was not part of a family. As the passengers spoke, he realized that most, if not all, were headed to strange-sounding places in America. He heard the names Boston, Chicago, and San Francisco. He wondered if any of these places were near Kulpmont. As the day waned, the scenic countryside gave way to more industrial settings and finally the train arrived at Naples.

Chaotic would be too mild a word to describe the scene that confronted the pilgrims on the docks of Naples. Thousands of humans pressed against each other as they attempted to gather the necessary information that would allow them to purchase tickets for the ocean voyage. The cacophony of language, sounds, and gestures added to a process that seemed to be without rhyme or reason.

Stefano saw an elderly woman struggling to carry her steamer trunk. Without hesitation, he assisted her. One of the steamship company employees noticed his kindness and motioned for Stefano and the woman to follow him. They arrived at the ticket office where they purchased steerage tickets on the *Giulio Caesare* steamship. With tickets in hand, they moved forward to the waiting area where an enormous ship was docked. Stefano marveled at the size in comparison to the tiny fishing boats back home.

After a series of checkpoints, Stefano walked up the gangplank and followed the masses to find a place in the bowels of the ship. The area became increasingly crowded. Once he had secured a cot, Stefano placed his tiny parcel down and wove his way back to the lower deck. After a seemingly endless number of people had entered, the gigantic ship's horn sounded and the seamen began taking off the mooring lines. The voyage was about to begin. Stefano gazed sadly on his homeland as the ship made its way out of the harbor to the open sea.

This initial part of the journey was calm and the waters were relatively mild, but that soon changed as the ship entered the rougher waters of the North Atlantic. Below deck, the trip was anything but smooth as the ship rolled up and down and side to side. This constant lurching caused many of the passengers to be seasick. After a short period of time, the entire steerage deck reeked of vomit. The stench, foul air, and cramped quarters made the voyage increasingly difficult, especially for children and the elderly. Stefano took every opportunity to go up to the steerage deck where at least the air was cleaner than below.

The days of rolling seas and the smell of vomit and human waste became a blur for Stefano as he wandered around the deck, peering at the limitless ocean. The faces of his family, now miles away, steeled his resolve that no matter what, he would meet the challenges of the new land.

After fourteen days at sea, he was lost in thought as he walked the deck. The morning fog lifted and the ship slowed to a crawl. He heard shouts in Italian that sounded like *"Liberta!"* and *"Gigante!"* As he moved toward the shouts, he saw in the distance a massive green statue of a woman holding a torch extended to the skies. Someone cried out that this was the Statue of Liberty. He stared in wonder as some of his fellow passengers wept. This statue was the symbol of the hope that had brought them to this new land. He would find a way to save his loved ones.

The voyage across the Atlantic had debilitated most of the passengers. Stefano felt better than most, but he still hoped this next part of the journey would be swift and soon he would be with Benjamin.

He gathered his few belongings and joined the masses that were slowly exiting the ship. In the water next to the ship was a series of barges that were filling up with passengers. He was overwhelmed by the size of the buildings in New York City. For a moment he wished his family could see this wondrous sight as he descended into one of the waiting barges. There was a babbling sea of humanity being fed into a tiny area with a cacophony of various languages trying to make sense of the process. He heard some Italian phrases but could not identify the other tongues.

Once the barge was filled with people, there was an air of anticipation. Soon they would meet their waiting loved ones on the shore. This hope quickly vanished as they spent hours in the rocking barge. High walls made it impossible to see outside. There were sounds of regurgitation and children crying. The claustrophobic setting caused panic among the passengers. No one had food or water. Stefano shivered with cold, wearing only a thin wool jacket that would suffice for a Calabrian night but was no match for the blustery port of New York.

After what seemed an eternity to Stefano, the barge began to move slowly. The trip was short, but the arrival presented new challenges. They disembarked onto what appeared to be an island, where they were greeted with a series of confusing shouts and herded into waiting lines by men wearing police uniforms. This did not scare Stefano, but it appeared that many others had come from places where the sight of a police uniform was frightening.

Once inside the massive building, the immigrants were ordered to place their belongings in a small baggage area where the items were tagged and numbered. The next step was to ascend a staircase that led to a massive room. On the stairs, men who appeared to be doctors were examining people. Some had a chalk mark placed on their clothing. Stefano was not marked. He had no idea whether this was a good or a bad sign. The noise in the room made it virtually impossible to hear, and he could feel the enormous level of anxiety.

Frightened people tried to adhere to the commands of the officers. Fortunately some of the officials spoke their languages. Stefano was examined a second time by a doctor and again did not receive a chalk mark. After a series of stops, a policeman who spoke Italian examined his papers. Finding them in order, he told Stefano that he must buy a ticket to the ferry station to Jersey City, where he was to be met by his cousin.

The ride to Jersey City was brief. As Stefano left the ferry in search of Benjamin, he felt excited. Finally, he was in the new land and ready to build a new life to help his family. He walked briskly to the waiting area, where he saw a familiar face carrying a sign that read "*Benvenuto* Stefano."

Although he had not seen him for years, Stefano immediately recognized Benjamin from the photograph his cousin had recently sent. He embraced his cousin and was thrilled to be able to speak freely in his native tongue. Usually a young man of few words, Stefano spoke nonstop to his smiling cousin.

Darkness was beginning to shroud the city as they walked to the area where Benjamin had parked an automobile. Stefano had heard about automobiles, but he had never actually seen one, let alone been a passenger in one. His cousin must have done well, indeed, if he could afford to own a vehicle. He watched as Benjamin expertly used the crank to start the engine.

Once inside, he settled onto the luxurious seat and watched through the windows as Benjamin drove away. Stefano was fascinated by the size of the buildings and the endless array of gas street lanterns. There was a glow to this new land that was so different from Esca. He wondered if Kulpmont would be like New York and Jersey City. As they continued on their trip, Stefano battled the urge to sleep, but finally exhaustion sent him into a deep slumber.

He had no idea how long he had slept when he awoke to the gentle voice of Benjamin, asking if he would like to have some breakfast and explaining that Kulpmont was still hours away and a rest stop would be beneficial to both of them. Stefano was astonished when he saw the huge portions of food that were served in the restaurant. A morning meal in Esca would be a little milk and a piece of bread.

After the breakfast stop Stefano noticed that the terrain had changed from an urban to an agricultural setting. In a small way the hills of Pennsylvania reminded him of Calabria, but the verdant green soon gave way to mountains surrounded by massive clouds of gray and black smoke. In front of these bleak hills was a series of low shabby buildings.

This was Stefano's first view of Kulpmont, a mining town in the industrial center of coal country. He silently took in all the surroundings as Benjamin informed him that he had arranged lodging in a local boarding house. Stefano had gone from a poverty-laced village with beauty to a soot-covered place of little beauty.

They arrived at a dilapidated boarding house with broken shutters and a sagging porch. Benjamin took him inside and introduced him to the landlady. She showed him to his room, a tiny cubicle in the attic with a narrow bed and a small bureau. The lavatory was one floor down and shared by six people. It was not much by some standards, but to Stefano it was a new, wonderful beginning. He would be eternally grateful to his cousin for all his acts of generosity.

As he walked Benjamin to his automobile, he thanked his cousin and inquired about employment. Benjamin explained that in the morning he would be taken to the coal mine and—he hoped—immediately hired. A thousand questions reverberated in Stefano's mind, but he decided that he would wait until he actually experienced the work of a coal miner.

Stefano spent a restless night and finally rose at about five in the morning. The house was quiet for another hour and then he heard the sounds of people preparing to have breakfast before work. He went downstairs and joined them for coffee and bread at a long table. The other residents were somewhat reserved, but one man who heard him speak recognized he was Italian and offered to take him to the mining office.

Stefano was led to the main office, where he was introduced to the head foreman. The man motioned for Stefano to follow him to the outside, where it looked like Calabria after an earthquake. There were huge mounds of black rubble and stones that seemed to reach to the heavens. The sky was black with smoke and everyone but the foreman appeared to be covered in soot and dirt. The foreman called over one of the miners to serve as interpreter. He told Stefano that he would begin the next day as a laborer in the mine.

Stefano knew what a laborer did in a farm community, but he had no idea what it meant in a coal mine. It didn't matter. He had quickly found work.

He left and walked up the hill, feeling a compelling urge to communicate with his loved ones. Before ascending the steps to the attic, he requested ink from his landlady. She graciously went into the parlor, opened a desk, and gave him a tiny inkwell.

In his small attic room, he sat on the bed, took out a pen from his satchel, and composed a letter home. He glossed over the hardships of the journey and reassured his loved ones that he would now be able to help them financially. He also repeated his counsel that Severio begin his education and stressed the fact that no matter what the cost he would find a way to finance it. As he finished the letter he felt a certain sense of accomplishment.

Early the next morning Stefano heard rain splattering against the roof and window. He was anxious to begin his new job, so he quickly went downstairs. He drank a cup of coffee and followed the miners to the office where he had been yesterday. He could not ignore the smells and dirty atmosphere of the area that seemed to cover persons and objects alike with heavy soot.

As he waited for the foreman, he noticed groups of men being lowered into the earth via some kind of basket. A man with an accent that was foreign to Stefano spoke a few words in Italian and motioned for him to follow. They went into a corridor where he took Stefano's passport and copied down the name and number. He placed a card with Stefano's name into a machine that had a clock above it. One of the other miners who spoke Italian explained that this clock measured the number of hours he would work.

Once this ritual was completed, the foreman grabbed Stefano by the arm and led him outside to the basket. With a group of others he was lowered beneath the surface of the earth. As the basket moved downward, the light from outside disappeared and was replaced with an orange glow that came from torches placed in the walls of the cave. The atmosphere seemed almost churchlike in spite of the deafening noise and foul-smelling air. Stefano had heard about the catacombs in ancient times and thought this place seemed similar.

When the basket reached the bottom, the men scattered to different areas. Stefano was led to a place where, through a series of motions, a man informed him that he was to take coal and load it into the huge bins in back of the mules until they were full. He would then push them toward the end of the mine.

Stefano could barely stand up straight because of the low ceilings. He was immediately aware of the falling rocks and creaking beams that were holding up those ceilings. Miners were using picks to free the coal. He found it difficult to breathe, often coughing, and placed a handkerchief around his neck and over his mouth. The only time he rested was at lunchtime. One of the other miners generously shared a sandwich and coffee with him. Stefano wanted to make a good impression so he worked feverishly for the rest of the day. Hour after hour he shoveled coal and pushed the carts to their exit places.

When the whistle that signaled the end of the day blew, he hardly had enough strength to make it to the basket that would take him back to the surface. Exhausted and dehydrated from the back-breaking work, he barely made it back up the hill. Upon arriving at the boarding house, he clung to the banister and slowly made his way to the attic. He opened the door to his room and collapsed into a coma-like sleep. The next sound he heard was the miners getting ready for work the next morning.

In a semi-trance he fumbled for his clothes. Half-dressed, he descended the stairs, gulped a mouthful of black coffee, and joined the parade of miners who were coming out of other boarding houses and company cottages on their way to the mine.

Stefano followed in their wake, now a grunt laborer far below the earth's surface in an industry that was sure to siphon almost every ounce of energy he possessed should he survive rock slides, cave-ins, explosions, and sheer exhaustion. Yet nothing could shake his commitment to his family in Calabria.

After two years, it became apparent to fellow miners and management that Stefano was not a run-of-the-mill employee. He had worked hard and done everything possible to improve his lot. After countless hours of nighttime solitary study, he could speak English fluently and could read and write in English. His facility for language and his leadership traits made him a magnet for other workers who sought his counsel. He would often write letters in Italian for those wishing to communicate with relatives back home. He was fast making a positive impression on his community as he found and strengthened the ideals that would mark every step of his life.

Chapter Two

Calabria, 1917

Walking barefoot down the slope, Severio barely noticed the sun rising over the Calabrian Mountains. He had wandered through the forest on countless occasions and had scaled down the many ledges that led to the main road, but today was different. This new venture that he had promised Stefano he would pursue filled him with trepidation.

His brother had given up much of his life in order to support his family in Italy, so they listened to his advice. Stefano insisted that despite Severio's age and lack of schooling, he must educate himself and secure a position where he would become a productive member of the community. The hardest part of this commitment was that Severio would have to begin at the beginning and would be with children much younger than he was. The fact that he had only one arm made the situation worse in his mind. If he had not promised Stefano, he would not be going to school.

As Severio reached the road, he was no more than ten minutes from the tiny schoolhouse. He had the urge to put the task off for another day, but he could almost hear the words of his brother pressing him to go on. When he arrived at the front door, he gently knocked, hoping that no one would hear, but a female voice said, "Come in."

As he entered the room, the children were reciting lessons in unison. They became silent at the sight of him, a tall, one-armed young boy without shoes. He paused uncertainly in the doorway.

The teacher stood at the back of the room. She smiled, nodding in encouragement. "I'm Mrs. Muffaletto. Who do we have here?"

Severio could barely breathe, but managed to utter, "I'm Severio Pittelli."

"Welcome to class." Mrs. Muffaletto turned to the other children in the room. "Greet your new classmate."

Severio listened to their greetings, but he still felt very awkward and anxious. Mrs. Muffaletto kindly ushered him to a seat at the back of the room in an attempt to put him at ease. He appreciated her help.

Initially all of the lessons were baffling for Severio because the only foundation he had was the informal teaching provided by Stefano. Sometimes the concepts all blended together. On numerous occasions he toyed with the idea of quitting school, but the commitment to his brother sustained him as he struggled with his studies.

After weeks of failure, it happened. A light bulb went on and the cloud of difficulty evaporated. He realized that Mrs. Muffaletto, who must have thought that she had inherited a child with multiple handicaps, now understood that he had more intellectual capability than either of them had guessed. He felt relieved that he wouldn't disappoint his brother.

Severio quickly grasped complex issues in all subjects. At the end of the second semester, he was the premier reader in the entire school. Not only was he intellectually gifted, he showed compassion and sensitivity far beyond his years. Coupled with all this he was a marvelous storyteller and would often be asked to tell the story of his accident, despite—or perhaps because of—the gory details, which he sometimes embellished to the delight of his listeners. He became a constant source of enjoyment for his fellow students.

One afternoon after school, Severio asked Mrs. Muffaletto what profession she thought he should pursue. She explained that he would succeed in any profession because he was a marvelous listener and easily able to make others feel special. He could be a lawyer, a teacher, or a doctor. He could even become a politician, but he was too forthright and honest for that job.

Severio mastered elementary classes in record time. With Mrs. Muffaletto's guidance, he received a full scholarship to attend the Catholic gymnasium at nearby Fortunato. In the course of his studies, he became fascinated with history and how leaders influenced the course of human events. His small village horizon was expanding into a fuller understanding of Italian culture.

As he grew in size, he also grew in stature in the eyes of the faculty and his fellow students. Perhaps it was his humility or his courage that led him to overcome his initial difficulties. Whatever it was, Severio was a born leader. Father Gregorio, the headmaster, once quipped that the students trusted Severio far more than they trusted him or anyone on the faculty. He also once ventured to say that he hoped his prize pupil would seriously entertain thoughts of becoming a priest. Severio had enormous respect for the clergy, but he gravitated to law, wishing to be part of the profession that implemented the ideal of justice for all, rich and poor alike. Also, celibacy was not an option because of his burgeoning interest in the opposite sex.

Chapter Three

Berlin, 1932

As Josef Goebbels undressed and prepared to enter his bedroom, he thought about the idea that he had come a long way from his childhood days in the Rhineland.

As a boy he had been the homely runt of the litter. This fact had been compounded by a club foot, making one leg three inches shorter than the other. Socially shy and overtly clumsy, he had been jealous of his peers, especially if tall and handsome. Josef had felt inferior in many ways and that had led to a constant internal struggle with self-esteem.

Despite his physical limitations, he had been an industrious student who had excelled at math and physics. Unable to participate in sports, he had spent most of his time reading and writing poetry. His parents, who were devout Catholics, had recognized his exceptional intellectual talents. His mother had provided constant support and encouragement. It had been the hope of his parents that he would enter the seminary and study for the priesthood.

After his secondary schooling, he had excelled at his studies at university. He had been active in student affairs. He had frequently attended daily Mass and had taught a religion class. He had to some degree remained a practicing Catholic. He had admired the symbols of Catholicism because they had the power to attract and retain loyal obedience, but he had also believed it was an archaic institution that did not offer sufficient meaning. Literature and the arts had attracted him, but despite frequent attempts to establish a career in literature, his writings had never been accepted for publication. In order to become independent from his family, he had taken a position as a bank teller, yet he had resented the menial tasks of merely doling out money to strangers. He had desired to become part of an organization that would give him prestige and meaning.

Dissatisfied with his lack of achievement in the literary and financial world, he had explored the field of politics. A brief flirtation with socialism had proved unsatisfactory, but through it he had gained critical knowledge. His first exposure to the National Social Party had been negative. He had thought that it was composed of thugs and hooligans. He had even written a series of articles condemning the movement. All of this had changed when he had been exposed to Adolf Hitler, the leader of the party.

Josef had been invited by a friend to attend a public gathering to hear divergent views of how Germany could contend with its economic woes. Adolf Hitler's dynamic speaking ability and inspiring presentation had enthralled Josef. Yet he had decided that those closest to Hitler were incapable of formulating his message to the masses. Josef had believed that with his literary background and comprehension of symbols, he could create a format that would attract the common man and allow Hitler to achieve greatness as a German leader.

No post or task had been too menial for Josef when he cast his lot with the Nazi Party. His initial roles in the party had been relatively insignificant, but his dedication and enthusiasm had been infectious. Daily he had cultivated the image of Hitler as a great leader by writing pamphlets that revealed Hitler's compelling vision for Germany. This image had been one that Josef could embrace fully. He had believed that Hitler's speaking ability was the key to captivating the masses. He had attached his journalistic abilities to Hitler's star and over time his talent for propaganda had been recognized and rewarded. In 1927 he had been awarded the powerful position of propaganda minister for the Nazis.

Josef chuckled at his musings. All of his turbulent beginnings were history. He was now the toast of the town. Despite his short stature and undistinguished features, he was being pursued by gorgeous women all over Germany because he was in charge of all art and communication within the Nazi Party. Determining who played significant parts in the theater and the arts was now almost totally under his jurisdiction.

Josef left the bathroom, and a smile traced his lips as he opened the door to his bedroom. A voluptuous twenty-seven-year-old actress lay in bed waiting for him to make love to her. He playfully began the session by slowly caressing her face before he kissed the nape of her neck.

Chapter Four

Berlin, 1932

Magda Ritschel came from a wealthy and highly cultured family. Her parents had divorced when she was three years old. After a short period of time, her mother had married Richard Frielander, a Jewish businessman. Magda had become attached to her stepfather and had the luxury of spending time with both him and her biological father. She had learned much from exposure to the different worlds and cultures of her father and stepfather.

In 1921 she had married Gunther Quant, a wealthy but somewhat eccentric and socially reclusive man. He had been extremely jealous and had imposed restrictions on Magda, a social butterfly. Her beauty and flirtatious manner had drawn most of the men who encountered her at social functions. After eight years of marital discord, Magda and Gunther had divorced. Ironically, they became closer friends after separation. Now she often sought his financial counsel.

Magda enjoyed her current freedom to date various men, but she was still dissatisfied with her life. Berlin at this time was alive with change and the worldwide financial depression had little effect on the upper social class. Like the city, she was waiting to bloom into roles that were vastly different from the traditional German image of a woman. She wanted a more exciting and challenging life but had not found ways to channel these desires.

She privately envied her friend Elsa because Elsa had rid herself of all the puritanical proscriptions that society imposed. Elsa was a delightful hedonist who experienced life's pleasures to the fullest and told Magda all about them.

Elsa had abandoned the docile image of sitting by the fireside doing needlework and planning her husband's favorite meal. She was involved in all of the traditional activities that men pursued, and she was proud of her sexual freedom. She was immersed in fashion and was truly a modern woman. Yet at her core, she was also fully German. This identity had recently found the perfect blend in her relationship with Wolfgang Oder, an active member of the Nazi Party. He had introduced her to the concept of the new Germany evolving to its rightful place as a world power. He had invited her to join in the coming revolution as a participant rather than a silent spectator. His prowess in bed was only part of the attraction because his fervor for a cause led her to new levels of excitement.

Magda wished for some of Elsa's wonderful life, but she'd been listless and bored for days. Nothing Elsa suggested doing seemed worthwhile, so she refused to leave her apartment.

Finally, Elsa showed up in determination. "My friend, we are going shopping, dining out for an early supper, and then you are going to be my guest at the Sportsplatz for a wonderful lecture."

"Oh, Elsa," she moaned, "You know that I have absolutely no interest in politics. Everyone who speaks about Germany is the same. Nothing ever changes."

"In this case you are absolutely wrong. Tonight you will hear a gifted speaker talk about the new Germany. I can assure you that it will not be boring."

"My heavens, Elsa, you remind me of those awful nuns at the Sacred Heart School. They were so pious and demanded absolute adherence to all their silly beliefs."

"I can assure you that what you will hear tonight is not silly. I am a different person since I have been exposed to those ideas. Get your coat and hat because today I will not take no for an answer."

"If you insist, I will go, but I promise I will be bored to tears." Magda went upstairs to her large and elegant bedroom. She shuffled through her closetful of fashionable clothes and settled on her warmest fur coat.

Elsa shouted up to her, "Come on, Magda. Let's not waste the entire day."

Magda walked down the stairs, smiling and teasing as she said, "You are worse than a nagging mother-in-law."

Arm in arm, they walked to Elsa's car. "Shall I put the top down?" Elsa asked.

"Are you crazy? It's freezing out."

"I know, but maybe the cold air will force you out of your stupor."

"Just drive, you clown."

To her surprise, Magda actually enjoyed the shopping spree. After three hours, Elsa suggested that they stop for lunch at a popular restaurant. Halfway through the meal, a handsome, tall, blond man approached their table. Elsa greeted him with an embrace and a kiss. She turned to Magda and introduced her darling Wolfgang. Magda shook his hand, admiring Elsa's choice of companion.

For the next hour Wolfgang spoke with great passion about the new movement in Germany. He persuaded Magda into joining Elsa for the evening spectacle at the Sportsplatz. Magda had thought that she would beg off attending the political rally and take a cab home, but she was unwilling to dampen Elsa and Wolfgang's enthusiasm. She had enjoyed the day and was somewhat energized by Wolfgang's zest for life.

Arriving at the Sportsplatz, Magda was shocked by the size of the crowd. There were thousands of people—every seat was taken. Many of the aisles as well as the corridors were filled with those who could not find a seat. Because Wolfgang was obviously a person of some importance, they were ushered to the front of the stadium with an unobstructed view of the speaker's lectern. There were brightly colored flags and banners everywhere. Magda marveled at the festive atmosphere.

After a musical interlude, the program began with the usual perfunctory introductions and identifications of notable attendees. Dr. Josef Goebbels, the minister of education for the National Socialist Party, was introduced as the main speaker. He began slowly, but his words were electric and his timing extraordinary to Magda and all who heard him.

"A blessing from heaven has fallen on the German people. Our whole hearts rejoice. It is a kind of joy that looks back with pride on what has been accomplished and that gives strength for new plans and decisions. The powerful movement that has seized the entire German people in the past year is a movement of life that is filled with a firm and faithful optimism that gives endurance and strength. We Germans have once more learned to love life in its entire splendor. We affirm it and accept all its demands, even if they be hard and pitiless. National socialism affirms life. It does not deny it. We draw from it the joyful strength that so wonderfully fills us in the last hours of the passing year.

"No one is left out. It fills the festive streets of the great cities and the lonely alleys and paths of our German villages. It fills huts and palaces, the rich and the poor. It fills the heart of the lonely wanderer who greets the New Year in the snow-capped and towering mountains, or those who are part of the crowds on Berlin's Unter den Linden. It was a blessed year. The German people found themselves once more and regained a hope that lets them look confidently into the coming year.

"What a difference from the New Year's Eve of a year ago. Then the Reich stood before the abyss. The people were torn by hatred and civil war. The parties and the government lacked the strength even to recognize the catastrophe, much less to deal with it. Collapse and desperation were apparent wherever one looked, and the specter of Bolshevism was everywhere. But today? The Reich is once more strong and powerful, the people more united and firm than ever before, led by a strong hand who is dealing with the problems we face. Where once there was hopelessness and despair, today a whole nation is filled with faithful devotion.

"A year of unprecedented victories and triumphs is behind us. What twelve months ago seemed the product of an overactive imagination has become reality. The flags of national renewal fly over the Reich, and a revolution of vast extent has captured the German people and given them back their true nature."

Magda could not believe how fascinated she was, not only with the words that Josef Goebbels was speaking, but with the man himself. Barely noticing his lack of stature or his limp, she found herself emotionally and sexually aroused.

After the speech, Elsa took Magda backstage to Wolfgang. On their way up to the second floor, Dr. Josef Goebbels and his entourage were descending. Magda briefly caught Goebbels's eye. She smiled as he glanced over his shoulder for a second look.

The next day Magda began to explore the possibility of becoming involved in the Nazi Party. Her involvement was somewhat hesitant in the beginning. She assumed basic secretarial functions at a local party office. Her exceptional interpersonal skills and natural intelligence made it obvious to the party officials that her duties could be enhanced. While working in the office, she began to read *Mein Kampf.*

Captivated by the words of Hitler, she soon moved from being a political student to a believer who wished to have a meaningful role in the development of the new Germany. She discovered that working on mundane tasks was less than fulfilling, but her opportunity to be more involved came when Dr. Goebbels visited the party office.

Sitting behind a desk, Magda was aware of a bit of commotion in the main corridor. She walked to the front of the building and was about to inquire as to what was happening when she saw the man who was responsible for her new awareness of politics. Dr. Goebbels and two of her colleagues were engaged in an animated conversation.

He turned and saw Magda. Almost as if no one else in the world was present, their gazes held, and for a brief moment they were fixated on each other. He quickly walked over to her and held out his hand.

"Good Morning, Fraulein. I am Josef Goebbels and I am pleased to meet you."

With her heart beating fast, she extended a trembling hand. "Magda."

The rest of the day Magda went through the motions of her office duties, but she felt as though she were caught in quicksand. She kept seeing Josef's blue eyes and hearing his magnetic voice. She didn't know this man and yet he had awakened in her feelings that she reserved for those she had loved in the past. Was this a foolish infatuation, like a schoolgirl who has been exposed to her first love, or was it real? *Will I see him again, or am I making too much out of that moment when he seemed as smitten as me?* she wondered.

When she was called to the phone, she picked up the receiver and said, "Good afternoon, this is Magda."

"Good afternoon, Magda, this is Josef."

Those few words began the whirlwind of countless lunches, dinners, and party functions. She had had many love experiences before, but never with the intensity that now possessed her. She was captivated by Josef Goebbels. Every time he gave a speech she could feel his penetrating gaze on her as she sat in the audience. She was more than a friend, but not yet the love of his life.

Josef was equally possessed by thoughts of Magda. His role as a leader in the Nazi Party had been the key to attracting women to his bedroom. The magnetism of his words always afforded him the opportunity to share the night with beautiful young women who would frequently offer their bodies to him. The years of sexual frustration dissipated with each new conquest. The power of the movement was an elixir that removed all inhibitions. He reveled in his newfound fame. All the obstacles of his youth had vanished. He was no longer the tiny boy with a limp. He was the golden Aryan warrior armed with the weapons of meaning and mission. Sex was one of the rewards for his devotion. Somehow Magda was different. It wasn't merely that she was beautiful. She was also intelligent, cultured, and high class. In her company he experienced an exhilaration that was far superior to mere sexual passion.

After innumerable dinners and walks together, he felt ready to commit to her. After a musical concert, they dined at the Drei Hussar. In the farthest corner of the restaurant, they sat as close together as possible. They spoke softly to each other and barely touched their food.

When they arrived at Josef's apartment, passion carried them from the foyer to the bedroom. By the time they reached the bed, they were naked. He fondled her breasts and kissed her lips. She was excited by the foreplay and reached gently for his penis. Their coupling was fast and the first entry brief, but it was followed by many moments of ecstasy during the night.

From that evening on, Magda was not merely one of the sexual conquests of Josef Goebbels; she was the woman who would be at his side on the path to glory and fame. No longer would she be an office worker in the shadows, but a significant part of the play that was being written. She was so personable and complemented him in so many ways that Josef believed that their being together was fate.

Once the relationship between Josef and Magda became public, it was obvious to all that this woman was different and that her path would be unique. It began with introductions to significant members of the Nazi Party. First and foremost, she was exposed to Adolf Hitler. Hitler was obviously impressed by her charm and beauty, and he realized that she could play a meaningful role in his desire to establish credibility in social circles where he had limited experience. Being unmarried, Hitler needed a woman to act as a primary hostess of the Third Reich. He was enthusiastic about Magda's relationship with Goebbels.

The courtship, which was volatile at times, led to marriage. Magda and Josef's wedding took place in Gunther Quant's farmhouse on December 19, 1931. The farmhouse looked enchanting. The main room was filled with colorful, fragrant flowers. There seemed to be a thousand candles flickering in the spacious rooms. Guests marveled at the snow-covered trees and spectacular views of the valley and the river.

Magda was radiant in white silk as she came down the main staircase to begin the wedding ceremony. Josef, in full uniform, beamed as he held the hand of his princess for the ceremony. He turned to his best man, Adolf Hitler, and said, "My Führer, this union will bring you new followers for the Reich."

Hitler embraced Josef, and then he bestowed a kiss on the woman who was to become the first lady of Germany.

Chapter Five

Rome, 1931

Cardinal Pietro Agnelli was the first son of nine children. He was born to a family of farmers on November 29, 1883, in Sopra Monte in northern Italy. He was a young boy of twelve when he decided to study for the priesthood after ten months as an altar boy. He loved the way Father Artioli, the pastor of Santa Maria's church, ministered to the people. He and two of his classmates had often accompanied the priest when he brought communion to the sick and food to the less fortunate in the village. Rooted to the land, he had a sense of the common people that never left him.

An avid reader and gifted student, Cardinal Agnelli studied for the priesthood at the Gregorian University in Rome. In 1910 he was ordained. He wanted to go directly to a parish, but because of his exceptional theological and linguistic abilities he was appointed secretary to Bishop Alfonso Como, an impassioned pastor of social justice. The bishop further developed Pietro's sense of fairness for all people and modeled a priesthood that was concerned with the concrete issues of his flock as well as their spiritual needs.

After five years as Bishop Como's secretary, Agnelli was appointed the spiritual director of Santa Croce Seminary. Engaged with the spiritual development of his charges, he imbued them with the knowledge that the priesthood was not a profession, but rather a call to serve others.

In 1927, when Agnelli was consecrated a bishop, he came to the attention of Pope Pius XI. The pope assigned him to be the apostolic delegate to Turkey. In this assignment Agnelli excelled at developing an ecumenical dialogue with the Orthodox Church. He was heavily criticized by the Vatican Curia as being too soft on heretics, but this did not influence his behavior at all. The pope was made aware by the more conservative members of the Curia that Agnelli was not, in their opinion, defending Catholic doctrine and was engaged in questionable theological pursuits with members who were not validated by the true Church. The pope never reprimanded Agnelli for his behavior, letting it be known that he appreciated the fact that Agnelli was a true pastor tending to the flock. The pope indicated his approval by making Agnelli a cardinal of the Church and appointing him patriarch of Venice.

The news of his appointment to Venice filled Agnelli's heart with joy, not because he had become a prince of the Church, but because he could now administer directly as a pastor to his flock. He was a frequent visitor to neighborhood parishes, and he had open dialogue with his priests about the social and religious concerns of the people. He often ministered the sacraments to the people, rarely wearing the ornate garments of his office. He was a priest, plain and simple, and any trapping that distracted him from service was discarded.

Cardinal Agnelli had a special place in his heart for his brother priests, especially those who had been led astray by human frailty. He welcomed opportunities to humble himself in order to raise the dignity of those who had stumbled in their ministry.

On one occasion he left the Episcopal residence to visit a priest who had suffered greatly from the abuse of alcohol. He asked if the priest would hear his confession.

The priest replied, "Your eminence, I am an unworthy drunk not fit to hear your confession."

Agnelli replied, "None of us is worthy to do the work the Lord calls us to perform. It is His love for us that enables us to grow as men and priests."

The priest was obviously overwhelmed by this act of humility and sought immediate medical help. Cardinal Agnelli regularly kept in contact with him, pleased that the intervention had been successful.

When Pius XI called Cardinal Agnelli back to Rome to become an adviser to the pope on political affairs due to Agnelli's personal contacts in many of the national embassies, the cardinal regretted leaving his pastoral role in Venice. Yet he was glad to be of assistance, since the Holy Father believed he would be useful as political tensions continued to mount in Europe.

Chapter Six

Rome and Berlin, 1931

As a Roman Catholic, Karl Hunsecker believed that there was no more satisfying job than being German ambassador to the Vatican and living in Rome. He had held various posts before 1927 that were far less desirable, in places such as Canada and the United States. He had trained as a diplomat, had studied Roman history, and had learned Italian to be more effective.

With his wife and three children, Karl now lived in a charming area in Trastevere, Rome. Being stationed in Rome also offered the Hunseckers the opportunity to visit both of their families in Regensburg and Zurich.

In the late 1920s the world had been facing serious economic problems, but the daily routine tasks of the German embassy had included very little stress. Communiqués from Berlin had been frequent but rarely urgent because the German Parliament had seldom involved itself in the political or theological issues of the Vatican.

In the course of his time in Rome, Karl had become somewhat of an expert on the ancient history of the Etruscans and Romans, spending significant time exploring its ruins. Coupled with this avocation, he had established friendships with other world ambassadors and with members of the hierarchy and the Curia.

Karl's favorite person in the Vatican was Cardinal Pietro Agnelli, a man who exhibited the finest character and humanity. Karl always enjoyed engaging in theological discussions with the cardinal, who frequently insisted that Karl was the more knowledgeable in theological matters. What Cardinal Agnelli did not know was that for a time Karl had entertained the thought of entering the priesthood.

Yet Karl's comfortable life was undergoing a big change. As he sat in his beautifully appointed office, he thought over the situation. He was keenly aware of the social tensions that existed among the various groups, along with the devastating effect that the world economic depression was having all over Germany. Staggering unemployment and a fragile government led by aristocrats who represented the nineteenth more than the twentieth century did little to help the ordinary German citizen. One out of every three Germans was out of work and there were increasing acts of vandalism and riots in many German cities. Karl was an idealist and an intellectual who could see that the conditions were ripe for political upheaval and possibly revolution.

At first, Karl had known little about the National Socialist Party, but one of his colleagues had mentioned a powerful speech by Adolf Hitler. The name had meant nothing to Karl, but his colleague was enamored with the content of the speech and had seemed absolutely sure that most of the Germany's ills could be traced to the wealthy Jews in Germany. This bigotry was unpalatable to Karl, so he had begun to explore the National Socialist Party and to delve into the history and political views of Hitler.

During this time, Karl's communications with Parliament had undergone significant change. The Vatican was no longer viewed as some idyllic island that had little relevance to Germany; there were social and political movements afoot that could be influenced by Vatican involvement. Also, through diplomatic channels, Karl came to understand that the anti-Semitism he thought was merely the bile of the uneducated was becoming more viable at every level of German society. There were even critics in the Vatican who openly expressed contempt for Judaism based on their readings of theology and history.

One such proponent was Bishop Alois Huldol, a member of the official Vatican family, but one who had never been assimilated into Italian life or customs. The bishop was the key liaison to the German hierarchy and a staunch supporter of the National Socialist movement. The undercurrent of anti-Semitism was very strong in the German Catholic and Protestant communities. Karl's position required him to have frequent social and business contact with Bishop Huldol, but Karl rarely enjoyed it. He was guarded about any opinions he had regarding the current struggles occurring in Germany because of the bishop's political connections to the Nazi Party.

In late 1931 Karl was called to Berlin for his annual meeting with the assistant chancellor. His visit to Germany quickly became a personal moral challenge. The speeches he read daily in German newspapers were so filled with hate and distortion that he believed Germany was headed toward a civil unrest that could cause serious internal and external consequences.

The second day of his visit he was to meet with Dr. Josef Goebbels, who was now in charge of information and propaganda. The title baffled Karl, who could not fathom why his government needed to cultivate propaganda.

At precisely ten thirty in the morning, he was ushered into the minister's office, which was decorated like a float in a parade. Flags emblazoned with the symbol Karl had come to associate with the National Party, a swastika, were on every wall, and there was a plethora of photos of parade-like settings. In back of the minister's chair was a large photo of Hitler and Dr. Goebbels.

To Karl, the minister appeared tiny and fragile with nondescript features. Dressed smartly in a uniform, he looked like a bellhop in a hotel.

"Good morning, Herr Ambassador," Dr. Goebbels said. "It is a pleasure to meet you."

Karl responded with his usual stock greeting, "It is also my pleasure to meet and to have the opportunity to discuss my duties with you."

Goebbels smiled and sat in his chair, which appeared to be on some kind of pedestal so that he actually appeared taller than Karl when they were both seated.

"Germany is undergoing the most magnificent change in its history," Dr. Goebbels stated.

Karl listened for the next fifteen minutes as Dr. Goebbels gave a lecture on the wonders of Adolf Hitler and the Nazi Party. There was no discussion, no opportunity for questions or for the exchange of ideas. It was as though Dr. Goebbels were dictating a memo.

Karl maintained his composure. Years of training enabled him to appear enthused by the minister's words, but he was appalled. How could this drivel and religious fanaticism have a positive outcome for Germany? Karl was particularly concerned about Dr. Goebbels's view of religion—Catholicism in particular. Although Dr. Goebbels was raised a Catholic, he obviously had complete disdain for the Church. He did not merely wish to minimize its influence but to destroy it.

Karl decided to listen attentively until he could better assess what his alternatives were. The session ended with Dr. Goebbels asking Karl to pass on his regards to Bishop Huldol, with a strong suggestion that the ambassador aid the bishop in cultivating acceptance of the Nazi Party within the German hierarchy. It was not the first time in his life that Karl was happy to be leaving Berlin. He was grateful that his children would not be schooled in the current climate.

The train ride from Berlin to Rome found Karl beginning to explore the personal implications of his meeting with Dr. Goebbels. There was no doubt left in Karl's mind that the Germany he knew and loved was beginning to wither and die. There were so many forces brewing that the cauldron of violence was about to overflow. The fear of Bolshevism, coupled with the economic depression, clearly defined the inability of the weak German government to deal with the struggling economy. Sensible leadership, discussion, and dialogue would soon be replaced by what he had experienced in the minister's office. The German people were ripe for the taking, and this Nazi Party was no minor phenomenon. The passion of Dr. Goebbels's words would surely inflame many, and in a time of uncertainty people would want certitude. A leader with a strong personality and a vision could easily capture the imagination of the German people, but where would this leader take them? Goebbels's views created serious concerns. What were the implications for the Jews? The belief that the Great War was lost because of the Jews was patently false, but it created a climate where they could easily become scapegoats. How could this possibly benefit Germany?

Karl pondered all this and came to the conclusion that the immediate outcome would be the social and physical estrangement of the Jews. If the rhetoric took hold, perhaps even violence might occur. Also, the concept that Germany could survive only if it gathered more land—*lebensraum*—was not a peaceful idea. It had never been attempted without leading to war. No one would give up territory without a fight.

Engulfed in these thoughts, Karl eventually arrived at their personal implications. What did it mean for him? Could he represent a government that deviated so fundamentally from his core convictions? Was there room for him to negotiate within it, or was it the proverbial cyclone that would swallow him and all he believed?

Upon his return to Rome, Karl was inundated with requests from Dr. Goebbels. Each communiqué evidenced increasing hostility toward all the groups that represented a perceived threat to the Nazi Party. Some were innocuous and could be ignored, but others had insinuations that Karl could not condone or support. The staff at the embassy appeared to welcome Berlin's increasing involvement in the daily activities of each German embassy. Rome was no exception, and despite its minimal size it warranted significant attention from party headquarters.

For the first time in his career, Karl felt compromised in what he could say to other staff members. He saw two of his staff wearing swastikas as lapel pins. He knew that soon he might be a minority of one in his home office. Strategic goals were no longer under his control, and increasingly the direction and objectives were developed in Berlin without input from the Roman staff.

In the embassy building, which in the past had reflected an appreciation of Italian artists, paintings were replaced either by works of German artists or large photos of major party members. His secretary suggested that in keeping with Berlin's expectations he should redecorate his office so that it would symbolize the direction that Berlin desired. Karl acquiesced, but not happily. All of these forces took a toll on his physical and mental health. The enthusiasm he had for his work was replaced by a methodical implementation of necessary tasks. No longer connected to meaningful strategy, he assumed the cloak of the bureaucrat. His entire career had engaged him in work that he had loved, but now he was rowing against a tide that threatened to carry him into a whirlpool of unthinkable actions.

Daily, Karl struggled with accommodations and tasks that were without merit. His mind whirled with questions: Where does one go when the known and tried become discarded without discussion? How can you implement behaviors founded in ideas that are contrary to your own core beliefs? Can you assume a holding pattern that conveniently removes you from personal responsibility? Is there any alternative that can justify silence, or is that silence to be interpreted as consent and support for what is occurring or is about to occur?

Karl chose to keep these questions to himself. He saw no reason to create pain and confusion for his wife and children. Rome still held all of the beauty that had captured his heart, and he was reluctant to ruin their world. Perhaps his fears would be transitory and there would never be a need to share his anxieties. Even as he pondered this hope he knew that it was not even in the realm of possibility.

Ultimately, either the accumulation of stress would force him to resign his position on grounds of conscience, or he would need to find a level that would enable at least moral equilibrium. The one person he knew he could trust with his fears was Cardinal Agnelli. Not only was the cardinal truly a man of God, he was also an experienced diplomat who had spent time negotiating difficult political questions in a multicultural setting. Surely Cardinal Agnelli had been confronted with situations that required difficult choices.

Karl decided to contact his friend. His request for a private meeting with Cardinal Agnelli was posed in his official documentation as an attempt to strengthen key Vatican support for the official politics of his government. He was certain that this would be positively viewed by Berlin because Cardinal Agnelli was very influential within the Curia and had often provided personal counsel to Pope Pius XI on world affairs. Because the regime in Berlin was created and staffed by loyalists and neophytes with limited diplomatic exposure, they would not be aware of the cardinal's record of tolerance and dialogue with those outside the Catholic community.

Karl had invited Cardinal Agnelli to meet him at his favorite restaurant, which was located in the Piazza del Popolo. They had more than occasionally dined there, discussing aspects of Roman art and culture. On some occasions, when the restaurant was relatively empty, they had sung Italian arias, much to the delight of the staff and the proprietor.

Now Karl waited for his friend to arrive, trying not to worry about growing Nazi political power and his own uneasy position.

Cardinal Agnelli swept into the restaurant and quickly sat down at Karl's small table in a quiet corner. With an an uncanny ability to immediately pinpoint the issues without meaningless chatter, he asked, "Karl, why are you burdened with such concern?"

Karl made no attempt to lead to his dilemma indirectly and launched right into it.

"Your Eminence, I am most troubled with the behavior that is expected of me from my government. The civility has evaporated and liberties are being stripped from law-abiding citizens daily. Hitler and my direct superior, Dr. Goebbels, have launched a series of attacks—primarily against the Jewish community—that are obviously illegal. There is not the slightest hesitation to implement these actions. I must tell you that the rule of law has been suspended by the German government. The daily mandates are not the whim of some isolated bureaucrat but rather the official policies of the government."

Cardinal Agnelli seemed oblivious to the appetizers that had been served and began to probe Karl's statement. "What is the foundation of these changes?"

"It is complex, your Eminence, but it is now in vogue to blame the Jews for everything.

"In my country there has been long-standing resentment of the residue of pain that the Treaty of Versailles has laid on the German people. Hitler has seized on this fact. Dr. Goebbels has orchestrated a rationale through the newspapers and radio that the Jews were the villains behind Germany's surrender. The complex has been reduced to the simple, and the end result is that his menu of hate is being digested in multiple German homes.

"Compounding this is the reality of unemployment in Germany. One out of every three Germans is out of work. The minister of propaganda has woven this statistic into a fable that says all the Jews are employed and doing well while there are merely crumbs on the tables of the ordinary German family. The churches by and large have added fuel to the fire by condemning the Jews for their rejection of Jesus and obstinately promoting a faith that relies on profit and greed rather than spiritual growth.

"I am telling you all this because you are an unbiased human being who rationally examines the facts. Dr. Goebbels has packaged his hateful distortions in ways that allow no other alternative but to hate the Jews. I have come to the conclusion that the ultimate goal of my government is to have every Jew leave Germany and perhaps even Europe."

"Do you believe this is even possible?"

"It is not only possible but probable. The instructions that cross my desk each day indicate a growing intolerance and an escalation of discrimination against all Jews."

The cardinal sipped his glass of wine, sighed, and took a few moments before he inquired, "Where does that leave you, Karl?"

"Somewhere between purgatory and hell. I have never felt like a character in Dante's Inferno until recently. I love my position, but I am racked with questions of conscience that plague me night and day. Even sleep is no escape, for obsessive thoughts and questions overwhelm me."

"What are your greatest fears?"

"I most fear that I am complicit in what is happening, and also what may happen. There are times when I attempt to calm my fears by trying to convince myself that this is temporary and the German people will never continue to allow these distortions of our constitution and way of life. Yet I don't really believe it. This is just the tip of the iceberg. Underneath what we have already seen is a mountain of inhumanity waiting to engulf Germany."

"Karl, what are you considering?"

"I have loved my position as an ambassador, especially my time in Rome. But I may not be able to continue. My faith has been my foundation, and residing in the city so close to the seat of Saint Peter has been its fulfillment. Now I am being asked to ignore that faith so that the voice of Christ will be silenced in the wake of this anti-Christian behavior. I am convinced that I will be used to aid Dr. Goebbels and Hitler in their mission to inflict pain on the Jews. I cannot accept this, but I am lost as to what else I can do. Outside of God and my family, this position has been the love of my life. It has given me fulfillment and direction. Now I believe I have lost that anchor."

Cardinal Agnelli leaned forward. "If you resign, will it change any of the behavior toward the Jews?"

Without hesitation, Karl responded, "No. Whoever replaces me—especially if he is a Nazi loyalist—will follow the letter of the law."

"Then perhaps our Lord is asking you to accept the cross of your office in order to implement His will."

"You don't seem to understand that I have no power to stop this madness."

"Maybe you cannot stop it, but you may find ways of helping the powerless who will be crushed by your government."

"I don't know how I could prevent it."

"Neither do I. If your assessment that it will get worse is correct, I am sure there will be ways to aid the Jewish community."

"I would like to believe that, but I must also make sure that any decision I make will not have negative consequences for my family."

"Karl, I want you to promise me that you will not resign before we have had opportunities to explore how you can stay."

Chapter Seven

Regensburg, 1931

The tiny village of Regensburg, once totally remote from the dynamism of political upheaval, was undergoing a sea change. The idyllic isolated hamlet was rapidly giving way to a cohesive part of the unified Germany. Years of apolitical status were being altered by circumstances that affected even the most remote parts of Bavaria.

The Richter household consisted of Johann Richter, Luisa Gruber Richter, and their nine children. Like all German families, they were involved in the political changes that had been created by the National Socialist Party. Events in Berlin were affecting everyone's daily behavior. The Richter household was a reflection of the tensions occurring in many other German families.

Johann Richter was a carpenter by trade and a devout Roman Catholic. He had rejected Hitler after examining the Nazi belief system and finding it lacked substance. His lord and master was Jesus Christ, and he took his worldview from the Church. Immersed in making a living for his family, he spent what little free time he had reading the Bible. He was a tall man with huge shoulders and incredible physical strength. Despite his imposing physical presence, he was a man of great kindness and consistently went out of his way to assist those less fortunate than himself.

Unlike his father, Georg Richter, the eldest son in the Richter family, was devoted to Hitler and the Nazi Party. Georg had attended Nazi rallies in Munich and had become overwhelmed by the words of Dr. Josef Goebbels, the minister of propaganda. This experience had led him to purchase and devour the bible of the movement, *Mein Kampf*. Now he poured over Hitler's book daily and accepted without question the beliefs held within. He spent hours going over the same passages, in particular focusing on the idea that Judaism was a major cause of Germany's problems.

This newfound data supported the personal experiences that Georg had undergone in Regensburg. Though his contact with Jews his own age was scant, he believed that their lives were far easier than his own. His father worked for a Jewish firm. Even though his father never complained about ownership, Georg became convinced that his father and all of the workers in Regensburg who were employed by Jews were oppressed.

Over a period of months, Georg made the conscious decision that he would abandon much of what he had been taught by his parents. His future was now eminently clear. He would embrace the Nazi Party. As the new Germany evolved, he would be an integral part of it.

Johann rarely imposed his will on his children. A mild, prayerful man, he believed that what he did was far more important than what he said. He was a good provider and strictly adhered to the Christian covenant, following all the rules and rituals. He had always believed that his good example would take root in all of his children, but recently he had become concerned about the behavior of Georg. Conversations at the dinner table had always been casual and frequently mundane, but lately Georg would enthusiastically lecture the family on his newfound love, the Nazi Party. This, coupled with his black clothing, Nazi Party necktie, and the ever-present swastika on his arm, could no longer be ignored. Johann decided that he must confront Georg at the dinner table that evening.

As the family ate their soup, Johann inquired, "Georg, why do you feel that you must wear that symbol on your arm at the dinner table?"

Georg proudly pointed to the swastika. "Because it is a public sign of what I believe."

"And what is it you believe?" Johann asked.

"I believe that we are involved in a great new movement that will change Germany forever."

"In what ways will the Nazis change Germany?"

"As a people, we will shed the yoke of the Treaty of Versailles."

Johann was incredulous at this statement. "What do you know about the Treaty of Versailles?"

"I know that it was meant to destroy Germany and was forged by Jews and Bolshevists."

"Do you really believe that nonsense? Germany lost the war and the price in human suffering was enormous for everyone."

"The real tragedy was the betrayal by the world Jewish conspiracy," Georg insisted.

"Where did you learn such drivel?"

"It may be drivel to you, but it is the foundation of the new Germany. Adolf Hitler will rectify the years of pain and suffering by dealing with the Jewish question."

Luisa attempted to halt the conversation at her dining table, which had become increasingly loud and agitated.

Johann signaled that she should not interfere, and continued, "How will you and this comical leader of yours achieve this?"

"You may think he is comical, but he will lead Germany and Europe to a Jew-free nation."

Stunned by this last statement, Johann pounded his fist against the table. "I did not raise you to spout such hatred. I forbid you to ever say these things again."

"I will follow my heart, Father. You are a good man, but you are living in the past."

Johann realized that further conversation was useless. "I find your allegiance to this nonsense un-Christian and misguided, but for the time being there will be no more political talk at this table. After all, we are family—despite disagreements."

Chapter Eight

Kulpmont, 1931

The past few months had brought significant changes that buoyed Stefano's spirit. He felt particularly happy that his sister Calista now lived nearby. She had married an Italian American who owned a small grocery business in Mount Carmel, Pennsylvania, which was the town adjacent to Kulpmont.

Calista had met her husband, Franco, when he had visited his parents last summer in a neighboring town in Calabria. They had been immediately serious about each other, and under the traditional Italian customs, Franco had courted Calista. The distance between America and Calabria had presented a significant problem, so the couple had decided to forego a long engagement period and marry.

After nine years, Stefano knew life in a coal mine was never routine. He had had his share of cave-ins, explosions, collapsed ceilings, and the constant breathing of foul air that had taken the health of so many of his friends and coworkers. But he had never complained. He had taken great comfort in the knowledge that his mother and brother were safe and becoming economically secure in Calabria.

Stefano felt proud of the fact that he had risen to the level of foreman, which was quite an honor considering he was the first

Italian to hold such a post. He had also become an American citizen. Though in his soul he would always be Italian, he had fully adopted the ideals and history of his new land and was intensely patriotic. In his time of dire need, this land had offered hope and opportunity. His gratitude would be everlasting.

Coupled with his growth and ascent into mid-management at the mine, Stefano was encouraged about Severio. His brother had not only finished his initial schooling, but had gone on to the university, where he had excelled in the law. With Stefano's help, the family had been able to move to a more commodious place in Soverato by the sea. In addition to all of this, Severio had become engaged and was soon to marry.

Stefano reveled in all the good news, but he yearned to have a family of his own in America. This desire did not lie fallow for long. On a bright Sunday afternoon, while sharing a picnic with his sister in Mount Carmel, he was captivated by a beautiful young woman walking with a couple he perceived to be her parents. She stopped to speak with Calista, smiled shyly at him, and then continued on with her parents.

Stefano could barely contain his emotion until he could find out about the young lady from his sister. Calista teased him, playfully insisting that she was not at liberty to share this information. When she perceived that this was not a laughing matter, she told Stefano that the lovely young woman was Caterina Torre, a sixteen-year-old Italian American who lived in Mount Carmel with her parents and attended Calista's church. Stefano decided he would visit Caterina's family and seek permission to begin the courting process.

The following Sunday, dressed in his best clothing, he ventured to the Torre home, an immaculate white cottage in the center of Mount Carmel. The yard had a beautiful garden filled with flowers and vegetables. He hesitated for a moment, straightened his tie, and, assuming an air of bravado, ascended the front steps. He knocked on the door but there was no response. He heard muffled voices coming from the back of the house. When the door finally opened, a middle-aged man looked out.

Stefano inquired, "Is this the Torre residence?"

The man responded in English with a heavy Calabrian accent. "Yes, it is. What can I do for you?"

"My name is Stefano Pittelli. I live in Kulpmont and I am one of the managers of the coal mine. I am here to ask permission to court your daughter."

"Please come inside."

Stefano suffered through an hour and a half of a polite but intensive interrogation by Mr. Torre. At the end of the grilling, it was clear that Stefano had passed the first hurdle and the possibility of courtship was now within reach.

Mr. Torre rose from his chair, went out to the kitchen, and returned with three cups of espresso. He set down the coffee, left the parlor, and went upstairs.

Stefano sat for what seemed at least fifteen minutes, but finally he heard Mr. Torre at the head of the stairs. He was followed by the beautiful angel from the park.

"This is my daughter, Caterina Torre. She has consented to meet you." Mr. Torre gestured toward the sofa. "Please sit."

Mr. Torre sat between the two young people, standard fare for the rest of the courtship. Stefano endured the separation because he became more enamored of Caterina each time he saw her, and he could see love for him in her eyes. The first time they were truly alone was on their wedding night. Until then, it was always Mr. Torre in the middle.

Life in the 1930s found the Pittelli family totally assimilated into the Kulpmont community. They had purchased their first home and had a son, Ernesto, who was now three years old. Caterina was pregnant with their second child. There had been constant letter communications between Stefano and his family in Italy. Severio, like his brother, was now married and had children of his own. Their aging mother lived happily with Severio's family.

Stefano and Severio, though separated by many miles, lived similar lives and developed similar viewpoints, including contempt for the political scene that was developing in Italy. Stefano kept abreast of all the political news by reading the Italian newspapers. From the beginning, he had serious reservations about fascism and Mussolini. He realized that whatever transpired in Italy, Sicily and Calabria would have little influence. Rome ruled and that was problematic enough without one man controlling Italy's destiny. Severio shared his brother's suspicions of fascism, but as a lawyer with a growing practice, he had to be very careful with what he said in public. The Italians were being caught up in the fervor of the concept that the Roman Empire could be revitalized. There was also a potentially frightening movement coming out of Germany, and though Italians had no passion for war, overtures between the German and Italian governments had begun.

There were also other trends in the new Italy that disturbed Severio. He was alarmed by the anti-Semitic laws that were being discussed in Rome. The possibility of racial laws had no relevance in the community of Soverato, and he hoped that no Italian would fall prey to such pseudo-scientific nonsense.

Like most of his male relatives, Severio was religious but not a regular churchgoer. He thought that no organized religion captured total truth and anything that punished another's belief was wrong.

While the brothers Pittelli lived in vastly different cultures, the bond of their common beliefs transcended time and place.

Chapter Nine

Passau, 1931

Sarah Lehman's world revolved around her family and music. At age fourteen, she was clearly an exceptional violinist. She would spend hours playing the most difficult pieces and her music professors would marvel at her interpretations of the classics. Sarah's parents recognized her ability and were somewhat conflicted about her future. At an early age, she was betrothed to Noah, the son of her father's dear friend. At seventeen, Noah was also an accomplished music student. He played the piano flawlessly, but there was nothing unique in his playing. The notes were hit with dexterity, but they lacked spirit. His fingers roamed the keys with Germanic precision but without Italian passion. When Sarah played the violin, she caressed it as though she were embracing a lover.

Sarah accepted Judaism as her religion, but she quietly resisted the part that a Jewish woman was expected to play. She did not belittle the roles of wife and mother, but she resented the belief that that was all she could be. Why should gender limit her dreams? Adolescent sexual awakenings stirred within her, and though she was not a free spirit, she was different from her parents and Noah. She liked Noah, but she found him to be dull and too predictable. The thought of spending her life with him was not repulsive but neither was it exhilarating. She wanted adventure, passion, new roads to explore, and instead she envisioned days, months, and years of sameness. Noah was a good man. She was sure that he would love her always, but that wasn't enough. She wanted to be adored and to adore. She resisted the belief that marriage deprived her of basic rights. Why should she sacrifice her identity for Noah or any man? Whenever anxiety about her future became obsessive, she turned to her music and played until exhaustion compelled her to stop.

Sarah also harbored a secret that she shared with no one. There was someone she had loved from the first day he came into her life. She dreamed longingly of him. Though he was unaware of her affection, she hoped that someday he would come to love her. That someone was Hans Keller.

As if yesterday were today, Sarah relived the first moment Hans stepped into her life. She was five years old when her parents brought home a young boy with golden blond hair. Sarah was told that his name was Hans and he would be living with them. Being an only child, Sarah was excited about another child living in her home.

In the beginning, Hans was exceptionally quiet and rarely spoke to her. Her parents explained that he was very sad because his parents were in heaven. Sarah was uncertain what that meant, but after a time it became clear that wherever it was, they were never coming back.

As time passed, she observed Hans building things with his erector set, and she marveled at how easily he built the most wonderful structures. Patience paid off because eventually Hans began to speak to her. It was the beginning of a friendship that would fill her heart for years.

Hans did not attend the Jewish school, but late in the afternoon Sarah would seek him out. They took endless walks and chatted about everything imaginable. Their relationship grew into that of older brother and younger sister. Yet she came to regard Hans less as a childhood playmate and more as a knight in shining armor. As an adolescent, however, she began to understand that nothing could come of the relationship for a variety of reasons. She was Jewish and betrothed to Noah; Hans was Christian. Intermarriage was not only frowned upon, it was forbidden by her Jewish faith. Her parents loved Hans like he was their own son, but the preservation of their heritage and faith superseded everything. Also, Hans never gave any indication that he cared for her in that way. He would tease her playfully and often touch her hair as he walked past, but he never did anything to indicate that he loved her.

For his part, Hans Keller believed that there was something important for him to achieve in the future. As a teaching assistant to Professor Lehman in the architecture department, he was not exactly bored, but he had a recurring fantasy that one day he would be part of a memorable project. Professor Lehman enjoyed an international reputation and had received plaudits from all over the world for his development of the parabolic city. As currently constructed, cities could not continue to grow without a host of economic and social challenges to overcome. The farther removed from the city, the more difficult it became for the citizens to commute to and from work. The parabolic center allowed the city's growth to be symmetrical and obviated the issue of commuting long distances.

Hans still missed his parents, although his memories of them had faded over the years. He had been told that their train had derailed near Leipzig and two of the six passenger cars had plunged into the river. The Kellers and eighty-seven others had been either killed by the fall or drowned in the icy waters. Their funeral was a blur except for the Lutheran pastor who had attempted to comfort him with the words that "God so loved your parents that he wanted them to come home and live with Him." At age nine, Hans had vowed that he would never believe in the monster that had stolen his parents.

After the accident, Aaron and Ruth Lehman had made consistent attempts to have Hans talk about his parents' deaths, but he always avoided the subject. The tragedy had been so painful that he could not speak about it. There were many missing pieces about his parents, but he had always felt uncomfortable asking questions directly. Maybe that would change.

As Professor Lehman walked into his office, he was troubled by an editorial in the morning paper castigating Jewish financial moguls for contributing to the worldwide recession. It was not the first time he had encountered such vitriol, but these types of articles seemed to be more frequent lately.

He put the newspaper down, poured two cups of coffee, and then carried the coffee to the drafting area where Hans was working on a set of architectural drawings.

"Good morning, Hans," he said.

Hans appeared startled. "Oh, good morning, Aaron. I was so focused on these drawings that I didn't hear you approach."

Professor Lehman smiled and responded, "Every day you become more like your father. There were times when he would go days without eating a normal meal. He had such a love for his work that I never failed to receive inspiration from him. Much of the praise I've received was in some way related to him and his brilliant mind. I miss that, but more than that I miss my friend."

"I miss him too, but there are times when I have trouble recalling his face. I only knew him when I was a child. I miss the opportunity to know him as a man."

Professor Lehman nodded. "In the past I knew you were not ready to talk with us about your parents. What would you like to know about him?"

"Well, first, how did you meet him?"

"We were in many of the same classes at the University of Munich and both of us had the privilege of studying with Dr. Gussmer. He was a dynamic professor who brought out the best in his students. Your father and I were his teaching assistants and spent many hours together. It didn't take long for us to become dear friends even though we were so different."

"In what ways?" Hans asked.

"We were different in almost everything. We held strong positions about architecture that often were in opposition, but we always were able to blend the designs. I believe that each of us grew as professionals because of our frequent disagreements." Professor Lehman hesitated, as if considering his next words, then continued, "When the accident happened, I tried to provide you with opportunities to talk about it, but you never seemed ready."

"I was so young and confused that I guess I just kept it all inside. Please tell me what they were like."

"Your parents were a special blessing for me. I could never have asked for two better friends. Your mother was the picture of elegance, with the rare ability to elevate everyone who had the privilege of knowing her. She had that wonderful gift of making you feel that you were the most important person in the world. She had a keen intellect and was a wonderful wife and mother. Your parents were more than husband and wife. They were also best friends."

Hans realized that this was the time to ask all the questions he had carried inside for years. "What were her interests?"

"Well, like your father, she was brilliant, and also an accomplished pianist. I think of the word spiritual rather than religious as far as her beliefs are concerned. I know that she was not a traditional Catholic like she was raised, and she had more than a casual understanding of the major religions. She and my wife were very close. Often they would take you and Sarah for picnics down by the river. You were the joy of her life. Nothing was more important to her."

"What about my father?"

"Your father was by far the most talented architect in Germany. He had the ability to maintain traditional principles and incorporate them into modern theories. There are designs that he created that are timeless because they represent the best of yesterday, today, and tomorrow. I learned so much from him, and though we would discuss and argue over everything under the sun, I admired and loved him. He was like a brother to me. We would sit over glasses of wine and discuss the merits of our beliefs. He was a phenomenal listener, but that mind of his was like a steel trap. I sometimes thought that except for the question of God, his philosophy of life was Jewish. He was truly a humanist, and I teased him that he could be a great rabbi.

"With regard to you, the only time he would be taken away from a pet project was when you appeared. He would spend hours playing with you, and together you would explore words, languages, and building models. Your language abilities stem from him, and I think even your architectural prowess."

Hans smiled. "I doubt that the world will ever see me as his equal."

"That would not be his goal for you. He would want you to be special in your own way."

"I wish I knew what that way was."

"You will find it, Hans, just as he did."

As they ended their conversation, Hans embraced his mentor. "Thank you for sharing them with me."

Looking deeply touched by the gesture, Professor Lehman said, "I would never try to replace them, but I have been blessed to be your second father."

"Thank you. I have been blessed by my second family."

After that, Hans felt even closer to his adoptive parents as he went about his work. He spent most of his days at the university, restructuring models that Professor Lehman had conceptualized. It required a great deal of precision and attention to detail, but it lacked the imagination that he desired. Somewhere in his wanderlust was the vision that at some point in his life he would be creating the cities of tomorrow.

The world had been immersed in economic hibernation, but one day the current economic woes would dissipate. Germany would once again flourish. Hans wasn't part of any political philosophy, but lately he had begun to think that one of the obstacles to the growth of architecture was a political atmosphere that represented archaic beliefs rather than contemporary opportunities. Germany still suffered from the remnants of the Great War, assuming an apologetic stance for its existence.

Professor Lehman represented the best of yesteryear, but Hans decided his mentor was incapable of leading Germany to its potential architectural significance. If his father had lived, would he be trapped in this traditional box, or would he have been a pioneer leading the way?

Hans rarely read the bulletin board in the Bonhauser Auditorium, but after he assisted Professor Lehman in an architectural lecture, he glanced at the speakers program. Next Tuesday evening there was to be a symposium led by an architect named Albert Speer and a ministry spokesman on education, Dr. Josef Goebbels. "The Architectural Future of Germany and the Age of Transformation" could be an interesting topic. Hans had been searching for some optimism in a sea of despondence. Germany's severe depression had recently become deeper, due to America calling in all the German loans. The world was in crisis. It certainly could do no harm to attend a lecture that could provide a speck of hope in a sea of gloom.

Arriving early, as was his custom, Hans decided to sit in the front row. By the time the lecture was to begin, there were scarcely fifty people in the massive hall, which could accommodate nine hundred. He gazed around at the meager group and saw one of Professor Lehman's graduate students, Josef Baumen. He waved at Hans and sat down in the front row.

Professor Wilhelm Schmidt, a senior member of the faculty, came out from behind the curtain on stage and briskly walked to the podium. Schmidt was one of the youngest members of the architectural staff and was somewhat radical. He had multiple disagreements with senior staff regarding the types of buildings that should be created in the current environment. Most of his colleagues were extremely traditional and dismissed his political exuberance as nothing more than the passing folly of youth. He had tried on many occasions to engage senior staff in dialogue, but due to his inexperience he had had little success.

Hans was not too surprised to see him there.

"Good evening ladies and gentlemen," Professor Schmidt said. "Tonight we are privileged to have two speakers who will enlighten us about the future of Germany in a world that is in dire need of vision and change. Our first speaker will be Dr. Albert Speer."

Hans listened attentively to Dr. Speer's lecture. Hans was somewhat envious of the work that Dr. Speer was undertaking. Dr. Speer's view seemed to be a blend of classic structure and untried modern that raised architecture beyond the tried and functional. Hans was a young professional drifting through a maze of predictable levels, and in listening to Dr. Speer he felt a momentary respite from his boredom.

When Dr. Speer finished, there was applause, but certainly not the banging on desks or excited whistling that Hans had expected. Once again, he was reminded of how staid this community was, how any vision of change was met by paltry applause.

"Thank you, Dr. Speer," Professor Schmidt said, "for your vision. We are grateful for such an exciting presentation. Now, ladies and gentlemen, we are privileged to have with us Dr. Josef Goebbels. Dr. Goebbels is a noted journalist and author who will address the growing influence that Germany will have in the world."

Hans was somewhat surprised at the physical appearance of Dr. Goebbels, who was slim, very short, and had a noticeable limp. Unlike Dr. Speer, this man did not create a positive initial impression. This impression was almost immediately changed by Dr. Goebbels's words. Hans found himself riveted by the vision of the new Germany. The style and energy of the talk were so dynamic that he felt Dr. Goebbels was speaking directly to him. The themes of rebirth, revitalization, and the courage to become free from the mire of economic and academic depression were so vital that Hans felt more alive than at any time he could remember.

When Dr. Goebbels finished, there was total silence, and then came the banging on desks and whistling in response to his words. Dr. Speer had been interesting, but Dr. Goebbels had lit a spark in the minds and hearts of the audience. Years of yearning to believe in something that mattered had been ignited by the magnetism of this man's words.

At the end of the speech, Hans saw Dr. Goebbels as a giant, not a runt with a limp.

Dr. Schmidt thanked both lecturers profusely and opened a question and answer period.

Hans was immersed in every response, as both men had the ability to articulate their vision with such clarity that what would have seemed impossible in Germany's recent past now seemed achievable. As an architect, Dr. Speer should have been more interesting to Hans, but he could not take his eyes off Dr. Goebbels. Hans absorbed every word like a religious zealot. After twenty minutes, Hans raised his hand.

"Dr. Goebbels, what role in your vision is there for a young professional like me?" Hans asked.

Dr. Goebbels smiled. "What is your name, young man?"

"Hans Keller, sir."

Dr. Goebbels wrote down the name before he responded with a ten minute answer.

Hans never took his eyes off the inspirational leader. The moment Hans had been searching for had arrived. There was a place for him in this new Germany. He made a silent personal commitment to find a meaningful role.

Dr. Schmidt once again thanked both speakers and concluded the evening with a few topical remarks.

Hans sat there for some time, feeling a high level of excitement. Dr. Goebbels had enabled him to see an alternative to meaninglessness. He would read everything that Dr. Goebbels had written on the topic.

Finally Hans rose from his seat and walked toward home. The night was cool with a silver glow from a full moon. Life had changed. He felt that exciting opportunities would be available in the future.

Chapter Ten

Berlin, 1931: Operation Nero

It was raining in Berlin. For the past two weeks the weather had been dismal. Josef Goebbels had just returned from a speaking engagement in Rome and was wistfully thinking about its beauty and climate.

As he had wandered through Rome, he had been intrigued with the history of the Roman Empire and had longed for the day when Germany would flourish in art and architecture. He had imagined the legions of Roman soldiers returning through the ancient arches, showered with flowers and the joyous cries of a thankful nation. The Capitoline Hill in all its grandeur had risen from the center of Rome. The Roman Empire had been a marvel built on the foundation of great leadership. The emperors had filled the common man with such visions of grandeur that no sacrifice had been too great for a Roman citizen.

Josef was still trying to fathom the underpinnings of such success. Of particular interest to him was the Vatican. How could an organization without the might of armies have such influence in every corner of the world? What mystique caused people to blindly follow the dictates of elderly men dressed in ridiculous costumes? His parents had been devout Catholics, and their fondest desire had been that one day he would enter the seminary and become a priest. This desire had no chance of success because he believed then and now that Christianity was merely a myth that brought hope to those without power. The real power was in the papacy and the clergy. In his efforts to transform Germany, he knew that at some point he would have to influence the Vatican and ensure that as the Führer's plans evolved there would be no resistance from the pope and his hierarchy.

As Josef sat at his desk in his austere office, he thought about his excellent adjunct, Erich Hanke. Erich was already a true believer and had left the practice of law to become a paid employee of the National Socialist Party. He was an avid anti-Semite who believed that every issue and challenge for the German people was intimately tied to the Jews. He hated anything that was directly or indirectly connected to Judaism. A soldier in the First World War, he believed without reservation that defeat had occurred because the Jewish financial wizards all over the world had sold out Germany. Erich also believed that if Germany were to be restored to her place as a leader of nations, she would have to purge herself of every vestige of Jewish influence. Erich did not yet subscribe to direct violence, but he fully supported making life in Europe so difficult for the Jews that they would willingly seek opportunities to immigrate to America, England, and possibly South America. Unlike many Germans who had personal or historical connections to the British, Erich loathed them almost as much as he hated the Jews, largely because his brother had died in the Battle of the Somme.

Josef summoned Erich, rose from his desk, and opened the top drawer of a filing cabinet. He rummaged through a series of files and took one out labeled "Operation Nero."

When Erich entered his office, Josef set the file on his desk so they could review it together.

"What progress have you made regarding our goals for Operation Nero?" Josef asked.

Erich took some papers from his briefcase and began to speak about a series of names on lists that he had compiled. Each name had personal data as well as comments regarding suitability for a role in Operation Nero.

Josef listened intently, and for each name he had questions.

"What has been his exposure to our cause?"

"Does he have the intellectual ability to be outstanding in an academic environment?"

"What is his facility with language?"

"How will his current employment mesh with the position he will be required to fill?"

"What are his dominant personal characteristics?"

"Does he have a religious affiliation?"

"What is his family heritage?"

"Can we establish that there is no pollution from any Jewish ancestry?"

As they discussed the various candidates, each one appeared to be more or less qualified, but both men lacked real enthusiasm for any particular individual.

Josef rose from his desk, walked toward the door, opened it, and said, "Good morning, Frieda. Would you please bring us some coffee?"

"Certainly, Dr. Goebbels," Frieda replied.

"Thank you." He hesitated, smiling. "You know how much I appreciate all your good work for me and the cause."

"Yes. I brag to all my friends that being your personal secretary for three years now is the best job in the world."

"I hope you continue to feel that way."

At short time later, the door opened again and Frieda entered with a tray of coffee and some biscuits. "Shall I pour, Dr. Goebbels?"

"No, Frieda, that won't be necessary. Thank you."

Erich stared at Frieda's shapely bottom as she closed the door behind her. He sighed.

"Don't you ever have a moment in your life when you put aside your sexual desires?" Josef asked.

"I try, Dr. Goebbels, but I am constantly aware of them."

"I certainly can relate to that. In Frieda's case, I am as pure as the driven snow. Mixing business with pleasure can be a huge mistake."

Erich smiled and said, "My father used to tell me not to shit near your own flagpole, but I believe you can if you watch where you walk."

Josef chuckled. He knew both of them had enormous sexual appetites. With the growing popularity of the Nazi Party, the opportunities to womanize were endless. "Enough of this frivolity. Let's get back to business."

"Do you have any additional candidates that you wish to discuss?" Erich asked as he closed the file.

"Ironic that you should ask that question. A short while ago I gave a lecture at the university and at the end of the formal presentation there was a question and answer period. One young architect asked if there could be a place for him in our movement. He was clearly intellectually and emotionally attuned to my responses. I know almost nothing about him, but I would like you to do a thorough investigation of him and his family."

"What is his name and where does he live?"

"His name is Hans Keller and he lives in Passau. Go there and check into his background."

Chapter Eleven

Passau, 1931

Erich Hanke was struck by the natural beauty of Passau. The town was built on a narrow strip of land near the confluence of three rivers: the Danube, the Inn, and the Ilz. He had the feeling that he had entered the Middle Ages. Passau was located on the Austrian border, approximately ninety miles from Munich. Unlike Dr. Goebbels, who was infatuated with creating new architectural wonders, Erich was duly impressed with the baroque character of Passau.

It was important for him to play a role and not be seen as representing the government or any political party. There was a high level of sophistication in Passau, but having been raised in a small village, Hanke knew there could be a reluctance to divulge information of a personal nature. He believed that the key to the information he sought was in the ancestral records, which he suspected were in the town archives.

Walking through the winding streets, he stopped to enter Saint Stephen's Church. There would surely be a caretaker or perhaps even a cleric who could provide essential leads. Entering the church, he used his recall to perform a blessing with the holy water and performed a perfect genuflection at the front of the church. He then went to one of the side altars and lit a candle. Kneeling, he bowed his head for a few moments before he rose and began to explore the area.

While examining the Stations of the Cross, he noticed an elderly man at the nave of the church folding a series of pamphlets and placing them neatly in the individual pews. He approached the man and said, "This is an absolutely beautiful church."

The caretaker paused in his work and smiled. "It is not only a beautiful church, it is also the home of the largest pipe organ in Germany."

Erich reacted as if impressed by this historical fact. This could be the perfect opportunity to explore whether the caretaker had any knowledge of the Keller family. "I'm searching for family roots. The name is Keller."

The caretaker scratched his beard and for a few moments seemed to be going through his memory. "Keller? I know that years ago there was an architect who was consulted regarding two of the bell towers that had some damage through erosion. I'm not sure, but I believe he was a professor at the University of Munich. Father Krautheim, our pastor, could probably tell you more, but unfortunately he is at a conference in Vienna."

Feeling confident that he was on the right track, Erich continued with his inquiry. "Thank you for being so helpful. Might I impose on you with one more question? Is there a place in town that contains records for the citizens who have lived here? I think that might tell me if these Kellers are related to my mother."

"If you walk down Blumenstrasse, which is the next street on your left, you will see the town hall. It is at 27 Blumenstrasse. When you enter the building ask for Herr Baumann. He is the archivist. Tell him that Otto from Saint Stephen's sent you."

Erich gave a deferential bow. "Thank you, Otto. My name is Erich. I am most grateful for your help." He was pleased at how much he had already learned.

The men shook hands and parted company.

Arriving at 27 Blumenstrasse, only a three-minute walk from the church, Erich was impressed by the splendor of the architecture and the views from the terrace. The building was located right on the Danube. As he ascended the steps to the main entrance, he stopped and read a brass plaque. In 1927 this spot was the high water mark where the river had risen. The mark was easily twenty feet above the river. Large tapestries depicting stories about the river and Saint Stephen adorned the high walls. The furniture was antique and far from his idea of comfortable. The main office area was to the right of the lobby and was staffed by what looked to be a young Bavarian man.

"Excuse me, but could you please tell me where I could find Herr Baumann?" Erich said.

"He is in the courtyard," the young man replied. "May I tell him who is asking for him?"

"Certainly. My name is Erich Hanke. Otto from Saint Stephen's suggested that I ask for him."

"Please wait, Herr Hanke. I will go and ask him to come to the office."

After a few minutes, an elderly man with snow-white hair came into the office. "Good morning. I am Herr Baumann. How may I help you?"

"Good morning, Herr Baumann. My name is Erich Hanke. I am hoping to find some of my mother's relatives. She died recently. My brother and I would like to reestablish connections with them. My mother and father grew up in Berlin, but they were born in Bavaria. My mother often told us what a beautiful town Passau was and how she enjoyed her many visits here."

Hanke had the impression that Herr Baumann did not have a lot on his mind and welcomed the opportunity to play historical sleuth.

"What was your mother's name and approximate date of birth?"

"Her maiden name was Keller. She was born on February 27, 1872."

"Well, come with me and let's search the town ledgers."

After walking up a flight of stairs, the two men entered the archive room, filled with registers dating back to the seventeenth century.

Baumann ascended a sliding ladder and positioned himself in such a way that the ledgers beginning with *K* were within reach. He dusted off a few of them, muttering, "The housekeeper has certainly not been at this level for a long time." After a few minutes he focused on two ledgers, pulled them out, and handed them to Hanke before he descended.

"Let's examine them on the table," Baumann said. "Pull up one of those chairs near the doorway."

The two men sat down side by side at a long wooden table.

Shuffling through the pages, Herr Baumann stopped and said, "Ah, yes, we have a few Kellers here. Let's see which dates of birth and death are most probable. Some of the listings are from the long distant past and others are so recent that they can easily be dismissed."

Erich waited, hoping he would quickly and easily get the information for Dr. Goebbels.

Baumann sorted through some more pages. "I believe that one name is the most probable. Heinrich Keller. Unfortunately, it appears that he is deceased as well as his wife. They had one son by the name of Hans. There is an address here. Perhaps you could go to that neighborhood and inquire."

"Thank you for your help." Erich quickly got up and left the building.

Now that Erich had the key to determining who Hans Keller was, he simply needed to find out whether Hans could meet the requirements of Operation Nero. The next step was to find a local café where he could explore his leads.

The Augsberg Café turned out to be the mother lode for his inquiries. Luisa Rau, the middle-aged owner, had grown up with the Kellers and had been a classmate of Heinrich Keller.

Erich sat down at a small table and ordered coffee with strudel, plying Luisa with questions. She was eager to talk.

She waxed enthusiastically about Heinrich's intellectual prowess and how he had become a successful and renowned architect. According to her, Heinrich was not only brilliant, but had also been endowed with an exceptional sense of humor. He had had an uncanny way of making light of even the most sacred and traditional beliefs. On one occasion he had so upset the local minister that he had been banned from attending Christmas services. She explained that Heinrich had been the only atheist in her group of acquaintances, and even as a young boy he had not taken the hell and brimstone rhetoric very seriously. Heinrich had believed in science, art, and architecture. He had thought reliance on the next world was an impediment to living life fully.

"Did Heinrich leave a son?" Erich asked, turning the conversation to his primary goal.

"Yes, indeed. Hans occasionally came here, but I haven't seen him for a long time."

"What is he like?"

"He is very much like his father. Handsome, bright, and also an architect. He teaches at the University of Munich just like his father did. After his parents died, Hans became a ward of one of his father's associates, Professor Lehman. I may be wrong, but I believe he still lives with them."

"Thank you. I hope you will not mention my inquiry because my client, a famous industrialist in Berlin, is searching for a young architect to build a combination plant and living community somewhere in Bavaria. He is aware of Heinrich Keller's work and had information that his son was also an accomplished architect."

Luisa looked surprised, raising her eyebrows.

"I know that you will keep this all a secret because if it becomes public knowledge I am afraid that young Hans will not be a final candidate. My client has not purchased the land for the project, and if it became public the cost of the purchase would be prohibitive."

Luisa nodded. "As the proprietor of a café, I have information about everyone in this town. My lips are sealed as if I had gathered the information from a confessional."

"You are very kind, especially to an orphaned young man."

Erich left the café with all the information he needed to satisfy Dr. Goebbels. In fact, he probably knew more about Hans Keller than anyone else in Germany.

Chapter Twelve

Berlin, 1931

Erich Hanke was in the propaganda office finalizing his report on the time he had spent in Passau when Dr. Goebbels entered the room, placed his coat on the rack, and reached out to shake Erich's hand.

"Good morning," Erich said, smiling.

Goebbels returned the salutation. "Well, Erich, why are you looking like the cat that ate the canary?"

"Maybe it's because it is not so cold outside, or maybe three days on the Danube and exploring Passau gave me new energy."

"Or perhaps in those three days you have found one or more *frauleins* to share your bed?"

"I was totally celibate during this assignment."

"If that is true, it only means that the opportunities were nonexistent."

"Duty blinded me to the attractions of the opposite sex."

"That would only happen if you were dead. Was your trip a success?"

"I believe it was—and critical to the outcome of Operation Nero. I don't think there was the slightest chance that I was viewed as uncovering information for the government. I had to be somewhat circumspect in exploring Passau, but I blended my story into a fable surrounding the search for long-lost relatives and the architectural needs of a client."

"Good. What did you learn?"

Hanke took out a file containing copious notes. "Well, to begin with, as much as can be determined with absolute certainty, the Kellers are all pure Germans. There is not one trace of Jewish heritage or any type of intermarriage. The family has deep roots in Bavaria and it appears that both his mother and father were extremely well respected.

"The father, Heinrich, had an exceptional career as an architect. Some of his designs can be found in Munich and Berlin. I uncovered some of his writings at the university, and it appears that he was a man of science first and foremost. There is no trace of political orientation in his writings. Local sources say he had no religious affiliation. There is some data that suggests he was an atheist.

"The mother, Charlotte, was one of seven children. Her father was a local businessman. There is nothing out of the ordinary in her background. She married Heinrich when she was nineteen. Two years later they had a son, Hans. Heinrich and Charlotte were killed in a train accident in Leipzig when Hans was nine years old. There were no close relatives living in Passau, so one of Heinrich's associates from the university and his wife accepted the role of foster parents. Hans has lived with them since that time.

"A lot of what I tell you is from conversations. I feel that it more than adequately gives us a real picture of Hans today. He is the perfect image of the German male that we are trying to recruit. He is tall with blond hair and, according to a café owner, has piercing blue eyes. Like his father, he is an architect and an assistant professor at the University of Munich. He is fluent in German, English, Italian, and French. There is no trace of any religious affiliation. His dating patterns are sporadic, and there is no indication that he is involved in a serious romantic relationship. He is a devoted sports fan, a moderate drinker, a nonsmoker, and quite a swimmer and soccer player."

Dr. Goebbels smiled. "I'm impressed. It is remarkable how you can gain so much information in such a short period of time. I hope the Führer never assigns you to establish a dossier on me."

"With all due respect, I would begin in the bedroom."

Both men chuckled at the implication.

Hanke paused, growing serious. "Do you think Hans Keller is the candidate we should focus on for this position?"

Goebbels enthusiastically replied, "Absolutely. Your information corroborates the impression I had of Hans that night at the university. If he is amenable, he will be an invaluable resource for the future."

Erich put down his notes. "There is one serious consideration. Since age nine he has lived with a Jewish family."

Chapter Thirteen

Berlin, 1931

The train was on time as it entered the Lehrter Bahnoff station in Berlin. Hans Keller had been told to go to the main information center and to ask for Ludwig Scheuer. As Hans made his way through the throngs walking toward the exit, he read the signs and saw that the information center was to the left. During the train ride he had experienced excitement and a certain degree of apprehension. Over and over, he had read the letter he had received the previous week.

Dear Herr. Keller,

I am pleased to invite you to Berlin to discuss a current project under the supervision of Dr. Josef Goebbels. After having met you at the University of Munich lecture, Dr. Goebbels believes you may be able to assist him in this project. It is our understanding that on February 1, the train from Passau to Berlin will arrive at 7:30 p.m. Upon arrival, please go to the main information desk where you will be met at 7:45 p.m. by Dr. Goebbels's chauffeur, Ludwig Scheuer.

Your hotel arrangements and travel expenses will be paid by our office. Because of the nature of the project, it is imperative that you share this information with no one. We rely on your ability to state, if you are asked, that you are spending a holiday in Berlin.

On February 2 at 7:30 a.m., a car will pick you up and transport you to Dr. Goebbels's office.

If you need further information or clarification, please contact me.

Sincerely,
Dr. Wilhelm Brenner

Hans wondered what Dr. Goebbels could want with his services. Surely in Berlin there were hundreds of qualified architects who could meet his needs. Dr. Goebbels could easily have asked Dr. Speer for a recommendation.

Arriving at the information booth, Hans stated his name and was informed by the attendant that the gentleman to the left of the booth had inquired about him. All went exactly as the letter stated, and soon Hans was seated in the back of an impressive limousine.

The limousine waded through the grand streets of Berlin until it arrived at Linden Street. Hans saw the Hotel Adlon Kempinski. In 1907 this legendary hotel was built next to the Brandenburg Gate. Hans thought it was an absolutely spectacular building. He was being housed in one of Berlin's most exclusive lodgings.

The chauffeur proceeded to take his luggage, open the car door, and escort him into the grand lobby. Hans was overwhelmed by its beauty. The area was spacious and filled with classical antique paintings and bronze sculptures. The plaster ceilings were elaborately adorned with floral decorations and two gigantic crystal chandeliers gave blinding elegance to the ornate surroundings. The main desk was carved out of black walnut, complemented by an Italian Carrara marble top.

The concierge examined his reservation. "Good evening, Herr Keller. Welcome to the Adlon Kempinski."

After being ushered to his room, Hans sat down in an ornate gilded chair in stunned silence. He had wanted something special to occur in his life, but in his wildest dreams he could not have envisioned what had already transpired. His level of adrenaline was so high that he wondered if he could sleep. He wanted to be at his best when he met Dr. Goebbels in the morning. Yet sleep came easily, and the next sound he heard was the phone.

"Good morning, Herr Keller, this is Ludwig Scheuer. It is 6:15."

"I am already up and looking forward to meeting Dr. Goebbels."

"I regret to inform you that a pressing engagement has arisen. Dr. Goebbels will be unable to meet you this morning. Instead he would like to see you at lunch."

"I understand. That is fine."

"He kindly suggested that I take you on a tour of the city of Berlin."

"I would enjoy that."

Though Hans could barely contain his curiosity about his visit with Dr. Goebbels, he welcomed the opportunity to explore the wondrous city. Despite the devastating effects of the world depression, Germany had become one of the true architectural wonders of the Jugenstil Art Nouveau movement. The recently constructed buildings were vastly different from the classic style of Passau. They were totally functional, but different completely from the staid architecture of the nineteenth century. The newer buildings focused on strict adherence of style to function. The ornate elements inherited from the influence of other European countries were lessened. Hans thought this new focus appealing because it represented progress rather than the repetition of standard models.

Soon he was enclosed in the warmth of the limousine, feeling astonished that he was being treated like an important man. As Ludwig drove through the Volkspark, Hans was enchanted by its vitality and beauty. Ludwig seemed as well versed as any tour guide as he explained that the Volkspark was the first municipal park in Berlin. In the 1840s the original section of the park was designed for outdoor enjoyment. Ludwig pointed out with great pride the beautiful Romance Fountain.

Hans was impressed with one of the stately Berlin churches and learned that it was the Memorial Church of Kaiser Wilhelm. Ludwig told him that it was well worth exploring and Hans agreed. Ludwig stopped and parked so Hans could explore the building.

Entering the vestibule, Hans thought how interesting it was that such marvelous architecture and art could be devoted to the fairy tale of religious belief. As he wandered through the grand edifice, he paid scant attention to the statues and side memorials. His mind was occupied with weight support and the beauty of architectural design. His training always came to the foreground. As he stood in the main center of the cathedral, he hoped that his visit with Dr. Goebbels would offer him some opportunity to contribute meaningful pieces to the vision Dr. Goebbels had presented at the University of Munich.

The next stop was the area surrounding Griebinitz Lake, considered to be the most exclusive residential area in Berlin. The homes were absolutely palatial, with carefully manicured lawns and gardens. Hans decided his favorite was a French manor house that had been originally built in 1760 and enlarged at the end of the nineteenth century. The owner was a personal friend of Dr. Goebbels. Hans was pleased to learn that this was where he and Dr. Goebbels would have lunch.

Ludwig parked the limousine and escorted Hans to the front door. The butler greeted them, taking their coats and hats. He invited them to be seated in the library. They were told that Dr. Goebbels had phoned and would be with them shortly. Ludwig excused himself and made his way to the kitchen where he would dine with the other servants.

The butler reappeared and inquired whether Hans would like something to drink. Hans requested coffee. While he waited, he glanced at one of the newspapers on the table next to the gigantic fireplace. He had been a guest in some of the most beautiful homes in Passau, but they paled in comparison to the elegance of this manor house. The wooden floor in the library was made from seven different woods, with geometric designs that bore the crest of the original baron who had built the manor. The fireplace was carved from white and gray Carrara marble, and it was so tall that even though he was well over six feet Hans could have stood in the middle without touching the top. In the fireplace, there was a roaring fire that heated the entire library.

The butler entered with coffee in a delicate china cup on a silver tray.

Almost simultaneously, Dr. Goebbels appeared at the library entrance.

"Good afternoon, Herr Keller," Dr. Goebbels said. "I apologize for not meeting you this morning. I trust that you had an enjoyable tour?"

Hans rose from his chair and shook hands with Dr. Goebbels. "Good morning. Yes, I thoroughly enjoyed the tour. Berlin is absolutely magnificent."

"Good. I'm glad."

"Dr. Goebbels, would you like anything to drink before lunch?" the butler asked.

"Coffee is fine. Please ask the cook to defer lunch for about thirty minutes so that Herr Keller and I may have an opportunity to chat."

The butler nodded. Within minutes, he returned with more coffee, then closed the door to the library behind him when he left.

Dr. Goebbels, who had been warming himself by the fire, proceeded to sit on a plush chair across from Hans. "I am sure you are most curious as to why I have invited you to Berlin."

"I am honored to have this opportunity, but of course there are a thousand questions that have been on my mind since receiving your letter."

"I can fully understand that. But before you find out the purpose of this visit, I would first like to learn more about you.

This evening you will attend, as my guest, a meeting that will be informative and hopefully instrumental in your total understanding of the purpose of my invitation. First of all, tell me a little bit about what you are doing now at the university."

"I am a teaching assistant in the department of architecture. My duties are to assist my professor in the design of building projects and to mentor the senior students with their final architectural theses."

"Do you find the work fulfilling?"

"I perform all of my work with complete adherence and focus, but I do not find it fulfilling."

"I understand that you are multilingual."

"I have a certain degree of fluency in English, Italian, French, and, of course, German."

"Impressive. How did you acquire this ability for language?"

"My parents were multilingual. When I was five years old, my father spent six months in Florence. I have always had a fascination for language and keep up my facility mostly through magazines and newspapers."

"Have you had any exposure to politics in Germany?"

"Not really." Hans picked up his cup of coffee and took a sip.

"Do you have any understanding of what my role is and what kind of work falls under my jurisdiction?"

"No, but I found your words at the university intriguing."

"In what way?" Dr. Goebbels sipped his coffee.

"When you spoke about the coming of a new Germany, I felt a fresh sense of energy and vision. I love my country, but, at least in Passau, it seems to be out of touch with change."

Dr. Goebbels dropped his cup back into its saucer with a clatter. He leaned forward with intensity. "That is precisely why I became involved with the National Socialist Party. Germany has for too long been mired in a museum of yesteryear. It must break out of these outmoded traditions and take its place as the head of the European nations."

Hans felt a renewed sense of excitement as he set down his cup.

There was a knock on the door and the butler appeared, announcing that lunch was ready. They were escorted into a cavernous dining area that could accommodate fifty people. Dr. Goebbels asked that they be served at one of the side tables so that they could more easily converse. Soon delicious food and fragrant wine was brought to them.

Goebbels again took the lead in the conversation. "What is your religious affiliation?"

"I have none."

"Does that mean that you have never had any, or that you are a nonbeliever?"

"My parents were nominally Catholic, but in retrospect, I believe my father was an agnostic. I have never been a member of any church and am, in fact, an atheist."

"Do you have any knowledge about the teachings of the Catholic Church?"

"I would have to say that my knowledge is minimal." Hans thought it somewhat strange that Dr. Goebbels would inquire about his religious beliefs, but there was so much mystery in this whole venture that he decided to continue to answer the questions with full candor.

"What about Judaism? I understand that you are working for a Jewish professor. Do you have any feelings about the Jews and their beliefs?"

"I have lived for the past sixteen years in a Jewish household, but I have formed no opinion about Jewish religious beliefs or traditions. I tend to think that their beliefs are as much wrapped in yesterday's fables as the Catholic beliefs."

"Where do you see yourself working in the next ten years?"

"I'm not sure. I have a strong desire to contribute to something that gives some meaning to my life, but currently I'm not sure what that is."

"Does it have to be in the field of architecture?"

"Not necessarily, but I don't know if there are any opportunities for me outside of my field."

Dr. Goebbels pushed his plate away. He smiled and said, "I don't want this to feel like an interrogation, so let me tell you a little bit about my background and what I am involved with now."

Hans took a sip of fine wine, anxious to learn more about why he was here. He struggled to keep his emotions under control.

"Like you, I come from a small town and was exposed to the academic path at an early age. After the completion of my studies, I began a career as a journalist and a writer. My initial entrees into this career brought only marginal fulfillment and success. My novel and plays were totally ignored. In 1924 I joined the National Socialist organization. In 1925 my life was inalterably changed when I met Adolf Hitler. I was not immediately enamored with the man and his message. He was surrounded by a group of thugs who had limited intellectual capabilities. I thought that perhaps the party was nothing more than a transitory phenomenon, but further investigation led me to believe that Hitler was unique and could become a great leader."

Hans nodded, even though he had not heard of Adolf Hitler. At all costs, he did not want to appear foolish, so he did not inquire about Hitler.

"I found what I had been searching for in Adolf Hitler and in his vision of a new Germany. He became—and is—my Führer and will be for all of Germany. My friend, you may be too young to have seen what has happened to Germany, but I will briefly try to help you understand.

"Germany was once one of the most formidable countries in the world, but for years she was mired in a series of events that have deprived her of her rightful destiny. At the end of the Great War—a war, by the way, that Germany would have won had she not been betrayed by the Jewish industrialists—Germany was forced to become a shell of her former power and influence. The Treaty of

Versailles was meant to embarrass her and kill the spirit and soul of her people. The superstition of the Church, the decadent democracy, the economic stranglehold of the Jews, and the annexation of lands that once were part of a glorious German Empire have made the common man lose hope.

"Adolf Hitler has burst open the scene with a vision that will lead us out of this quagmire. To achieve this, it is imperative that we control information and bypass powers like the Church, the Jews, and the intelligentsia in order to shape the message of Hitler's vision. The current government has failed Germany and only works for the rich and the influential. The common man and his family do not even have crumbs to survive while the leeches suck the blood out of us.

"Over the coming years, we intend to control the government and the Church. Then we will deal directly and forcefully with the Jewish question."

Hans did not understand the reference to the Jewish question, but he thought that it certainly had nothing to do with average people like the Lehmans. Surely Dr. Goebbels was referring only to wealthy Jewish industrialists.

Hans caught himself leaning forward, trying to capture each of Dr. Goebbels's words as though he had a butterfly net chasing the golden creatures in the hills of Passau. He had not felt such excitement in years, and though he had an abundance of questions, he sat there absorbing this new gold mine of information.

It was late afternoon when the conversation finally ended. Hans barely had time to freshen up before the limousine picked up Dr. Goebbels and Hans to attend the meeting that Dr. Goebbels had referred to earlier. Adolf Hitler was to be the key speaker.

When they arrived, the building was surrounded by hordes of people dressed in uniforms. Dozens of flags emblazoned with swastikas snapped in the breeze. They did not use the main entrance but rather a door at the end of the building that was guarded by security.

Dr. Goebbels led the way. Soon Hans found himself seated alone in the first row of the balcony, a prime location. The room below was packed to the brim and the roar of enthusiastic voices sent a chill down his spine. The stage had a simple platform, but the backdrop was filled with banners, flags, and placards. The noise level rose as a party of uniformed men made their way down the aisle to the main stage. Behind them were two others. One was Dr. Goebbels and Hans surmised that the other was Adolf Hitler. Dr. Goebbels and the unidentified stranger ascended the steps leading to the platform to the excited clapping of the audience.

Soon everyone stood and applauded, growing louder and louder. Hans could not say why, but he found himself standing and applauding wildly as well. The mystery man was seated with his arms folded while Dr. Goebbels stood at the lectern, clapping with the rest of the audience.

After a few minutes, Dr. Goebbels motioned to the crowd to be seated. After a series of requests for quiet, he began introducing the main speaker.

"You have the privilege of being here this evening to listen to the words of a prophet, one who has suffered at the hands of those who oppose the righteous destiny of the German people. Tonight we are more than blessed to have with us a leader who will rid Germany of the greedy rich who have sucked the blood out of our veins for years. Here is a man who sees the future and will achieve glorious feats for the new Germany. It is my pleasure to give you my Führer, Adolf Hitler."

Uniformly, the crowd rose again with shouts of "Heil Hitler!"

The man stood up and appeared to be soaking in the adulation; he made no attempt to limit it. He remained motionless, waiting until there was absolute silence. Finally, he uncrossed his arms, walked to the podium, and began to speak. Initially he lectured in a deliberate, slow rhythm, but his voice gradually rose until it was filled with intense emotion. He began to gesticulate wildly as he walked back and forth on the stage. He sweated profusely. His face became beet red and his eyes bulged. His voice cracked with passion as he shouted about the evils that had befallen the German people.

"Now is the time for the citizens of Germany to rise up and support a new government. The moment has come to embrace a vision that restores Germany to its rightful place. It is a fight for an idea—*weltanschauung*—and in the forefront stands a fundamental principle. *Men do not exist for the state; the state exists for men.* First and far above all else stands the idea of the people. The state is a form of organization of this people; the meaning and the purpose of the state are through this form of organization to assure the life of the people. And from this there arises a new mode of thought and thus necessarily a new political method."

Hans was taken by surprise at the dynamism of the presentation. It seemed that Hitler had perfected more than just words, for his timing was flawless. He knew exactly when to pause and allow the audience to shout their approval. Although Hitler had spoken for over an hour, Hans had lost all sense of time. Sitting on the edge of his chair, he was spellbound by the words and concepts that flowed so powerfully across the auditorium. When Hitler finally finished, the audience broke into enthusiastic applause and shouts of "Heil Hitler!" For twenty minutes, the Führer stood soaking up the adoration of his loyalists.

Hans was so overwhelmed by the words of the Führer that he began to understand the passion of Dr. Goebbels's earlier discourse. This was by far the most exciting night of his life.

Hitler's raised arms signaled the end of his presence on stage. He began to descend the steps into the main area of his audience. It seemed as if this crowd would have followed him through the gates of hell. Hans believed that he had found the answer to his own quest, a way to be more than an imitator of the past. He was signed, sealed, and delivered. Whatever Dr. Goebbels requested from him would have his wholehearted consent.

When Hans glanced to the side, he saw Dr. Goebbels's assistant, Erich Hanke, waiting at the end of the aisle. He motioned to Hans and ushered him down the stairs. Instead of leaving, they took a right turn at the bottom of the stairs and proceeded to the back of the stage. There were a number of armed men who saluted Hanke before moving aside from a door where they were obviously standing guard. Hanke knocked on the door.

A voice that Hans recognized as Dr. Goebbels's said, "Come in."

Hanke motioned for Hans to lead the way.

As Hans entered the dressing room, he stopped abruptly in front of Adolf Hitler and Dr. Goebbels.

"Come in, Hans," Dr. Goebbels said. "My Führer, I would like to introduce you to my friend and hopefully new colleague, Hans Keller."

Hitler extended his hand, smiling beneath his dark, clipped mustache. "Welcome to our political party. You are in good hands with Dr. Goebbels. I am sure you will contribute much to our cause."

Hans was speechless with shock, barely managing to shake the great man's hand. Fortunately Dr. Goebbels engaged the Führer in conversation while Hanke led him out of the room and into the waiting limousine. Hans expected to be taken back to the hotel, but instead he was escorted to Dr. Goebbels's apartment and informed that Dr. Goebbels would soon join him.

Hans sat down heavily in a chair, his head spinning with conjectures about how he could be involved in this movement. His initial thoughts about perhaps assisting Dr. Speer in designing buildings that would represent the new Germany dissipated. The demand for secrecy obviated them. There was a hint of cloak and dagger to this whole process, and he was beginning to enjoy the mystery. As he sat quietly in the living room, he realized that his life was about to radically change.

When Dr. Goebbels arrived, he placed his hat and coat on the ornate coat rack in the hall and proceeded to a chest that held his liqueurs. He deftly removed a bottle of cognac and two crystal glasses. He sat down across from Hans, poured two glasses of cognac, and handed Hans a drink.

He pinned Hans with a hard gaze. "What did you think of the Führer's speech?"

Hans took a sip of the smooth cognac, gathering his thoughts. "Magnificent. What most impressed me was his ability to take profound and complex thoughts and make them simple and clear."

Dr. Goebbels nodded in agreement. "Did you mentally subscribe to what the Führer offered?"

"Yes, I did. To be frank, I am excited about the possibility of having a role in his vision."

"Before I tell you what we have in mind, it is critical that you understand the importance and value of the Office of Propaganda."

Dr. Goebbels walked over to his desk and took up a large writing tablet. "Information is power, and the ability to influence will be critical in establishing the new Germany. We know that the changes we envision will be met with fierce resistance, and so we must take preemptive steps to overcome this resistance. We will be opposed by the present government, which will fight to the last gasp to maintain power. We will confront this resistance through the ballot box. Our entry into the political arena will grow, and eventually we will have one political party with one focus.

"One of the first steps will be to neutralize the media. The newspapers and journals are now filled with untruths about our movement, but as we grow in power we will ultimately control them. Hitler has given me the authority to eventually regulate all forms of the media in order to ensure that our message is heard and understood by every German. We will use the radio as the vehicle to reach the German public."

Dr. Goebbels became more animated as he continued, as though he were delivering a lecture. "The wealthy and influential Jewish community will resist us and will try to buy their way into sabotaging everything we stand for. We will meet this head-on by making life in Germany difficult for the Jews. As we limit their influence, they will have no choice but to immigrate to countries where they have a foothold. The long-range goal is a Jew-free Fatherland."

This statement about the Jews troubled Hans, but he dismissed it. He was reluctant to ask for clarification—this was his opportunity to play a meaningful role in this movement. He was so caught up in the vision that right now the Lehman family was the least of his concerns. He loved them deeply, but he was not about to discuss them at this time.

"Bolshevism will continue to try to cultivate the people with its promise of a utopian society," Dr. Goebbels continued. "We will destroy this illusion by creating jobs all over Germany. We will completely rebuild the German infrastructure and become self-reliant. We will also demand the return of land that was illegally stolen from the German people under the Versailles Treaty."

As Dr. Goebbels delineated the plan, Hans felt himself becoming ready to say yes to any and all assignments that he would be required to undertake.

"And last but not least, the Church will resist us. Years of superstition allowed them to create power by guilt and threats about the next world. Their God and all His illusions have for too long been a monstrous chain around Germany's neck. In particular, we must prevent the Church of Rome from being a roadblock to our aspirations."

Hans sensed that Dr. Goebbels was finally coming to the real reason he had been privy to all this information.

Goebbels rose with his glass in hand and gestured for Hans to rise. "Let us toast the Fatherland." He clinked his glass against Hans's snifter, and then both men drank the last of their cognac.

"Dr. Goebbels, I am privileged beyond words to be here, but please tell me what you want me to do."

Goebbels smiled. "I want you to become a priest."

Hans laughed at the obvious joke, but quickly realized the man was serious. "But what does being a priest have to do with your department and the Nazi Party?"

"It has everything to do with it. We need someone on the inside of the Church who can help shape their thoughts and actions. He also needs to be a source of information about their plans and their reaction to our policies. The pope and his secretary of state, Cardinal Pacelli, are opposed to all of our principles. We need someone on the inside of the Vatican who can prevent the Church from public condemnation of our policies."

"Are you asking me to be a spy?"

"In a way, yes. Yet I can assure you that when we come to power, you will be able to drop this charade and assume a position at the highest level of the Nazi Party."

"But Dr. Goebbels, I know nothing about the Catholic Church, much less the priesthood."

"You have been chosen because of your keen intellect, your language ability, and because you are not weighted down with infantile beliefs. Your transformation to a devout Catholic will be arranged in the next four months. When you enter the seminary, you will be an expert in Catholicism."

Hans felt as if a rug had been jerked out from under his feet. Not in his wildest dreams could he have imagined this moment.

"I will need to know by noon tomorrow whether you will accept or not. You have been given the opportunity of a lifetime to shape history and mankind. I envision the new Germany lasting for a thousand years, and I would give every ounce of my blood to achieve it. No sacrifice will be too great for any of us to have the opportunity to serve the Führer. It is my deepest desire that your answer will be yes. I must entrust you with the solemn promise that you will share this information with no one. The only people who know about what I have requested of you are myself, Hanke, the Führer and, of course, yourself. Obviously, because this role is so critical for the party, if you refuse there will be serious consequences. At the least, you will not be able to return to Passau. You will be retained indefinitely in Berlin. For now, my chauffeur will take you to the hotel. I will eagerly look forward to your response tomorrow."

Hans felt dizzy, but he managed to stay upright. "Good night, Dr. Goebbels. Please know that I am overwhelmed by your offer, but I—"

"Sleep well. We will talk tomorrow."

Hans hardly remembered how he got out of Dr. Goebbels's house, into the limousine, up to his hotel room, and into his bed. Everything whirled as he drifted in and out of tormented sleep.

Lying in bed as the first light of dawn appeared, he tried to figure out if last night had been a dream. He had spent two days that would in one way or another shape the rest of his life. For months he had struggled with where his life and career would ultimately lead, but this set of circumstances was not in any remote way connected to what he had imagined. He felt terrified that he had walked into the middle of a dangerous situation. If he refused, there was the strong possibility that he would not leave Berlin alive. But how alive had he been in Passau? He had been totally frustrated there. What did the future hold for him in Passau anyway? He might eventually get an appointment to the university or maybe even a full professorship. But what difference would his life make? Here was an opportunity far beyond his hopes and dreams. Something vital was happening in Germany, and he was being invited to participate at the highest level.

At a few minutes before noon, Hans sat in the large chair in front of the table that held the phone. There was no longer any time left to reflect. It was the moment to make the decision that would launch him into the whirlwind of the unknown. He raised the receiver, asked the hotel operator to call the Office of Propaganda, and took a deep breath.

The phone rang twice and was picked up. "Dr. Goebbels here."

Breathing as though he had just skied down a double black at Kitzbuhl, Hans said, "It is I, Hans Keller. My answer is yes."

"That is wonderful news. Return to your home. You will be contacted in the next few days regarding the next steps. Heil Hitler!"

"Heil Hitler," Hans responded.

Josef Gobbels almost waltzed around his office after the phone call. He was on the crest of a wave that would launch him into fame and fortune, along with all of Germany.

He paused to reflect on the days of growing up Catholic in a home where his parents' fondest wish was that he would enter the local seminary and be ordained a priest. The irony of the current situation made him laugh out loud. He remembered their disappointment and shock when he rejected the Church and sought a new divinity to worship.

He strutted across the room. "They prayed that I would become a priest. Instead I have become a bishop capable of selecting a candidate for the priesthood. Now that is power."

After he poured a cup of coffee, he summoned his adjunct to his office.

Erich Hanke entered and said, "How may I help you, sir?"

"My friend, you are going to be a busy man for the next few weeks. Operation Nero has begun."

Chapter Fourteen

Passau, 1931

Sarah Lehman and Hans Keller were enthusiastic fans of canoeing. They had often picnicked on the banks of the Danube River. On this beautiful day in May, the temperature was rising and the water was glistening from the rays of the sun. They had spent hours on the river, chatting and laughing as they had done when they were children first learning to swim.

Today, however, their river frolic seemed distant, as if already in the past—especially for Sarah. In two weeks, she would be married and soon all the camaraderie she had experienced with Hans would be altered. She knew a love relationship with him would be a scandal, but emotionally her fantasy life seemed more real than anything else. Besides all the reasons that forbade the relationship, there was also the problem that she believed Hans loved her only as a younger sister.

Sarah felt torn between telling Hans how she felt and dealing with the risk of scandal. Even more troublesome, what if he rejected her? All of these turbulent thoughts streamed through her while Hans sat near her on the riverbank, feet trailing in the water.

"It's actually quite warm for this time of year," Hans said. "Maybe I'll take a swim after lunch."

Sarah placed her hand in the water. "You may think it is warm, but I would rather swim in August."

"By then you'll be a married woman and you won't have all this free time."

Those words hit her like a slap. She felt an overwhelming urge to cry. She quickly turned and feigned a sneeze. Hans did not seem to notice her agitation.

"*Gesundheit,*" he said, opening a bottle of beer.

They lunched in relative silence, secrets swirling around them.

At last, Hans stood up. "Let's take a canoe down the river. We can go to the center of town, leave the canoe there, and walk back here to get the car."

"Wonderful!" Sarah welcomed his suggestion as a way to get her mind off her indecision. "The day is perfect for canoeing."

They walked to the pier and were greeted by Herr Ackerman, the local boat owner, who had a thriving rental business in the spring and summer.

"Be careful today," Herr Ackerman warned. "The current will be swifter and stronger than usual because of Tuesday's rain. You may have a difficult time returning the canoe at the Panbourn Pier. Also, I noticed yesterday that there were large branches in the water. Please be vigilant."

"We'll take care," Hans agreed.

Sarah was an experienced boater and swimmer, as was Hans, so she had no apprehension as they slid a canoe into the wide river. As they paddled down the glittering water, she appreciated the beauty of their hometown. The Danube was the focal point that allowed residents and tourists to see the wonderful sights of Passau: the castle, the shops, and all of the church steeples pointing upward into the magnificent blue sky.

After a few minutes on the river, Hans asked, "Are you excited about the wedding?"

"What do you think?"

"It's hard for me to imagine that you are so grown up that you are about to enter a new life."

"Do you think you will also marry in the near future, Hans?"

After a few moments of silence, he said, "I don't think that I will ever marry."

Sarah could not believe her ears. "How can you be so sure?"

"I have my reasons."

"Hans, I've known you almost my whole life. I cannot understand that someone as wonderful as you would forego being a husband and father."

"I have only excluded one of those roles."

"I don't understand. Which one?"

"I will not be anyone's husband."

"But then how will you be anyone's father?"

"I will be everyone's father."

"Hans, you're not making any sense."

"I didn't want to tell you before your wedding, because I wanted the spotlight on you, not on me. Sarah, I have decided to become a priest. I will someday be Father Hans."

Sarah felt as though she had been struck by lightning. "But Hans, you're an atheist!"

"I was until recently, but I've had a complete change in my beliefs."

Sarah caught his blue gaze and held it, willing him to make sense in some way she could understand.

In the next moment, a log speeding down the river hit their canoe, tipped it over, and caused an oar to hit Sarah's forehead. Momentarily dazed, she could not keep from submerging under the canoe.

Hans dove under the canoe and reached for her. He fumbled but finally got a strong grip around her breasts and stomach. He quickly kicked hard, forcing them to the surface. Sarah had a gash on her forehead, but she was conscious. He noticed that the current had carried them to the middle of the river. He would have to swim toward the shore while aiding her.

"Sarah, are you strong enough to grasp on to my belt?" he asked.

She nodded.

"Hang on. I'll get us to safety."

After what seemed like an eternity, Hans reached the bank. He dove underneath Sarah and pushed her up so that she could scramble up the embankment. After she was safe, he climbed up the side of the river bank. She reached out, took his hand, and helped him stand. He glanced over her wet, shivering form. Other than cold, she appeared to be fine.

As Sarah looked into his eyes, she suddenly leaned forward and kissed him on the mouth. He passionately returned her kiss until he remembered their divergent futures.

He reluctantly stepped back. "Sarah, we mustn't."

Chapter Fifteen

Passau, Two Days Later

Aaron Lehman sat in his study, thinking that the life he had known in this house was about to change. He and Ruth had lived here almost all of their married life. After finishing his studies at the University of Munich, he had received a small architectural commission that eventually blossomed into a distinguished career, making him one of the most famous architects in Germany. His talent brought not only fame but, to a certain degree, fortune.

After the tragic deaths of Heinrich and Charlotte, this house had become a home for Hans, their only child. Aaron had come to love Hans as if he were his own biological son. These walls had been filled with the joy of raising both Sarah and Hans. Yet they were both grown now and would soon be leaving home. Aaron felt a deep sadness that surprised him.

Sarah was to be married in a week to Noah, a young man Aaron had known from birth. Aaron knew that Noah was in for a surprise because Sarah was not the dutiful wife type. She had always had an independent streak that put her into conflict with teachers and even with their rabbi. She was never contentious on purpose, but her zest for life did not accept gender limitations. Aaron adored Sarah's spirit and reveled in her musical ability. He often thought that if

Sarah had been a man, the world of classical music would have been her oyster. When she played the violin, he felt the presence of God and the angels.

He was still stunned that Hans planned to enter the seminary and study for the priesthood. Until the moment Hans had told him, Aaron had never had any indication that Hans even believed in God. Respecting the culture of Hans's parents, the Lehman family had made no attempt to convert Hans to Judaism. Aaron had many unspoken questions about Hans's decision, but he had simply congratulated Hans.

Now the time had arrived to celebrate the future of Sarah and Hans with a lavish farewell dinner. The dining room had never seemed so splendid, with every piece of crystal, silver and elegant dinnerware evident. The room glowed with the flickering of multiple candles. The meal had been carefully prepared. So that his wife, Frau Lehman, could enjoy the food, Aaron had asked their maid and cook to perform the functions of servers and sommeliers. Aaron wanted this to be a memorable night that would reflect the love and joy that were in his heart.

Sarah sat across from Hans with Aaron in his usual place at the head of the table and Frau Lehman at the opposite end. Aaron stood up. "Before we begin this sumptuous repast, I would like to make a toast. First to my wife of twenty-seven years, I raise my glass in gratitude for the love and warmth you have brought into my life from the first moment I saw you in your father's bookstore. There has never been a moment when I did not feel your love and support. You have not merely assumed the roles of wife and mother; you have created them in such a singular way that you have no competition from anyone in Passau.

"And to you, my lovely daughter, I wish you a lifetime just like the joy that your mother and I have experienced. You will never know how much fulfillment you have brought into my life. I pray that you and Noah will someday experience the miracle that only a child can bring.

"And to you, Hans, last but not least. I loved and admired your parents, and considered it a great privilege to help raise you after their tragic deaths. I never tried to replace them, but I have loved you as if you were my own son. Bless you as you embark on your spiritual journey, and may you touch the lives of others as you have touched ours."

They all stood and clinked crystal glasses. Both Frau Lehman and Sarah wiped tears away, smiling at the bittersweet moment.

"All right," Aaron said, also feeling the loss that came with gain. "The moment for tears must give way to glorious food and wine."

Hans appreciated the superb meal, and the wine flowed so freely that at one point he realized he was more than half drunk. Yet he was already home, so he knew that he could lean on the banister and slowly wend his way to his room at the other end of the house. Even if he stumbled, he was far enough away that no sound could be heard by the Lehman family.

Sarah told the story of their recent escapade on the Danube where Hans had to rescue her from the turbulent waters. As she spoke, Hans could not help but notice that she was staring into his eyes. It was probably the wine, but she seemed especially beautiful to him this evening. Noah was a fortunate man, for soon he would have the pleasure of Sarah in his bed. Hans, on the other hand, would remain alone with only fantasies as his source of pleasure. He tried to block these thoughts as he agreed to the maid refilling his wine glass.

When the family grew quiet, Aaron stood up, filled four small glasses with schnapps and passed them around. "I wish to make one final toast. To a wonderful evening and a fitting way to end all of the delightful times we have spent together around this table."

Frau Lehman was the first to leave, hugging Hans, kissing his cheek, and then repeating the embrace with Sarah. Aaron followed suit, and then he and Frau Lehman said their good nights and headed upstairs to their bedroom.

Sarah made no attempt to leave as the servants cleared the table and closed the dining room doors.

"Well, I guess it's time for me to go upstairs also," Hans said.

"Stay a while. It's really not that late." She got up, pulled two towels out of the sideboard, and tucked them over her arm.

"I'll stay a few minutes, Sarah, but I may have trouble making my way to my room after so much potent wine."

"I can assist you at least past the first landing."

"Thanks."

After they talked a short time, Hans knew he had to get up or never make it. He stood up and felt a little wobbly. Sarah looked at him in concern and walked with him to the stairs. He placed one hand on the banister and the other hand around her shoulder. As they began the ascent, he accidentally brushed his hand across her breast. He immediately drew it back; the movement caused a momentary stumble. Sarah reached out to help him regain his balance. She again slipped his arm around her waist, and this time his hand was squarely at the bottom of her right breast.

When they arrived at the landing, Hans reluctantly removed his hand from around her. She quickly kissed him, first on both cheeks, and then full on his lips. She pressed her warm body against him. He felt a sudden rush of blood in his loins. He pushed her away, then turned and stumbled into the safety of his room, slamming the door shut behind him. He stripped off his jacket, kicked off his shoes, opened his shirt, and undid his tie. In a matter of minutes, he was naked and on top of his bed. It was such a warm evening that he kicked off the blankets and partly covered up with just a sheet.

As he began to doze off, he became aware that someone was in the room. He opened his eyes and saw Sarah standing above him.

"What are you doing here?" He kept his voice low so as not to attract attention to them. "This is insane. Your parents—"

"They are asleep and cannot hear anything from this end of the house."

"Sarah, we can't be here like this." He wanted to reason with her, but felt befuddled with alcohol and a growing need to hold her.

Sarah captured his face with both hands and kissed him soundly on the mouth. He wasn't strong enough to resist. Their kiss was soft and gentle, but the prolonged effect of her tongue inside his mouth aroused him to full erection. She jerked away the sheet that covered him, and she gently placed her hand on his penis. He moaned with pleasure, but in a last moment of rationality, he pushed her away.

"Sarah, you are getting married in a few days. I'm leaving for the seminary next week. Let's be sensible."

She caressed his hand. "Hans, I knew that this could never be forever, but I've loved you for a long time. Soon we will be separated by vows that we both will make. Please, I need us to make love this one time. I will carry the memory in my heart for a lifetime."

"I've never been able to resist you."

They kissed passionately while Hans fully embraced her, pressing against her soft, warm body. Sarah removed her nightgown, spread the two towels on the bed, and lay back on them. She pulled him toward her. Her kisses transported him to a place of perfect ecstasy. He fondled her breasts and covered her body with kisses before he placed his hand between her legs. Soon he rose above her and thrust into her moist depths. She cried out with pain and then moaned with pleasure as he spent his seed deep inside her.

They both lay there silently for a while, and then they made love again. Finally, she rose, removed the towels, and kissed him one last time.

"Hans, I'm happy for you, but know that this night will be the most special of my entire life."

Chapter Sixteen

Belfast, 1931

Patrick O'Hara's inner-city Irish neighborhood had seen more than a lifetime of hardship and poverty. The Catholic minority had experienced years of unemployment and job discrimination. Large families struggling to survive were the norm rather than the exception. There were too many deaths from inadequate food, housing, and medical care. Centuries of resentment boiled slightly below the surface while sporadic attempts at unionization ended in bloody tragedies. It was difficult in the Catholic community to discern who was more hated, the Protestant majority or the English might that supported them. Children learned almost from the moment of their weaning that any contact with the heretics or their prostitute Brits would be grounds for social excommunication.

The O'Hara family was typical of the families on Waverly Place. It was composed of eight children with a devoted mother who, though only forty-two, looked to be in her sixties. The father, John O'Hara, was a morose man who spent most of his life working at menial jobs. He had a healthy taste for the drink and was in many respects a father in name only. Mary O'Hara was a devout Catholic who never once whined about her station in life. She felt blessed that the Lord had allowed her to be the mother of such a large family and hoped that one day He would reward her with a son who would be ordained a priest. This honor she had hoped would be bestowed on Michael, her eldest, but he had neither the desire nor the intellectual ability.

Patrick, the youngest of the litter, was the least of all the candidates. Throughout his childhood, he was always one step away from being thrashed and thrown out of parochial school. With his peers, he was more than a legend. While he was in the fourth grade, Sister Joseph Evangeline told his mother that it would be a miracle if Patrick were to make it to purgatory.

Father Mooney, on the other hand, appreciated the devilish spirit that Patrick evidenced at many church events. On one occasion, while saying the Hail Mary, Patrick added his own version which provoked raucous laughter from the other children. He said, "Holy Mary, Mother of God, chase the chickens out of our yard." This was typical of Patrick with the angelic face and marvelous wit, so filled with blarney that he could outwit the devil himself.

Unlike Father Mooney, Mr. O'Hara had no appreciation of Patrick's wit. Once Patrick told him at the dinner table that Jesus was not Jewish, he was Irish. Falling for the ploy, Mr. O'Hara said, "That's ridiculous. Why would you believe that?" Patrick said, "He had drinking buddies, was single living at home, and his mother thought he was God."

The entire dinner table had erupted with laughter—with the notable exception of Mr. O'Hara. He had leapt from his chair, grabbed Patrick by the scruff of his neck, and took him to the woodshed for a beating. Even though Patrick was so sore that he could not sit down for days, he did not learn his lesson and did not let up on his drive to be the neighborhood's biggest smart-ass.

In his adolescent years, Patrick was like every other boy his age. Any mention of the female body created a pulsation in his veins. Every time he glanced at Eileen Kielty in class he would get an erection. He wasn't the only one who focused on Eileen and her developing body. Johnny Farawell would sit mesmerized by her in class. Once while Johnny was immersed in his sexual fantasies, Sister Evangeline called on him to read. Annoyed at his lack of response, she said, "Master Farawell, stand up straight and take your hands out of your pockets." Sheepishly, Farawell, who had been trying to hide an erection, took out his hands. Patrick said, "Hey Johnny, you forgot a finger!" For that, Patrick received another few cracks across his knuckles and another day spent in detention.

Despite his gregarious, carefree manner, there was a side to Patrick that was disposed to protecting the defenseless. One of his classmates, Billy Walsh, had a stuttering problem and was often the butt of taunts and ridicule from a group of boys led on by the chief bully, Ripper Collins. Ripper was at least five inches taller than any of his classmates and had the reputation of a tough, dirty street fighter. He particularly enjoyed making Billy Walsh's daily life miserable, and he sought out ways to embarrass and demean him. On various occasions Ripper and his gang of misfits would trip Billy in the corridors. One wintry day, they stole his pants and forced him to walk home half naked. Some of the other students were repulsed by this constant cruelty, but they were intimidated by Ripper so they remained silent.

One day in the school playground while all of the students were at recess, Ripper smacked Billy in the back of the head. Billy fell to the pavement. Ripper laughed at his victim and poured a carton of milk on his face. Ripper's followers were convulsed with laughter when a voice from the other side of the playground said, "Leave him alone."

Ripper was obviously shocked that anyone would have the gall to interfere. Patrick O'Hara helped Billy to his feet while wiping the milk from his face. Ripper rolled up his sleeves, preparing for fisticuffs, and yelled, "Get ready to have your ass kicked!"

Once it was obvious that Patrick was not going to run, Ripper confronted him with clenched fists. The two circled each other as Ripper's fan club gleefully anticipated the fight. The dancing was brief. Patrick threw the first blow, which Ripper easily deflected.

Ripper laughed and moved closer to Patrick in order to take advantage of his height. He threw a left-hand jab that missed Patrick, but it set up a vicious right cross that shattered Patrick's nose. This was followed by a series of body blows. Patrick fell to the ground bleeding. Amid the cheers of his fans, Ripper raised his hands in triumph and began to roll his sleeves down.

Yet Patrick slowly rose weakly from the ground and moved forward with clenched fists. Ripper warned him off, but Patrick swung wildly. Ripper hit him with such force that two of his teeth flew out of his mouth. He tried again, but he was knocked to the ground. He crawled to his knees. Leaning against a bench, he tried to get up. "That's enough," Ripper said, turning away. He and his friends never tormented Billy Walsh again.

With tales like these, no one in the neighborhood thought Patrick O'Hara would even consider the priesthood. Handsome, fun-loving, and a brilliant athlete, he seemed more likely to be a bartender or perhaps a soccer player. This all changed when Father William Donahue was assigned to the Church of Saint Michael.

Sunday Mass had always been something that Patrick endured, but on a blistering hot August Sunday his world changed. The sermon usually allowed him to fantasize about Eileen Kielty, but this day it bore into him as if Father Donahue were speaking directly to him. It wasn't the usual horse crap about heaven and hell that had no relevance; it was about the neighborhood and the need for social justice. Father Donahue talked about Jesus not as a timid caricature with his eyes peering up to the heavens, but rather as a man spending his time with ordinary people and fighting for justice. He talked as if the Beatitudes were part of a union struggling against the power brokers. From that day forward, Patrick had a hero that he wished to emulate.

Patrick's transformation was not like Saul of Tarsus, knocked off his horse and blinded by words he could live by. Patrick loved to drink, fight, smoke, and flirt, but now he had found something and someone that changed his life. For days after the sermon, he thought seriously about what he wanted to do with his life. Through the words of Father Donahue he had found Christ, but he was unsure of how to follow Him.

After months of soul searching and prayer, Patrick came to the rectory and explained to Father Donahue that he wanted to become a priest. Father Donahue was obviously somewhat shocked and explored the reasons for Patrick's decision. After many hours of conversation and counseling, he understood and supported Patrick's decision.

Patrick went to the seminary. His first two years in Dublin were difficult for him because he felt stifled by all the rules, but he kept his eye on the goal of being like Father Donahue. At the end of his second year, he presumed that he would go to the major seminary in Dublin, but apparently the Holy Spirit and his bishop had other ideas.

It was the custom in Patrick's minor seminary for two outstanding candidates to be selected to study theology at the Gregorian University in Rome. The faculty recommended two safe candidates who evidenced the highest degree of scholarship and piety. Yet Bishop Thomas Boland wanted a candidate who appeared to embody the future, not the past, because times were changing in Ireland. One of the seminarians assigned to his office the previous summer had impressed him. The young man appeared to have exceptional leadership ability that was complemented by a marvelous sense of humor. The parishioners flocked to him at parish functions. His winning smile and gregarious nature were infectious. Bishop Boland ignored the faculty's recommendation and selected Patrick O'Hara.

When the news reached Saint Michael's convent, Sister Evangeline almost fainted, proclaiming that the Lord often works in strange ways. Mary O'Hara rejoiced at the news, but her husband, in his usual drunken stupor, thought the Church had gone to the devil. The rest of the family was happy for Patrick but also sad because he would be so far away in Rome. However, Bishop Boland assured the family that he would provide financial help to allow Patrick to spend summers in Ireland. Patrick's going-away party resembled an Irish wake. Never one to pass up a free drink, he boarded the boat the next day with a splitting headache.

Chapter Seventeen

The Gregorian University, Rome, 1933

The first few months at the Gregorian posed a large challenge for most of the young seminarians, but not for Hans Keller. Each day brought him closer to his ultimate goal of being a shaper of the Reich's destiny.

"*Benedicamus domine.*" Hans heard those words in the darkness from his prefect and responded, "*Deo gratias.*"

Hans had been well schooled by the time he arrived in Rome, and he behaved as though he had spent his entire lifetime preparing for this spiritual encounter. The last four months prior to his arrival in Rome he had spent studying every aspect of Catholic doctrine for eight hours a day. His photographic mind and ability to master complex philosophical and theological theories placed him clearly as the most prepared of the new seminarians. Some of his classmates seemed to him to be rather juvenile. They could regurgitate what they learned, but they were easy targets in discussion and debate.

The daily schedule posed no threat to Hans. After being roused at 5:30 a.m., he had twenty minutes to get ready before going to the chapel for morning meditation. This exercise was meant to provide solitary time where the seminarians would focus on the Lord in silent reflection. For Hans, who was able to mimic total trance behavior, it was a time to more deeply reinforce his relationship with the Führer and the lofty goals of *this* world, not the next.

Seminarians were sheltered somewhat from the everyday realities of German politics and had no opportunity to read daily newspapers, but Hans had developed a methodology for garnering news from the outside. As an assistant librarian in the German house of studies, he had weekly access to the German newspapers and journals. He had also been trained over the summer in sophisticated codes so that he could easily understand the personal letters from Dr. Goebbels containing party information. Hanke would also periodically send him letters detailing information directly from Dr. Goebbels.

Dr. Goebbels understood that four years in the seminary without specific tasks and goals could have a powerfully negative effect on Hans's commitment to his critical role, so he devised ways that Hans could be involved before ordination. Seminarians were allowed infrequent visitors. Dr. Goebbels saw to it that Hans's main visitor was Erich Hanke, who brought specific tasks for Hans.

Hans's primary duties were to monitor Vatican publications like *Observatore Romano* for anti-Nazi sentiment and to develop dossiers on any Roman cleric who voiced opposition to the burgeoning revolution in Germany. Dr. Goebbels's plan was to try to maintain the Roman Church's longstanding tradition of noninvolvement. Pope Pius XI was a man to be feared, so any information Hans could procure prior to its being disseminated was extremely valuable to the party. Dr. Goebbels also wanted Hans to identify clerics who were involved in organizations that openly opposed the growing German incursions into the life of the Jews.

Classes in the Magna Aula were boring, at best. Hundreds of seminarians from all over the world would sit there for hours listening to some professor read from a Latin textbook that he had written. Some of the students were extremely attentive while others slept. Hans had a blank cover over what appeared to be the text, but it was really a detailed series of lectures that Dr. Goebbels had given in the past. By the end of the first semester, Hans had committed the entire series of lectures to memory. More importantly, he had ingested Goebbels's words into his soul.

Unlike Hans, Patrick O'Hara's adjustment to life in the major seminary was anything but smooth. He was constantly plagued with doubts. He observed that most, if not all, of the other seminarians were holier and more worthy than he. The Jesus that he wished to follow seemed vastly different from the one presented in all of his theology classes. The content seemed altogether otherworldly. His attraction to the priesthood was more focused on service to the poor than on prayerful meditation. The humanity of God incarnate confronting those who had ignored the poor and those forced to live on the margins was what motivated him. This was the magnet, and yet it seemed that the Church almost ignored the dynamism of the message and portrayed God as completely removed from this world. For Patrick, the core of the Christian message was rooted in the Beatitudes. In a series of letters to Father Donahue, he more than hinted that perhaps he should leave the seminary and return to his home.

Father Donahue was not surprised by the content of Patrick's letters, so he decided to visit Patrick in Rome. He could relate to the personal doubts that Patrick was experiencing because he had almost left the seminary on numerous occasions. The regimented life could take a toll on a free spirit like Patrick. Father Donahue had found the rigid discipline almost intolerable at times. He had readily accepted the vow of poverty, but obedience and chastity would remain challenges for a long time.

Father Donahue's visit to Rome was providential and timely because Patrick had more or less decided to leave the seminary. Father Donahue received permission to take him into the city of Rome for an overnight visit. Patrick was excited to be outside the seminary walls and welcomed the opportunity to convey to his mentor the doubts that were besetting him. Neither of them knew much about Rome, so they relied on the recommendation of the concierge at Father Donahue's hotel. He recommended a quiet *trattoria* located in a less than luxurious part of Rome called Trastevere. The restaurant had once been a prison and the dining room tables were set up in individual cells. This provided almost absolute privacy and made it possible to have meaningful, uninterrupted conversations.

After they sampled the local appetizers, Father Donahue asked, "Well, Patrick, how are things going? From your letters, I have the impression that it has been a difficult transition for you."

Patrick nodded. "Father, I'm not sure I belong here. I've really tried, but I doubt that I have a calling to the priesthood. Every day we're told that we were chosen by God, but I don't feel that way."

Father Donahue smiled, understanding in his sharp eyes. "So you have doubts."

"Hundreds of them. Every day I pray that they will go away, but they don't."

"Do you think you're the only one who has doubts?"

"I don't know, but the other seminarians seem so sure of themselves. They accept everything at face value."

"Like what?"

"Like the image we get every day in theology classes that Christ was a goody two-shoes always looking to heaven. I thought Jesus was a radical, but pardon my words, Father, he's presented as a powder puff."

"Patrick, would it help you to know that I almost left the seminary at least fifty times for similar reasons?"

"I thought you probably sailed right through."

"Why would you believe that?"

"At Mass and in your sermons you seem so sure of yourself."

"Patrick, I almost quit because in many respects the Christ that was shown to me was vastly foreign to the one I wanted to serve. Prayer and meditation are essential to the priesthood, but so is service and activism. I am a living example that both can exist within you side by side. The seminary was the most difficult part of my life because the day-to-day living was pulverizing. There were days when I almost couldn't bear the thought of the schedule.

"There was almost no real freedom to express myself. I felt as though I was the least worthy candidate in my class. They seemed to accept this way of life with certitude while I constantly struggled with doubt about my vocation. It was difficult for me to accept that I would never have a wife or children."

"Thank you for sharing your doubts with me. To know that I'm not alone helps a lot."

"Give the Gregorian more time." Father Donague smiled. "Make friends."

"I will. You've offered me a way to grow into a spiritual human being who will be able to serve both heaven and earth."

Patrick followed up on Father Donague's suggestion to make friends with other seminarians. He met Hans Keller at the café near Saint Eustachio, noted for the best cappuccino in Rome. The seminarians, in full cassock, were celebrating one of their infrequent excursions outside the seminary. Being the most gregarious, Patrick attempted to address Hans in his best Italian. Hans actually smiled and responded in flawless English.

"Are you a Brit?" Patrick asked in utter amazement.

"No, actually I'm German."

"Shite, you speak better English than I do!"

"I doubt that, but it's nice of you to be so kind."

"Not kind at all. You sound great." Patrick glanced around and picked out a table. "Let's get cappuccinos and share our life stories."

"You get the table. I will get the drinks," Hans agreed.

After they talked for some time, Patrick decided to share his earlier priesthood doubts. "I went to my spiritual adviser one night and told him that I was plagued with uncertainty. He calmed my fears and told me everyone goes through the dark night of the soul, even Camillis Delilis. Blimey, I thought he was referring to a senior theology student, but he meant some bloody spirit from the Middle Ages. Glad I didn't ask to speak to him!"

Hans chuckled, somewhat taken with this blustery fellow who differed with him over a host of issues. He wondered how this dynamic rogue could believe all the fables that were rationed out daily. Did Patrick leave his rationality at home, or was he here because the priesthood was a relatively easy life?

After Patrick shared everything from his family history, including recounting his impure thoughts about Eileen Kielty, it was Hans's turn.

"Compared to you, my life sounds very dull. Graduate architect and late bloomer with regard to Christianity. In all of my schooling and career choices, there was always something missing."

Patrick nodded. "Boy, I can relate to that. I thought the hocus-pocus stuff by men in dresses was a bunch of shite, but one day I heard a sermon from Father Donahue and the priesthood became a real option. I could see spending my life in the service of others. For me, the priesthood is about caring for the people who have no voice or power. I have a hard time with the way Jesus is portrayed in most of our theology classes. I see him as one who came to shake things up. I really relate to his confronting all the powerful forces in his land. By the way, speaking about powerful forces, I'm glad you're not a Brit. Where I come from, they've had their boots on our necks for centuries."

"Somewhat like the Jews have had us in their clutches for years."

Patrick looked puzzled. "You're not occupied by Jews, so how is it the same?"

"It's complicated, Patrick. They control the financial world. In many ways historically they are responsible for the terrible economic climate in Germany. The financial woes are caused by wealthy Jews who care little about the economic conditions of the common man. This must change if we are to have a just society that benefits all its citizens."

Patrick finished his cappuccino. "Cheerio, my good man. I hope we have the chance to speak again. I'll look for you in the Magna Aula. Maybe we can share a cigarette break."

"I'd like that," Hans said, knowing he would enjoy a trusted friend. Patrick posed no threat to Hans's mission, for Ireland was not a country that figured into the designs of the Führer. It would be refreshing to occasionally chat about trivia and not have to be perfect all the time.

Chapter Eighteen

Passau, 1936

Professor Aaron Lehman sat in his office struggling to believe the letter that he had just received from the University of Munich's chancellor. He knew racial laws were being implemented in Germany, but he did not believe they would apply to him. He was a full professor with an international reputation as an accomplished architect, but apparently that did not matter. He had been aware that younger Jewish members of the faculty had been forced to resign, but he had hoped that seniority and years of dedicated service would protect him. He read the letter again.

Herr Professor Lehman,

The academic board of the University of Munich is obliged to fully implement the racial purity laws which are to be applied without exception. Your Jewish heritage dictates that you can no longer have the rights or privileges of a member of the architectural staff at the university.

As of the date you receive this letter, you are officially removed from all of your duties as a professor of architecture. It is imperative that you vacate your office immediately. As of your receipt of this letter, you will have no further contact with students or faculty.

Aaron slowly rose from his chair and began to assemble his belongings. Thoughts raced through his mind as he put personal items into a box: *How does one leave a life's work when there is no rational cause? Are my architectural contributions to be obliterated because of my heritage? What does being a Jew have to do with architecture? Do my buildings care whether they were designed by a Jew?* His thoughts moved to his family and the future. *What if this is only the tip of the iceberg? I must find a way to protect myself and my family. Perhaps the racial laws are being carried out only in outlying areas; they most assuredly will be ignored in Berlin. I think the most reasonable thing for me to do is to move my family to Berlin and explore teaching opportunities at the university. I have given countless lectures there, and surely my friends and colleagues there will help me.*

After packing as many of his belongings as he could carry, Aaron left the office. He turned back to look one last time at the place that he so loved. He felt a tear trickle down his cheek as he realized that this might be the last time he saw it.

As he walked down the corridor, a group of students appeared. Seemingly embarrassed to see him, most of them turned away. However, one of his graduate students hurried up.

"Professor Lehman, you are the finest professor I have ever had and I will miss you."

"Thank you. Continue your studies and you will do well."

After the student walked quickly away, Aaron continued down the corridor. He saw another small group of his students. These avoided eye contact with him. The silence was deafening as he walked past them.

Aaron went home, even thought it was the middle of the day. He opened the front door to the sound of piano music. He quietly walked down the hallway and observed two of the people in the world that he most loved. His wife Ruth and his grandson Micah.

Ruth was spending the entire afternoon with Micah while Sarah gave music lessons at the Temple. At age four, Micah was an amazing child. He had been blessed with his mother's zest for life. He already was considered a child prodigy at the piano. Though Micah was exceptionally handsome, he bore little resemblance to their family and none to Noah's family. Somewhere over the centuries there must have been a Jew with blond hair and blue eyes in their families.

"Nana, want me to play for you?" Micah asked.

"Yes, please, my dear boy."

Ruth sat down on the piano bench beside him. Piano notes wafted through the air, the music sending away cares and concerns.

Aaron watched the innocent child who brought beauty and joy to their lives. Micah's tunes created a momentary hope that the turbulence would soon evaporate and once again the life they loved would be restored.

He must have made some sound—maybe one of hopeless despair—for his wife turned, saw him, and leaped to her feet.

"My God, Aaron, what is the matter?"

"It will be all right, Ruth. Things will get better."

Chapter Nineteen

Berlin, 1936

Magda Ritschel had agreed to ignore Josef's constant infidelities, but she grew increasingly furious at how blatant they had become. There wasn't the slightest trace of discretion in his behavior. Early in their marriage, he had told her that his sexual exploits had nothing to do with his affection for her. Magda was not without her own sexual secrets, but unlike Josef, she had kept the fact that she had a lover to herself. Part of this was pride, part discretion, but the main reason was that her lover was none other than Erich Hanke, her husband's primary assistant.

Her relationship with Erich had begun months before when she had confided that she was beginning to tire of Josef and his obsession with sex. Hanke had begun by listening, but before long he had stated that if he had such a wonderful wife he would forsake the bed of every other woman in Germany.

Magda reached her boiling point when Josef moved his current mistress to the guest quarters on their villa property. This new liaison was more than the casual two-week affair that Josef had paraded on countless occasions. The intensity of the relationship and its longevity indicated that Josef was in love. As the mother of his children, Magda was furious at the idea that he might have a child with another woman.

One afternoon while Josef was out of town, Magda had gone to the guest quarters and demanded that the mistress, Lida Barova, pledge never to have a child with Josef. Lida had reluctantly agreed, but the confrontation had done nothing to ease Magda's discomfort.

For the first time in her marriage, Magda pondered the possibility of a divorce. Because of her role as the de facto First Lady of Germany, she could not even raise the possibility with Josef without conferring with the Führer first. She traveled to the Berchtesgaden, hurried inside, and poured out her pain and anguish to Adolf, one of her best friends. Hitler listened attentively without saying a word, but he appeared more and more concerned with every word.

Finally she took a deep breath. "I want to divorce him."

"Magda, there will be no divorce. The image of your perfect marriage is too important to Germany. However, I make you a solemn pledge that Josef will immediately end this relationship. He will resume his role as devoted husband and father."

"Thank you so much. You are so kind to help. Actually, I really want my marriage to last. And I do apologize for creating a difficult situation for you."

Hitler kissed her on both cheeks, smiling in a fatherly way. "I am pleased that you had such confidence in me that you could openly share your unhappiness."

"You know I have total confidence in you, now and always."

With her life returned to order, Magda swept out of the Berchtesgaden and headed back to Berlin.

After she left, Hitler went into a rage, tossing chairs about. "That goddamn runt will get rid of that whore or I will have him castrated."

Hitler summoned his secretary to place a call to Dr. Goebbels.

Josef and Lida woke slowly after a long night of making love. She placed one arm over his shoulder. With her other hand, she fondled his erect penis.

"My God, you are insatiable," he said with admiration.

She smiled sweetly, preparing to mount him when there was a loud knock at the door.

"Yes, who is it?" Josef called.

"Dr. Goebbels, there is a phone call for you."

"Have the person call back."

"But, sir, it is the Führer."

Josef jumped out of bed, put on his robe, and answered the phone.

Lida put on Goebbels's hat, stood on the bed, and gave a salute, imitating the Führer. Josef was not amused by her antics. "Yes, my Führer. I will leave immediately."

When he finished talking to Hitler, Josef took his robe off and started to get dressed.

Lida pressed herself against him.

"I have to go."

"Not before you make love to me." She pushed him back on the bed.

The past month had been exhilarating for Josef. Not since his early days of marriage had he experienced such love. He had actually entertained the thought of divorcing Magda, giving up his post in the party, and leaving Germany.

For now, he must hurry to Hitler. The Führer's voice had indicated that he was displeased about something.

All the way to the Berchtesgaden, Josef explored the possibilities in his mind, but he had no clue as to what was wrong. Why had the Führer's voice on the phone sounded so different? In the few words he had spoken, it was clear that this visit was mandatory and not a casual occasion to discuss trivial issues. What had gone wrong in the past few days that could put Josef in a vulnerable position? He was constantly worried that Goering or Himmler would replace him as the Führer's most trusted advisor. This was certainly a possibility, but the Führer knew that it was Goebbels who had been largely responsible for his popularity with the German people. Goebbels had structured the election campaigns. Goebbels had organized the massive rallies. Goebbels had taken control of the entire German media. Hitler was intensely loyal to those who served him well. Goebbels was a member of the inner circle. What could he possibly have to fear?

The limousine entered the oval driveway of the Berchtesgaden, stopped, and the chauffeur opened the door. Josef grabbed his briefcase, saluted the guard at the door, and entered the building. He was shown to the drawing room. It was but a few moments before the Führer entered the room, closing the door behind him.

Josef rose from his chair and saluted, saying, "Heil Hitler."

The greeting had no effect on Hitler. He motioned for Goebbels to sit. Hitler began to pace up and down, waving his arms. Suddenly he turned and shouted, "Have you lost your mind, you pervert?"

Josef sat stunned and speechless. What was the Führer referring to? What had he done? Fear froze him in place.

Hitler stood over him and screamed, "Why have you let a whore make you a laughingstock? Has your penis destroyed your brain? I have ignored your sexual dalliances before, but now I am furious at your behavior. You and Magda are the perfect emblems of the Aryan family. You and your children are supposed to be the images of the new Germany. Your lust for this Czech whore has placed that image in jeopardy. Your wife has begged me for permission to divorce you. I tell you now that will never happen."

Josef was both mortified and terrified. He loved Lida, but he also loved the power and position of his office. He was one of the most powerful men in Germany. Now his sexual relationship had placed him on the precipice of failure. At that moment, he not only feared for his position, he feared for his life. He would not be the first to be found dead in an alley, the victim of anonymous murderers.

He opened his mouth to speak.

"Be silent!" The Führer's rage seemed somewhat lessened, but still the tone was anything but friendly. "You are to remove that whore from your residence immediately. She is to leave Berlin today. I forbid you to have any further contact with her. Also, you will apologize to Magda. You will arrange newspaper and magazine articles featuring your wonderful family. Do you understand everything I have said here this morning?"

Josef felt faint, but he managed to rise from his chair. "My Führer, I am most sorry that my behavior has led to your need for this meeting. I will fulfill your commands at once."

Hitler still seemed angry, and he did not offer any additional words that would indicate forgiveness. He turned and left the room.

Josef saluted the Führer's back. As he put on his coat and hat, his hands were trembling. He could not control his anxiety. It took him a few moments to find the opening to his coat sleeves. He quickly left the Berchtesgaden.

The ride to Berlin seemed endless, and Josef wondered if he could ever be in the good graces of the Führer again. He had always believed that the power under his roof resided with him. Now he realized that in a confrontation with Magda, he would be the loser.

He entered the guest house and walked to the patio. Lida was having coffee, looking as beautiful and sensual as ever. She turned and happily rose to greet him.

But she was not for him—not now, not ever again.

Chapter Twenty

Rome, early 1937

There was a slight tap on the door. The pope said, "Come in."

Dressed similarly to the pope, in a black cassock, Cardinal Eugenio Pacelli, the Vatican's secretary of state, entered. It was apparent that this meeting was in no way about pomp and circumstance.

"Good morning, Holy Father," Cardinal Pacelli said as he placed his hat on the coat rack.

"Good morning, Eugenio. I asked to meet you here so that we will be uninterrupted."

Pacelli nodded. "Holy Father, it was clear from your note that you have serious concerns about what is happening in Germany. I share your belief that the situation is worse than I initially thought."

The pope frowned. "There is no longer any doubt about what is transpiring in Germany. I seek your counsel as to how we should intervene. News about the treatment of our Jewish brethren is alarming. There is never any justification for the deprivation of personal or property rights, but daily acts of brutality are frightening."

"This is a most delicate situation because the German people are embracing this new political movement. The Jews have become a target and convenient scapegoat for all of Germany's past problems."

"What has happened to the civilized culture that produced such masterful literature and music?" the pope inquired.

Pacelli shook his head. "I fear that the Nazi Party has discredited the intelligentsia. The movement is largely led by men without intellectual skills who are so blinded by bigotry that their rationality has been suspended."

The pope rose from his chair and slowly paced the room. "Tell me about Adolf Hitler, Eugenio."

Pacelli opened his briefcase and took out a large folder. "I have been keeping a file on Chancellor Hitler. I have come to the conclusion that he soon will have complete control over the German people. His speeches are filled with anti-Semitic rhetoric, and it appears that his ultimate goal is to rid Europe of its Jewish population."

"I don't understand. What does this mean?"

"I believe Hitler has decided to make life in Germany so difficult for the Jews that they will be forced to emigrate. He repeatedly links them with Bolshevism and blames them for the consequences of Germany's defeat in the Great War."

The pope began to scribble some notes on a pad, then looked up. "He is not the only one who fears Bolshevism, but coupling atheism from the east with European Jewry makes no sense."

Pacelli nodded. "True, your Holiness, but the entire Nazi movement is not based on rationality. It is rooted in fear, ignorance, and hate."

"Eugenio, no one here knows more about the German people than you. Do you believe they will follow Hitler's lead in all of these matters?"

"Your Holiness, they have depicted him as the Messiah come to lead his people out of the darkness. It has taken on the cloak of a demonic cult and demands blind obedience."

The pope seemed completely baffled by this assessment. "I have heard that Hitler and many of his inner circle are actually Catholics. How can they reconcile their behavior with the tenets of the Church?"

"They were baptized, but they have nothing but hatred for the Church. They have no allegiance to Catholic doctrine. They are Catholic in name only. They will seek to neutralize you and every form of belief system that opposes their path to power."

The pope tapped his fingers on the desk. "Where is the German Church with regard to the National Socialists?"

"Are you asking about our bishops or all of the Christian churches in Germany?"

"Let us begin with our bishops. What is their attitude and behavior toward Hitler?"

"I fear many of the bishops have publicly embraced Hitler. After living in Germany for many years, I can attest to the national loyalty many of them evidence. They differ from the Italian bishops. In Italy, there is no overall binding nationalism. Italy is still a group of city states. In Germany, those individual differences are blended into a homogenous love of country. Hitler has reawakened the past glory when the Church and the state were one. Also—and it pains me to say this—there is an aspect of anti-Semitism in the German Catholic hierarchy that appears in sermons and public pronouncements."

The pope was incredulous. "How can they be anti-Semites? We are all spiritual Semites, and everything that is sacred and holy has its roots in Judaism! Hating Jews and loving Christ is totally incompatible. Loyalty to country over morality can never be viewed as the will of God."

Pacelli nodded. "We must directly intervene with the German bishops and alter their current posture, but how will we do that, your Holiness?"

"I want you to write an encyclical that will decry the evils of racism, in particular, the Nazi philosophy that is the root of all the horrors occurring in Germany. You must do this in such a way that no one but you and I will know of it."

"I accept, your Holiness, but what will we do when it is finished?"

"First it must be written in German. When it is completed and reviewed, it must be smuggled by couriers into the hands of the hierarchy and mandated that it be promulgated from every pulpit in Germany."

Pacelli seemed troubled by this strategy. "Holy Father, there is great risk to the Church in Germany if we publicly create a confrontation. My assessment is that the Nazis will take direct actions that will be harmful to the Church."

"Eugenio, I have no illusions about changing their beliefs, but we are commanded by God to not stand by and have the children of Abraham be pitched into this maelstrom of evil. It is our duty to confront these evil actions regardless of the consequences. We cannot guarantee outcome, but we can guarantee witness."

"I agree, but I believe that a large segment of the Catholic population will not follow our lead on these issues. Even some bishops may resist."

The pope shook his head. "He did not say, 'I will build this Church upon a rock, but if things are difficult, avoid them.' We are the shepherds. We cannot run from the wolf because we are afraid." The pope paused, then asked, "What about the Protestant churches in Germany? Will they resist Hitler?"

"I think that, by and large, they are akin to German Catholics. Hitler has captured the imagination of a large segment of the population, but so far he has not tampered with religion directly. Also, the words of Martin Luther and his loathing of the Jews seem to be an integral piece of the Protestant fabric." He paced the floor and then turned to the pope. "How will we balance this criticism of the National Socialist movement with our opposition to Bolshevism?"

"I will depend on your intellectual and writing skills to develop the encyclical so that in no way does it give support to Bolshevism."

"Your Holiness, God has blessed us with your leadership, and I pray that you will be able to see us through this crisis." He knelt and received the pope's blessing.

"Go in peace, Eugenio, and may the spirit of the Lord fill your pen as it did with the four Evangelists."

Chapter Twenty-One

Rome, May 29, 1937

Cardinal Pietro Agnelli had been troubled by the situation in Germany, fearing that the plight of the Jews there would continue to worsen. The growing popularity of Hitler alarmed him because he had read *Mein Kampf*. He knew that the book's belief system was rooted in blame and hate. An optimist, the cardinal searched for things that would balance his concerns. This day was one of them.

Today he would ordain forty-two graduates of the Gregorian University in Saint Peter's Basilica. He found comfort and joy in the realization that even in the current climate of world crisis, men could still be attracted to the peaceful message of Christ. Today he would lay hands on forty-two young men who would take up their crosses to alleviate the suffering of others.

At 8:15 a.m., Hans Keller left the German house of studies. He was not due at the Basilica until 9:30, but on this beautiful morning in Rome he wanted to gather his thoughts. Many of his classmates had undoubtedly spent the night tossing and turning at the thought of assuming the roles of priest and minister. He had no such thoughts, so his sleep had been deep and undisturbed. The tedious years of the seminary were behind him. The real work of his dedication to the Reich would soon begin. The other forty-one men to be ordained with him would live in a spiritual world following the preaching of a dead Jewish carpenter, but he would help shape policy developed by a true leader who lived and ruled in the here and now.

Arriving at the square in front of the Basilica, Hans marveled at the magnificent edifices Catholicism had created. As an architect, he appreciated every aspect of the square and the Basilica. He looked first at the two beautiful fountains in the square, and then he gazed at the center where the tall obelisk from the thirteenth century gave height to the oval square. The outline of the colonnade created the impression of embracing the onlooker. From the top of the colonnade, 140 statues of saints peered down on all who entered the portals of the Basilica. He hoped someday to be part of creating such magnificence to honor the Führer. As he approached the entrance on the side of the Basilica, he showed his clerical pass and was saluted by the Swiss Guards.

Saint Peter's Basilica was already filling up, and he could hear the joyous sounds of people who had traveled many miles to see the ordination of their loved ones. There were families from Europe as well as the United States and South America.

Hans had only three people who were there for his ordination. Erich Hanke, plus Magda and Josef Goebbels, were the substitutes for both of his families. Magda had no knowledge of the role that Hans was to play in Germany's future. She understood simply the story that Hans was Josef's good friend from Passau. Only four people in the world knew why he had embarked on this journey: Hans, Hanke, Goebbels, and, of course, the Führer.

As Cardinal Agnelli entered the main altar from the sacristy, the Vatican choir began to sing the hymn that has been sung in Latin at every ordination in this hallowed place, *"Tue es sacerdos in eternum,"* or "You are a priest for eternity."

For the past four years, Hans had accepted his role as a challenging step toward his future position in the Nazi Party. He had played the part of the outstanding seminarian perfectly. Excelling in his studies, he had been selected in his final year to be responsible for the initiation of ten new seminarians. This selection was based on the faculty's belief that direct contact with Hans would help develop the spiritual and intellectual development of these seminarians.

Now the day had come when Hans would finally be finished with the first phase of his commitment. He was anxious to contribute directly to the goals that Dr. Goebbels had outlined in their initial meeting.

Cardinal Agnelli remained seated until all of the candidates sat down, and then he rose and greeted them and all of the visitors. "There is no more joyous charge for me than to welcome all of you to this wondrous occasion. Today we will continue to call new disciples to the ministry of our Lord."

He turned and began to celebrate the mystery of the Eucharistic sacrifice. After the reading of the Gospel, Cardinal Agnelli ascended the steps to the pulpit and began to speak directly to the candidates.

"My brothers, in a few short moments each of you will hear your name called. You will prostrate yourselves on the floor of this altar and present yourselves for ordination to God's holy priesthood. You are being ordained not for yourselves but for others. The road will not always be easy, and especially in the world today there will be pain and suffering. But may the joy of this day with your loved ones and friends enable you to grow in compassion to live the beatitudes that our Lord has challenged us to embrace.

"Your priesthood is not about power or glory. It is about service to others. In that awesome responsibility, you will find the fullness of meaning you seek. May the Prince of Peace bless you in the name of the Father, the Son, and the Holy Ghost."

One by one the seminarians uttered the statement, *"Adsum,"* the Latin words of total acceptance.

When it was Hans's turn, he murmured to himself, *"Adsum,"* and he then added under his breath, "my Führer."

Like many other professions, there was the overriding anxiety about new circumstances and responsibilities. The academic part was over. The newly ordained priests were now about to be immersed in the pastoral and spiritual needs of their flocks.

Unlike his peers, Hans was not anxious; his role had been determined long ago. The seminary had been a four-year costume party for him. While others had been praying for spiritual growth, he had been immersed in the political aspirations of the National Socialist Party. All the skills that he had developed were tools of subterfuge that could manipulate others into the wishes of his superiors. The seminary had been a prelude to the real goal: a meaningful role in the implementation of the Nazi vision.

Chapter Twenty-Two

Rome, July 1937, First Assignment

Bishop Alois Huldol was the perfect mentor for Hans. He was influential in Vatican circles, and from 1920 to 1927, he had been an auxiliary bishop in Munich. He was a physically impressive man, topping six feet by five inches with chiseled features and a deep baritone voice. An ardent student of history, he aspired to return the Church to the golden eras when the Church and state were synonymous. He had visions of the Vatican once again being the core of the empire with piety being secondary to power. The dawn of a new opportunity had arisen in the homeland of his birth, and he was determined to assist the body politic in establishing harmony between Berlin and Rome.

Bishop Huldol had been a chaplain during the Great War. He still harbored resentment over the capitulation to the Allies. Just like many German soldiers, he never accepted the defeat of Germany.

The bishop attributed his great nation's surrender to the power of international Judaism. He perceived the Jews as a persistent obstacle to the dreams of a glorious German reign in harmony with the crown and the cross. Jews had been a temporary part of God's universal plan, but their role was no longer relevant. In his mind the plan had been fulfilled. The prophetic part had been achieved.

There was no longer any value in the rituals and message of Judaism. The wait was over. The stubborn refusal of Jews to accept Christ as the fulfillment of God's word relegated them to the status of heretics. Their unwillingness to accept the good news was because the lust for money and power had replaced a true understanding of the prophets' messages. Money was the real god of Judaism. The power and privilege that money purchased were the obstacles to the Church accomplishing its potential.

He believed that Jewish money compromised the dream of a glorious German Empire largely because of the weak posture of the German government toward the Jews and the Jews' undermining of any attempts to change the status quo. Most, if not all, of Germany's problems were directly related to the Jews.

This fervent belief had been pulsating through the bishop's veins for some time, and finally his desire to influence change had become a possibility. There was a whirlwind of change occurring in Germany. The corruption and ineptness of the chancellor and his minions were being challenged. A new political party, the National Socialist Party, had emerged. What had started as a minor annoyance for the Parliament had become a dynamic alternative.

The party's leader, Adolf Hitler, was a dynamic speaker with a vision of Germany's future that was taking hold in the average German soul. Bishop Huldol had had the opportunity to hear Hitler speak in Munich. He had found it easy to subscribe to all of Hitler's views and policies. The yoke of Versailles and the penalties that had been imposed by the victors must be removed. The real enemies of the people were the philosophy of Bolshevism and the financial power of the Jews. Hitler was never timid when he spoke about the source and the solution. It was Bishop Huldol's great hope that as he had found his spiritual master in Christ, he could find his political master in Adolf Hitler.

The Vatican offered a dual platform: one was information and access to the ambassadors of multiple nations and the second was the ability to affect public opinion both within and outside of the

Church. Bishop Huldol's presence in the German hierarchy could shape resistance and create a fertile field for the Nazi Party by minimizing the Vatican's opposition to policies.

The bishop was well aware that the current pope, Pius XI, had serious reservations about the Nazis, for on many occasions he had voiced opposition to the perceived growth of anti-Semitism in Germany. Bishop Huldol scoffed at the pope's obsession with the Jews. As an Italian, the pope had no real sense of German history. The Italians had not suffered to the degree that the Germans had from the Treaty of Versailles. Plus, the pope was insulated from the political accommodations that were necessary between Church and state.

Bishop Huldol had a keen awareness that direct opposition to the Vatican's dispositions on these matters was useless. Subterfuge and secret alliances within the Church and the diplomatic world were far more effective than confrontation. He was ecstatic about having Father Hans Keller become his secretary and assistant. He had been made aware of the young priest through a dinner last year at the German embassy. Erich Hanke, a member of Dr. Goebbels's staff, had spoken glowingly of Father Keller's talents.

Hanke's assessment of Keller had proven to be accurate. The bishop had spent time in the last six months at the German house of studies in Rome and had investigated the background and qualifications of then seminarian Keller. The rector had been effusive in his praise and had ventured the opinion that in his ten years at the German house of studies, Hans was easily the most outstanding young man he had ever taught. Hans was a brilliant scholar, a master linguist, and a dynamic speaker who carried himself with confidence. He was viewed by his peers as the class leader. To add to all this, he was a superb athlete.

Bishop Huldol had found the ideal person to be used in the essential missions that would bond the Church in Germany with the Nazi Party.

Chapter Twenty-Three

Rome, 1938

The lecture hall was filled with professionals from every walk of Italian society. Attendance at the two-day seminar on the racial laws was not optional. Anyone who did business with the central government of Italy was obliged to attend the conference and proof of presence was required.

Due to his official status as an attorney and the mayor of Soverato, Severio Pittelli had received instructions to attend. During the rise of fascism, he had successfully negotiated a position of noninvolvement. Yet he walked a fine line, because it was critical not only for his family but also for the citizens of Soverato that he not be seen as one who opposed the government in Rome. He personally detested Benito Mussolini and believed that ultimately his relationship with Adolf Hitler would have dire consequences for Italy. The constant bombardment of Rome's propaganda machine promoted the ideals of ancient Rome and stressed the racial purity of Italian blood. He was convinced that Mussolini would ultimately lead Italy off a cliff into destruction.

Severio believed that Mussolini's initial posing as a caring father building a successful series of programs that would lead to a better life for all had been replaced by a dictator's blind thirst for power.

This vision was constantly fostered from the balcony over the Piazza Venezia by the man who aspired to be the new Caesar.

Severio feared that young men all over Italy would be sacrificed in the coming years. He had heard Mussolini's bellicose speeches from the balcony of the Piazza Venezia along with the band playing and all the fawns praising Il Duce. The temporary suspension of people's rights worried Severio because he knew that once the government interfered in the private lives of its citizens a progression of denied freedoms would quickly follow.

That day the auditorium was filled with colleagues exchanging pleasantries, but soon the noise gave way to Dr. Alfonso calling the meeting to order. He pounded his gavel until total silence allowed him to address the audience.

"For the next two days we will be privileged to hear Europe's most expert authorities address the issue of racial purity. As leaders in your professions, it is essential that you have the latest scientific data so that you may enforce the spirit of the racial laws as well as understand the guidelines."

As Dr. Alfonso spoke, Severio took a quick 360-degree look around the auditorium. He could not believe that this drivel was being taken seriously. As the day wore on, he heard endless droning about the purity of blood and the need to prepare the culture for an elevated populace. To Severio, this was nothing more than sheep dung thinly covered by pseudoscience. There was no such thing as the Italian race. For centuries the Mediterranean land had hosted countless tribes and peoples. The years of intermingling made it impossible to make any claim about purity of blood. In all parts of Italy there were so many shades and shapes that if the goal of penalizing the Jews was not so frightening, it would be laughable.

Severio instantly recognized the emerging pattern of the speakers. No matter what their expertise or what their data indicated, the conclusions were always the same. The pollution of the Jewish race had curtailed the greatness of Italian potential, so ultimately Jews must be ostracized from Italian mainstream society. The premise that the future generations would have pure blood, all the same features, and enhanced academic ability once Semitic blood was purged was so outrageous that Severio could not fathom how any intelligent person could subscribe to such bigotry.

At the end of the conference, the purveyors of this tripe were lined up onstage and greeted with thunderous applause. Severio clapped his hands along with everyone else, but he vowed that this poison would never be drunk by the citizens of Soverato while he was the mayor.

Chapter Twenty-Four

Kulpmont, 1938

Stefano Pittelli had pleaded with the management of the coal mine for months to invest in a series of safety precautions that would benefit both miners and management. He had carefully explored the cost of these improvements. He had established data indicating that despite the expense, there would actually be financial gain from these improvements. So far, the mine had been spared a major tragedy.

Yet at least twice a month, there was a work stoppage due to insufficient beam support. Also, the ever-present danger of explosions and fires could shut the mine down for days. Even though Stefano's attempts were frequent, he rarely heard back from management; when he did, the answer was always no.

On a Thursday, no different than thousands of days that preceded it, a living nightmare came to the Kulpmont community. One of the mules stumbled in a mine, and the entire load of coal fell from the rear of the truck and dislodged two torches from the wall. These fell into a bale of hay that ignited the dry grass, setting the entire mine ablaze. A series of explosions from the coal gas in the air trapped a group of miners deep within the bowels of the earth.

Stefano reacted immediately and managed to rescue five of the miners closest to the entrance, but the fire spread so rapidly that those furthest from the original blaze were overcome by intense flames and smoke. Despite the intensity of the fire, Stefano raced through the flames and rescued two unconscious men. Though badly burned, he attempted to penetrate the fire again, but the heat had become too intense. He wept at the cries of the miners who were being smothered and burned alive.

Two days before the funeral of the twelve miners killed in the fire, Stefano woke up not so much from the pain in his burned arms but rather from the dry cough that had plagued him for weeks. Not wanting to disturb the family during his coughing attacks, he went downstairs and attempted to sleep on the sofa.

At dawn, he gave up and started making coffee, but he coughed so severely that he dropped the coffeepot as he was about to put it on the stove. The water extinguished the gas burner and spilled all over the kitchen floor. When he finished mopping up the mess, he coughed hard again, noticing that there was blood as well as coal dust in his handkerchief. The coal dust was a constant, but this was the first time he ever noticed blood.

Stefano would see the doctor later to have his bandages changed, so perhaps it was time to discuss the source of his coughing. He knew that years of breathing in coal dust affected every worker, but because he did not smoke cigarettes, he had always thought the lung damage would be minimal and could be controlled.

As he drove to the doctor's office, his thoughts raced between what had happened to twelve of his miners and the fact that if he had serious lung difficulties he would need to give up mining. With all its difficulties, the mine had allowed him to support his family. It was the only work he had ever done in this country. If he had lung disease, he would have to find some other way to support his wife and children.

After he parked his automobile behind the medical clinic, he strode into the doctor's office with the gait of a man who could conquer the world.

Dr. Schicatono warmly greeted Stefano. After examining the burn wounds, he asked, "How long do you think you can hold your breath to mask the coughing spell in your throat?"

Stefano had been trying to hide the cough so that the conversation would not focus on the real cause. Realizing that trying to fool the physician was an exercise in futility, he found relief in a series of hard coughs.

"How frequent are the coughing spells?" Dr. Schicatono asked.

"Often. I have trouble sleeping at night."

"I'm not surprised. I'm ordering a series of X-rays this afternoon. As soon as I have the results, I will call you, but I am almost certain that you have black lung disease. If that is so, you can no longer work in the mine."

Though expected, the words hit Stefano with the force of a sledgehammer. Yet right then he could not dwell on the prospect. His first duty was to comfort the grieving families at the funeral in two days. After that, he would formulate a plan for his future. "I'm not surprised, Dr. Schicatono. If that turns out to be the case, I'll deal with it. For now, I would like to keep this between us until you are certain."

"I completely understand. Now get dressed and take this note to the X-ray department at the hospital."

The ride to the mine, which was closed until after the funerals, was a blur as Stefano went over and over in his mind the incidents of that day. He entered the building and began to formulate the eulogy he would deliver. He would survive whatever the outcome, as he once had survived the harshness of life in a village without work and without a father.

The loss of the twelve men weighed heavily on Stefano. The fire left some burn scars, but these paled compared to the anger he felt about the lack of safety precautions that caused the deaths of his friends. Stefano was, above all, a man of reason who rarely allowed his emotions to interfere with his work—but this utter disregard for human life demanded a response. That opportunity would be the eulogy that the relatives of the dead miners had asked him to deliver.

On the morning of the funerals, Saint Antonio's church was filled to overflowing. Built by the wave of immigrants who came at the beginning of the century, it was reminiscent of German architecture. The stained glass windows depicted scenes from the lives of Irish and Italian saints. This holy place was still the sanctuary for those who came from Europe, and it contained the records of the main events of life and death. In this church the miners were married, had their children baptized, and buried their dead. It was a place whose floors had been washed with countless tears of sorrow and joy.

Today the main and side aisles were filled with the coffins of those who had perished in the disaster. There was certainly sorrow in those in attendance, but there was also a seething anger that these men who had given so much were betrayed by the greed of those who lived off the expense of their labors. The men in these coffins had come to America with the hope of a better life and had stoically endured the hardships of coal mining. They had known pain, suffering, bitter cold, and intense heat that only the brave could confront day in and day out. They ate cold food out of steel lunch pails so that their children would have a warm supper each night.

When the mass ended, Stefano left his pew and walked to the stairs that led to the ornate pulpit. As he readied himself to speak, he felt a lump in his throat as he viewed the coffins and the weeping families before him.

"We come here today in this holy place to honor the lives of our brothers who died in the mine on Thursday. I have no words that can capture the sorrow that all of you loved ones feel. You have lost wonderful husbands, fathers, sons, relatives, and dear friends. None of us can replace these good men, but we can pledge to you that we will not forget them or you. This is a community of people who truly care for each other.

"We will also not forget how they died and will continue in their names to create a better and safer mine. We owe it to their memory. We realize that mining is hazardous, but we must never accept less than the best we can provide for those who have the courage to enable the rest of the country to thrive. We must do this not just with anger, but also with reason. These men and many of you are the backbone of an industry that creates heat for homes and power for manufacturing. Without us, the country would come to a standstill. We must have no more coffins lining the aisles in coal country.

"In closing, I would ask you to pray for my brothers and their families." Before leaving the pulpit, he read the list of names of all who had died.

After the funerals, Stefano received a call from the doctor confirming the original diagnosis. He began to think about the next step in his life.

For weeks, as the pittance that the mine gave him as severance was running out, he went over and over the possibilities. After a great deal of soul searching, he finally settled on an idea. Somehow, he would reach back into time and bring forth the knowledge of the land that he had learned as a young boy in Italy. At present, his garden was considered a marvel in Kulpmont. He felt an almost spiritual uplifting when he nurtured plants to reach their full potential to aid his family and friends. His mother and priest had taught him that life was about more than simple survival. He wanted to help others, too. He would find a grocery store somewhere in Pennsylvania where he could continue to provide food, shelter, and educational opportunities for his children and those in need of assistance.

Black lung disease was no match for Stefano as he began to put together the building blocks for Pittelli's Grocery Store and Delicatessen.

Chapter Twenty-Five

Normandy, 1938

Most of the last year since ordination had been intriguing, but Hans was eager to be part of more serious involvement that would have significant meaning for the cause and for him as well. When he received a summons to a secret meeting with Erich Hanke, he hoped that the opportunity was at hand.

Rain covered the entire coast of Normandy as Hans drove to his weekend meeting. Visibility was so limited that he thought he might have missed the side road that led to Stuttgart Cottage, his destination. He had been to this area before, and it was so secluded that there was no chance that he would be observed. Without his clerical garb, he felt more like himself. It was refreshing, at least for a weekend, to be free of the charade. There were moments when he felt like he had multiple personalities: architect, priest, diplomat, spy. Whatever disguise might be necessary, he would gladly undertake whatever was required to meet the expectations of Dr. Goebbels.

Turning around because the odometer indicated that he had gone too far, Hans observed a small sign for Stuttgart Cottage. He turned right and negotiated the winding turns of the narrow road. He opened his window so he could hear the sound of the sea.

He always found it amazing how the sound of the waves created the feeling of power and peace at the same time. He had always been enamored of places situated on water. He loved Rome, but he missed his many ventures on the Danube River.

Thoughts of the Danube brought Sarah to mind, especially their last canoe trip together that led to their intense sexual experience. It had been years since they had any direct communication. He wondered about her and whether she was living in Passau. He hoped she had a happy marriage and that her kind parents were in good health.

These thoughts ended when Stefano arrived at Stuttgart Cottage. He had met Hanke in Normandy before to discuss strategy, but each time it had been at a different location. The cottage was exactly as had been described. As far as summer places go, it was common and somewhat stark. Even on this gloomy day with the driving rain, he could see the sea pounding on the rocks beneath the cottage. He hoped the rain would pass so that tomorrow he would be able to enjoy the view and perhaps even climb down to the sea.

When Hans drove into the circular area in front of the cottage, Hanke emerged from inside. He opened the door and assisted Hans with his luggage.

"Good afternoon, Father," Hanke said, not sparing sarcasm in his use of the title.

Hans shook the rain off his jacket. "For heaven's sake, Hanke, please don't call me that. For the next couple of days I am just plain Hans."

"Fine. I will make a deal with you. I will call you Hans, but you must refer to me as the Führer."

Hans was surprised. The last thing he would have said about Hanke was that he had a sense of humor. "I think I will mention that to Hitler the next time I see him."

Hanke saluted. "If you do, I will tell the Gestapo that you are secretly a Jewish agent and should be tortured."

Hans burst out laughing. "I think we've reached a stalemate."

After they went inside, Hanke motioned for Hans to warm himself by the fire crackling in a large stone fireplace. He poured cups of black coffee.

Hans accepted a cup and eased his tired body onto an over-stuffed lounge chair. "What is happening in Berlin?"

Hanke grinned gleefully. "Every day we move closer to the Führer's goals. We are achieving wondrous things, even beyond our wildest dreams. The Führer has been able to outsmart and outbluff the weak-kneed politicians who shudder at the thought of war. It is more and more apparent that merely by the threat of the possibility that Germany is willing to go to war that Hitler has them retreating on every issue."

"Is Dr. Goebbels intimately involved in all of these negotiations?"

"He is the backbone of everything that the Führer accomplishes. The Führer readily acknowledges that his work ensures our ability to anticipate and neutralize every issue through the use of propaganda. You are here today because Dr. Goebbels has need of your services in Vienna. I actually envy you. I am aware of all of our plans, but you will be directly involved. In many respects, you are Hitler's priest and will end up being one of his closest counselors."

Hans leaned forward, eager to learn how he was to be involved in a real mission. The duties of clerical messenger and diplomatic social butterfly were necessary but held no excitement for him.

Hanke picked up and opened an envelope marked with a "Top Secret" red stamp. He read aloud the next step in Hitler's plan to reestablish lost German territories and added, "The Führer has a deep affinity for Austria because it is his birthplace. He harbors strong resentment against the Austrian government because they have taken the dictates of the Versailles Treaty literally. Austria has become a shadow of its former self and is currently being exploited by wealthy Jews and bureaucrats. The Führer wishes to make Austria a province or colony of Germany."

Hans blinked in astonishment. "How will this be achieved?"

Hanke grinned and made a prayerful gesture with his hands. "Not by prayer, my good Father, but by pressure and internal manipulation. We already have many German members of the party placed in the Parliament and every government office. Through the newspapers and magazines, we have also written a great many stories addressing the plight of German citizens living and working in Austria who wish to be united with the Fatherland. We have mounted a campaign against the Treaty of Versailles and the world Jewish conspiracy that currently controls the destiny of Austria."

"That is an amazing amount of collaboration."

Hanke nodded. "I am sure that by now you realize this is not merely a history lesson I am sharing with you. If I were you, I would want to know what this has to do with me."

"You missed your profession. You should have been a psychic."

Hanke made a gesture as though he was gazing into a crystal ball, but then he appeared serious. "All joking aside, you will have a most important part to play within the Catholic Church in Austria. As you probably know, the country is largely Catholic, so it is critical that the annexation not be resisted by the Church. This is not the time to neuter the Church or to remove it from its position of influence. That time will come. Currently, the goal is to engage and influence the Austrian hierarchy, especially the head of the delegation, Cardinal Innitzer. He is the most influential cleric in Austria. Unfortunately, he is less than enthusiastic about being reunited with Germany. Your role is to influence him and help him understand that it is in the best interest of the Catholic Church to openly support the Nazi Party. His endorsement will have a huge influence over the Catholic unions and student leagues."

"I understand the significance of reclaiming Austria, but how do I gain access to the cardinal?"

"Dr. Goebbels has met with Bishop Huldol and suggested that in order to maintain a civil dialogue with the Austrian Church, an ambassador must be sent to Vienna for a month to be the liaison between the German hierarchy and the cardinal. The bishop realizes that his pro-Nazi views might be a stumbling block for the cardinal, so someone new and unknown would better serve the goal."

"What about the Vatican? Will they be involved?"

Hanke vigorously shook his head. "They certainly will meddle, but your role is unofficial and should not be discussed with anyone in the Vatican. Dr. Goebbels has major concerns that the Vatican's secretary of state, Cardinal Pacelli, will try to prevent Cardinal Innitzer from welcoming the annexation. Remember also that Bishop Huldol knows nothing of your real role, so be as vague as you can with him. You can act surprised when he informs you about your assignment. Any further questions, Father?" Hanke asked with a huge grin.

"No, my Führer."

Both men chuckled, shaking their heads.

Hanke walked into the kitchen and then returned with a bottle of white wine from the Moselle region. He poured two glasses, handed one to Hans, and toasted, "To the Fatherland and the taking of Austria."

"To the glory of the Rhineland!"

Chapter Twenty-Six

Vienna, 1938

Vienna, Austria, was another new experience for Hans. At one time his entire life had revolved around Passau. Occasional trips to Munich had been his only cosmopolitan exposure. Vienna's center was exquisite. As a student of architecture, he found himself captivated by the Ringstrasse and the overpowering presence of Saint Stephen's cathedral. He had read that it was impossible to be lost in Vienna because all one had to do to establish a focal point was to look for the steeple of Saint Stephen's. Bishop Huldol had arranged for him to stay at Cardinal Innitzer's residence, which was attached to the cathedral.

As the taxi briskly made its way to the residence, Hans read the instructions that he and Hanke had discussed at Stuttgart Cottage. The overt part of his mission was to represent Bishop Huldol and the bishops of Germany in order to bring about a unified front regarding the Church's relationship with the Nazi Party. The underlying objective was to ensure that Cardinal Innitzer's response to the future occupation of Austria would be one of enthusiastic support. The dossier he read indicated that the cardinal probably would not oppose Hitler's desires, but would be cautious in his public support.

There was also the question of the Vatican, which always loomed over any agreement between the Church and Hitler. Dr. Goebbels had made it crystal clear that the Vatican should not meddle in the Austrian question, and he had insisted that Hans keep him informed if any Vatican diplomat or delegation visited while Hans was in Vienna. He was also to be alert for any communication from Secretary of State Cardinal Eugenio Pacelli, who had a great deal of influence within Germany and had recently been less than enthusiastic about national socialism. Coupled with this concern was the fact that the pope had made official and unofficial pronouncements that were interpreted as criticisms of national socialism.

When Hans arrived at Cardinal Innitzer's residence, he noticed that the building reflected the cardinal's personality and the manner in which he represented the Church. The residence gave the impression of royalty and power, both in its size and its magnificent baroque structure. Austria was predominantly a Catholic country, and in many ways, the policies of the state and the Church were identical. The Treaty of Versailles had decreased the physical size of Austria, and in some sense the mammoth city of Vienna was too large because the nation no longer encompassed part of Czechoslovakia. Still, it was a sovereign state where the Catholic Church had tremendous influence.

Hans felt nervous, wondering what Cardinal Innitzer's response would be to a low-level cleric being involved in delicate political matters. Would he view it as interference, or would he welcome the opportunity to explore his options with a neutral observer?

Hans had been invited to have breakfast with Monsignor Rietz, the cardinal's vicar general, before his meeting with the cardinal at ten. Monsignor Rietz was a career chancellery bureaucrat who had never spent any time in a parochial setting. Canon law was his area of expertise. It was said that his approach to every question would be to "follow the rules." One of his priest colleagues had quipped that "Rietz is more German than Austrian and blindly adheres to whatever the book says." Hans hoped that this assessment was literally true because it would make it easier to attain the outcome Dr. Goebbels desired. With the advent of Nazi power, the Austrian rule of law would be dead, but there would be no need to share that information with the good monsignor.

Soon Hans realized that breakfast with Monsignor Rietz would not be one of his fondest memories. The food and coffee were excellent, but the conversation was stilted because Monsignor Rietz had limited social skills. The overt reason for the breakfast was that Monsignor Reitz was to prepare him for his meeting with Cardinal Innitzer. Hans concluded that the covert reality was that Monsignor Reitz desired to reinforce his political position and influence with Bishop Huldol.

After about twenty minutes, Hans was pleased when the housekeeper entered the dining room and informed Monsignor Rietz that his appointment had arrived. The monsignor excused himself, and Hans was left to examine the portraits of all the cardinals that adorned the walls. Dressed in full splendor, the portraits made him feel as if they were watching him. He laughingly thought that they might know why he was really there.

At precisely ten in the morning, Cardinal Innitzer appeared in all his church finery. He invited Hans to join him in the main office.

As they entered the large room, Hans understood why the cardinals were referred to as the princes of the Church. The office alone was more spectacular than any Hans had seen in Berlin or Rome. The entire ceiling was a major work of art comprised of various biblical images carved of rare wood. The huge chandeliers were obviously made of fine Italian crystal, and the luxurious furniture and oriental rugs were fit for a king.

Hans thought it strange that during normal working hours, Cardinal Innitzer was dressed in full formal church garb. The cardinal stretched out his hand and Hans kissed the ornate gold ring. They exchanged formal greetings and then the cardinal motioned for him to sit.

Hans selected a plush chair near Cardinal Innitzer. His initial impression was that the cardinal was probably sixty years old and in relatively good shape. He had read in the cardinal's dossier that he was an avid skier and sports enthusiast. If the conversation ever became difficult, this information would be valuable because Hans enjoyed sports, too.

Soon Hans found the cardinal to be most welcoming and open about discussing the current crisis confronting the Austrian Church. He realized that the cardinal feared the German government more than he feared the Vatican. Cardinal Innitzer would know that Bishop Huldol had tremendous influence in the German hierarchy and was very much in support of the Anschluss. As Bishop Huldol's representative, Hans could certainly provide essential information that would be critical to the cardinal's decisions.

"Father Keller, I'm glad that you have come to Vienna," Cardinal Innitzer said. "This is a perilous time for the Church and Austria as well. I am sure you are aware of the ongoing political negotiations."

"I have been made aware of them by Bishop Huldol."

"Good. I would like to explore what the Church in Germany is experiencing with Herr Hitler and the National Socialist Party."

Hans cautioned himself to lead the cardinal to a positive disposition slowly and not betray undue enthusiasm for the Nazi Party. "I have learned much from Bishop Huldol. In his estimation, the Church in Germany has little to fear and much to gain from the current political situation. The key enemy of the Church in Germany, as well as all of Europe, is atheistic Bolshevism, whereas national socialism has its roots in Christianity."

"I have heard from clergy in Germany that some behavior on the part of party members has been very physical toward those who have other philosophies."

"In the past six months, I have been a frequent visitor representing Bishop Huldol. My current assessment is that, by and large, the German bishops have overcome their initial concerns about

Herr Hitler. In fact, many have actually become members of the party."

Cardinal Innitzer took off his glasses and cleaned them with a soft cloth. "I find that encouraging because in Vienna there are constant stories about the Nazi mistreatment of Jews. You may not know it, but though we are predominantly a Catholic country, Vienna has a large and influential Jewish population."

Hans recognized that the cardinal was probing about the reality of the rumors, so he attempted to address his comment with diversions. "Your Eminence, I believe that much of the rhetoric stems from the German people's resentment over the unfair burden of the Versailles Treaty. There is a strong belief at every level of German society that wealthy Jewish Bolshevists were behind Germany's defeat, and that Jews still profit from a number of Germany's problems. Many members of Germany's Catholic and Protestant hierarchy subscribe to this belief. Much of what is being fostered in newspapers is nothing new."

"What would happen to the Jewish community in Austria if we are reunited with Germany?"

"I am not a politician, your Eminence, so I cannot answer that except to say that perhaps the Church would gain additional influence because of the concordats that Hitler has signed with Rome."

Cardinal Innitzer appeared puzzled. "Father, what is Rome's position on these delicate issues? I am in the middle of very powerful forces. The Vatican—in particular the pope and Cardinal Pacelli—are obviously not enthusiastic about Hitler even though they have signed a concordat with the Nazis."

This was delicate and dangerous ground. Hans needed to choose his words carefully. "Your Eminence, I represent Bishop Huldol, and to some degree the German hierarchy, so it would be presumptuous on my part to speak for Rome. I will say that I have had the opportunity of attending state affairs of many of the European nations in the past few months. Without exception, they have determined that the National Socialists are becoming the most powerful political force in Europe. At times Rome seems to be isolated from what is happening. Of course, there is the danger that being neutral may support philosophies that should be of more concern than national socialism. The Nazi Party has been beneficial in many ways to the common concerns of all German citizens."

"Are you referring to Bolshevism?"

"Yes, I am, your Eminence. The Bolshevists have clearly evidenced a hatred for the Church. At some point there will have to be a major confrontation between opposing philosophies."

The conversation was far more open than Hans had anticipated, and he thought it was now appropriate to lead the cardinal to some major decisions. "May I ask, what is your most serious consideration today?"

"I fear that Hitler may try to nationalize religion and that he will stifle the growth of the Catholic unions and student leagues."

Hans saw the opening he needed. "Would it be beneficial for you to protect all of your organizations by anticipating what will happen instead of reacting to what will happen?"

"I'm not sure I understand your point, Father."

"You appear to believe that Hitler will unify Austria and Germany. If that is the case, I would suggest you explore the possibility of enthusiastically supporting it before it happens. If you only react after it happens, you will lose influence and power."

"Following that possibility, what specifically would you suggest that I do as head of the Austrian Church?"

Hans deliberately drew back before pushing further. "Your Eminence, I am only a messenger. It is not my role to suggest policy."

"Father, I am asking you a direct question and I need a direct answer."

Hans cautioned himself to hesitate and act as if the question made him uncomfortable. Finally he broke his silence. "Communicate directly with Hitler and welcome the unification. Publicly inform your people about why you are doing this. I would counsel you to even go so far as to greet the German chancellor with a phrase that has become a sign of affection in Germany: 'Heil Hitler.' If the union takes place between Germany and Austria, I would advise every church bell in Austria rung to indicate the Church's support."

Cardinal Innitzer rose, ending the meeting. "Father Keller, you have given me a great deal of information to ponder. I would appreciate further opportunities to explore your counsel in the next two weeks."

"I am fully at your disposal, Your Eminence." Hans knelt and received the cardinal's blessing.

As he left the building Hans could not help but smile. Now he fully understood why Dr. Goebbels had placed him in such a powerful position.

Chapter Twenty-Seven

A Vienna Synagogue, 1938

Seated in his office, Rabbi Mendelsohn found it increasingly difficult to control his emotions. Shabbat had always been a joyous part of his week, but this evening he would face his congregation with misgivings. Steeped in the Jewish traditions of tolerance and respect for others, he had always been able to see past imperfections to the inner goodness of everyone. Yet right now in Vienna he found it almost impossible to see any goodness in the Germans. For the first time in his life, the rifle seemed more appealing than the olive branch, but he was reluctant to meet violence with violence. What could he do to lessen the pain and anxiety of his people? After much thought, that evening he stepped before his congregation to speak the saddest of truths.

"Dear brothers and sisters, I come to you this night with the heaviest of hearts because now that we have been taken back into Germany our lives will never be the same. For the longest time we hoped with all our being that the German government would not continue to erode our rights as citizens and free people, but that hope is now but a tiny flickering flame. Already our daily lives have been so disrupted that we find the most common and ordinary things that we once took for granted are now forbidden. These limitations are not merely the criminal acts of isolated fanatics. They are the policies of what we once believed was a civilized government. What have we done to deserve this despicable treatment? Why are our innocent children punished because of their birth into our families? How does a man deprive another of visiting a café or a park without cause? Why have we been removed from occupations where we have served others for most of our adult lives? Is the Jew less a physician today than before the racial laws? Is the merchant who sold reputable goods to others suddenly a thief? We have lost the basic right of due process, and we now are unable to flee into safe environments.

"I fear that these laws only mask the deeper intent of the government. If they cannot force us to leave, they will force us to cease to exist. We need each other more today than ever before, and our heritage of caring for each other is the hope that will enable us to survive these dark days. I cannot stand here tonight and act as though there is nothing to worry about, but neither can I abandon you any more than I can abandon myself. I believe in you and your goodness. I believe there is a loving God. I pray that sanity will be restored before the unimaginable happens. I do not have a magic wand. I do not presume to be a Moses who can lead you to the Promised Land. I am your rabbi, and I pledge my undying devotion to serve you no matter what tomorrow brings."

Joshua and Miriam Abrams sat listening in the synagogue with tears streaming down their cheeks. After the service, they slowly walked home, discussing the fact that the future for Jews in Austria appeared hopeless. They had lived for twenty years at Ten Bolzmangasse, a typical Viennese apartment building that housed seven families. Built in the late nineteenth century, it was an ornate edifice, but through the years it had experienced only the barest maintenance on the exterior. In contrast, the interior apartments were elegant, with hardwood floors, crown molding, high ceilings, and a marble fireplace in every room.

Joshua was forty-seven years old and had a tailor shop in Vienna. The business had thrived for years, but in the last six months many of his non-Jewish customers had stopped utilizing his services. Miriam was only three years younger. She was a marvelous cook who had an exceptional singing voice. Her love for music had been genetically and socially implanted in their twin boys, Isaac and Solomon. Both had attended the Vienna conservatory and until recently had been members of the philharmonic orchestra.

Joshua had initially thought of leaving Vienna because of the increasing difficulties of being a Jew, but after the Anschluss he could not get an individual visa, let alone travel permits for his entire family.

After Austria became part of Germany, new acts of abuse and violence rained upon his family each day. The twins had been beaten on their way home from a Jewish concert, and Solomon's cello had been destroyed in the skirmish. Some of the tenants in their building had ceased speaking to them. Their closest neighbor called them names when she saw them on the stairs. The final tipping point for Joshua had come when he witnessed a group of thugs cutting the beard off an old rabbi near the Ringstrasse. After they had cut his beard, they had beaten him with their fists. When he had fallen to the ground, they urinated on his semi-conscious body.

Helpless to intervene, Joshua had cried as he turned away, trying to avoid the eyes of those who were enjoying the spectacle. Something in him died that day. For the next week, he had discussed his thoughts, once unthinkable, with Miriam. After hours of tearful exploration, they had agreed on a course of action.

On the Thursday after listening to Rabbi Mendelsohn, they began the night with the lighting of the candles. Miriam had prepared a most delicious dinner. The Abrams family ate, laughed, sang, and listened to the wonderful sound of Isaac's violin. After dinner they reminisced for hours, leafing through the photo albums that captured happier days. As the embers glowed in the fireplace, Joshua left the parlor and returned with four glasses of wine. He hugged and kissed each member of his family. They held hands and prayed to the God of Abraham to embrace them.

With one last look into each other's dark eyes, they all drank fully of the glasses. One by one, they slumped to the floor, holding hands in death as they had in life.

Chapter Twenty-Eight

Rome, June 1938

Nothing weighed as heavily on the aging Pope Pius XI as the plight of the Jews under the Nazis. Despite deteriorating health due to diabetes, heart issues, and a plethora of compounding side effects from medications, he was determined to speak out in such a direct manner that there would be no danger of misinterpretation.

In the pope's mind, Hitler was at least equal to the threat of atheistic Bolshevism—and perhaps would be more barbaric in the long run. He was not oblivious to the danger that direct opposition would pose for the Church. Yet he had concluded that any concordat or agreement of the past was meaningless, and even if it were honored, it would not be worth the cost of innocent Jewish blood. The roots of Christianity were irrevocably bound to the children of Abraham. He had publicly and repeatedly stated that we are all spiritually Semites.

He knew his death was imminent, so he wished to leave a testament that would alert the world to the horrors of Nazi Germany. The course of this contribution would not be simple. If the writing of an encyclical were made public, it would engender tremendous resistance, not only from the National Socialists and the German hierarchy but from members of the Curia as well. The encyclical would have to demonstrate the courage to openly deal with universal racism.

After a great deal of reflection and private counsel with Cardinals Agnelli and LeFebbre, the pope selected one of the Jesuits to form an encyclical. He chose an American, Father John Lafarge, who had written about the evils of racism in America. The pope had read Lafarge's most recent book on the subject and thought the work profound. He was particularly disposed toward Lafarge because of his longstanding and courageous opposition to the treatment of Negroes in America.

Pius XI sent for Father Lafarge. The pope was often confined to his bed, but he mustered all of his physical strength for a private meeting.

When Father Lafarge arrived, the pope said, "Good morning, Father."

Lafarge dropped to his knees. "Holy Father, I am thrilled to meet you. May I have your blessing?"

Pius XI raised his right hand and made the sign of the cross over Lafarge. He then tapped him lightly on the head, indicating that he should be seated. "Father, I am not long for this valley of tears. Soon I will be summoned before our Lord who will ask me what I did to alleviate the suffering of his most helpless children."

"I pray that the Lord will keep you well so that you may continue His work on earth."

The pope smiled. "My days are almost done, but it is imperative that I seek your help in one last monumental task."

"I am at your complete disposal, Holiness."

"I want you to write an encyclical abhorring the cancer of racism. I am familiar with your work regarding the Negroes. I admire your ability to influence men of goodwill to look in the mirror and see that we are all children of God, regardless of race or belief. I want this encyclical to focus on denouncing German national socialism and the harm it is inflicting on the Jewish people. There is to be no doubt or equivocation in your pen, Father. This evil must be called what it is, regardless of the consequences for the papacy and the universal Church. Because of my physical condition, it is imperative that your work begin immediately. I have already informed Father Ledochowski of my desire that you write this encyclical. He has offered two other Jesuit scholars to assist you in this work. Now go, my son, and may the Lord inspire you as He did the four evangelists."

"It is my great honor to serve you." Father Lafarge knelt and once again received the pope's blessing.

The pope embraced Lafarge as he rose and looked directly into his eyes, communicating with more than words. "I cannot be clearer with you, Father, than to tell you that you must be direct in this work. Do not couch the truth in diplomatic words. Write this as if you are the pope speaking from his heart without fear of the consequences."

Chapter Twenty-Nine

Rome, 1938

The encyclical written by Father Lafarge was completed and submitted to the general of the Jesuit Order, Father Ledochowski. Bishop Alois Huldol was concerned about the encyclical's contents. He had learned that Father Lafarge had done extensive research on the Negro in America, so Huldol had presumed on that basis that Lafarge would reject the tenet of Aryan supremacy. Once Huldol had received a rough copy of the encyclical through his contacts, he had been astounded to find that some of the passages were blatantly condemnatory of the German government.

Dr. Goebbels would be livid if this encyclical focused negative light on the Nazi Party. It was imperative to delay its promulgation.

Huldol knew that Pope Pius XI was gravely ill, so he hoped there was a way to make the encyclical totally vanish. He decided to have his associate, Father Keller, contact the Jesuit vicar general and discuss the dire implications of its publication.

Huldol read one passage aloud, realizing it alone was enough to make Hitler go ballistic.

"Millions of persons are deprived of the most elementary rights, denied legal protection against violence and robbery, exposed to every insult and public degradation. Innocent persons are treated as criminals; even those who in the time of war fought bravely for their country are treated as traitors. This flagrant denial of human rights sends many thousands of helpless persons out over the face of the earth without any resources."

Bishop Huldol shuddered at the implications of the encyclical. He must enlist Father Keller's aid to ensure that it never saw the light of day.

Father Ledochowski, the Jesuit superior general, was a former Austrian military officer and an austere man with sharply chiseled features. Standing well over six feet tall, he dwarfed many of the priests in the Jesuit community. A staunch conservative theologian, he had a passionate commitment to oppose Bolshevism with all the means at his disposal. The official posture of his office regarding any opposition to the German government was that the Jesuit community should refrain from any public or private statements on political issues. He was not an anti-Semite, but he made no attempt to decry the treatment of the Jews in Europe. His paramount responsibilities were first to protect the Church and second to protect the Jesuit order.

He had been less than enthusiastic when he had been informed by the pope that Father Lafarge had been assigned to write an encyclical. Even though the Jesuit order was at the beck and call of the Holy Father, he had felt angry that he had not been consulted as to the selection of author and content of the encyclical. To maintain some influence in this project, he had assigned two other Jesuits to assist Father Lafarge. He had also ordered Father Lafarge to give a finished copy to him as well as the Holy Father.

After reading the encyclical, Father Ledochowski had been concerned that this document would cause great harm to the Jesuits in Europe, as well as the German Church. Minister Goebbels was sure to react violently to the sections that condemned the Nazi Party's treatment of the Jews.

In that frame of mind, Father Ledochowski had been delighted to hear from Bishop Huldol regarding the encyclical. He had eagerly agreed to meet with Father Hans Keller to discuss an over-all strategy.

When Father Keller arrived, Father Ledochowski indicated that Hans should be seated across from him.

"Are you aware of the contents of this document?" Father Ledochowski asked as he skimmed the pages of the encyclical.

"Bishop Huldol has briefed me on the main thrust of the work."

"Does the bishop have any opinion on what the German government's reaction will be?"

"He is most concerned that there will be a severe negative reaction by the Propaganda Ministry and serious consequences for the German hierarchy and the entire Catholic community. He fears that the Jesuits in Germany will experience direct and indirect acts of persecution."

Father Ledochowski frowned. "Unfortunately I have the same reservations."

"Bishop Huldol is also concerned that this work will give support to the enemies of the Church in the Bolshevist communities. The attack on the Nazi Party could be construed as support for Bolshevism. The consequences would be to aid the growth of a far greater danger to the Church."

Father Ledochowski nodded in agreement. "There is no greater evil in the world than Bolshevism. If in any way this work aids that heresy, it must be destroyed."

"I know that the Holy Father is gravely ill as we speak. Bishop Huldol does not wish to interfere in any way with his desires, but would it not be prudent to wait until the pope is either restored to health or, if God wishes, for the new pope to decide after the pope's death?"

Father Ledochowski knew that, barring a miracle, Pius XI's remaining days on this earth would be few. "I agree that the most prudent course of action is to suspend the document during this period in order to await God's disposition."

Father Keller knelt, asked Father Ledochowski for his blessing, and then left.

Father Ledochowski felt satisfied that he had done what he could to protect the Church and the Jesuits. The Jews would need to find their own protection.

———————————

In the waning days of his pontificate, Pope Pius XI was confined to his bed, but he asked to see his dearest friends and associates. He retained clarity of thought and concern for his flock despite the erosion of his health. One of his closest friends and advisors, Pietro Cardinal Agnelli, was allowed to see the Holy Father.

As Cardinal Agnelli entered the room, he saw the Pope wave and smile, but the cardinal was shocked at the emaciated image before him. This man had once been his inspiring hero and beloved mentor. Even though the cardinal was terribly saddened by the sight, he managed to muster a smile and an affectionate greeting.

The Pope attempted to sit up in bed. "Good morning, Pietro. I am happy that you have come to see me before I make my final journey."

"Your Holiness, I pray every day for your total recovery."

The Pope laughed gently. "I believe our Lord has heard your prayers, but He has other plans for me. It is my time, Pietro. Yet before my final moments, I ask you please to continue to help the children of Abraham. They are suffering far more than I am."

"What would you have me do?"

"First, please adjust my pillows so I may speak face to face more easily."

Cardinal Agnelli quickly complied with the Pope's request.

"Thank you. See to it that the words of Father Lafarge are spoken from every pulpit in Christendom." The pope's breathing became labored and he slumped back into the pillows.

One of the attending physicians moved from the back of the room to his bed and injected him with insulin. "Please go now. It is imperative that the pope rest."

With tears in his eyes, Cardinal Agnelli kissed the hands of the Pope and gave him his blessing, knowing that it was the last time he would see his friend alive.

Cardinal Agnelli knelt down to say his prayers at the side altar in Saint Peter's Basilica. He begged the Lord to provide another great leader to face the challenges confronting the world. As the pope lay in state, the clouds of war loomed over the entire continent. The glittering rays of the Roman sun did little to brighten the future.

The cardinal believed that the German leader salivated for war. Each day there were implications that diplomacy had failed. Hitler lusted after Poland, and the contrived question of Germans suffering in Danzig was his latest ploy to annex territory. The Treaty of Versailles had always stuck in the German craw. Hitler craved land which he stated rightfully belonged to the German nation. The British and French had caved on every issue, betraying thousands in the hope that at some point Hitler's appetite for new land would be satisfied. In fact, these spineless decisions had the opposite effect; they enabled the bully to know no bounds. Beginning to believe he was infallible, Hitler escalated new demands daily.

All of these fears weighed heavily on Cardinal Agnelli as he made his way to celebrate a Mass for the dead in memory of his beloved friend and mentor. The loss of Pius XI was especially tragic at this time because Agnelli knew him to be a man who would not bend to any form of tyranny. When the pope ceased to breathe, the world and the Church lost a voice of strength and reason.

Cardinal Agnelli prayed that the Holy Spirit would guide the cardinals in their search for the new pope. He hoped that they would select one who would continue Pius XI's stance, not only against Bolshevism but against Nazism as well. As he went into the conclave, he was aware that the prevailing view was that the Church needed a diplomat rather than a leader who would confront the evolving dangers.

The question of the essential role of the Church was the key to Cardinal Agnelli's search for the will of the Holy Spirit at this time. He believed the successor to Saint Peter must not be an explosive cleric who would be abrasive on major issues, but neither should he be one who merely sought to protect the interests of the Roman Church. The key role, in his opinion, was to bear witness and to protect all children of God.

As the Mass ended, the cardinal appealed to the sisters and pilgrims to pray for the cardinals as they assembled in Rome to elect the next pope.

Chapter Thirty

Paris, November 1938

On October 27, Zindel Grynszpan's family was ousted from their home and their possessions confiscated because they were Jewish. They were forced to move to Poland.

Zindel's seventeen-year-old son, Herschel, was living with an uncle in Paris. Unbeknownst to his family, Herschel was a homosexual who had recently gotten involved with an older man who had a penchant for adolescents. In the past month, the older man had spent two evenings a week in local bars and restaurants with Herschel, wining and dining the young man. These evenings had usually ended with Herschel going to the man's apartment, where they would have sexual relations.

It was imperative that the two men not spend the entire evening together. Herschel did not want his family to know about his sexual orientation, and the older man was an employee of the Nazi Party. The man, Ernst Van Rath, would have lost his post—and perhaps his life—if his relationship with Herschel was made public.

When Herschel learned of the fate of his parents, he called Ernst and implored him to help them return to Germany. Ernst agreed. Over the next two weeks, despite constant requests, Ernst ignored Herschel's pleas. Yet the sex continued. Herschel became more upset with each passing day and began to berate Ernst. He even threatened Ernst with exposure to his Nazi friends if he did not help. Ernst ordered Herschel to leave him alone. Herschel finally realized that perhaps he had been too hasty in his threat. He attempted to apologize. Ernst warned Herschel that if he ever tried to make their relationship public, not only would it have severe consequences for his parents, but Herschel also would suffer at the hands of the police.

The next week found Herschel in a state of deep confusion and depression. He frequently called Ernst's office, but even though he left messages, Herschel never received a return call. He even ignored Ernst's request that he never call his home unless it was an emergency. For Herschel, nothing could be more of an emergency. Depression and powerlessness made Herschel feel used and furious. He wanted Ernst to feel the pain that he was experiencing. He wanted Ernst to pay a price for not helping Herschel's parents. He decided to go directly to the German Embassy and denounce Ernst Van Rath as a practicing homosexual. He would take his uncle's revolver in case there was an attempt to incarcerate him after the disclosure.

Arriving at the embassy, Herschel demanded to see the ambassador, but he was told that the ambassador was not in the building. Herschel made a commotion, so a secretary ran down the hallway to ask for Ernst Van Rath's help. Herschel was taken to Ernst's office, upset and frenetic. They quickly got into an argument.

"Calm yourself, Herschel. Do you realize what could happen to you by coming here?" Ernst asked.

Herschel could feel blood pounding in his brain. "You lied to me and did not lift one finger to help my parents."

"Herschel, I will send out a letter today requesting the return of your family to Germany."

"You are a liar! You're just saying that to get rid of me. Well, I will stay here until the ambassador returns. I will denounce you."

"If you do not leave this instant, I will have you arrested. Do you believe that anyone will take the word of a deranged young Jew against a loyal officer of the Nazi Party?"

The way Ernst spat out the words "young Jew" was the final straw for Herschel. He reached into his jacket, pulled out the revolver, and fired three shots.

Ernst slumped to the floor, bleeding. Security personnel rushed into the office and immediately disarmed and arrested Herschel.

Herschel later learned that on November 9, two days after the shooting, his former lover died of his gunshot wounds.

Chapter Thirty-One

Berlin, November 1938

When Dr. Goebbels learned about the murder of Ernst Van Rath, he told party members that this act was orchestrated by the world Jewish conspiracy. He vowed to make Jews pay for the assault.

Over the years, Josef had made sure that dynamite was strategically placed in Germany. Now he had the match he needed to light the fuse. He secretly gave the order to organize violence against the Jews all over Germany. It was to be staged in such a way that it must look as though it spontaneously came from the people.

Josef had felt outside Hitler's inner circle since the time when the Führer had berated him. He was worried about the growing influence of Goering and Himmler on Hitler. This was his opportunity to please the Führer and get back in his good graces. Hatred for the Jews was fertile ground that Hitler would surely wish plowed.

At that evening's Nazi Party dinner, Josef would inform Hitler as to what was transpiring. He would lie about his direct involvement because he wanted the issue to appear to be outside his or the party's influence. He feared that the Führer would be upset to know that he was the author of these actions, since there was a risk that the actions were orchestrated by his office without consultation. Hitler hated the Jews, but he was very careful to project an image of being a man of peace who detested violence. This charade insulated him from the countless atrocities committed in recent months. The safe approach for Josef would have been to ask the Führer's permission beforehand. It was a risk he was willing to take because he needed to be vital to Hitler again.

Just as Josef had anticipated, when he told the Führer about the demonstrations, Hitler said, "Let the Jews feel the anger of the German people." The Führer immediately left the dinner, even though he had been billed as the primary speaker.

Feeling powerful again, Goebbels was free to leave, too. As he was driven to his hotel in his limousine, he felt jubilant at the sight of the red sky. He knew synagogues and Jewish businesses were burning all over the city. As his limousine passed vandalized shops, he witnessed shattered glass everywhere. He felt like a child opening presents on Christmas morning. Once an unenthused anti-Semite, he had assumed his master's policies with a full heart. Destroy the Jews and obliterate every trace of Judaism from Europe.

Goebbels knew well that the seeds of anti-Semitism were not sown solely by the Third Reich. They had been an intricate part of the fabric of Germany for centuries. The Jews had been the focus of hatred in small towns as well as major cities. Martin Luther had denounced them. From many pulpits throughout the land, there had been constant condemnation of the Jews. Only Hitler had the brilliance to use hatred and fear to rebuild Germany.

Chapter Thirty-Two

Vienna, Evening of Kristallnacht, November 1938

Aaron Lehman was in Vienna on business the evening of Kristallnacht.

He had received a letter from Wilhelm Krieden, a colleague from years ago, asking him to spend a few days in town to discuss the possibility of collaborating on an architectural project. Aaron knew that it was forbidden for him to be part of any German business project in Munich, but perhaps the rules were different in Vienna. In fact, they weren't. Wilhelm was offering him an opportunity to participate in the design of a new complex, but without personal identification. Although Wilhelm abhorred the current state of affairs, he told Aaron that in no way could Aaron's name be attached to the project. If he agreed to participate, Wilhelm would find a way to pay for his services in cash so that there would be no trace of the transaction.

Aaron was grateful for Wilhelm's offer. As he returned to his hotel, he pondered the possibility that perhaps the worst was over and the current restrictions would soon be lifted. He went to his room to freshen up before seeking a local restaurant for dinner. As he changed his clothes, he became aware of street noises that seemed unusual for this quiet neighborhood. He left the bathroom and walked to the French doors that led to a tiny balcony overlooking the street. There appeared to be a red glow in the sky, and his initial thought was to wonder how a sunset could be in the sky this late in November. This gave way to the realization that what he was observing was a fire. The building down the street was ablaze. It was one of the oldest synagogues in Vienna. The street was mobbed with people shouting and destroying everything in their path.

He shuddered in horror. What could have unleashed this frenzy? Why weren't officials trying to contain it? It was then that he noticed part of the mob enter the hotel, shouting and screaming. He could not make out all of the words, but "Jew" seemed to be the most prevalent word.

Choices at that moment were few. He could not make his way out of the building, so he decided to put out the lights and hide in the closet. The sounds of breaking furniture and shattering glass throughout the building terrified him. He remained perfectly still and quiet in the dark for nine hours.

When he left in the morning to return to Passau, he was aghast at what he saw on his way to the train station. The streets were strewn with shattered glass and broken furniture. The air was filled with the smell of burnt wood and steel. The sky was overcast with a slight drizzle. As he walked near the Ringstrasse, he made no attempt to look at anyone. He prayed that he could emerge from this battle scene without being identified or harmed.

Aaron had always thought of himself as a German citizen who had a Jewish background. His family had deep roots in Germany. Some of his relatives had even shed blood for the Fatherland in the Great War. Educationally, socially, and even as an architect, he had never felt that being Jewish had been an impediment to partaking fully in life as a German citizen.

When Hitler appeared on the scene, Aaron truly thought that the man's vicious words would never reach the hearts and souls of the German people. The flight from traditional values would not last and like all those before him who had appealed to the baser side of human nature, Hitler would be an embarrassing memory.

Everything changed that November. Kristallnacht jarred everything that Aaron believed. He was incredulous at the stories he heard that were pervasive in the Jewish community: wanton behavior, random violence, murder, beatings, the open destruction of synagogues, Jewish businesses confiscated daily. He could no longer conclude that the worst was behind the Jewish community. Even in Passau, he had already experienced the pain of losing his position at the University of Munich.

Aaron could not jettison his German roots, but he concluded that it was critical for Sarah, Noah, and Micah to immigrate to a place where they could experience the fullness of life.

Noah had frequently participated in international music conferences and had many friends throughout Europe and America. Past relationships with the departments of music at the universities might lead to his receiving a musical commission either in London or the United States. Finances would not be an issue because even though Aaron was not rich, he had lived a life without ever being extravagant. His savings were substantial, and he still had connections in the world of architecture that could speed up the necessary visas and paperwork. It drained his heart to have those that he most loved leave home, but their safety stood above all other needs. He knew that his wife would be heartbroken by his decision, but there was little time to act. Comfort and the closeness of his loved ones would have to be sacrificed in the face of expediency. He went straight from the station to Sarah's home.

Chapter Thirty-Three

Passau, 1938

After curfew one night, Sarah was talking with Noah when she heard a light tapping against the front door. She quickly turned out all the lights in the house before Noah slowly cracked open the door.

"Noah, quickly let me in."

He opened the door, and Aaron Lehman darted inside.

Sarah hurried forward and embraced him. "Father, what's wrong? What are you doing here at this hour? What if a Nazi saw you?"

"I'm safe. It's you and your family that I'm worried about."

"But we're fine."

"No, you're not. I want you, Noah, and Micah to leave Germany while there is still time."

"What do you mean?" Noah asked.

"Please, Father, sit down. Let me get you something to drink," Sarah said.

Aaron sank heavily onto a soft chair, and then he told them what he had witnessed in Vienna. They appeared horrified and scared. He handed Sarah a satchel that contained money and heirloom jewelry.

"If you take your family and go, my heart will be heavy, but I will know that you are safe. I now believe there is nothing that can stop the mistreatment of Jews."

"Father, let us all get out together."

"There is not enough money for all of us. Besides, I love Germany. I do not want to leave the land of my birth. If I stay here, I may be able to help others."

"I don't see how I can leave you," Sarah said.

"Noah, please listen to reason and take your family away from this madness." Aaron hesitated, tears in his eyes. "You are all that your mother and I have in the world. It would be a great comfort to us to know that you are safe."

"I believe you are right," Noah said. "Thank you for making our escape possible."

Sarah nodded in agreement, hugging her father in tearful silence. "Do not go back into the night. Stay here where you are safe. I'll call Mother and tell her that the pony is safe and will be fed and back in the pasture tomorrow. She will understand the coded message and be relieved that you are safe."

"Thank you," Aaron said. "Now that this responsibility is off my shoulders, I am weary with relief. I want to go on to bed. You two make plans."

After her father went upstairs, Sarah sat in the dark with Noah, weeping with the full realization that her father was right, with a profound sadness that they were abandoning their loved ones to the whims of the Nazis.

In the morning, Sarah promised her father that she would take the money and make immediate reservations to leave. He counseled her to contact Max Levy, his attorney, who would know how to go about it. Sarah did not have to contact Levy, because the following day he came over with the arrangements for a train ride to Geneva on Friday morning. Sarah was stunned by the imminence of this departure. Max Levy insisted that even the delay of a few days could be a grave mistake. He shared with her that he too would be leaving, and that to miss this opportunity would violate her father's wishes. She thanked him profusely and then called her father to ask him to meet them at the train station in the morning.

The day was overcast, as are most days in November. As they met at the railroad station, Sarah steeled herself to act as if this were just a weekend trip. Her mother and father were dressed in their best clothing, bringing chocolates for Micah. When the train was announced, Sarah's heart dropped and she felt the panicky urge to cancel the trip. Aaron picked up one of the suitcases and walked toward the train. He placed the suitcase onboard and motioned for them to enter.

When Sarah reached her father, she hugged him hard, pulling her mother into the embrace. She never wanted to let them go, but her father finally pushed away before he hugged Micah and Noah. Her mother courageously held back her tears, but Sarah could feel the breaking of all their hearts.

Once onboard, Sarah pressed her face against the window and stared at those two wonderful human beings as the train began to lumber out of the station. Her father gave her a salute and her mother blew a kiss. She could not leave the window as long as she had sight of them, for she knew it might be the last time that she ever saw them. Those two loving people who once again had given life to her were left to face the inevitable by themselves. The only comfort was hugging her son and the realization that he would be safe somewhere else.

Chapter Thirty-Four

Berlin, 1939

The original intention to wage war in Europe was that once Germany had fully rearmed, Adolf Hitler could become the ruler of every European nation. At first the grand design was based on real world time lines and military assessments, but the initial series of land usurpation without shedding German blood made Hitler believe that he had messianic powers. He had bluffed his way into annexing the Sudetenland and Austria and the world had stood by without any real intervention, so he cast away his initial plans.

Surrounded by fawning subordinates and terrified military leaders, Hitler lived in a bubble of infallibility. Consultation was merely an echo of what he wanted to hear, regardless of the subject. His growing hatred of those he considered impure had infected those closest to him. As he bathed in his plans for expansion, he lusted to test the world once again by threatening to invade Poland. The scenario followed the same rationale as his prior aggressions: to protect poor defenseless Germans living in environments where they were being persecuted.

Hitler had decided that the rest of the world, especially France and England, would do nothing if he decided to invade Poland. English and French ambassadors had asked to meet with him, but they had been refused an audience. Buoyed by the successes in Austria and the Sudetenland, he now intended to unleash his complete plan for Lebensraum.

On August 31, Hitler summoned the Reichstag. He entered the chamber amid chants of "Heil Hitler." The atmosphere resembled the cheering of the throngs as the legions entered Rome after one of their many conquests.

The Führer strode to the podium and, with a wild gesture, announced, "As I speak, German troops have entered Poland. It is my pleasure to announce to you that I have declared war on Poland. We will obliterate Poland and rescue the German people who have suffered under the yoke of Polish tyranny."

Hitler immediately left the podium and was driven to the Kroll Opera House. Dressed in a field gray jacket, he made his way to the central auditorium. As he entered, there was a spontaneous shout of approval. The applause was thunderous. Goering beamed as he embraced the Führer and then introduced him as the great leader who would lead Germany to the Promised Land. Hitler stood at the podium for a time with his arms crossed, soaking up the adulations of the crowd. Finally he raised his hands to silence the cheering.

"I have always been a man of peace, and I have done everything in my power to avoid war, but I stand before you to announce that Poland has forced my hand. It is not I who has declared war on Poland. It is Poland that has declared war on Germany. We must fight this war because Germany's survival depends on total victory."

Hitler stood amid the thunderous applause of his National Socialist Party. He left the Opera House with the sounds of "Heil Hitler" ringing in his ears.

On the morning of September 3, Hitler received word that England and France had declared war on Germany. His reaction was instant rage. He ranted and raved to his cabinet members.

"The French and the British are merely posturing because they know they are powerless to prevent the inevitable. The French with their so-called impregnable Maginot Line will be crushed by the

Wehrmacht. The British are hypocrites. They conquered country after country and ruled without pity. They never believed that the East Indians or Sudanese were truly human beings. They kept them as slaves and never allowed them to be integrated into British society. And now the French and British have the unmitigated gall to act on behalf of the Poles and Slavs. These filthy creatures who do not deserve to breathe the same air as the German people are scum. I tell you now that we will act as the British have in the past. We will behave as they did in their conquered territories. There will be no distinctions made as we obliterate Poland. There are no noncombatants, and I wish to exterminate every man, woman, and child. There are no laws. Every act of killing, raping, or destruction I view as an act of patriotism. My invasion of Poland is based on what the British have done for years. For them to oppose me is the height of hypocrisy."

Dr. Goebbels and his propaganda machine went into full operation. He told Hanke, "The German people still have an aversion to war, so it is critical that the Führer be seen as a man of peace who has been *forced* into this conflict."

Hanke said, "We must bombard the people with images of how filthy the Poles are, and that we are employing a policy of total destruction. There must be absolute clarity that these people are subhuman and pose constant threats to the security of Germany. It is critical that the Führer be seen as one who has made endless peace overtures, but the Polish refusal to negotiate left him no other alternative. We must publicize the Führer's recent speeches focusing on his desire for peace in order to neutralize the people's aversion for war."

Dr. Goebbels added, "We must also remind the public that, after all, Danzig is purely a German city, and it should not be occupied by Poles and Jews. Our goal is to portray the Führer as a diplomatic genius and a man of peace."

As time passed and German troops invaded Poland, Hanke became increasingly tired of responding to endless requests for different approaches to propaganda. Dr. Goebbels depended on him to cultivate the German people's appetite for war. He realized that he was bored. Even his love life had dramatically changed. His ongoing relationship with Magda Goebbels had ceased once Hitler demanded that the Goebbels family reconcile. He had been fortunate that Goebbels never found out about the heated love affair that he had with Magda.

The daily reports from Poland were thrilling. Hanke believed that there would be a total purge of all non-Germans in the entirety of Poland. He hoped that if he positioned the data properly, he would be able to visit Poland and actually participate in the process. He knew that Goebbels relished direct accounts, so he suggested that he spend time at the front so that the propaganda would be rooted in actual incidents. Under the directive of the Führer, the Schutzstaffel—SS—units were following the Wehrmacht, and he wished to observe the work of these groups firsthand.

Dr. Goebbels concurred with Hanke and dispatched him to Poland on an extended fact-finding tour.

Chapter Thirty-Five

Poland, 1939

Erich Hanke left immediately for Poland and caught up with the SS in the town of Lublin. Before the German invasion, the town had approximately 7,000 Jews and 4,500 Germans living there. Hanke arrived in time to go to the edge of town where he heard the constant firing of machine guns. He followed the sound and arrived at a wooded area with a large field.

At the end of the field, there were large open pits. As far as he could see, there were groups of naked men, women, and children. They were organized in two lines and were being prodded toward the ditches. Once the first group arrived at the ditch, twenty-five of them went to the edge and the machine guns opened fire. As the bodies fell, men with shovels pitched a white substance onto them.

On the other side of the field, there was a crowd of local Germans who had created an almost festive atmosphere. They were raising their children on their shoulders so that they could have a better view. Hanke was pleased to see that there were no distinctions being made in the process. Women and children were being killed, young and old—Jews were Jews, whether they were infants or elderly.

Hanke went to the local commander in the field and, after showing his credentials, asked to man one of the machine guns. Once permission was granted, Hanke fired for the next ten minutes. He felt a physical surge of pleasure. He was not merely reading reports far from the action; he was actually killing Jews.

The violence in Poland was different from prior acts in Germany. There was certainly criminal behavior in Germany, but there was still a semblance of the German legal system. There were no restraints to overcome in Poland, no powerful lobbies to consider, so any and all acts of violence toward defenseless civilians were totally endorsed by the Führer.

Chapter Thirty-Six

Berlin, 1939

When Erich Hanke returned with films of the Polish campaign, he shared the images with Adolf Hitler and Josef Goebbels.

As the films played, Hitler stroked his German shepherd dog. Dr. Goebbels rejoiced in the unshackling of the old order and said, "We now have the power and the mandate to liquidate the impurities that endanger the future of the Third Reich. There is no Parliament blocking the eradication of the Jews and no world opinion strong enough to neutralize our might."

The killing had become so commonplace that the SS viewed their work as simple daily chores. There were no moral discussions about their behavior. Any initial pangs of conscience had dissipated. They were just following orders like factory workers or any other employees would. The erosion of personal responsibility was furthered by the Propaganda Ministry's relentless depictions of the Jews as responsible for all of the problems in Germany. The Jew was portrayed as a rat, a thief, a traitor, and a rapist of young Aryan girls. Over and over through journalism and film, these images were imprinted in the minds and souls of the German people. The SS units were no longer killing human beings; they were inoculating the German people against a dangerous virus.

There was a clear division of earlier SS moral codes into a duality that allowed the young men to lead two distinct lives. Their personal lives were still grounded in traditional values, but their military world had only one moral guideline: the will of the Führer. They murdered Jewish children by day and played with their own children at night. The moral duality was not the only reason for their choice to obey; it was also the exhilaration that came with the power of their position.

These experiences were singular; before the war most of the SS had led ordinary lives. The lives of others were now suddenly in their hands. They could decide merely on a whim whether a person would live or die. They could beat, rob, rape, and kill with impunity. They could experience the rush of power as they gazed into the terrified eyes of a Jewish mother pleading for the life of her child. No rules, no guidelines. They reacted merely to the impulse that they felt at the moment. They could spare or condemn without consequence. Daily life had changed from merely following orders of superiors to the realization that never before and perhaps never again would they possess this supreme power.

One member of the SS in Poland told a colleague, "What I do every day fills me with a sense of power more intense than any sexual experience I have had. I can force the Jews to do unimaginable things. I can make them lick dog shit off the street or get them to urinate on their holy books or whatever else comes into my mind."

The madness had been inhaled and sanitized as the higher good for the Thousand Year Reich.

Chapter Thirty-Seven

Rome, the Vatican, November 1939

Rabbi Solomon Abraham sat in the corridor fidgeting with his hat in a high state of nervousness. He had been traveling for days, and it was difficult to remember when he had actually slept in a bed. He had spent much of the past two months traveling through Eastern Europe. With forged papers, he had been able to pass himself off as a German merchant. He had worked for his father in Danzig years ago in the furniture business, so his knowledge base was sufficient to bluff his way through simple border crossings or passport reviews on trains. His years spent as an adolescent in Germany and his fluency in German made him familiar with local customs.

The rabbi had spent many years in Turkey, and he had become very friendly with then-Bishop Agnelli. The two had convened an informal ecumenical group that excluded no one who was affiliated with a religion. Initially most of the members of the group were reluctant to participate because through the years there had been unresolved theological questions. Each member in the group viewed the others with suspicion.

Over time, all of them grew in trust and respect for the purpose of the group. Rabbi Abraham gave most of the credit to Bishop Agnelli, but if one had asked the bishop who was most responsible for the success, he would have said it was Rabbi Abraham. The two had formed an immediate bond, and their cultural and familial similarities had contributed to their developing a deep friendship. Bishop Agnelli had said that it was almost impossible to tell a Jewish family from an Italian one. The only area where they had disagreed was which group had the best food. Rabbi Abraham was sad when his dear friend was called to Venice, but he was also thrilled that such a kind man of God had been so honored.

Today the rabbi was not at the Vatican on a social call. He was not sure whether this visit would solve his current problems, but he had nowhere else to turn. He was consoled only by the fact that his immediate family had left Poland and was now living with relatives in Chicago.

The rabbi heard the clock above his head strike ten, and almost simultaneously Cardinal Agnelli opened the door.

The cardinal opened his arms and embraced the rabbi. "It is wonderful to see you, Solomon."

"I am thrilled to see you, Your Eminence."

"Your Eminence! Please, I am still Pietro. This garb was never meant to have dear friends treat me as royalty."

The cardinal offered the rabbi a seat, asking, "May I get you some coffee?"

The rabbi sat down and nervously twisted his hat. "No, thank you. I wish nothing right now."

"And how are your wife and children?"

"They are in Chicago, Pietro. I am fortunate to have a brother living there. They left before the Nazis invaded Poland."

Cardinal Agnelli sighed, shaking his head. "I'm glad that your loved ones are safe, but I'm sure that many others in Poland are not."

"Pietro, you cannot imagine the horrors that my people are experiencing. I have been exposed to eyewitness accounts that are so barbaric that I fear no one will believe these things are happening daily."

The cardinal rose from his chair and sat next to the rabbi, who was weeping.

"I am sorry, Pietro, but the shock of these stories is so devastating that I cannot even sleep without having nightmares."

The cardinal patted the rabbi on the arm. "Please go on, Solomon."

"I spoke to a man two days ago from a village in Poland that had seven thousand Jews. It was occupied last month by the Nazis. They began their occupation of this village by gathering all of the Jews into the main part of town. Once gathered, they singled out the rabbi and the elders, forcing them to do shameful acts in front of the rest of the people. In the middle of these inhuman behaviors, they had the Torah and other blessed items from the temple brought to the square. They forced the rabbi and elders to urinate on them. If they refused, they were beaten with rifle butts.

"The Nazis laughed until they became bored and lusted for a higher degree of violence. The man who saw what was happening had been patching a chimney in his neighbor's house and thus avoided being herded into the square with the rest of the Jews. From the window in the attic, he could see all that was occurring. This is what he reported to me.

"He said that the soldiers then split the townspeople into three groups. Old men, old women, and children were in one group. The second group was all of the young men. They were marched out of town first. The man said he could hear the sounds of gunfire in the woods outside of town. Next they took the older men, women, and children, where the process was repeated. Again he heard the distant sounds of gunfire.

"As he peered through the window, he saw the soldiers forcing the younger women left in the square to disrobe. He was looking at his wife and two younger sisters standing naked with hundreds of other young women. Even though he was some distance away, he could hear the shrieks and cries of the women as they were herded into the synagogue. He told me that he sat there, feeling like a whimpering coward because there was nothing he could do.

"After what seemed an eternity, the soldiers came out of the synagogue, laughing. Some were putting their shirts back on or pulling up their suspenders. The witness could only imagine the horrors that had occurred to these innocent women. He hoped that the lust of the soldiers for murder and rape was finally satisfied and they would leave, but the worst was yet to come.

"The soldiers shut the doors to the synagogue and rolled huge horse carts in front of the exits. They poured gallons of liquid around the entire structure, and then lit it so that in moments the building was an inferno. He could no longer watch and tried to suppress the sounds of agony that were piercing the town square by covering his ears. In disbelief, he looked one more time and saw the soldiers laughing and drinking from wine bottles. The witness cried himself to sleep. When he awoke in the morning, he realized the nightmare was not a dream. He looked out the window, and it appeared that the soldiers were gone.

"He walked to the synagogue and slowly removed the charred remnants of the carts in front of the remains of the doors. He edged his way into the building. He vomited and then shouted like a madman when he saw the heaps of burned corpses. It appeared that in a panic, the women had attempted to reach the windows before the fire killed them. Burned beyond recognition, they were indistinguishable from one another. He went outside and wept. When he was able to regain some strength, he walked from the main square to the woods that surrounded the town. He arrived at a large field and again he saw a sight that no child of God should ever see. There were the rest of his friends and people from the village. All had been murdered."

Cardinal Agnelli was also weeping as he leaned over and embraced Solomon. For moments the two men were as one as they cried for all those innocents.

"I had heard some rumors, Solomon, but I had no idea that there were these kinds of atrocities."

"Pietro, it is happening in every Jewish town, village, and city in Poland. They want to kill every Jew, and there is no one to stop them."

The cardinal took out his handkerchief and wiped the tears from his glasses.

"We have nowhere else to turn. I thought perhaps with your diplomatic contacts, you could help the Jews."

"Do you think protesting will help?"

"I'm not sure, but obviously the Germans have abandoned the rule of law."

Cardinal Agnelli was momentarily silent, shaking his head at the horror. "I cannot imagine why anyone would do this to innocent people. The story you have told me could never be justified because of this war."

"It's easy when you make a race less than human. They have found a convenient scapegoat in the Jew, and Hitler uses it to its full advantage."

Cardinal Agnelli again shook his head. "It is particularly frightening when this violence is associated with religious fervor. For centuries, Christian sermons have supported the linking of Christ's death to the Jews."

"That is nothing new to a Jew. We have always been a target for Christians who need someone to blame."

"But it is wrong and totally false." Echoing the words of Pope Pius XI, he said, "We are all spiritual Semites."

"You may believe that because you are like a brother to me, but many who wear crosses today are killing my people."

Cardinal Agnelli rose and paced back and forth, deep in thought. "I can still travel with my Vatican and diplomatic passports. I will try to determine what assistance we can provide in Poland and neighboring countries. Do you have anyone I can contact directly once I gain more information?"

"You can contact me directly here in Rome. I will be staying at the main synagogue."

As the rabbi moved to leave, the cardinal embraced him. "Shalom, my friend."

Father Patrick O'Hara had mixed feelings about being assigned to the Association for Religious Development. On the one hand, he loved the glorious city of Rome and would be assisting the man who had actually ordained him, Cardinal Agnelli. On the other hand, he missed the rumble-tumble of his involvement with the Catholic minority in Northern Ireland. His indomitable will, his zest for a good fight, and his insatiable drive to create justice for the "little people" had been fulfilling. He wondered if academic or ambassadorial assignments would ever give him such a sense of purpose and fulfillment. Still, his new responsibilities gave him access to some of his old friends at the Gregorian University. Once he was settled, he intended to contact Father Hans Keller, who was also part of the Vatican's official family.

He mused that Hans probably needed Patrick to drag him over to Chicerrachio's in Trastevere to drink barrels of wine and rant about their seminary days. But then he corrected himself because though he found the rules and regimentation of seminary life suffocating, Hans, being a buttoned-up German, probably enjoyed them. It was strange how they could be so different and yet such good friends, not to mention fierce competitors on the football field. Hans was more than his match in football, and, though he feigned good sportsmanship, on more than one occasion he had tripped Patrick deliberately—the cunning bloody character never seemed to get caught.

It was almost lunchtime when Patrick finished writing a report for Cardinal Agnelli, so he decided he would go to the refectory for another one of those wonderful meals that the Swiss nuns prepared. Growing up in Ireland, Patrick had believed food was something that was necessary merely for survival. In Italy, it was an art form that was to be discussed, savored, ingested, and then further discussed.

When he arrived at the refectory there were only a few priests that he knew. He settled in with Frank McNulty, a priest from America who taught at the American College and lived outside the Vatican at the Graduate House of Studies on Via del U'milta.

Frank was a charming man with a delightful sense of humor, who loved to tease Patrick about his Irish brogue. Patrick's response was always the same, "Where did you pick up that awful accent?"

Patrick had no sooner sat down and prepared to engage Frank in conversation when he felt a tap on his shoulder. He turned and saw Cardinal Agnelli. Both he and Frank stood to greet the cardinal, but he motioned them to be seated.

"Pardon me," the cardinal said, "but I need to speak with Father O'Hara privately."

Frank, who never let an opportunity to stick in the needle pass, whispered to Patrick as he was leaving, "Finally found out what a fraud you are! They'll probably send you to back to Northern Ireland."

"In your dreams, McNulty," Patrick replied as he picked up his tray and prepared to join the cardinal in a nearby private dining room.

"Patrick, I'm sorry to encroach on your lunch," Cardinal Agnelli said as they sat down at a table, "but I must speak to you about a most serious matter."

Patrick could not imagine what the cardinal was about to reveal.

"Before I begin, I would feel more comfortable if you would call me Pietro instead of Your Eminence. We are brother priests and equal in the sight of God. The other titles are trivial."

Patrick nodded, adding, "It's not easy to call you by your first name, but I'll do my best."

With this, Cardinal Agnelli recounted the horrible tales that Rabbi Abraham had shared with him.

"Those bloody bastards! I thought the Brits were bad." Patrick clenched his fists in fury.

He realized the impropriety of his words, and said, "I'm sorry, Your—Pietro—but that story makes my blood boil."

"No need to apologize; there are no words in any language strong enough to express the anger and revulsion I also feel at this moment. I told you this because I cannot in good conscience stand by and do nothing. There is no apparent way that I can prevent these atrocities, but I must bear witness that these horrors cannot be ignored. These acts against innocent civilians must be brought to the world's attention. In the meantime, we must provide direct assistance."

"What do you have in mind?"

The cardinal reflected a moment. "I'm not sure, but I've had extensive dealings in Eastern Europe and many of my clerical friends live either in Poland or neighboring countries."

"I'm completely at your disposal. The memory of occupation in my own country is deep in my soul, so I'm totally with you."

Cardinal Agnelli nodded. "Thank you, Patrick. Please know that this is not an expectation or command of my office. It is rather a request that together we fulfill the mission for which we were ordained."

"Pietro, I feel privileged that you would share this opportunity with me, but I have one question."

"What is that?"

"Can I share this information with anyone?"

"Like whom?"

"Like one of my classmates from the Gregorian who now is stationed as a liaison for the German bishops."

"Is he assigned to Bishop Huldol?"

"I believe he is."

"Then, Patrick, I would use great caution. Bishop Huldol is a very strong supporter of the German government. I have it on good authority that he has been influential in deflecting criticism of the Nazi Party within the Church groups. Be careful with any member of his staff."

"I'll sound out his leanings and will not share anything unless I feel he can be helpful."

"Good. Thank you for accepting my offer. Now go and join your colleagues."

"Bless you, Pietro, and by the way, the minute I go through that door you become Your Eminence again."

The cardinal laughed. "If you ever change professions, I think you could be a fine comic."

Patrick rejoined Frank McNulty, who immediately greeted him with, "Can I assume that the good cardinal informed you that your hope for the papacy is nil?"

"No, he informed me that the entire American Church is going to be excommunicated and all of your people are being sent back to Northern Ireland where you will report directly to me."

Frank roared with laughter. "Once a smart-ass, always a smart-ass."

Chapter Thirty-Eight

Rome, the Casino Valadier, December 3, 1939

Patrick was deeply disturbed by the graphic details that Cardinal Agnelli had shared about the fate of the Jews in Poland. The stories triggered memories of violence that he had witnessed in Northern Ireland, but those paled in comparison to the Nazi crimes. Surely no one connected with the Church could sanction, let alone embrace, a political party that was inflicting such pain on innocent civilians. He had trouble believing that his classmate and friend espoused such positions regardless of who was his superior. Bishop Huldol may have been a Nazi, but certainly Hans Keller was not a devotee of Hitler.

Patrick decided that not only would it be to his advantage to pick his friend's brain on the matter, he would also welcome his company over dinner. To make it impossible for Hans to refuse a dinner invitation, Patrick made reservations at the most exclusive restaurant in Rome, the Casino Valadier. He justified this extravagant setting with the rationalization that he was doing the Lord's work.

Hans arrived precisely at eight in the evening. Scanning the marvelous edifice, he thought that the Italians must have a larger entertainment budget than the Germans. The Casino Valadier was situated on the ancient Collis Hortulorum, the highest point of

Pincio. For many years, Roman families owned the most beautiful gardens in Rome, which were adjacent to the restaurant.

The restaurant was built between 1816 and 1837 by Giuseppe Valadier, a well-known Roman architect and urban planner. He was involved in the important restoration of Piazza Del Popolo and Pincio in Rome. Now one of the most famous restaurants in the city, the Casino Valadier was built on the remains of an ancient Roman cistern. The building was incredibly beautiful and had a magnificent view of the city. After the Great War, it became the most fashionable place in Rome.

Patrick was already seated, and he rose to meet his old friend. They exchanged pleasantries. The head waiter came over and recommended a red wine while informing them of the specialties. After sampling the antipasto and sipping the robust Gattinara wine, they gossiped about former classmates and agreed that perhaps they had received the best assignments in their class. When the main courses came, Patrick moved the conversation to a more serious level.

"What have you heard about the situation in Poland? Hans, I have it from reliable sources that the Jews of Poland are being massacred by the German Army. These acts are not battle-driven casualties, but rather the direct murder of innocent men, women, and children."

Hans slowly sipped his wine, and after a few moments, he finally responded, "I have seen countless reports about Poland and a good portion of these are unfounded rumors or gross exaggerations."

"Are you saying that my information is unfounded?"

"Patrick, once you confided that your world was turned around by a champion who openly opposed the injustice of the British. I believe his name was Father Donahue."

Patrick shook his head in wonder. "Your memory is remarkable."

"German citizens have been abused in Poland for years. The city of Danzig is the core of this abuse. On countless occasions, the German government sought peaceful remedies to these abuses, but each and every time the Polish government refused to engage in meaningful dialogue. Hitler offered the olive branch over and over again, but it was ignored. He is a man of peace, but he had no choice after the Polish soldiers attacked German troops at the border. Also, your old nemesis, the British, as well as the French, made the situation worse by unjustly declaring war on Germany."

"Suppose I concede your premise. How does that justify the killing of civilians?"

Hans did not hesitate. "I am not justifying the action of rogue soldiers, but the reality is that civilians unfortunately die in every conflict."

"Can I ask you a personal question?"

Hans smiled. "When did you ever need permission to be yourself?"

"Where do you stand regarding Herr Hitler?"

"What do you mean?"

"Do you believe he is a man of peace or a tyrant leading an entire continent into war?"

There was a pause. "I would say that I view him as you view your hero, Father Donahue. Your man fights against the oppression and occupation of the British, whereas Hitler fights against the unjust Treaty of Versailles. Now can we finish this political parrying and just enjoy the company and the marvelous food?"

Patrick nodded, saying nothing more, for the words of Cardinal Agnelli's counsel rang in his ears.

Chapter Thirty-Nine

Florence, Italy, 1941

The view of the Arno at this time of day was beyond description. Romeo Benedetto had walked over the Ponte Vecchio a million times, but he never ceased to be amazed at the beauty of the river set in the red glow of the Tuscan hills. Even in the midst of this insane war, his architectural business was flourishing. Despite his complete disdain for Italian fascism, he had been awarded major contracts to build the city of the future on the outskirts of Florence. He had daily contacts with officials of the Italian government without involving himself in political discussions. He could not fathom why the Italians had become allies with the Germans. He was absolutely disgusted at the implementation of the racial purity laws in Italy. Recently the Italian way of life had become more and more threatened. First the German occupation had caused trouble. Now the Allies had landed in Italy, so there would soon be fighting throughout Tuscany.

Once inside his car, Romeo was temporarily removed from the realities of present day Europe as he wended his way around the endless curves toward his farmhouse outside the city of Greve. The Tuscan hills had always provided him with a sense of peace, and he longed for the day when this land would be free from outsiders who wished to superimpose a way of life incompatible with the Italy he knew and loved.

Arriving at the gate to his farm, he waved to Antonio, the caretaker, who was busy mending the fence that encircled the horse barn.

"*Buona sera*," Antonio called without losing the rhythm of the stroke of the hammer pounding nails into the main post.

Romeo parked the car. As he entered the house, he took deep breath and let out a joyful sigh. "Ah, it appears that we are having pasta carbonara this evening."

Hearing their father's footsteps, the children ran to greet him and leaped into his arms. His wife called out her hello from the kitchen. Carrying both children, he walked to the stove and gave her a kiss.

"It is so good to be home," Romeo said, "and far away from the problems of the city."

Rosalia nodded in agreement while stirring the cauldron of pasta. "Someday, my love, this will all end and we will once again live in peace."

Placing the children down on the floor, Romeo poured two glasses of red wine and proposed a toast. "From your lips to God's ears. After dinner, my dear, I need to talk to you about one of my professors who is in dire need of our help."

"Why not now?"

"I would rather wait until the children are asleep."

After dinner, Romeo heard Rosalia singing a lullaby upstairs to their children. He wished that life could be as simple as that song. Hearing her footsteps on the staircase, he moved to the living room and sat down on the sofa.

Rosalia entered the room and sat beside him. She tucked her feet underneath her, and said, "Well, Mr. Man of Mystery, what do you wish to discuss?"

"Rosalia, you know I have always felt that a large part of our success was because I had a wonderful mentor and friend, Aaron

Lehman. Well, that friend is in grave danger. I would like to reach out and help him and his wife."

"What kind of danger?"

"They are Jews and will probably meet the same fate as the Jews in Germany."

"What do you have in mind?'

"I would like to rescue them and bring them here to live with us."

"How will you arrange that, Romeo?"

He moved closer to her on the sofa and confided, "I have high-level contacts within the Italian government. You know I believe fascism is nonsense. I could arrange the necessary papers, but I would not do it without your full support."

Rosalia was pensive for a few moments, but then spoke with great emotion. "I hate this war because it has already cost me my brother. Luigi died on some desert dune, and for what? That bastard Mussolini deserves to be crucified for getting in bed with the Nazis. I am not one who welcomes danger, but I will fully support bringing them here. If it was our family, I would hope someone would reach out and help us."

Overwhelmed by her courage, Romeo embraced her and whispered, "You are my greatest treasure."

Chapter Forty

Passau, 1941

Hans Keller now thought Passau seemed to exist in a different time, certainly a different life for him. He had been exposed to the exciting cities of Rome, Berlin, and the other capitals of Europe. Passau was nothing more than a tiny, insignificant village. The archbishop of Bavaria had invited him to be the main celebrant in the cathedral during the feast of Saint Stefan. This was a significant honor for one who was not a member of the hierarchy. It entitled him to lead the processional before the Eucharistic celebration and to deliver the homily at the high Mass. From a clerical career point of view this was a singular honor, but like all other activities in a cassock, this was a means to an end. Hans never lost sight of his main goal.

After the ship docked in Passau, Hans walked down the gangplank and gazed at the place he once called home. The waterfront seemed tiny, with very limited space for ships and commerce. The Danube River, where he had enjoyed so many canoe trips and picnics, seemed like a trivial part of his past. It was an idyllic place for those who were content to repeat the mundane lives of yesterday, but his restless spirit had yearned for a more cosmopolitan life with challenges and meaning. If Dr. Goebbels had not spoken at the university, he might still be in a tiny office replicating architectural drawings. He shuddered at the thought.

Walking away from the ship, he noticed the canoe rental shop, and his thoughts turned to Sarah and her parents. He had often fantasized about that evening here with Sarah and wondered about Aaron and Ruth, but he had never contacted them. Hanke's words about there being no exceptions regarding friendships with a Jew had guided him in ignoring their attempts to contact him. He still cared about them. Yet due to his position, he knew he could do little in the way of assisting them.

Two clerics motioned to Hans as he stood at the square. They introduced themselves as curates at Saint Stefan's and led him to a black limousine where they placed his luggage in the trunk. The two priests seemed very young and ill at ease with their task of escorting him to the rectory. Knowing that being an official member of the Vatican carried a great deal of prestige, he attempted to put them at ease by recalling memories of his youth in Passau. As he reminisced, the subject of his family arose and he quickly steered the conversation toward questions about their priestly duties. Clearly it would not be a good idea to reveal that he had been raised by a Jewish family. Yet he knew that had it not been for the Lehman family, he would have been raised in an orphanage. This thought disturbed him at deep a level. For a moment, he considered visiting them, but then he dismissed the idea out of hand. Contact with Jewish friends or family would not be looked upon favorably by his superiors.

As Hans put on his vestments, preparing for the liturgical celebration, the sounds of the largest pipe organ in Europe filled the church with fugues from Bach and Handel, creating a wave of peace and serenity. Hans marveled at the beauty of the sound in this opulent baroque edifice as he left the sacristy and walked to the rear of the church. The procession began as he neared the baptismal font, and he walked up the aisle with all the gravity and confidence of a Vatican celebrity. When he reached the altar and ascended the steps, he turned and greeted the assembly, which was packed with parishioners, pilgrims, and clergy.

He began the liturgy and performed it as though he were engrossed by the words and gestures of the Mass. He had learned well how to fake the role of pious cleric. After the first part of the Mass was completed and the gospel for the day read, Hans ascended the ornate pulpit that overlooked the nave. He began his sermon with a warm greeting.

"I am thrilled to be in the enchanted village where I was raised as a boy, and I come to you this morning with a heart filled with endearing memories of Passau. It is here where the earth and the heavens meet that I am reminded of the words in the New Testament, 'Render to Caesar the things that are Caesar's and to God the things that are God's.' As we assemble here this morning we are one family bound by blood and the water of baptism. We are citizens of the Christian and German communities. We are not wandering through life without connections, but rather we are part of the building of heaven on earth. Our inspiration comes from two leaders sent by the Father to guide us. We are enlightened by the words of Jesus, the son of God, and our leader on earth, the Führer. The worlds of matter and spirit are no longer fractured, but have been welded in our faith, binding the Church and the government. We will find our total humanity in behaviors that support the goals of the New Testament and the new Germany. Our destiny is found not solely in prayer, but in actions that enable us to be part of a wondrous kingdom where there will be peace and prosperity for a thousand years. This vision calls for dedication and sacrifice. At times it will be most difficult because many will resist our activities. They would like to keep the Church and the government separate, but it is in this unification that we will fulfill the promises of the prophets. As we break bread this morning, let us remember our sons and brothers who at this moment are willing to risk their lives to achieve the vision we all desire."

After the Mass, Hans had breakfast with the archbishop of Bavaria and all of the attending clerics. Most, if not all, were supporters of the Nazi Party and his sermon had been enthusiastically received. His return to his place of birth had been a remarkable success. As he left the rectory, he realized that this place was still special for him.

He intended to walk to the waterfront and spend a few hours roaming the streets that once were part of his daily life. He turned the corner and ventured down a side street where he spotted Aaron and Ruth Lehman standing on the opposite corner. The whole town had been aware that he would be at the church this morning, so the Lehman family must have waited hours in order to see him. Jews were forbidden to enter the church, so they had positioned themselves in the background with a clear view of the rectory entrance. They were relatively safe in this area, and they would still have a perfect view.

It was obvious that they had seen him, so Hans decided not to pretend that he had not seen them. As he walked toward them, their unease was apparent. Hans ended the suspense by smiling and opening his arms. They ran to him and embraced him as though he were their son come back from the dead. And in a way, he was.

Wiping away their tears, they both asked if he could visit them. He glanced at his watch, explaining that he was on his way for coffee. He asked if they would join him, even though he knew that they were forbidden to enter cafés. Aaron replied that they could not enter a café, but would be thrilled if he would come to their home. Hans agreed to meet them at home.

When he arrived, he was struck by how shabby the outside had become. This place was once stately, but today it almost appeared abandoned. The door opened before he knocked. Apparently they had been peering out the window, waiting for his arrival. They quickly ushered him into the living room. Ruth immediately apologized for the lack of pastries as she poured him a cup of coffee.

"I did not come here for pastries," Hans said. "I came to see you."

With tears in her eyes, Ruth smiled sadly. "We have so missed you."

Hans was touched by this statement, but he also felt guilty because he had rarely thought about their plight and how difficult life was for Jews in Germany.

"What is it like living in Rome?" Aaron asked, obviously avoiding difficult issues.

"It's been far beyond my wildest dreams. As an architect, you can appreciate the magnificence of the buildings. Not just the ancient buildings, but the new city that Mussolini is building is breathtaking."

Aaron appeared wistful. "I wish I could see it with you."

Hans decided to change the subject. "Tell me about Sarah."

Ruth stood up, went to a side table, and took out a photo album. "She is well and enjoys living in America. She loves her life, but she misses us as much as we miss her. These are recent photos of Micah, her son."

"She is happy with her family?"

"Yes, very much so." Ruth held out the album. "You can see that in these photographs."

Hans graciously gazed at the photos, remembering Sarah's intense beauty. He was mildly surprised to note that Micah looked more German than Jewish.

The conversation continued to be pleasant, but Hans realized it was time to leave. He warmly embraced Aaron and Ruth. "I hope that someday you will be able to see me in Rome."

"We hope so, too," Aaron said. "What we wanted to tell you today is that we are very proud of you. We know your mother and father, if they had lived, would be, too."

"Thank you," Hans said, wanting to be free of the past they represented. "I appreciate all you did for me as a child."

With those words, he quickly left the house and walked away.

As he moved forward with his important life, he realized that he had once felt a loyalty to the Lehmans, but now those feelings had been replaced by pity. They had become the tragic remnants of a Germany that no longer existed. He had passing thoughts about their welfare from time to time, but he had abandoned the Lehman family psychologically and physically.

Hans adhered to Erich Hanke's counsel that it was impossible for anyone in the National Socialist Party to care about the plight of any Jew.

Chapter Forty-One

Greve, Italy, 1943

Living in a farmhouse above the idyllic community of Greve, Ruth and Aaron Lehman were somewhat removed from the horrors that the Jews were experiencing in other parts of Europe. The Italians, for the most part, had not enthusiastically embraced the racial policies of the Nazis. There were certainly restrictions on Jews in Italy, but acts of overt violence had not yet become a part of daily life.

One of Aaron's former colleagues, Romeo Benedetto, had provided him with work for the last four years. Their architectural collaborations were kept totally secret during this time period, but Aaron felt a surge of intellectual vitality every time he and Romeo became immersed in a project. The Benedetto family had no use for Mussolini or his alliance with Germany, and they believed that it was beyond disgraceful that a man such as Aaron Lehman could be removed from his world-renowned work.

Aaron missed Passau and the life that he once knew, but above all he missed Sarah, Noah, and Micah. As painful as their absence was, the knowledge that they were safe and removed from Nazi clutches made it worth the sacrifice.

Sarah sent frequent letters to the Benedetto family, using an Italian name to protect the anonymity of her parents. These communiqués were an emotional lifeline for the Aaron and Ruth. Every photo of Micah was a treasure to be savored. Aaron and Ruth would spend hours talking about their family as they longingly looked at the most recent picture of their grandson.

Though the war seemed to be turning against the Germans, there appeared to be more of a German presence, even in the hill towns of Tuscany. Romeo had recently noted that Florence was filled with Germans, especially around the holidays. Soldiers stationed in Florence had greater access to their families, and during the Christmas season there was an influx of German women and children.

Aaron found it ironic that the Germans so enjoyed life in Italy without seeing the contradictions between the two cultures. The warmth and openness of Italians to strangers was totally incompatible with the superior race vision. He wondered what madness had blended the Italians with a people who could wantonly murder women, children, and the elderly. Aaron observed the devotion to children in Greve and the reverence that was afforded to the elderly in sharp contrast with images of people being put in cattle cars destined for mass execution. He remembered the beginning of the brutal treatment in Germany, and he hoped that the same would not happen here as the German presence grew.

For the Jews, each waking moment was filled with the anxiety that there could be a knock on the door, or that in the middle of the night you could be whisked out of the warmth of your bed and cast into the back of a truck as though you were a sack of potatoes. There was never a respite from this fear. Each breath was filled with uncertainty as to what the day would bring. Now it was prohibited for Jews to have commerce with Aryans. Years of building positive relations were dismissed in the blink of an eye. The second wave of anti-Semitism now involved the question of life itself. Initially the curtailment of basic ordinary rights seemed petty, and Aaron believed that it would soon pass. As time progressed, the changes gradually moved from annoying restrictions to serious interventions into commerce and social life. Customer bases were diminished in his beloved Germany. Now it was not only prudent to mark the Jew for extinction, it was meritorious. This made Aaron treasure all the more what Romeo was doing for him and Ruth. He knew that his friend had taken a great risk in inviting them to come to Italy, and he prayed that this respite of safety would last until the end of the war.

On the morning of February 15, 1943, Romeo left for his office in Florence while Rosalia, Ruth, and Aaron shared coffee at the kitchen table, discussing plans for the day. There was a loud knock on the door. Everyone froze.

"I'll check," Rosalia said, getting up, hurrying to the living room and drawing back the drape over a window to peek outside. She rushed back to Ruth and Aaron, tears in her eyes. "Two men dressed in long black leather coats accompanied by two German soldiers. I must keep my family safe. I'm so sorry, but I have no choice but to open the door."

"Do what you must do, as will we," Aaron said gently, clasping Ruth's hand.

When the door was open, the taller of the two men said, "We wish to speak with Aaron Lehman and Ruth Lehman."

Rosalia stepped aside as the two men politely entered the house.

Aaron embraced Ruth as she wept against his shoulder. "Be strong, my love," he said against her soft hair.

"Herr Lehman, we need to speak with you," a hard male voice called.

Hand in hand, Aaron and Ruth walked into the living room.

Both men in black coats showed their credentials, and the leader said, "There is no need to be frightened, Herr Lehman, but you and your wife are required to come with us."

Aaron asked, "Where are you taking us?"

"I am not at liberty to say, but I have orders to treat you as a guest of the German government. Please gather enough belongings for two weeks. If your stay is longer, you will be permitted to return for additional clothing."

Aaron ascended the stairs with Ruth, trying to comfort her. After they placed some clothing in a valise, Aaron embraced his wife again, but she was inconsolable.

Urged by the soldiers in the hallway, they descended the stairs and made their way to the car. Entering the back seat, Aaron could not help but admire the beauty of the Tuscan hills. He hoped desperately that some day he would have the chance to walk these hills with his grandson, Micah.

Aaron had no immediate sense of the ultimate destination of this trip, but he surmised that the limousine was headed for Germany. His impression was confirmed when they arrived at the Italian–German border. The stop at the border was short. If he had been trying to get through the border as a Jew, the wait would have been interminable and the results would have been disastrous. There was no conversation coming from the front of the limousine, and Ruth was curled almost in a fetal position. His attempts to comfort her were in vain. The only saving grace was this thought: *If they wanted to kill us, why go through all this trouble of transporting us back to Germany?*

Caught in bizarre situations, the mind can create scenarios that seem plausible. Perhaps because of his world reputation, Hitler needed his services as an architect. Aaron was aware of Hitler's desire to create a magnificent new German city and was familiar with the work of Speer. Whatever gave respite to the fears that dominated in these troubled times was welcome.

Ruth Lehman had no such comforting fantasies. Her lifeline to the next breath was the picture of Micah she held in her hand. In the midst of her grief, she tried to recall the moments in Passau when he would play the piano; she would marvel at his talent and spoil him with delicacies after his recitals. She had known joy with Sarah as her daughter, but the thrill of a grandchild was truly one of God's greatest blessings.

Night had fully covered the land when the limousine arrived at what appeared to be a building snuggled deeply in the woods.

It was just a guess, but when Aaron estimated driving time and direction from the border, he believed they were approximately two hours from Berlin. Perhaps he was right. Perhaps he was about to be commissioned to build a monumental building, even though he was a Jew.

Chapter Forty-Two

Philadelphia, 1943

Sarah felt as though she were living a schizophrenic existence. Life in the Jewish community in Philadelphia was totally without fear, but her mind and heart were fixated on what was happening to her parents in Europe. Noah's music career had blossomed to the point where he was not only viewed as an exceptional teacher, but he had also secured a full-time position with the prestigious Philadelphia orchestra. Micah had already been recognized as a child prodigy in his music studies, but he had been captivated by American baseball. The time not spent on his schooling and music lessons was devoted to the sandlot.

Sarah loved the freedom and anonymity of being a Jew in America. She had heard from people at temple that there was anti-Semitism in America, but she had never encountered a problem. Even if it did exist, everything was relative to the horrors in her native land. At times, she would have to pinch herself as she wandered the streets of South Philadelphia. No anti-Jewish signs, no forbidden points of entry. She could stroll through a park, stop at a café, and buy produce from any grocery store. Jews in Europe lived with exclusion and fear every day, and that knowledge created a sense of guilt that Sarah could not wish away.

Her life in Philadelphia also rekindled her interest in Judaism. Growing up, she had perceived herself as more German than Jewish because she viewed the traditions and limitations of the Jewish culture as impediments to her growth and development. She aspired to be a modern woman, not bound by the restrictions that were part of the Judaism she had known. Judaism in Germany had little appeal to her free spirit. The purge by the Germans had changed all that, and what she had viewed as a yoke around her neck was now a source of strength and comfort.

This receptivity to her faith came about because of Rabbi Sanford Hahn, the magnetic rabbi of Temple Emmanuel. Rabbi Hahn was so welcoming that Sarah felt an instant connection. His sermons were so moving that she almost believed he was speaking only to her. It was more than mere eloquence; it was a profound understanding of human nature. He worked tirelessly at trying to get the American government to act regarding the plight of the Jews in Europe, but never once did he counsel his congregation to hate the Germans. He was a man of peace, entrenched in the finest traditions of the Torah.

The situation in Eastern Europe weighed heavily on Rabbi Hahn. He had a sister living in Warsaw and cousins in Poland and Germany. A man of true compassion, he was beset with a feeling of rage that he had never felt before. Generally, he was able to see and understand the other side, but the current situation differed from any that he had known. He could not find a scintilla of evidence that supported the Nazi purge of the Jews. His embedded conviction that there is goodness in all people was being badly shaken by the events in Europe. He related to the suffering of his people so much that he was lost as to what message he could bring to his congregation. At the visceral level, he wished to demonize those who waged war on his people, but he was uncomfortable with that posture. Wouldn't hate versus hate create even more hate? Naïveté did not blind him to the political pressures that Jews in America must bring to bear on their government, but he wanted to find a way to instill love into the equation that confronted him.

His personal story was not singular in his community. Many had relatives who could not leave Europe and were targets for the Nazi net, which was tightening daily. He had spent numerous hours listening to the personal concerns of those in his temple. Sarah had shared her story with him.

In one of the sessions devoted to reintroducing Sarah to Judaism, Rabbi Hahn showed her the last communiqué that he had from his nephew after the Nazis invaded Poland. Reaching into his filing cabinet, he took out what appeared to be a diary, which he treated as though it were part of the holy Bible. The diary had been smuggled out of Poland and was the only remnant of his family that he had left.

Handling the diary gently, he said, "I had encouraged my nephew Zvi to become a writer and to describe the wondrous life that he was living in the rural valley of my birth. I had hoped that at some point he would perhaps come to study in Philadelphia, but this excerpt from his diary is the last time I heard from him or any member of my family. He somehow smuggled it out of the ghetto, but I have not heard from him again."

Rabbi Hahn handed Sarah the diary, and she carefully read his nephew's words aloud to him.

My father's easygoing ways had been replaced by periods of complete silence. My mother seemed so sad and there were times at night when I could hear her weeping. My oldest sister, Rachel, approached me and asked if I had heard anything about the war or the Nazis coming to the village. She had overheard my father talking to my mother, and it seemed that they were afraid if that happened, we would be forced to move away from the farm. During the conversation, Rachel also heard them say that we would be moved to a settlement camp near the city, and that when the war was over, we would be able to return home. She said that the very thought of moving seemed to terrify my parents, but my father had cautioned my mother not to do or say anything that would upset us. But Rachel and I had been aware for a while that things were changing in the world.

It began with my father taking us into the city to sell his produce. We always looked forward to those trips because the city was such a magical place. There were lights all over and the sound of music wafted through the streets as if flowing on a magic carpet. The merchants and the bustle of daily life had initially startled me, but I grew to love the frenzy of it all. Often, while helping father sell the vegetables, I would dream of living in a splendid house in the city where all of my relatives would visit and be overjoyed at my success. These dreams were the harmless musings of a fifteen-year-old boy, but they became so real that in time I grew to believe in them.

I didn't really understand why my father now went alone, except to think that perhaps it was the incident in July when a huge, burly man refused to buy from my father because he was a Jew. The man seemed to have a real hatred for Father and publicly insulted him, warning other shoppers not to do business with him. I could see that my father was afraid and tried to avoid any contact with this livid man. I was filled with anger. Even though the man was a giant compared to me, I was tempted to respond, but I knew that my father would not tolerate that type of disrespect. Later in the day, I tried to ask him about what had occurred, but he just brushed it off as if it had never happened and told me to tend to the matters of youth and to leave the adult world to the grown-ups.

The weeks following the end of summer were anything but ordinary. When it came time for us to prepare for attending school, my parents informed us that there had been some changes due to the local laws and we would now go to school with the Weiss children, who were our neighbors, and all of us would be taught by Mrs. Weiss in their home. I thought this was strange, but there was

S. J. TAGLIARENI

no provision for discussion and we did what we were told. Rachel and I went for a walk after being told the news. She said that she thought there was more to this than just a school issue. She had heard from Josef Weiss that the Nazis, a group that I knew nothing about but whose mention always seemed to strike fear into the hearts of all the adults in our neighborhood, had broken through the defenses of our army and were treating everyone in their path horribly. I thought this was awful, but I naively did not see what effect this would have on us as children. Rachel, who was almost seventeen, told me that I really didn't understand the situation and that we children had as much or more to lose than our parents. I felt fearful as her words began to penetrate. Rachel knew something that I didn't, and she was trying to prepare me for the days ahead. I had the feeling that she had heard my father discussing more of his concerns with my mother.

It was November 28, a cold and gloomy day that began with a heavy snowfall. The beauty of the snow glistening on the trees greeted us as we trudged our way to the Weiss farm. While we walked, I sang a song that made my younger sister, Rebecca, smile. When we arrived, the wondrous smell of bread and oatmeal greeted us before we began our first day of private lessons. We were treated to a magnificent breakfast. It felt like a celebration, a stark contrast to the pall that had been cast over our lives for the past few months. Mrs. Weiss was almost too happy. As she served us, I observed that she seemed to be forcing herself to behave in such a festive manner. Halfway through the meal, Mr. Weiss entered the room, shook off the snow from his clothing, and summoned Mrs. Weiss into the parlor. At first I thought he was cross with her for providing such an extravagant breakfast without any reason, but apparently it was much more serious than that. I heard him say he had received a notice that he and his family were to prepare for relocation within three weeks. They were ordered, under threat of severe penalties, to go to the city, where living arrangements would be made for them. Mrs. Weiss gasped when he told her the news, but upon her return, she tried to show us the smiling face that made me want to stay in her presence forever. However, after a few moments, I noticed a tear on her cheek. She appeared to be struggling not to cry in front of us.

We continued to eat the delicious delicacies that she had prepared, but the taste was no longer as sweet as before. I knew something bad was happening, but without knowing how or what to ask, I continued eating and waited for whatever it was. Our lessons were short that morning, and Rachel and I walked home in total silence. We suspected that upon our arrival there would be news like the news the Weiss family had received. Unfortunately we were right.

After taking off our coats and hats, we were summoned to the kitchen, where father urged us to sit by the roaring fire to warm ourselves. Mother sat motionless at the kitchen table, and we could tell that she had been crying. Father told us that we would have to leave the farm for a while, but as soon as the war was over we would be able to return home. He said this was common in situations like this. It was only temporary, and we should not be overly concerned. By the look on both their faces, we knew this was far more serious. Rachel began to cry and my mother was jolted out of her stupor, quickly moving to reassure Rachel and the rest of us. Rebecca asked if she could take her favorite goat with her, and father gently told her that he would see if that was possible. The rest of that day and the following week were a blur. Now that I look back, it was blissful compared to what was about to befall us.

The bitter cold of that December morning is indelibly branded in my brain. I can still hear the sounds of the horses, their hooves clomping as they plowed their way to the road that was the beginning of our relocation. That word created terror in me. I feared the so-called relocation was the first pretense that would lead to the ultimate horror, the torture and death of our way of life. We talked in muted tones along the way, but mother, who had recaptured her equilibrium, led us in singing folk songs and reading passages from the Holy Book. Yet the images of so many like us trudging to the city constantly took our attention away from her valiant attempts. We were a homeless people wandering through the snow, going to a destiny fraught with unknown dangers. A trip that usually took six hours was slow to the point that my father decided it was foolish to continue this trek in the dark. The roads were jammed with others. Some of them were known to me, but the only recognition I received from any of them was the mere shrug of shoulders or a trancelike stare. The quiet of that trip was eerie, and without the occasional sound of the horses or the wagon wheels straining against the snow and ice, it would have been totally silent. Never had so large a group been without song or chatter. This was a nation of music and dance, but now we were silent, overwhelmed by the events that had befallen us. What was hovering over all of us transformed who we were, and we were powerless to deal with these changes. My brain was exploding with questions that begged to be asked and answered, but in deference to those whom I loved, I remained silent. I prayed that this was just a dream that would find me in a cold sweat upon waking, but happy that the goblins were unreal and the harmony of our agricultural community had been untouched.

The driving wind assured me that this was not a dream, and the future would not find me waking in a warm room to the familiar sights and sounds that I loved. This was a living nightmare. My reflections were shattered by the words of my father, who was shouting to the Weiss wagon to follow us when we reached the next fork in the road. He remembered that this fork led to an area that was protected from the cold winds by a series of caves. I gathered that it was my father's intention to spend the night in one of those caves and to proceed to the city in the morning.

Sliding down a hill that we once picnicked near did not trigger fond memories because I was obsessed with the cold and the unknown fate that awaited us in the morning. As I helped the children settle into the caves, I was saddened by the confused looks on their innocent faces. They were so young, and yet they were caught in a net of insanity that forced them from their homes to go on a journey in the cold night to a cave. The howling wind and the intense cold were hardly mitigated by the layers of clothes that my mother had dressed them in. I tried to be extra kind to them and to make it seem like they were launching into a wonderful adventure, but even the young ones saw through my ruse. Once I had managed to settle them, I followed my father to find any scraps of wood that we could use to start a fire. There were many boughs broken from the weight of the snow and before long we were all situated around a roaring fire. After a paltry supper, I drifted slowly into a fitful doze that left me more tired in the morning than when I went to sleep.

The morning was strikingly bright and temporarily the clarity of the sky and the absence of the winds allowed us to feel some hope that that we might have some control over our destiny.

We started out toward the city with renewed vigor, and as we approached the outskirts, we felt a little calmer. My mother spoke as though this journey would be a short one, and we would soon be back on the farm, laughing about our great adventure. I tried to go along and thought about the things I would do on my return. I suddenly remembered the animals at the farm and wondered who would tend to their needs. They could not survive without help in the winter. The momentary hope that Mother had created slipped away. As I mused about the horses, there was a sound like shouting ahead of us. As we approached, the garbled words spewed into such venom that we were all overwhelmed by fear. A large group of men and women were raining insults and rocks on those that were in front of us. As we got closer, I saw people bleeding and trying to protect themselves from the stones that were hurled at them. What kind of insanity was this? I had never seen any of these people in my life. Yet they were calling us Jew pigs and trying to hurt us. I looked to my father for guidance. He shouted for us to place blankets and canvas over our heads as we got closer to the stone throwers. The fury reached its crescendo as we crossed a tiny bridge over a stream that was an entry to the city. I heard my father grunt with pain as one of the stones struck him. The crying of the children under the blankets was almost unbearable. I was terrified, and yet I was filled with a rage that I had never known. I wanted to leap from the wagon and physically make them stop, but I knew that was impossible. I was better off trying to comfort the little ones. Thankfully the sounds of the mob began to trail off, and I realized we had passed the worst. I peered out of the blanket to see my father, his scalp oozing blood, steadfastly holding onto the reins as he guided the horses. He motioned for me to be silent and to take the reins while he wiped his head and tied a piece of canvas around the wound to stem the flow of blood. He then told everyone that they could now uncover themselves. I asked him why they referred to us as Jew pigs, but he did not answer me.

The rest of the ride went by without incident until we got to the railroad station, which was mobbed with people like us who were registering with the authorities. I didn't know who these authorities were, but most of them were dressed in black. There were flags everywhere. I had never seen this red and black flag before, but I feared that it might belong to the people that were called Nazis.

The wait for Father's return seemed endless, and I estimated that he had been gone for at least five hours. We tried to comfort ourselves with the thought that things would get better. But the reality of what was happening could not be so easily dismissed. What kind of craziness were we a part of? How could we go from milking cows in paradise to being the target of rocks and insults? What had we done to merit all this? Was heaven playing a joke on us? I felt the need to pray, begging God to step in and rescue us from this misery.

When Father returned, he looked totally worn out. I had seen him weary from all the work on the farm many times, but I had never seen him look this sad. He told us that we had been assigned housing. He knew which section of the city it was in, so he would have no trouble finding it. As we traversed the city, it began to be clear that we were not headed for a desirable location. Wending our way down a series of small alleys, we encountered hundreds of families searching for addresses that had been given to them by the authorities. Finally we arrived at a dilapidated building. The address was the one written on the paper. After checking it several times, Father decided that this was to be the place where we would be housed. He gently reached into the wagon and lifted my mother to the ground. With all her courage, she could no longer conceal the broken heart under her shawl. She sobbed uncontrollably. We took our personal belongings and followed Father inside.

The halls were lined with strangers shouting, crying, and trying to make some sense of it all. I entered the building, and I was immediately aware of the terrible smells and the dampness. Our farm animals had better living conditions than this, and I could not believe we were expected to live there. After my father negotiated with a host of strangers, we wound up in one room on the third floor—all of us. There are no words to describe the feelings that flooded me at that moment, but at the very end of the day, I felt a cold hand grasp mine. It was Rachel. She said that we would get through this together and that we must be brave for the younger ones. I marveled at her courage and just nodded. Sleep came as a welcome visitor that night and dulled our fears of the future. We drifted into the night, huddled together as though the closeness of our flesh and blood could stem the growing tide of hate.

Sarah finished reading the tragic diary, although it seared her very soul. "I cannot imagine how difficult it is for you, Rabbi. At least I have a way to contact my mother and father."

When she went home, Sarah took out the letters she had received from her parents and caressed them. Communication with them had been a great source of comfort to her. She did not know exactly where they were, but she knew they were safe for now in Italy. They were living in the Italian countryside with her father's colleague. The lifeline for her was a sophisticated process of mail between a fictitious American name and the office of her father's colleague. Her letters bore the return address of one of the non-Jewish musicians who had befriended Noah at the Curtis Institute. Having a Jewish name on the return address could pose a serious problem for all involved, so they avoided it.

The letters, though infrequent, provided opportunities for her parents to share in the development of their grandson. In case the letters were ever opened by a German censor, Micah was referred to as John. There was never any Jewish content or political data, only the notes that a daughter would send to her parents. Her ending was always the same, "Until we meet again. Love, Elizabeth," which was her pseudonym. She had not received a letter in the past month, so she felt constantly concerned that something had happened that threatened their security.

One day a letter finally arrived, but her initial relief was short lived as she read the text out loud.

Dearest Elizabeth,
Sorry that we have not written recently, but we were visited by friends from Germany and are joining them for an extended vacation. We will write once we know our itinerary. Love.

Sarah felt stunned. The transparent message from the Benedetto family was obvious. Her parents had been arrested in Italy and transported to Germany. What had happened to them? Were they in a concentration camp? Had they been murdered? Being this far away and powerless, where could she turn? The two who had given her life and love were now in the depths of hell, but all she could do was weep. Over and over, she wondered if there was anyone who might be able to help, but nothing seemed plausible. At last, she remembered a possible contact.

Maybe Hans Keller could intervene on her behalf. She'd had very little communication with him in the past two years, but when he wrote, he was always cordial and friendly. With his diplomatic contacts, perhaps he could assist her parents. He had every reason to help them, as they had once helped him, and she was sure that a plea on their behalf would be well received. The challenge was how to send him a message without it being intercepted by the German censors.

She asked Rabbi Hahn for help. He inquired at the bishop's office in Philadelphia, and his friend, Father Reynolds, informed him that the message could be sent from his office as part of a diplomatic parcel to the Vatican. She quickly composed a short note.

Dear Hans,

I know it has been a while since I have written, but as you know, I am now living in America. Though we have communicated infrequently, there is not a day that I do not think of you and the wonderful life we shared in Passau.

The current situation in Europe has worsened for the Jews, and I fear for the safety of my parents. They were living in Italy, but I have been made aware that they were recently arrested by the Gestapo. I have no way of knowing where they are or if they have been harmed.

You are certainly aware of how much they love you, and I am asking you to come to their aid. I know that you have diplomatic relationships in Germany, and I hope that you will be able to protect them. I hate to burden you with this, Hans, but I have nowhere else to turn.

I have another secret to share with you. I would have taken this to my grave, but circumstances have made me change that decision. You and I have a son, Micah. My wedding was so close to our lovemaking that no one suspects he is not Noah's child. Hans, he has so much of you in him. He looks exactly like you did as a young boy.

Please allow him to know and love my parents as we did.

Love, Sarah

Chapter Forty-Three

Berlin, February 1943, the Sportsplatz

The Battle of Stalingrad completely altered the course of Germany's war. What initially appeared to be a brilliant strategy by Hitler turned into a colossal military blunder. The Führer became erratic after the defeat, and on frequent occasions, he retreated to his room for days at a time.

Dr. Goebbels feared for the welfare of his beloved leader. After great consideration, he came to the conclusion that Hitler needed a vote of confidence on the part of the German people. He instructed Erich Hanke to plan a huge public meeting at the Sportsplatz with the themes being total war and dedication to the Führer.

Hanke did a superior job of orchestrating the critical propaganda meeting. The enthusiastic crowd was composed of true believers positioned to express their loyalty and devotion to the Führer. The walls and stage were adorned with huge flags displaying the party swastika to remind the audience of past victories. The hall was filled with thousands of attendees when Dr. Goebbels made his grand entrance from the rear of the building. Shouts of approval and applause erupted as he made his way to the stage. He waved, allowing the audience to bellow out their love and affection for ten solid minutes. Finally he strode to the podium and called for silence with a wave of his hand before he spoke.

"The tragic battle of Stalingrad is a symbol of heroic resistance to the revolt of the Bolshevists. It has not only military, but also intellectual and spiritual significance for the German people. Here for the first time our eyes have been opened to the true nature of war. We want no more false hopes and illusions. We want to look the facts in the face, however hard and dreadful they may be. The history of our party and state has proven that a danger recognized is a danger defeated. A merciless war is raging in the East. Our battles there will be fought under the sign of this heroic resistance. It will require previously undreamed of efforts by our soldiers and our weapons. The Führer was right when he said that in the end there will not be winners and losers, but the living and the dead.

"Total war is the demand of the hour. We must put an end to the bourgeois attitude that we have seen in this war. The danger facing us is enormous. The efforts to meet it must be just as enormous. The time has come to remove the kid gloves and use our fists to make the truth plain.

"In order to establish what the truth is, I will ask a number of questions of you, my fellow Germans, which you must answer to the best of your knowledge and convictions. When my listeners indicated their spontaneous approval of my demands of January 30, the British press the next day claimed that it had been a propaganda spectacle and was not representative of the true mood of the German people.

"Well, to this meeting today I invited a cross section of the German people. In front of me there sit row on row of wounded soldiers from the Eastern front: men with scarred bodies, men with amputated legs or arms, men blinded in action who have come here with their Red Cross nurses, men in the prime of life whose crutches are standing in front of them. I count as many as fifty wearers of the Oak Leaf Cluster and the Knight's Cross, a splendid delegation from our fighting front. Behind them, there is a block of armaments workers from Berlin's armored car factory. Behind them, there sit men from the various party organizations, soldiers from our fighting forces, physicians, scientists, artists, engineers, architects, teachers, officials, civil servants from their offices and studies, proud representatives of our intellectual life on all its levels. Distributed over the entire auditorium of this Sportsplatz I see thousands of German women. Youth is represented and so is venerable age. No estate, no profession, no age group was overlooked when our invitations went out. Thus I can truthfully say that facing me is a cross section of the entire German people, at the front and at home.

"You, my listeners, are representing the nation at this moment. And it is you to whom I would like to pose these questions. Give me your answers, along with the German people, before the whole world, but particularly before our enemies.

"The British claim that the German nation has lost its faith in victory. I ask you: Do you believe, with the Führer and with us, in the final, total victory of the German people? I ask you: Are you resolved to follow the Führer through thick and thin in the pursuit of victory, even if this should mean the heaviest of contributions on your part?"

The crowd screamed, "Yes!"

"Second: The British claim that the German nation is tired of the struggle. I ask you: Are you prepared to continue this struggle with grim determination and, undeterred by any circumstance decreed by fate, to continue it with the Führer as the phalanx of the home front behind our fighting armies until victory is ours?"

"Yes!"

"Third: The British claim that the Germans no longer wish to accept the ever-increasing amount of war work demanded of them by the government. I ask you: Are you and the German nation resolved to work ten, twelve, and if need be, fourteen or sixteen hours a day if the Führer should command it, and to give your all for victory?"

"Yes!"

"Fourth: The British claim that the German nation is resisting the government's measures of total war, that what the Germans want is not total war but Germany's surrender. I ask you: Do you want total war? Do you want it to be, if necessary, even more radical than we are capable of imagining it today?"

"Yes!"

"Fifth: The British claim that the German nation has lost its confidence in the Führer. I ask you: Is your confidence in the Führer more passionate, more unshakable than ever? Is your readiness to follow him on all his paths and to do whatever is necessary to bring the war to a successful conclusion absolute and unconditional?"

"Yes!"

"I ask you my sixth question: Are you prepared henceforth to devote your entire strength to providing the Eastern front with the men and materials it needs to give Bolshevism its mortal blow?"

"Yes!"

"I ask you my seventh question: Do you swear a solemn oath to the fighting front that the country stands behind it and will give it everything necessary to achieve victory?"

"Yes!"

"I ask you my eighth question: Do you, especially the women, want the government to see to it that German women, too, give all their energies to the pursuit of the war, filling jobs wherever possible to free men for action and thus help them at the front?"

"Yes!"

"I ask you my ninth question: Do you approve, if necessary, of the use of the most radical of measures against a small group of draft-dodgers and black marketeers who profit in the midst of war and exploit people's sufferings for their own selfish purposes? Do you agree that a person who interferes with the war effort shall lose his head?"

"Yes!"

"As my tenth and last question I ask you: Is it your wish that even in wartime, as the party program commands, equal rights and equal duties shall prevail, that the home front shall give evidence of its solidarity and take the same heavy burdens of war upon its shoulders, and that the burdens be distributed equitably, whether a person be great or small, poor or rich?"

"Yes!"

"I have asked and you have given me your answers. You are a part of the nation. Your response has demonstrated the wishes of the German people. You have told our enemies what they must know lest they abandon themselves to illusions and misinformation."

There was thunderous applause. Everyone in the arena was standing and shouting their total support.

Hans Keller was no different from any other attendee in that by the end of the evening he had almost lost his voice because of the numerous times he had shouted with full fervor his total commitment to the Führer. He felt himself singularly blessed that he was one of the privileged few that sat in the propaganda minister's box during the speech. He felt even more honored when he was ushered backstage to spend time with Dr. Goebbels.

Entering the dressing room Erich Hanke, Hans noticed that the minister appeared tired but also extremely pleased with the evening's outcome. He offered his hand to shake.

Hans enthusiastically grasped it with both hands and said, "Heil Hitler, Dr. Goebbels."

Goebbels gestured for him and Hanke to be seated.

Ordinarily Hans would let Dr. Goebbels take the lead in conversation, but his enthusiasm could not be contained. With great fervor, he said, "Dr. Goebbels, that was the most magnificent speech I have ever heard. You captured every heart and soul in the arena and I am sure the total listening audience in Germany."

Goebbels smiled. "Thank you, Hans. I am sure you know that the speech was not merely theatrical rhetoric. It was meant to pierce the heart and veins of every German to make an absolute commitment to the Führer and our cause."

Goebbels stared into Hans's eyes. The force of his presence was nearly overwhelming. "Hans, are you ready to make the ultimate commitment to Germany?"

Without hesitation Hans replied, "I am, Dr. Goebbels."

"Even if you are commanded to perform an act that you could never conceive of in the past?"

"Yes, I am your loyal servant."

"You realize that if you say yes to my request there can be no turning back. Every loyal German must go beyond all the trivial moral taboos to reach our ultimate goal. We must show the Führer that we will give every ounce of ourselves to him and the cause."

"I am willing to give my life for you and the Fatherland."

Goebbels smiled. "Before you return to Rome, you will accompany Erich Hanke on a journey where you will receive instructions on the next step toward full commitment. I am extremely pleased with your contributions in the past and can assure you that there will be ongoing opportunities for you to continue to contribute. Now I must change my clothes and return home."

Hans rose, shook Goebbels's hand, and left by giving the traditional salute.

The ride back to the hotel found Hans eagerly chatting with Hanke. He had learned not to ask what assignment he would be given. That would be divulged at the appropriate time, but once this mission was accomplished it would place him high on the list for a major post at the end of the war. Tonight there would be no apprehension and sleep would be sound.

In the morning, the ride to the mysterious destination was breathtaking. Hans particularly noticed the beauty of the terrain once the limousine left the confines of Berlin. On this crisp winter day, the road was bracketed by endless forests covered with snow and ice. The sun's rays bouncing off the snow almost blinded him as he gazed out the window. Hanke apparently was not interested in the scenery and had fallen asleep before they left the city limits.

The forests, which went on for miles, suddenly opened to the majestic view of a gigantic lake. The blue water seemed to caress what Hans imagined were beaches that would be filled with vacationers in the summer months. The lake was surrounded by elegant villas. At this moment he started to search his brain for plausible tasks that could relate to this locale.

Soon the limousine pulled off the main road and entered a long driveway that led to a magnificent mansion overlooking the water. The car approached the portico and went halfway around the circular drive. Hanke awakened. The driver got out of the car and opened the door on Hans's side. He left the car and waited for Hanke. A servant opened the front door and assisted the driver of the limousine with their luggage.

Once inside, Hans, ever the student of architecture, marveled at the beauty of the interior. He was unaware that this was the villa where a year ago the architects of the Final Solution had assembled to address the Jewish question. Here, under these vaulted ceilings, it had been devised and was now being implemented. The beauty of the furnishings and the art masked well the ugliness of the outcome of that conference.

After Hans was ushered to his room, Hanke told him that dinner would be served in the main dining room at seven that evening. As it was only early afternoon, Hans decided he would walk around the lake and reflect on his thoughts. As he strolled down the wooded path to the water, he could not help but marvel at the life he had assumed. He had dined in ambassador suites, traveled first class on his frequent trips to Germany, had the city of Rome and all its wonders at his feet, and was intimately involved in the strategic plans and desires of the Third Reich.

He smiled, thinking how inconceivable this was for a struggling architect from Passau. For a rare moment he reflected on what his father would have thought of him. Secondhand information had led him to believe that his father was apolitical, and by reviewing his professional relationships and friendships, certainly not an anti-

Semite. Hans dismissed this probing into the past as an exercise in futility. His father was dead and he was alive and on the crest of a brilliant career.

Dinner was delightful. Every favorite food of his was on the buffet table. He engaged Hanke in small talk throughout the entire meal. Hans kept cautioning himself not to inquire about what mission was in store for him tomorrow. After coffee and a selection of German desserts, Hanke invited Hans into a small drawing room off the dining room and poured both of them an after-dinner drink.

Hanke settled into a large, comfortable chair and toasted the Führer.

Lifting his glass, Hans responded in kind.

For a while, the two sat in silence, basking in the glow of the fireplace.

Finally Hanke said, "Tomorrow you will leave here with me and travel a very short distance to the other side of the lake. Upon arrival you will receive instructions and operational directions. I must remind you tonight that regardless of your feelings you have pledged a total commitment to implement whatever the assignment is."

Hans wondered why there was so much emphasis on whether he would follow through on his commitment. Surely his accomplishments to this point had proven his dedication to the Fatherland. Why was so much effort put into preparing him? He thanked Hanke for a delightful evening and started up the magnificent stairway leading to his bedroom. He was sound asleep in a matter of minutes.

In the morning, Hanke telephoned and instructed him to wear comfortable clothing and not the formal attire he had worn last evening at dinner. Hans went through his normal morning toilette and then he walked downstairs to the breakfast room. Excitement at what was to transpire made him more interested in coffee than food. Caffeine had a marvelous energetic effect on him. He guessed that there might be a physical component to the day, hence the comfortable clothing request. He ate very little but drank three cups of coffee.

After breakfast, he was informed that his suitcase would be placed in the limousine by one of the servants and that he should be at the front door in ten minutes. He did not need the additional time so once again he walked around the mansion, soaking in the architectural design and structure. After a few minutes he glanced at his watch and headed for the front door.

As the servant opened the door, the limousine made its appearance at the circular drive. Hanke was already in the backseat when the driver stopped the car and opened the door.

"Good morning," Hans said. "Today is not as nice as yesterday."

"The weather will not affect your task," Hanke replied.

Those were the last words they spoke in the limousine.

Finally the driver made a left turn off the main road and pursued a dirt lane leading toward the lake. Two German soldiers indicated that the car should stop. The chauffeur rolled down the window and gave one of the soldiers a document. Hans saw the soldier salute and heard him say, "We were expecting you."

About a hundred yards behind the soldier was a large cottage. The limousine pulled up adjacent to the side entrance. Hanke stepped out, carrying a black leather bag. Hans followed him, glancing around at the deep forest.

Entering the cottage, Hans could easily see that this was not like the luxurious accommodation where he had spent the night. The appointments were functional; there were no charming features to the interior. It was rather warm inside due to a very large wood-burning stove.

"You may remove your coat and be seated," Hanke said formally.

Hans felt short of breath as he sat down. This was the moment of truth and his opportunity to clear his last hurdle after all the long years of hard, dedicated work for the Nazi Party.

Hanke sat down, placed the leather bag on the table and began the instructions without preamble. "You are here this morning to finalize the process of initiation into a select level of members of the National Socialist Party. You have pledged to perform without question the task which I will assign to you. Do you understand and readily consent?"

"Yes." His heart was pounding hard. He did not know if it was anxiety or the caffeine from the coffee he had consumed at breakfast.

Hanke continued, "In the next room are two enemies of the state. They are Jewish vermin who do not deserve to live. Your mission is to kill both of them without hesitation."

Thoroughly shocked, Hans blurted, "But I've never killed anyone before."

"Then it's time you lose your virginity and join the rest of us." With that Hanke reached into the black leather bag and pulled out a revolver. "Remember, you have no choice in this matter."

Hans clasped the Luger. Though he had hunted in the Bavarian woods, he had never fired at a human being.

Hanke stood up and opened a door. "Your targets are inside."

Hans walked over to the open doorway. He could never have imagined the sight before him. In the room stood Aaron and Ruth Lehman, pale, frail, and frightened.

"No choice." Hanke pushed Hans into the room and closed the door.

Hans heard the latch shut behind him and quickly hid the Luger behind his back.

Aaron stood up, holding Ruth close. "Oh my God, it's you, Hans! I cannot believe my eyes! Our prayers have been answered! When we were arrested, we thought it was the end. Was it you who arranged to bring us here? I told Ruth that the Germans would not go to so much trouble if they merely wanted to kill us." He glanced down at Ruth, who was smiling through grateful tears.

"I told you miracles still happen," she said, running up to Hans and putting her arms around his neck.

Hans could not speak or move. He had pledged to give even his life for the cause, but who could have ever imagined this? "Please be seated."

Ruth quickly stepped back and clasped Aaron's hand, appearing frightened again.

"Hans," Aaron said, "why are you not telling us what's going to happen to us? Have you arranged for our safe passage out of Germany?"

Hans could not respond. He felt the cold steel in his hand. His finger was inching toward the trigger. He lurched forward and aimed the Luger at Aaron.

"My God, Hans, what are you doing? You can't . . . we raised you! I—"

Hans pulled the trigger. It was hard to determine which was louder: the sound of the gun or Ruth's scream. Aaron fell to the floor, missing most of his face. Ruth dropped down beside her husband and cradled him in her arms. Hans calmly and coldly leaned over her and once again pulled the trigger. The back of her head exploded and pieces of her brain splattered the walls.

Hans felt so sick that he vomited on both corpses. He was totally unaware when the door opened. He had no recollection of how he made it back to the limousine. The ride back to Berlin was a blur. While Hanke slept, Hans felt waves of nausea so strong that at one point he asked the driver to stop. He got out of the car and vomited again. He could feel the Luger inside his jacket, confirming that this was not a dream.

He had killed Aaron and Ruth Lehman.

Chapter Forty-Four

Rome, Three Days after the Murders

Hans now realized that he had ignored the growing inconsistencies in the Nazi Party for years, making accommodations to avoid the underlying discomfort he had felt about the repressive and cruel behavior that he had been a part of. Blinded by ambition, he had rationalized that these so-called atrocities were being grossly exaggerated. Surely the upper echelon of the party had not endorsed such behavior. His relationship with Dr. Goebbels and other high-ranking officials had always been highly civilized and refined, as had all of those he had dealt with on a regular basis.

All of these layers of self-protection from the horror he had just committed could no longer protect him from the truth. The questions he had suppressed rose with crushing force to a devastating consciousness. He had become a veritable monster, murdering the very people who had shown him only kindness and love.

Sarah's letter was the final straw; he now had the additional burden of knowing that he had killed his son's grandparents. Micah would never know those wonderful people who had loved him unconditionally and there was nothing he could do to change that fact. How could he have been so mired in his devotion to the Third Reich that he had totally lost his moral compass? He realized that he had become a dummy for Dr. Goebbels, the master ventriloquist. Visions of that last dinner with the Lehman family and the wonderful moments he shared with Sarah that evening now haunted him. His hands were covered with the blood of innocents. How had he ignored the obvious? How could he have disbelieved reports about how Jews were treated in Vienna after the Anschluss? The Jewish suicides and the escalating brutality all over Europe were there for him to see. He had heard the rumors, but he had blocked them out because he was so immersed in his own goals.

He had silently mocked the beliefs that were taught in the seminary, but now they did not appear to be so ludicrous. Men like Pietro and Patrick, who had dedicated their lives to these beliefs, were not on the brink of suicide. They were troubled by the suffering of others but at peace with their convictions. He felt lost because there was no avenue to peace, and he now lived with the belief that he was a minister of evil.

Part of the hell that he inhabited was his memory of what loving people his father and Aaron had been. What would be *his* legacy to his unknown child? What would happen if his son ever learned what he had done? And Sarah? How could he respond to her letter? There was no way back from the road he had chosen; nothing could restore the lives of the two people he had brutally murdered to further his own goals.

What had changed in him over these years that had enabled him to look into those terrified eyes without renouncing his monstrous task? How had he forgotten all that the Lehman family had done for him? When had he embraced the anti-Semitism that had allowed him to negate their humanity? What was so terribly flawed in his character that he could associate with leaders who demanded that kind of barbarism?

It wasn't only this single terrible act of murder that now haunted him. He began to ruminate over his role in shaping policy that doomed others to their deaths. Did his influence in Austria contribute to the deportation of innocent Jews? Was his ability to sway the cardinal to support the Anschluss connected to the number of Jews in Vienna who chose suicide? Did his work to suppress the Lafarge encyclical pave the way for the Final Solution?

In his quest for meaning and significance, Hans had traded the person he could have been for the automaton that craved fame and recognition. He had denigrated the loving message of people like Cardinal Agnelli and his classmate Patrick O'Hara. Their lives, committed to a gentle Nazarene carpenter, did not offer a seat with the powerful and the privileged. Instead of openness to their convictions, he had chosen the bloody trail of the war king and the propaganda minister. The lure of the parades and drums had blotted out the shedding of his humanity. He had his eyes on the prize, which was a prominent place in the history of a glorious nation. Now he realized that his honored seat was at the table of those who were committed to the world's most heinous acts of genocide.

The only way he could stop thinking about what he had done was to drink enough wine to enable him to pass out. Sleep, even with its nightmares, was not as devastating when he had consumed a bottle and a half.

Sunlight seeped through the curtain and was reflected brightly in Hans's face. The dreaded night was finally over, but a new day offered nothing more than the continuance of self-hatred. He slowly sat up, pausing before getting out of bed. He felt dizzy as he walked slowly to the bathroom, and he was shocked at his appearance in the mirror. The image of an unshaven, disheveled human being stunned him. He realized that he could not hide in his bedroom indefinitely. He had heard the phone ringing the last two days. He needed to contact his office and concoct some story about having food poisoning. Despite his mental and physical condition, he could not avoid the responsibilities of his office. Besides, this was the week before Pentecost Sunday. He was scheduled to hear confessions in Saint Peter's Basilica.

Chapter Forty-Five

Saint Peter's Basilica, One Week Later

Hans entered the darkness of the confessional with the hope that for the next two hours he would find respite from his mental anguish. He had scoffed in the past at this practice, viewing it as a mechanism created by the Church to use guilt as a way of controlling members. Now he wished that he could adhere to the belief because there could be no one as riddled with guilt as he was.

For the first hour he listened to the ordinary mundane human frailties and would only respond when the penitent stopped speaking. He mumbled the words of forgiveness and doled out the same minor penance regardless of the severity of the sins.

"Bless me, Father, for I have sinned," said a strong male voice, followed by loud sobbing. "Father, I don't believe I can be forgiven, but I don't know what to do."

Hans could not imagine what the man was referring to and thought that whatever it was would pale next to his own actions. "What is it, my son?"

There was a long silence, and finally in a trembling voice the man responded, "I have murdered women and children."

Hans knew that the penitent was a soldier.

"I have personally murdered women and children in Poland and I cannot stop seeing their terrified faces. No matter what I do, I can't stop seeing them. I can't eat, sleep, or concentrate on anything else. Father, I have a wife and three children in Germany and I cannot believe what I have become."

Hans wanted to bolt from the darkness, but like the soldier, where could he go?

"Father, can God forgive me for what I've done?"

If there was a God, Hans did not know how He could forgive either of them.

The silence of both murderers was broken by the man's renewed sobbing.

Hans muttered some words of God's goodness and forgiveness. He only wished he could believe the words he spoke.

Chapter Forty-Six

Rome, Spring 1943

Ambassador Karl Hunsecker was still trying to process the reports from Germany regarding the escalating purge of the Jews when he realized that he could no longer influence the outcome. Up to this point he had been able to divert some resources such as passports and travel visas. He had on numerous occasions intervened through third parties, but this was no longer possible. He believed he had thus far evaded suspicion, but his entire staff was made up of loyal Nazis and it was just a matter of time before his true convictions would be discovered. He had anticipated the worst by concocting a fictional family illness in Geneva that required his wife and children to leave Germany to care for his ailing father-in-law. He had traveled with them to ensure their safety, and he had spent four days in the company of his in-laws in the tranquil countryside, feeling heartened by the knowledge that his loved ones were safe.

On his first morning back in Rome, he rose at daybreak and walked through the Piazza Navona, which had always been his favorite city square in Rome. Years before, while spending the autumn semester in Rome as an art history major, he met Solange, his future wife, at a famous restaurant, Tres Scalini. In that moment his world changed forever. He was enthralled by her natural beauty, but most of all he was drawn to her artistic spirit and brilliant mind. Although they had just met, he felt as though they could explore any topic without reservation. On their second date they held hands and talked for hours in Piazza Navona, where they marveled at the magnificent work of Bernini and Borromini in the Fountain of Four Rivers in the center of the piazza. They were married three years later in Sant'Agnese, the church where he was about to attend Mass this morning.

Sant'Agnese in Agone, Borromini's masterpiece, was Karl's sanctuary and the source of many meditative moments that enabled him to withstand the intense pressures of his position. As he entered the small church, he felt peace settle over his shoulders like a mantle, and he knelt in the back. As he prayed, he gazed upon the statue of Saint Agnese with her long hair flowing down to cover her nakedness. The sunlight was streaming through the windows of the cupola, casting its brilliance on the multicolored marble columns. Ordinarily he would spend time feeling the uplifting of the marvelous Glories of Paradise frescoes painted by Corbellini and Baciccia, but this morning he had no time for such reflection.

As he knelt before the statue of Saint Agnese, he prayed that she would fill his heart with the courage that had enabled her to die for her belief in Christ. At this moment there was a high probability that he would die for his involvement with the Jews. This frightened him, but it paled against the pain he felt about what was happening in his beloved Germany.

He could not understand or accept the series of degradations inflicted on neighbors the German people had known for years. Why had they been silent instead of confronting the madness, and why had the Vicar of Christ been silent? Was it not the role of the Church to protect those who could not protect themselves? Despite the lack of answers to his pressing questions, being in this holy place and receiving the body of his Lord gave Karl renewed strength.

After Mass he left Sant'Agnese feeling a peace that had been absent for months. He walked alone through the streets of Rome as the city became alive with merchants and pilgrims, making his way toward the Vatican to meet with his friend, Cardinal Agnelli.

Arriving at the Porto di Bronzo, Karl showed his credentials to the Swiss Guard and entered. Walking up the staircase leading to the Cortile di Dimaso, he made his way to Cardinal Agnelli's office.

The cardinal was standing in the hallway and quickly led the ambassador to a side chamber next to his office. Little time was spent in formal greetings. The ambassador began the conversation.

"Your Eminence, I am losing what little control I've had over the treatment of Jews in Italy. All of my current staff are devoted Nazis, and though I pretend to be one of them, there is a real possibility that my involvement with you may be discovered. Because of this, I have sent my family to live temporarily with my wife's parents in Geneva."

"It was a wise decision. I would never wish to place your loved ones in harm's way. Being older and single does have some advantages in this crazy time. If I am caught, others who are innocent will not have to suffer."

"I've made plans to remove the largest Jewish group ever from Nazi clutches. We have arranged to have 250 passports and travel visas dispensed at the feast of San Antonio of Padua in June. The monastery outside of Florence will be filled with thousands of tourists and will provide the perfect cover for our plan. I have it on the highest authority that there may be a second front in France. When this happens, many troops will be reassigned to Italy and it will be impossible to avoid the German net. Some anti-Nazis in Germany hope that this will bring the government to the peace table. However, after my recent meeting with Dr. Goebbels, I do not believe this is possible. Hitler and his staff are committed to total war. In my opinion, that means the total defeat of Europe. Nazis will continue to massacre Jews until the end."

Cardinal Agnelli shook his head in dismay. "I cannot understand why the world is silent, knowing what is happening to Jews all over Europe. The Vatican has not openly condemned the atrocities. I know the Holy Father personally and he agonizes over this, but I believe he has decided that speaking out will worsen the plight of the Jews."

"With all due respect, your Eminence, how can it be worse? My government is committed to killing every Jew in Europe and they are well on their way. I am appalled at the world and especially my church for not openly condemning Hitler and the Nazi Party. Why doesn't the Holy Father at least excommunicate Hitler and Goebbels? They're both Catholics." Karl paused and then blurted out, "I wish you were the pope!"

Cardinal Agnelli vehemently shook his head. "God forbid! I wouldn't know where to begin. We must pray for the pope and believe that he will do what is needed. I've spoken to the pope personally and know that he has privately supported the countless acts of heroism on the part of priests, nuns, and laymen. He is in a very difficult position because he fears that if he publicly speaks out, the Nazis will punish Catholics around the world. Nothing he does publicly will lessen the brutality toward the Jews. The pope is in an untenable position because in many respects he is alone in this matter. The governments around the world are surely aware of the situation, but they are silent. The pope is also aware of what happened to the Jews and Catholics in the lowlands when the bishops spoke against the Germans. The situation became worse and because of this, many of the bishops have begged the pope not to speak out. I have firsthand knowledge that he consistently acts behind the scenes to aid the Jews. It is a burning moral issue for the pope, as it is for us, but his involvement is far more complicated."

"I will always respect the office of Saint Peter," Karl said, "but when I die I hope Saint Peter will help me understand why the pope does not act now."

"I will inform Father O'Hara and wait for your signal before leaving for the monastery," the cardinal, said, studying the detailed plans for the escape in Florence. "Now go in peace and may God protect you."

The ambassador knelt as the cardinal raised his right hand and blessed him.

Chapter Forty-Seven

Rome, September 1943

The Gestapo in Rome were relieved that they no longer had to cooperate with members of the Italian military. There had been a distinct aversion to the racial purity acts; in fact, by and large, the Italian population ignored the guidance of the Führer with regard to the Jews. Now that the Italian government was collapsing, the Gestapo no longer had to satisfy the Italian sense of justice. The milieu in which the Gestapo was forced to operate in Italy was cumbersome and showed few positive results. Too many Italians took it upon themselves to deliberately sabotage the goal of registering, harassing, and ultimately arresting Jews. In particular, members of the Catholic clergy all over Italy had flagrantly disobeyed the orders of their German ally and had in many cases provided sanctuary and safe transport for Jews.

Members of the Vatican were particular thorns in the side of Colonel Edmund Schiller, the ranking German officer in Rome. The situation was somewhat delicate because of the mixed messages his office was receiving from Berlin. The official tone was always condemnatory toward any form of collaboration between the Vatican and the Jews, but there was always a precautionary provision attached to every one of these documents. Colonel Schiller was particularly concerned about two Vatican prelates. He believed they had established a sophisticated system for hiding Jews. He had been aware for months that it was impossible for so many Jews to slip through the net at random. It required diplomatic assistance, money, and a series of safe houses to allow the Jews to evade the plans of the Gestapo. He was certain that he knew the designers of these plots, but he lacked concrete evidence.

On Wednesday, thanks to interrogations performed by the Gestapo on three Italian partisans, he received the evidence he needed to trap the collaborators and identify those who were behind the Jewish escape system. If they were Vatican officials, their diplomatic immunity presented a challenge because the world outcry would be severe if he arrested them on sovereign soil. Actually, he found that restriction amusing because territorial limits had never been an impediment to German behavior in this war. However, it would be essential to capture them in the act. He believed that he would soon have all the information he needed to bait a trap.

Colonel Schiller entered the prison and was escorted through a courtyard to a stairway that led to the basement. The sounds and stench of men being tortured filled the caverns of the narrow hallway. The escorting guard took a key from his belt and opened a large steel door that led to a torture chamber.

Three men of the Third Riech entered the dank, cold, small room. An Italian prisoner was chained to a wall in such a way that his feet did not quite reach the floor so that every limb in his body was stretched to the breaking point, leaving him in constant, agonizing pain.

Two of the Gestapo released the prisoner from his chains and eased him onto a chair. He blinked as if having difficulty focusing through eyes almost swollen shut. His eyeglasses lay shattered on the floor.

The colonel sat down across from the prisoner, cocking his head in consideration. "I am Colonel Schiller. I am in charge of this prison. I am your only hope. If you help me, perhaps I may help you. First show me how cooperative you can be. What is your name?"

The prisoner mumbled something through bloody, swollen lips.

"I cannot hear you. Speak louder."

"My name is . . . Sergio Caputo."

Colonel Schiller lit two cigarettes and offered one to Sergio. "See how easy that was?"

After a moment of hesitation, Sergio accepted a cigarette, took a deep drag, and coughed.

"Sergio, do you know why you are here?"

No response.

"You are here because we know that for months you have been involved with helping priests protect Jews. Isn't that right, Sergio?"

Still there was no response.

"I am a very patient man, Sergio. I can also be kind. I admire your bravery, but I require you to give me the information I seek."

Sergio puffed deeply on the cigarette, but he also raised his shoulders as if in anticipation of more physical blows.

Colonel Schiller nodded, and then played his ace in the hole. "I know that you are a family man, Sergio. Let me see if I have this right. Your wife is named Sophia, and your children's names are Maria, Paolo, Arturo, Giuseppe, and Angelina."

Sergio's bruised and distorted face revealed panic.

"Do I have that correct?"

Sergio finally nodded, tears filling his eyes.

"I want you to know that your family is safely under house arrest. You can either save them or seal their fate. If you tell me what I need to know, you will be released and no harm will come to your family. That is my kindness to you. Do you understand me?"

Trembling all over, Sergio nodded.

"Good. Now please tell me the names of the Catholic priests involved in hiding Jews in Rome and Florence."

Sergio's head slumped forward against his chest. He said nothing.

Colonel Schiller stood up. "I am sad that you choose to reject my kindness." He started to leave and then turned back. "You do understand that without your help, I cannot help your family. They will be dead by tomorrow evening. My soldiers grow weary of Italian lies, so I regret to inform you that the deaths of your wife and children may be most unpleasant."

"Please, wait." Sergio dropped to his knees, bowing his head in supplication. "They have done nothing wrong. I am guilty. They are innocent. I beg you not to harm them."

"I am not the one who will harm them. If you do not tell me what I want to know, understand that you—and you alone—will have murdered your loved ones." Colonel Schiller motioned to the guard to open the cell door.

"Colonel, please. I will tell you whatever you need to know. Just save my family."

"Very well." The colonel sat down again. "If you tell me the truth, I will see what I can do."

For the next hour, Sergio gave chapter and verse about who was involved and how they successfully avoided being found out by the German authorities. The backbone of the system was twofold: Father Patrick O'Hara and Cardinal Pietro Agnelli. Sergio even gave specific details about how the Jews were notified and how, in many cases, the actual presence of Father O'Hara and Cardinal Agnelli facilitated the participation of the convents and monasteries.

Colonel Schiller patted Sergio kindly on the shoulder and then rose to leave.

Sergio pleaded again, "Now that I have told you everything, you will see that my family reaches safety, won't you?"

"I will personally see that you and your family receive everything they deserve."

"Thank you."

Colonel Schiller left the cell, a slight smile on his lips. He motioned for one of the guards to come forward. "Shoot the Jew-lover and deal with his family, too."

"Yes, Colonel. It will be done immediately."

As the colonel ascended the stairs, he heard a single shot. It had been a fruitful evening for him. Soon he would be rid of Agnelli and O'Hara. Now it was time to dine at one of the excellent Italian restaurants near the prison.

Chapter Forty-Eight

Berlin 1943, Office of the Minister of Propaganda

Erich Hanke enthusiastically presented the latest report to Dr. Goebbels regarding the resettlement of Berlin's Jews.

Goebbels skimmed through the report and settled on the number of Jewish homes that had been confiscated to meet the requirements of the Führer's new contemporary city. To adhere to the schedule of Hitler's architect, the entire northern section of fashionable homes had been either condemned or purchased for paltry sums. The report stated that Dr. Speer was absolutely gleeful about the progress that had been made and had reported it to the Führer.

"As your good friend, Dr. Speer gave you total credit for the revised schedule," Hanke said.

Dr. Goebbels strutted around the office. "I am pleased to hear that, because the Führer has recently been inundated with negative reports. I am sure this will buoy his spirit. I have major concerns about his health because, unlike us, he is faced with woeful incompetence on the part of the general staff. It is amazing to me that these generals so poorly serve the greatest leader in the world. The new Berlin models that Dr. Speer is developing will allow Hitler to see the outcome of his glorious vision."

"I agree," Hanke said, sifting through reports. He stopped at one page. "I know you are well aware of the Catholic Church meddling in the Jewish question and providing sanctuary for countless Jews. I have received word from a Gestapo colonel in Rome, Colonel Schiller, that he has uncovered the prime network responsible for this resistance. Two Vatican clerics have been responsible for saving thousands of Jews. One of the leaders is a cardinal stationed in the Vatican."

"Despicable! What is his name?"

"Cardinal Pietro Agnelli."

Dr. Goebbels pounded his fist on the desk. "That swine has been a constant critic of national socialism for years. He is the one who ordained Hans and had the audacity to imply in his sermon that the German government was dangerous. I knew that someday we would have to deal with him. What does Colonel Schiller propose to do to correct this situation?"

Hanke put down the report. "He is seeking guidance because he is concerned that this is a direct attack on a prince of the Church and may trigger international protests. Also, there could be a public denunciation by the pope. The colonel is asking that we give him the desired end result and he will then implement a plan."

Dr. Goebbels removed his glasses and cleaned them with his handkerchief. "I am most impressed with Colonel Schiller's assessment of the situation and believe he should receive recognition for his work. Not now. After the process is complete, recommend to Himmler that the colonel be promoted. Don't do it immediately because if you do Himmler will take the credit that is rightfully ours."

Hanke jotted down Dr. Goebbels's requests. "Maybe we should involve Hans in this matter. His position as an insider in the Vatican may be invaluable to Colonel Schiller."

"I did not intend to use him again so soon," Dr Goebbels said.

"I was not certain he was completely committed to us, but killing those two Jews puts him at the head of the loyalty list. His action symbolized the commitment that every German needs to make at this critical time. I think it may be worthwhile to ask Colonel Schiller if he needs Hans's assistance."

"Go ahead."

Hanke closed his portfolio and left the room.

Chapter Forty-Nine

Rome, late April 1943

Father Patrick O'Hara found that more and more of his time was spent coordinating the underground process of hiding Jews. His administrative tasks in the Ecumenical Office suffered, but it mattered little because he reported directly to Cardinal Agnelli. The current problem confronting him was that the German occupation of Rome had made it increasingly difficult to move freely without the Gestapo intercepting those he was trying to save. Ambassador Hunsecker easily forged the documents and travel visas, but recently Hunsecker was having more difficulty providing the necessary documents.

Also, since the Italian government was collapsing, the borders had tightened through the use of German guards. The pressure to provide safe haven for those fleeing was more urgent than ever because the Germans were building a detention center in Calabria, a temporary stop before the residents were sent to their deaths at Auschwitz.

The network that Cardinal Agnelli and Father O'Hara established centered on a series of safe houses between Rome and Florence. Monasteries and convents were only notified at the last second in order to prevent German spies from picking up the trail. The network was successful, but the dominant German presence in Italy made the work more dangerous.

Since Patrick had become involved in saving Jews, he had grown to hate the Germans more than the British, something he never would have thought possible.

Chapter Fifty

Rome, late spring 1943

Colonel Edmund Schiller was almost salivating over the realization that he was about to eradicate the source of Jewish escapes in Italy. Through a series of fortuitous events and strategic planning, he had clearly identified the pipeline that moved the Jews from Rome to Florence and ultimately to Switzerland. His information had been authenticated through torture and the information of well-placed informants.

Colonel Schiller knew that to kill the resistance it was necessary to sever the head of the organization. In other words, Cardinal Agnelli and Father O'Hara had to be caught actually transporting Jews. Arresting them in the Vatican presented too many diplomatic issues. It was essential that their capture and ultimate deaths be unrelated to the German government. To camouflage their deaths, two prisoners who resembled them physically would die in a staged automobile accident. The automobile would be completely incinerated and items identifying Agnelli and O'Hara would be placed nearby. The key to the plan was the assistance of Dr. Goebbels's inside agent, who would guarantee the presence of the clerics.

Erich Hanke left Berlin and made his way to Rome to have a face-to-face meeting with Hans Keller. They had had no contact since that fateful day when Hans had proven his total loyalty to the Nazi Party.

Hanke carried with him the detailed plans for the Jewish escape, which was to occur on the feast of San Antonio at a monastery near Florence. The plan was to have Hans learn the schedules of the two clerics and notify Hanke.

Father Hans Keller had agreed to meet Erich Hanke at the Hotel Raphael located a block from the Piazza Navona. At the thought, he felt a wave of nausea like the one he had experienced after he had murdered Aaron and Ruth Lehman. He wondered what new monstrous act would be asked of him to serve the Fatherland.

He had been so drained after his last meeting with Hanke that for many days it had taken all of his energy just to get out of bed. Yet he'd had no choice but to continue his charade.

For some reason, he was experiencing a totally different feeling when he said the daily Mass. It had always been a part of the pretense, but no more. He had begun to feel a sense of connection to this ritual and it ceased to be merely a part of his actor's role. Yesterday as he raised the host he experienced tears, and he wondered if he was losing a grip on his sanity. Was he actually starting to believe in the sacraments he had previously dismissed?

Hans steeled himself before entering the Hotel Raphael. In ordinary times he would have stopped at his favorite café in the Piazza Navona, but today he barely noticed the Fountain of the Four Rivers, his favorite in Rome.

Hanke was seated in the lobby. On seeing Hans, he motioned for him to walk toward the elevator. Once they arrived at Hanke's room, Hans sat down. An awkward silence engulfed them.

"Are you all right?" Hanke asked

"Cold coming on," Hans mumbled.

"Jewish germs." Hanke shook his head. "I have news. The Gestapo has concerns about certain Vatican clerics. There is overwhelming evidence that Cardinal Agnelli and Father O'Hara are the masterminds behind the plot to save Jews in Italy."

Hans felt pure horror race through his body. He feared that he would be asked to murder Agnelli and O'Hara. Where would this madness end? Would they soon ask him to murder the pope? He struggled to refocus because Hanke was describing Colonel Schiller's plan to capture the clerics.

"We want you to alert us to their schedule on the feast of Saint Anthony because we know that the exodus will take place in a monastery outside of Florence."

"What will happen to them after they're caught?"

"That's the beauty of this plan. There can be no trace of German involvement in their deaths."

"How will you achieve that if they're missing? Everyone in the Vatican will know."

"The colonel in charge of the Gestapo in Rome should have been a novelist because he has devised a superb plan. After the two clerics are captured, two prisoners with similar physical character-istics will be placed in a car that will go over a ravine in Florence. Documents indicating their identities as Agnelli and O'Hara will be found nearby after the car is incinerated. The clerics will be inter-rogated to determine if there are other prelates involved, and then they will be killed and buried somewhere in the woods near Flor-ence. It will appear to the world that they died in a tragic accident. Your job in this is simple but important. You must call me if they do not leave the Vatican for the feast of San Antonio. Now, before you go, would you like some cognac?"

Hans shuddered at the thought. "No, thank you. I must return to the Vatican."

Chapter Fifty-One

Rome, June 1943

Colonel Edmund Schiller received with satisfaction the information that guaranteed he would break the back of the clerical conspiracy once and for all. The location for the mass escape would be the Benedictine Monastery of Vallombrana outside of Florence during the feast of San Antonio. This would be the perfect opportunity to collect all of those involved in the network en masse. The feast was only a two-day event, so it would be easy to orchestrate ongoing surveillance.

The key factor would be the affirmation from Erich Hanke's inside person that the clerics under suspicion were in attendance during the raid. The method was simple. The operation was a go unless Hanke's man notified him that the cardinal and priest in question were not scheduled to attend the feast. If there was no such notification, the plan would be operational. The monastery was located in a secluded area and would not be noticed by partisans or locals who were not feast-goers.

Identifying the Jewish women and children would be relatively easy, but the men in these escapes were usually in clerical garb. Only when they were stripped would it be obvious which men were Jewish.

On the day before the feast Colonel Schiller visited the area with his staff and organized a plan of attack for the entire operation. The only difficulty he perceived now was waiting the twenty-four hours before he could capture the conspirators.

For Father Hans Keller, this assignment was the final test to ascertain for himself whether there was any morality left in him. He was no longer hypnotized by all that had destroyed what was decent and honorable. There would be no more blood on his hands. Regardless of the cost, he would not betray the cardinal and his dear friend. He struggled with how he could warn them without divulging his sordid past, but no matter what, it was time to do the right thing. If he allowed them to be caught, it would be like murdering Aaron and Ruth Lehman all over again. If he warned the clerics, he had no illusions about his fate. He would be signing his own death warrant, but that thought almost brought him relief. His life had evaporated the moment he pulled the trigger. Even though he was terrified at the physical torture he would endure at the hands of the Gestapo, he knew he must warn his friends.

He reached for his phone and called Cardinal Agnelli. "Pietro, this is Hans. I need to speak to you and Patrick this evening. I can't tell you any more over the phone, but it's critical. I will be at your residence within the hour."

When Hans arrived at the cardinal's residence, he was greeted at the door by Pietro and led into the parlor where Patrick was seated on the sofa sipping an espresso. Both men were dressed in casual clothes.

Hans felt his hands tremble as he refused the offer of an espresso. "I have come here this evening on a matter of the greatest importance to both of you. I am aware that you have been involved in a network that secures safe passage for Jews out of Italy. I also know that your plans involve the monasteries near Florence and that you are planning a major escape on the feast of San Antonio."

Both men looked dumfounded.

"How did you learn about this?" Pietro asked.

"That's not important, but it is imperative that you realize the Gestapo knows every detail of your plans. They have set a trap to catch you and all of the Jews that you plan to escort. Your plan is doomed to failure."

Patrick stood and punched the wall with a fist. "How the hell did they find out? We've been so careful!"

"There are so many spies in Rome that I'm surprised you weren't discovered earlier."

After a few silent moments, Pietro asked, "Hans, I am deeply indebted to you for making us aware of this, but how can we abandon the two hundred people we plan to free? Is there any other way?"

"If you continue your involvement, you will soon be dead," Hans said bluntly. "The Gestapo will be merciless with you and any of your accomplices."

Pietro looked hard at Hans. "I am an old man and death will come with or without the help of the Nazis. I do not fear death. It is doing nothing that really frightens me."

"There is no way you can avoid them catching you," Hans insisted. "Please, in the name of common sense, promise me you won't involve yourselves any further in these rescues."

True to his nature, Patrick said, "I'm not sure I can make that promise. I appreciate the warning, but I must find other ways to help."

"I completely understand, but please believe that what I told you is absolutely true." Hans glanced sorrowfully from one to the other. "And I've put myself in danger to warn you."

"Thank you." Pietro rose from his chair, embraced Hans and made the sign of the cross over his head.

"Watch your back," Patrick said. "We'll do what we can to keep your involvement secret."

Hans shook Patrick's hand and left through a side door, relieved but fully aware that his discovery as a traitor was, most likely, imminent.

After Hans left, Patrick could not contain his anger. As usual, he reverted to his stubborn way of approaching life. He appreciated the warning and had no desire to be a hero, but he recalled the words that Father Donahue had spoken to him about leadership just before he was ordained. He knew what he had to do.

Part of the original group that was to be rescued from the feast of San Antonio was being hidden in the Benedictine convent, a four-hour train ride to the border in Lugano. Sister Regina Coeli, the mother superior of the convent, had been hiding thirteen Jewish families at great peril to them all.

Patrick and Dr. Giuseppe Morano, a physician and one of the collaborators, decided to smuggle only the children at the convent out of the country. The two men were distraught at the thought that they would not be able to save the parents, too. It was literally impossible to have such a large group evade the Nazi net. The plan was to have Dr. Morano sedate the children, who would be presented as extremely ill and being transported from local Italian hospitals to a convent in Lugano where they would receive the medical attention they needed. Dr. Morano could not travel with the patients because of the upcoming wedding of his daughter, but he would prepare Patrick to pass himself off as a pediatric specialist. Most of the regular German physicians were at the Russian front, but, at worst, Parick would be perceived as merely a medical student.

Patrick requested a few days of vacation. He did not inform Cardinal Agnelli of his plan so as not to make him vulnerable if it failed.

The first part of the escape one evening went flawlessly, but the most difficult aspect for Patrick was observing the pain on the faces of the parents as they bade farewell to their children. Once the children were sedated, they were wrapped in blankets and arranged in ambulances to drive them to the train station. The children were accompanied by Patrick and six nuns. This part of the plan seemed credible. They all hoped that they would encounter little resistance from the Germans. Dr. Morano insisted that Patrick take his Luger in case there was a confrontation.

The group arrived at the station fifteen minutes before scheduled departure. At first everything seemed to be going smoothly, but as the train arrived and the nuns were putting the children in their compartments, a German captain and two armed soldiers suddenly appeared on the platform. Patrick met the soldiers onboard with all the essential paperwork. The German captain scrutinized the paperwork, returned the travel visas, and began to inspect every compartment.

When he returned, he said, "I congratulate you on your clever ploy, Dr. O'Hara, but I do not believe these are ill children. My suspicion is that you are smuggling Jewish children out of Italy."

Patrick was tempted to deny the allegation, fall back on his pugilistic training, and physically attack the captain, but he realized that the armed soldiers would intervene and probably kill the children and the nuns. He had removed the Luger from his luggage while the captain was walking through the train and had hidden it under his coat. First he attempted to fool the captain by using the medical terminology that Doctor Morano had rehearsed with him, but it was clear that the captain remained unconvinced. Summoning one of the sisters, Patrick gave her medical instructions that were to be administered before the train left. Still, the captain repeated his initial suspicions.

Departure was minutes away. Patrick decided to appeal to the humanity of the man. "Captain, these innocent children have suffered more than you and I have in our entire lives. They have done nothing to deserve this pain, and human compassion demands that we do what we can to minimize it. The sisters and I have pledged to make them comfortable and to give them the hope that their innocence deserves. If your hunch is right, you may receive a temporary reward, but you will have to live with their deaths for the rest of your life."

"If I am right, would you be willing to die for these children?"

Patrick did not hesitate. "Not only that, but I would be willing to kill if it meant saving one of them."

"Are you a Jew?"

"No, I am not a Jew, but that is not the issue. At this moment we have the opportunity to be fully human or beasts that kill innocent children. Which will it be?"

The conductor came onboard. "Captain, may the train now proceed?"

The captain had one hand on his Luger, but he never took his eyes off the face of the man willing to die for a group of strangers. The tension warped the world into a deafening silence.

Patrick held the captain's gaze and did not blink at all.

Finally, the captain took his hand off his Luger. "Conductor, you are free to go." He quickly left the train.

Chapter Fifty-Two

Vallombrana Monastery on the Eve
of the Feast of San Antonio, June 1943

The Benedictine Monastery of Vallombrana was founded by Giovanni Gianini in the eleventh century. Its beauty derived from the simplicity of its architectural style and its setting in the magnificent Tuscan hills. The main structure had tall windows that allowed sunlight to penetrate the entire interior. The ornate frescoes that adorned the walls of the hallways were created by students of the Roman and Florentine schools of art. The buildings reflected the synthesis of the Gothic and Romanesque periods with simple symbols from multiple Italian and Greek sources. The beauty of the monastery was complemented by the resonant Gregorian chant that flowed from the chapel through the woods and surrounding valley.

Dressed in civilian clothing, Colonel Edmund Schiller marveled at the splendor of the grounds as he played the role of a tourist visiting the monastery. He was particularly impressed by its serenity. Spending the night at a neighboring inn, he had gone over the final plans for the invasion of the monastery that was to take place during the afternoon Mass. Once he was satisfied that all systems were in order, he dressed in his formal uniform and made his way to a local restaurant. Seated on a terrace overlooking the monastery, he ate a leisurely lunch and marveled at how beautiful the Tuscan hills were. Someday when Germany ruled the world, he might consider retiring to this area.

As the day progressed, he witnessed the festive activities below him. His men were already positioned for the afternoon intervention. They had successfully hidden themselves in the neighboring woods. The plan to enter the monastery was foolproof because all of the pilgrims would be contained in the large courtyard. Once the Mass started the soldiers would enter the courtyard and require the presentation of passports and travel visas. The colonel assumed that the entire process would take about two hours. Trucks would be present to take all prisoners to a detention center.

At four that afternoon, Colonel Schiller was joined by two other officers who informed him that the Mass would soon begin. The colonel left the terrace and made his way to the monastery. When he saw that all the pilgrims had entered the square, he gave the signal for the soldiers to enter. The soldiers raced into the square and forced all of the pilgrims into three groups: men in the first group, women and children in the second group, and priests and brothers in the third. One of the monks protested the intrusion but was quickly silenced by a rifle butt.

Colonel Schiller walked to the center of the square and announced, "Pardon the intrusion. This is a simple procedure to check passports and travel visas. If all is in order, you will be able to resume your activities."

The soldiers began to process the papers while six men in full-length leather coats singled out the clergy members and ordered them to go inside to the main refectory. Once inside, the clerics were forced to disrobe and were physically examined to determine whether they had been circumcised.

The square was chaotic. The peaceful religious environment had turned into a nightmare for the Italian pilgrims. They had come with hopes that San Antonio would hear their petitions and instead found themselves at the receiving end of bayonets and automatic weapons. After approximately two hours, the lieutenant and one of the other Gestapo members approached Colonel Schiller, who was seated in the courtyard.

The lieutenant spoke first, apparently hesitant and nervous. "Colonel, I regret to inform you that we did not find one unauthorized person in the square. Most of the people here live in neighboring towns. There is not one Jew in the entire crowd."

Colonel Schiller was stunned by this news. He questioned the Gestapo representative about Jews in clerical garb and two special clerics, but still did not receive a positive answer. He was furious. How had his meticulously detailed plan failed? In sheer rage, he shouted, "This fiasco is the work of a traitor. I will find out what happened!"

He immediately called Erich Hanke.

Chapter Fifty-Three

Berlin, June 1943

Erich Hanke answered the phone, listened intently, and then slammed the phone down in a fury. "We have a traitor in our midst," he yelled. "I don't know who it is, but I will find out."

After he calmed down somewhat, he called Hans's office and left a message for him to come to Dr. Goebbels's office in Berlin as soon as possible.

When Hans received the message, he knew that his fate was sealed. He hoped he might be able to bluff his way out. If not, his life was over anyway.

Hans took the same train that he had taken years ago when he was invited to meet Dr. Goebbels. The first trip had been filled with excitement and hope; this time it was filled with shame and fear. Arriving in Berlin at midday, he went directly to the Propaganda Ministry. He observed numerous German soldiers in the lobby. As he entered, Dr. Goebbels's secretary announced his arrival and escorted him into the main office. Hanke and Goebbels were seated and did not even casually greet him.

Hanke immediately lunged with a question. "Hans, do you have any idea why Cardinal Agnelli and Father O'Hara did not participate in the feast at the Benedictine Monastery on Sunday?"

"I'm not sure, because when last I spoke with them that was their intention."

Hanke drove straight to the point. "Why didn't you call me and indicate that they had not left for the monastery?"

Before Hans could answer, Dr. Goebbels intervened and said, "Let me handle this, Hanke." He fixed Hans with a sharp gaze. "Only a few of us knew about the plan to capture those two men. It was well planned, but it turned into a huge failure. Someone obviously warned Agnelli and O'Hara. Was it you?"

"How can you ask me that after what I've done for the Fatherland?"

"It is certainly true that you have done great things, but we are not talking about past performance. There is never a point when any man can rest on his laurels. These two men are enemies of the state. They are directly involved in thwarting the will of the Führer and they must be dealt with. It is a delicate matter because we cannot kill them within the Vatican without diplomatic repercussions."

Hans saw an opportunity to steer the conversation away from his involvement. "Dr. Goebbels, it would be a grave mistake to assassinate them because sooner or later it would become obvious why they were killed."

"I know that, Hans, and in order to kill two birds with one stone I have devised a way to free you from suspicion and at the same time remove these two swine."

Hans did not need psychic powers to know what was coming next. He felt his heart sink with despair.

Dr. Goebbels smiled. "You are to dispose of both of them personally. Find a pretext of taking them somewhere in Tuscany and then notify Hanke where and when you will arrive. We will arrange to have their deaths appear to be a tragic automobile accident."

Hans realized that Dr. Goebbels had laid the perfect trap. There was no move left that he could make, but perhaps, at least for one moment, there could be some redemption left for him.

"I cannot and will not do it."

Hanke pounded his fist on the table. "I knew it was you. You will regret this, you fucking traitor!"

Dr. Goebbels seemed more sad than enraged. "Hans, why have you given up the opportunity of a lifetime? You were positioned to enjoy a marvelous future within the Reich and you have forfeited this for a group of Jews. Why, Hans, why?"

With nothing left to lose, Hans said, "I made a horrible decision when I allowed myself to live an illusion for personal gain. Because of that decision I did things that now I despise. For years I fooled myself with rationalizations, but this cause is evil and we can never wash away the blood of all we have slain."

Hanke could no longer be silent. "Do we have to listen to this Jewish horseshit?"

Hans braced himself and faced Hanke. "The worst part for me is that I have become you, totally committed to the hypnotic ravings of a lunatic."

Hanke's face turned bright red and the veins bulged in his neck. He reached for the Luger in its holster at his waist.

Dr. Goebbels stopped him with one word. "Enough! I have heard enough. Hans, you will never see Passau, Berlin, Rome, or any other place again. Hanke, call the guards and have him taken away."

Hanke opened the door. "Take this traitor to Gestapo headquarters."

After Hans was taken away, Hanke was beside himself. "Why didn't we kill him here?"

Dr. Goebbels answered, "Anger solves nothing, my friend. We must always plan rather than merely react. Follow the strategy that was intended for the other clerics. Take one of the prisoners that fits his description and implement the car accident scenario."

"What should we do with Hans?"

"Send him to Dachau. There are no names for priests there, just numbers."

Chapter Fifty-Four

Train headed to Dachau, August 1943

The metallic sounds of train wheels clattering against tracks echoed through the boiling hot freight car packed with silent human cargo. The men were crowded into limited space, pressed against each other like mollusks on stone, with no room to sit. They had been riding for two days and nights. There was no food or water and the suffocating smells of urine and feces had turned the air acrid. To the Nazi régime, these men were the cancers that must be removed to purify the Aryan race and rid it once and for all of the dangers that these unbelievers presented to the Third Reich.

These silent shadows of humanity had been collected from every occupied country in Europe. Their crimes had not been aired in courts of law; their punishments were the outcome of Nazi justice. The rule of law had been replaced by the arbitrary hate of all that was deemed subversive. This car, once reserved for cattle on their way to slaughter, had been utilized to transport these "enemies of the state" to their final destination.

For a change, Train Number 187 was not transporting Jews, Gypsies, or homosexuals. It was filled with Catholic priests. Men like Father Wilhelm Benzinger, a Scripture scholar from Leipzig who had dared proclaim from the pulpit that the murder of innocent civilians was an abomination. Men like Monsignor Paul Presacki, the stalwart vicar general of Plazoa, who had been convicted of the crime of harboring a Jewish family in his rectory.

Father Anton Weigel had been a pastor at Saint Stefan's in Regensburg for twenty-seven years. Short in stature with a soft body that evidenced a weakness for strudel, he was the moral pillar of the entire Regensburg community. Long before it was fashionable he had reached out to members of every religious community and had often ignored strict prohibitions from the ecclesial authorities against these activities. His initial resistance to the treatment of the Jews in Regensburg was quiet opposition within his intimate circle, but soon his views became public. His articles in the parish bulletin cautioned Catholics against participating in anti-Semitic behavior. He reminded them that Christian principles of love demanded acceptance of all groups. His flock was not surprised to see him well up in tears when the choir sang Bach's beautiful "Cantata 39" inspired by the *Seven Works of Mercy*.

After Kristallnacht, Father Weigel's involvement became more overt and included providing hiding places for Jewish families in Regensburg and in convents and monasteries throughout Bavaria. Eventually Father Weigel was questioned by the Gestapo. He was candid about his anti-Nazi beliefs, but he was not arrested because the local mayor and businessmen pleaded with the Gestapo to ignore these transgressions. He was warned that any further interference with German policy would have dire consequences. True to character, Father Weigel promised nothing and delivered less. The afternoon he was released from prison, he formulated an action plan to create a series of protests and interventions. When he was next arrested by the Gestapo, he was tried, convicted, and sentenced to Dachau.

Father Paul Koestler was dragged from his pulpit and beaten because he gave a sermon that sympathized with the plight of the Jews in Germany. He had been pastor of his parish for eleven years and was known to be a kind and saintly man. Many of those who rained blows upon him were the same parishioners who had received Communion from his hand for many years. Three days later, Father Koestler was visited by the Gestapo, who ushered him into their dank headquarters, where he was interrogated and tortured for days before receiving a life sentence to Dachau.

Many so-called Catholics had found a new Messiah; Hitler replaced Christ in their hearts and minds. To oppose the Führer's gospel was a heresy that could be punished by death. The New Testament had been replaced by *Mein Kampf*. The rule of law had been replaced by the rule of jackboot. The initially covert suspension of religion, especially the Church of Rome, had exploded into full-blown hatred. Hitler loudly complained, "Catholicism is only an extension of the Jewish plague. It was the Jews who gave us Christ, and everywhere we turn in Germany the Catholics are preventing us from achieving our vision."

As the train lurched around curves, the physical pressure of bodies crammed against each other increased. One of the priests attempted to raise his hand in order to make the sign of the cross on the man who was pressed against his chest. The man's face was blue, and though he was standing erect it was obvious that he was dead.

"Requiescat in pace," the priest uttered. Even though he was unable to raise his hand for a blessing, he was joined by others in the car in reciting the traditional, powerful Catholic prayers for the dead. "Pray for us sinners, now and at the hour of our death. Amen."

In a civilized world this death train might merely be a figment of a deranged imagination, but this train was far from unique. It was one of many headed to the ultimate hell on earth: Dachau.

Only one of the priests in the train car believed that he deserved the hell that awaited him. That man was Father Hans Keller, for he was Hitler's priest.

Chapter Fifty-Five

Dachau, August 1943

As the priests staggered off the cattle car, they were immediately greeted with a derisive welcome from the German guards who smacked the backs of their heads and forced them to pick up the pace as they walked into the camp.

One of the guards shouted at the last man to disembark to pick up the body of a dead priest on the floor. Three of the priests attempted to lift the body, but they were so weakened that they dropped the corpse. The soldiers began beating them with batons. One priest fell, bleeding profusely, and the guards kicked him harder.

This brutal introduction to the concentration camp was the first of endless days of psychological and physical abuse. Hitler's hatred of the Catholic Church and its priests had been clearly conveyed to the camp guards. They took every opportunity to make life in Dachau a living hell. Stripped of their freedom, the priests would soon lose their names and be known solely by the tattooed numbers on their arms.

Life in Dachau was a nightmare. In the summer the barracks were like ovens. In winter there was little heat and the threadbare clothing issued did little to prevent frostbite. Coupled with the cramped living arrangements and the work details, wanton brutality often brought life to a violent end. In another time and place, the hard physical work would have been performed by beasts of burden. The priests were forced to carry loads that could not be carted even by healthy human beings, and they were severely punished if they dropped a load. The guards indiscriminately gave out prolonged pain and suffering as if relishing their brutal acts.

For some gentle priests the stress was too overwhelming to bear. As they crossed themselves, they embraced the electric wire that surrounded the camp. Others struggled courageously to keep the faith, staying alive until disease or violence claimed them. Despite the cauldron of horror, many survived. They sustained each other with continual acts of love and charity. On many occasions someone who procured a crust of bread would give it to a sick prisoner rather than devour it. The Eucharist was celebrated in secret.

Father Hans Keller was one of the men who was strong enough to remain alive. He marveled at the love and faith of these beleaguered priests. He believed he had no right to share anything with these good men. They served the Lord Jesus, who offered life and ultimate redemption, while he had aligned himself with the devil in the guise of Adolf Hitler.

In the still of the night one of the bishops in Father Keller's barracks tapped him on the shoulder and asked if he would hear his confession. Hans wanted to ask the bishop to seek someone else, but respecting the risk the bishop had taken, Hans agreed. He heard the man's confession and found himself silently weeping. Hans knew that this man deserved comfort, so he raised his hand in absolution.

Suddenly he felt a peace that he had not experienced for months. In the darkness and despair of Dachau, he clearly heard in his head the words of Cardinal Agnelli, "There is never a moment when He will not open His arms to you, no matter what you have done." Hans wanted to believe this with all his heart and soul. Could there be redemption, even for a sinner like him? For the first time, Hans prayed for faith.

Hans was aware that there was particular hostility toward him on the part of the guards and the head capo because they knew that he had once been a prominent member of the Nazi Party and had betrayed the cause. Every day he was singled out to perform the most demeaning and disgusting work assignments. One of the guards especially enjoyed having him clean the dog kennels, and he would often put his boot on Hans's neck while he was scrubbing the floor so his face would be pushed into dog excrement.

"You are Dog Shit Number 621644 and belong with all the dog shit on this floor," the guard would scream while kicking and punching Hans. On one occasion the guard fashioned a crown of thorns out of rusty barbed wire and forced it on Hans's head. "If you want to be like Jesus the Jew, you should look like him," he taunted.

The barbed wire tore into Hans's scalp and blood oozed down both of his cheeks. Though the pain was excruciating, he never made a sound, thinking, "I deserve this for what I've done."

Over and over Hans ruminated on how he had worshipped a false Messiah, and in the course of his devotion, he had committed unspeakable crimes. These priests worshipped a God who had built his temple on love. Hans desperately wanted to believe in this God and take a leap of faith. Yet he believed that even if their God was real He could not forgive betrayals. Hans had assassinated those who had loved and raised him, while contributing to the deportation of countless innocent Jews. He had also deprived his son of the love and affection that Aaron and Ruth Lehman would have provided their grandson. There was no ritual that could wash away his sins. Dachau was a terrible place, but the pain of living there was less than the pain of his tormented soul.

Late one night Hans heard a loud noise at the front of the barracks. Startled by the sound, he sat up on his mattress only to have a flashlight thrust in his face. Blinded by the light, he could not immediately see who was standing over him.

"Get up, you piece of shit," a voice commanded.

Hans recognized the guard who constantly abused him. He stumbled out of bed and was smashed on the right side of his head with the heavy flashlight. The guard grabbed Hans by the neck and pushed him toward the door. He kicked Hans down three steps and smashed his face into mud.

As Hans tried to stand, he smelled liquor on the guard's breath.

"Tonight, Jew priest, you are going to have a new experience. Stand up and take off your trousers." He chuckled, spotlighting Hans with his flashlight. "Now bend over."

Hans obeyed the command and shivered in the cold night air.

The guard unzipped his pants. "I'm going to fuck you in the ass, priest!"

Hans knew he would be killed if he fought back, so he braced for the impending rape. Instead of penetrating him, the guard hit Hans violently on the head with the flashlight. Hans fell to the ground, hurting and bleeding from the wound.

Standing over Hans, the drunken guard said, "On second thought, I would rather fuck a pig than a Jew priest."

After the guard left, Hans sat with his head in his hands for what seemed like an eternity before he could attempt to stand. He placed his hands in the mud and applied a layer to his scalp for protection. He crawled back into the barracks, staggered inside, and fell into a deep sleep on the floor beside his mattress.

The next morning was like every other morning except that one of the priests who had returned from the infirmary had heard the guards speaking about a list that was being compiled. If you were on the list you would be killed at a designated spot outside the camp. One of the capos was in charge of selection. If you bribed him with some food, he would take your name off the list. Hans ascertained which capo was in charge of the list. For the next three days he did not eat his meager ration of bread. Instead, he hid the bread under the floorboards along with two potatoes he found that had been discarded in the garbage bin near the barracks.

In the pouring rain, Hans approached the capo in charge of the list. While other guards were having a cigarette. Hans took the opportunity to speak to the capo. "I know that you're in charge of the list that will send ten of us away next week."

The capo turned, giving Hans a dispassionate look. "It's true. Now get out of here before I crack your skull open. If you want to give me something to keep you off the list, come and see me in the barracks tonight."

"I will give you two potatoes and five pieces of bread if you put me on the list."

The capo stared at Hans in astonishment. "Are you mad or joking?"

"Neither. These good men have done nothing to deserve death, but I have."

"Why don't you just run and grab the wire to end your life?"

"For once I want to have my life mean something."

The capo agreed, completing the transaction.

The following Tuesday, ten numbers were read at the morning roll call. Those men selected were marched to a waiting truck. As they climbed into the vehicle, Hans felt for the first time in his life that the hand of God had finally touched his heart.

Chapter Fifty-Six

Dachau, July 7, 1943

Field Marshal Schutzen sat in the rear of his chauffeur-driven limousine as it wended its way in the darkness through the German countryside. Because it was dangerous to use headlights due to the constant presence of Allied fighter planes, the trip took much longer than usual. The parking lights shed just enough light to negotiate back roads at a snail's pace. Schutzen tapped a cigarette against the sterling silver case that bore his family crest. It was a gift from his father and bore the inscription, "To my son Wolfgang on his eighteenth birthday. Love, Father."

Schutzen had been a career soldier with impeccable bloodlines on both sides of his family. For centuries the family had been part of the Bavarian aristocracy. In his military circles he rarely spoke of his privileged background or of the fact that he was raised a Roman Catholic and was still devoted to his faith. At one point in his youth he seriously considered becoming a Jesuit priest, but family expectations and the burden of celibacy tilted the scale in favor of a military life. All of the male members of his family were graduates of the Bavarian military academy and had served with distinction for centuries.

Unlike most of his colleagues at the academy, he was not a blind adherent to Hitler's vision of world domination, but love of country and dedication to duty forced him to remain silent about his convictions. He had enjoyed an idyllic childhood in the bosom of wealth and privilege. Part of his growth and development had been entrusted to people whom he had loved as if they were blood relatives. In particular Elizabeth and Solomon were his favorite caretakers. He knew they were Jewish, but that had never been an issue. Now in the eyes of the Führer and his colleagues they were vermin that must be murdered. He detested anti-Semitism. The irony of his life was that his current position was connected to the Final Solution. Prior to this post he had lived his life according to the strict moral code of a soldier and field commander, but this issue with civilians tore at his very soul.

Schutzen finished his cigarette and crushed the remains in the ashtray. "How much longer before we reach the camp, Sergeant?"

"Twenty minutes, sir."

He had plenty of time to comb his hair and put on his overcoat. The camp would certainly require his credentials, so he reached into his satchel and pulled out his travel visa and identification. He also slipped several chocolate bars into his pockets.

At the main gate, the guard carefully examined Schutzen's papers. After returning them with a salute, he raised the gate and the driver drove to officer barracks. The stop was just a formality; with Schutzen's high rank all his requests would be honored. The real purpose for this visit had nothing to do with government policy; it was solely to arrange the release of a prisoner. Father Gustav Rahner was a Jesuit priest who had been Schutzen's primary mentor at the university. He admired the man beyond words. Although advanced in years, Father Rahner was apparently involved in antigovernment activities and was arrested after he preached a sermon against the Nazi treatment of the Jews.

After sharing a cup of coffee with the officer on duty, Schutzen asked that Father Rahner be brought to him. As he lit a cigarette, he wondered how his government could justify a place like this. No one understood the scars of war better than he, having been a field commander, but this place and all like it were inhuman hellholes that could never be justified.

Finally there was a knock on the door. As it opened, he was horrified to see the emaciated and stooped body of his once tall and strong mentor. The priest barely resembled the giant of a man who had bested him skiing down the mountain at Kitzbuehl. He helped Father Rahner sit down.

They eagerly talked, words flowing in conversation as if they had just seen each other yesterday. This kind and gentle man had opened the world of wonder and knowledge to Schutzen. Now his government was depriving the priest of freedom and perhaps life itself.

"Father, as a senior field marshal I have the authority to see that you are released. I will arrange for you to stay safely with my family in Bavaria."

Father Rahner smiled sadly. "Do you have the authority to free all of my brothers and sisters in this camp?"

"Unfortunately, that is not possible, but I can arrange for your immediate release."

"Thank you, Wolfgang, but if you cannot free all of us I choose to stay here."

Father Rahner tried to rise to his feet, but he needed to be assisted by the field marshal. "It is wonderful to see you." He raised his right hand and added, "May the good Lord watch over you and keep you."

Despite the stench of Father Rahner's body and the dirt on his clothing, Schutzen embraced the priest with tears in his eyes. "I wish I could do more for you, but at least take these." He quickly pulled out the chocolate bars and thrust them into the priest's hands.

The ride back to his headquarters took place in total silence. He could not remove the image of that saintly man from his mind.

Chapter Fifty-Seven

Florence, Italy, July 9, 1943

Field Marshal Schutzen arrived at his office in Florence early on Monday morning, feeling thoroughly exhausted from a weekend of personal recriminations. As a field commander he was obliged to follow orders even when they doomed soldiers to certain death. He had always been able to retain his dignity by scrupulously following the dictates of his conscience and the Geneva Conventions.

Despite pressures from Berlin, he would not tolerate or condone actions that were opposed to an honorable military code of conduct. He had carefully selected members of his staff who, though patriotic, adhered to the ethical treatment of prisoners and civilians. It had been difficult at times because even in his battalion there were devoted Nazis who did not believe in any code of behavior except their own lust for power.

Schutzen's new assignment posed the biggest moral dilemma of his career and required more than evasion and moral juggling. Despite his request that he continue to be assigned to a field unit, he had been put in charge of civilian affairs in Italy, which in reality meant that he was required to deal with Hitler's vision of a Europe free of Jews. His initial task was to build four detention centers that would provide temporary living quarters until further transportation could be arranged. He clearly understood that these centers were merely stopping points for Jews on their way to the death camps. He had been selected for this post because he had an impeccable reputation as one who strictly followed the highest code of ethical behavior.

Himmler's intention was to have an officer of high moral repute as the head of civilian affairs in order to give the impression that the treatment of the Jews was not harsh. Schutzen had held a series of military attaché appointments during his career and had many friends and associates in Italy. Himmler believed that the field marshal could facilitate the necessary compliance that the centers would require. Schutzen saw clearly that his role would be to provide a veneer of humanity to the greatest of human crimes. If he complied, the blood of many would be on his hands. If he opposed, he and his family would probably be the victims of Nazi justice. There was no facile solution to his dilemma.

He fumbled with the reports on his desk and opened a new pack of cigarettes. Never before had he smoked so much nor had he consumed so much wine and schnapps. Neither took away the tension he felt daily, but as yet he had not found any better palliative. Though he knew that the war was lost, it would certainly drag on for months and possibly years.

Caught up in these thoughts he barely heard the knock on the office door. The subsequent knock was louder and snapped him out of his trance. "Come in."

The door opened to reveal a short, stocky, steely-faced German officer. He entered and snapped a salute with an enthusiastic shout, "Heil Hitler!"

Schutzen mechanically returned the greeting.

"I am Colonel Georg Richter reporting for duty. Here are my orders."

Schutzen scrutinized the orders and motioned for the colonel to be seated. "Would you like some coffee?"

"Yes, I would."

"How do you take it?"

"Black. I am wedded to the basics, spending so much time at the front. I actually drink seven or eight cups a day."

Schutzen poured two cups of coffee and handed one to the colonel. "Where were you stationed?"

"Initially Poland, but I spent the last year on the Russian front."

The field marshal had also been at the bloody and deadly Russian front. He was still aghast at Hitler's stubborn ability to ignore the recommendations of his generals. Schutzen had concluded while in Russia that Hitler's refusal to adjust battle plans had cost the Germans untold losses of human life and materials, not to mention time. He had come to the conclusion that after Stalingrad the war was lost.

"It turned out to be such a tragic campaign," Schutzen said mildly to probe Richter's beliefs. "The beginning was so easy that I thought we would all be home for Christmas, but Stalingrad changed everything."

"I blame the spineless generals and the Jewish conspiracy for those temporary setbacks, but the Führer will overcome their cowardice and treachery."

So that was the way the wind blew with this colonel. Schutzen turned the conversation to the mission in Italy. "I know that it is the explicit desire of the Führer and Himmler that we solve the Jewish question in Italy, but it will be more difficult than in Poland or Russia."

Richter furrowed his brow, appearing confused by that assessment. "I'm not sure I follow you, sir."

The field marshal chose his words carefully. "The Italians, by and large, have not supported harsh measures against the Jews, so I do not believe they will cooperate with us. In fact, we must be careful that we do not encourage active partisan resistance. Italian citizens will oppose the taking of civilians, especially the elderly, women, and children."

"Who cares what the Italians think? They've been a liability to Germany and personally I'm glad they're out of our way."

Schutzen took a deep breath, deciding to try another approach. "We must avoid Vatican involvement in the issue at all costs."

"With respect to your view, sir, the Church has been and will remain powerless against us. We have a pact with the Vatican, and they have much to gain from our war against the Jews."

"Are you a religious man, Colonel?"

"Hardly. When we finish with the Jews, we will deal with all the clerics who hide them."

"I believe it is my duty to counsel restraint, Colonel."

"Are you tying my hands, sir?"

"Not at all. Yet if the only tool in your chest is a hammer, you will see all the world as nails."

"Sir, I can tell you from firsthand experience in Poland and Russia that the best way to get compliance is to hang anyone who blocks our will."

Schutzen had heard this many times before, but it still staggered his imagination that a soldier in arms could believe that there are no boundaries. "Colonel, as your superior I will not tie your hands, but I will provide you with essential assistance that will enhance the mission."

"I'm not sure what you mean."

"I am going to place a lieutenant on your staff. He is fluent in Italian and understands the culture. His name is Franz Wolfe. He is a decorated veteran of the North African campaign. I have the utmost respect for his skills and recommend him to you without qualification."

Chapter Fifty-Eight

Florence, July 11, 1943

The sun was setting over the Ponte Vecchio as Lieutenant Franz Wolfe walked along the path that led to his favorite picnic spot near the Arno River. This peaceful place reminded him of the countless joyous festivities that he shared with his beloved Nonna before she died.

For the first nine years of his life, Franz's parents lived in a small house above Florence. His mother was raised in a village called Barberino, barely an hour from Florence. She first came to Florence to attend university. There she met her husband, who was finishing his graduate studies in Renaissance art. After a two-year courtship, they were married, and Franz was born two years later. He learned both German and Italian, eventually becoming fluent in both as well as English and French. His parents spoke all four languages and would frequently go back and forth from one to the other in daily conversations with their son.

When Franz was nine, his father received an appointment to the University of Passau. Franz was enrolled in a German-speaking school. Culturally, Passau was vastly different from Florence, but Franz quickly made friends; thanks to his father's family the transition was practically seamless. His early years of schooling in Passau were conventional. In the 1930s, significant change occurred in German education. There was an increased focus on German history and prolonged lectures on the value of the new Germany. Franz's parents were not political, showing little interest in the movement, but Franz, an accomplished athlete, was attracted to the physical culture of the Hitler Youth. His parents thought his attendance at summer camp would be rewarding, but they were unaware of the depth of indoctrination that occurred at the camp. Franz became imbued with the desire to be part of something exciting and developed a growing allegiance to the tenets of Germany's plans for the future.

After gymnasium, Franz attended university and pursued the study of chemistry. In many of his classes there were devoted members of the Nazi Party. He did not adhere initially to some of their radical positions, believing that such behaviors would moderate in time. When war broke out, he did not wait to be called. He enlisted. He was sent to officer candidate school because of his academic achievements. When he received his commission, he was immediately assigned to a combat unit in North Africa.

Franz found a vast difference between the comfort of the military academy and the reality of the battlefront. Strategic victories and tactics often worked perfectly in the sterile environment of a classroom, but they were a bigger challenge when men had to endure the sound of anguished screams, the sight of shattered limbs, and the smell of smoldering corpses. There was no adequate preparation for the pain of shrapnel ripping through your body or the agony of holding the hand of a dying comrade as he breathed his last. No one who wasn't there could imagine the look of horror on an enemy soldier's face as your bayonet worked its way between his ribs. Soldiers lived with these realities day and night, and the images often interrupted what little exhausted sleep they managed to get.

North Africa was light-years away from the parades and fawning crowds of Nuremburg. It was a zone where Franz moved restlessly between endless days of boredom and terror. The first time the shelling occurred he felt a horror that was beyond belief. The sounds of the cannons mixed with the screams of men searching for their limbs as their torsos writhed in the final moments of life haunted his sleep—as well as his waking hours. Despite all of this, however, he was committed to the concept that his country was involved in an honorable conflict and the shedding of blood was a prerequisite for the new Germany.

For weeks Franz's division would contend not only with enemy fire but with the constant heat. Insects, poor food, and body rashes took their toll on all the soldiers. The endless number of funerals also weighed heavily on the officers. Franz realized that these same difficulties plagued the British Army, but according to intelligence the British had something that was becoming scarce in the German camp: fuel. The British had severed the main German supply lines and without fuel the Panzers and the foot soldiers would become sitting ducks. Petrol became an obsession of the officer corps and a plan was concocted to raid the British petrol center near Tobruk.

Franz and two teams of ten volunteers were assigned this delicate and most dangerous mission. Arriving under the cover of nightfall, Franz peered through his binoculars and determined that the perimeter of the depot was patrolled by four sentries. Killing them would be the easiest part of the plan. Neutralizing the two adjacent barracks filled with at least sixty armed men would be a major challenge. The element of surprise was critical.

As they crept forward on their stomachs, Franz gave the order to kill the closest guard. The plan was to then put on his uniform and pose as a sentry. When the other guard came around the perimeter, they would kill him quietly and then gain access to the compound. However, when the second guard returned he immediately saw that Franz was an impostor. The guard blew his whistle. Even though he was shot six times, the whistle had aroused both barracks. In various stages of dress the British soldiers rushed into the courtyard and opened fire. There was no choice but for

Franz and his men to go back to their mechanized vehicles. As they retreated there was a loud series of explosions. Franz was felled and knocked unconscious. One of his men carried him to safety. Bleeding profusely from his neck and shoulder, he was barely alive when he reached the German camp.

Franz spent months recuperating in Germany before being reassigned to assist Field Marshal Schutzen in Italy.

Chapter Fifty-Nine

Soverato, July 14, 1943

The idea of being assigned an adjutant did not sit well with Colonel Richter, but he was ambitious so he needed to please Field Marshal Schutzen. This task, given to him directly by Himmler, was his ticket to a high-level staff job in Berlin. If he had to gain the support of the field marshal, so be it.

Richter was needed in some of the major cities in Italy and would therefore have to delegate the Soverato detention center to Lieutenant Franz Wolfe. He knew little about Wolfe except that he had been awarded the Iron Cross for valor. Wolfe's dossier showed that he was an exemplary officer who always went beyond expectations, so Richter did not anticipate any difficulties. He was aware that the lieutenant was fluent in four languages and surmised that, unlike himself, Wolfe had been raised in a privileged environment.

In order to fully assess Lieutenant Wolfe's ability to take over the Soverato project, Richter invited the lieutenant to join him at Vittorio's trattoria for dinner.

When Lieutenant Wolfe arrived a little before the scheduled meeting time, he admired the magnificent view from the trattoria. He gazed out the window as the sun was setting over the sea. Colonel Richter had not yet appeared, so the owner asked where

Franz would like to be seated. The owner's impersonal tone changed dramatically when Wolfe told him in perfect Italian that his mother was Tuscan and he loved being stationed in Italy.

"I wondered how a German could speak Italian so perfectly," the owner said.

Wolfe smiled, leaning over to the owner and whispering, "Don't tell anyone, but the better half of me is Italian."

The proprietor laughed and crossed his heart. "Your secret is safe with me."

"Please keep it that way or I'll be in trouble."

"It is time I brought you some wonderful Italian wine."

"Thank you, but please wait until my guest comes because I'm not sure whether he will want white or red."

In a few moments Colonel Richter entered the restaurant, briskly strode past the proprietor, and made his way to the corner table where Wolfe was seated.

Wolfe looked away from the window and stood up, crisply saluting. "Good evening, Colonel Richter."

"At ease, Lieutenant Wolfe." The colonel removed his cap and sat facing the front of the restaurant with his back to the magnificent view of the sea.

"What kind of wine would you like, sir?"

"I would like a white wine from the Moselle Valley."

"Sir, I don't believe they have German wines here. Would you like to try a local Calabrian white wine?"

"If that's all there is, it will have to do."

Franz motioned to the waiter, who brought the menus. "We would like a carafe of local white wine."

The waiter nodded and recited the specials of the day.

Colonel Richter commented, "It's obvious that you're fluent in Italian. How did you acquire such facility?"

"I spent the first nine years of my life in Italy. My mother was born and raised in Tuscany. My father was at the University of Munich and received a fellowship to study Renaissance art in

Florence. My parents met at the university, married, and lived in Italy until my father received an appointment to the University of Passau. We then moved to Germany where I spent the rest of my childhood."

"So the better part of you is German," Richter probed, raising an eyebrow.

"I love my country," Franz said, avoiding possible entanglements.

"What was your initial exposure to the National Socialist Party?"

"I was a student at the university. I'm a chemist by training. I had no interest in politics until one day I was invited to attend a study group looking at the implications of the new Germany and its vision."

"What was your reaction?"

"I was fascinated by it. A month later I had the good fortune to hear the Führer speak at Nuremburg. From that moment on, just like every other young person, I sought to be part of a meaningful cause."

"When did you enlist in the army?"

"Right after I completed my university studies. I was sent to officer training in Dusseldorf and ultimately assigned to a combat unit in North Africa."

"How long were you in North Africa?"

"I was there for eleven months, and then I spent four months in a hospital near Dresden."

"Were you severely wounded?"

"Compared to my comrades my wounds were minor."

"I understand your wounds were quite severe."

Wolfe shrugged, dismissing the idea.

"I'm sure that you received some decoration because of your wounds."

"Everyone who was wounded was decorated."

"You are modest. I know that you received the Iron Cross. Perhaps you will do well under my supervision. Now tell me about your combat unit. Was it comprised totally of German soldiers or were there Italian troops assigned to the unit as well?"

"Sir, we had both. All of the troops were under the command of Field Marshal Schutzen."

"I am sure he found the Italians to be useless. Italians are only good in parades; they have neither the discipline nor the courage of German soldiers." He took a sip of wine. "How did you get assigned to this mission?"

"While I was in the hospital recuperating, Field Marshal Schutzen was kind enough to visit me. After my hospital discharge, he asked me to join his staff."

"Do you know the purpose of the mission?"

"All I know is that we are responsible for building a detention center in Soverato."

When the waiter walked up to the table, Richter glanced at Wolfe. "Please order for us." Wolfe quickly placed their order in effortless Italian. He stoically waited for the colonel to continue his relentless interrogation, hoping he would soon be satisfied with Franz's qualifications and let him enjoy his meal in peace.

Colonel Richter took another sip of wine. "Detention center is a euphemism. The Jews will be kept there only until we can arrange transportation to their final destinations."

"I'm not sure what that means. What are their final destinations?'

"Concentration camps. In this case it will be Birkenau-Auschwitz."

"Will they be military prisoners? Civilians?"

"Lieutenant, I am shocked at your lack of knowledge. These will all be Jews. Men, women, and children will be temporarily retained until we can dispose of them."

"Dispose?"

"You have obviously been too long out of Europe to know what is happening here. The Jews will all be gassed in order to meet the Führer's goal of a Jew-free Europe."

Wolfe was silent for a moment, feeling stunned. "Then the rumors I heard in the hospital are true?"

"I don't know what you heard, but the plan to exterminate the Jews is ahead of schedule. Minister Himmler has chosen me personally to rid Italy of Jews. Frankly, I relish the task."

"But what about the Geneva Conventions? These people are civilians."

"The Geneva Conventions are archaic and have no relevance. They are for ministers, not soldiers."

"I have to tell you, sir, that the Italian people will never support this policy. They have a reverence and respect for women, children, and the elderly."

Colonel Richter took a long sip of his wine. "I could care less about the outmoded morals of the Italian bourgeoisie. Read your history, Lieutenant. The Jew is the center of all of Germany's problems, past and present. The Treaty of Versailles, written by Jews, embarrassed our entire nation. They have robbed and raped the people of Germany for too long, but it ends now. The rich Jews will cease to exist."

"Colonel Richter, I grew up in a community in Germany where only a few Jews were rich."

"It's all relative, Lieutenant. As a child of privilege you were not aware of the pain they inflicted. I grew up and saw my father and others exploited daily by the Jews. While we struggled, the Jews in our town had an abundance of everything."

"Sir, I completely understood the reasons for combat. Killing the enemy is part of my duty as a soldier, but I am puzzled by this mission."

"That is because you are not burdened with the responsibility of leadership. The Führer has clearly set out the path and your orders have been laid out by your superiors. Your duty is to assist me and bury your childish misguided principles. When you truly understand the wisdom of this plan you will revise your thinking."

Franz nodded, unable and unwilling to say more.

"Ah, here is our food." Colonel Richter ate with relish as he provided still more details of the mass murders that lay ahead.

As they left the restaurant, he turned to Wolfe and said, "I am glad that we had the opportunity to break bread together and for me to clarify my expectations. I trust that you will reflect on our conversation and dedicate yourself to the work." He raised his arm. "Heil Hitler!"

Lieutenant Wolfe responded with much less enthusiasm. As he slowly made his way to the beach, he muttered, "What the hell have I gotten myself into?"

Chapter Sixty

Soverato, the Mayor's Office, July 22, 1943

Mayor Severio Pittelli and the head of public services constantly attempted to derail the detention center being built outside of Soverato. The pressure to complete the center had grown exponentially in the last month. What was at one time relatively easy had became a mission fraught with severe consequences. Roman bureaucrats had been replaced by sharp-eyed German officials. The recent surrender of Italy felt like a mixed blessing to these two officials as they tried to assess their next steps.

As was their custom, they stopped at the local café for an espresso before going to the office. This morning, instead of sitting at the front of the café, they chose a secluded table in the rear for privacy.

Severio, who looked tired and worried, began the conversation in a low voice. "Salvatore, we both are to report directly to the German commandant."

Salvatore had already gulped down his coffee and nervously spun the spoon in his hands. "Why did Mussolini get in bed with these bastards?"

Severio raised his palm in the time-honored "who knows" gesture. "Idiot thought Italy and Germany would rule the world."

"Rule the world, my ass. He couldn't even beat the Ethiopians and all they had were big sticks."

Severio pondered the question. "The only thing I can come up with is that he fell in love with the salute."

Salvatore leaped to his feet, thrust his middle finger into the air, and then angrily raised his other middle finger. "This is the only salute I have for him. How the hell could he believe we have anything in common with the Germans? We hear music and dance. They hear tubas and goosestep."

Severio chuckled. "Your total lack of respect for our occupiers reminds me of a story I heard about a German general in North Africa. When the general first went there he noticed a mangy camel tied to a post in back of the building. He asked about the camel and was informed that the men used the camel for sex. Disgusted by this information, he marched into his office. But after seven hot, lonely months in the desert he asked if the camel was still available. His sergeant replied affirmatively and was ordered to bring the camel to the rear of the building. Later in the day the general arrived with a large box, climbed up on it, and had sex with the camel. When he finished he asked the sergeant, "Is that the way the men do it?" The sergeant replied, "No sir. The men ride the camel to the brothel."

Salvatore laughed heartily and sat down. "From here on, I'll tell that story as my own."

"It's yours."

Severio finished his coffee. Time to get serious. He opened his briefcase and took out the complete blueprints for the detention center. The main part of the structure was far from finished. Their explanation was that in wartime it was always difficult to get building materials. They purposely sent the materials to the wrong destinations, and then they complained to Rome that bureaucrats lost the order.

"What happened to the last requisition?" Severio asked.

"My cousin sent it to the station at Rocco Palumbo in Sicily where it sat for three weeks on the platform. It was then unloaded and taken by donkey to the Piazza in Cammarata at the top of the mountain. My cousin waited two weeks before he notified Rome of the error. Meanwhile, the load was so great that one of the donkeys died so it took him another week to replace it. Then, of course, my cousin had to take an inventory and check it every day for a week before he could use the official stamp on the requisition."

Severio shook his head, marveling at the ability to compromise the system. "We would make excellent bureaucrats in Rome."

"Are you kidding? Even at this pace we would probably be employees of the month."

"Seriously, Salvatore, the game has changed. This new commandant will have a completion date in mind. I'm sure they will require the name of every Jew in the area. I think it's time we involve all the town leaders."

"No. That's too dangerous. I think we should keep it close to the vest."

"I disagree. Certainly we have to include the rabbi and Monsignor Donato."

"Can we trust Donato? I'm not a fan of any priest. Maybe we should be more cautious."

"Salvatore, you are the model Catholic male Italian. You go to church when you're hatched, matched, and dispatched."

"That's not true. Sometimes I go on Christmas and Easter."

"The monsignor is a close friend of the rabbi," Severio said. "He may be able to get the Church in Rome to make some form of protest."

"I could kick Mussolini in the ass for bringing the Nazis to Italy."

"You would have to get in line and many in the line would be former ass-kissers. I never believed in all the rhetoric, but as mayor I had to walk a fine line. Mussolini was afraid to be left out so he made a deal with the devil."

"In the barbershop, we say his shit didn't stink." Salvatore shook his head. "What totally confuses me is that the Germans are so cultured. How can such learned people allow such horror? Could it be that many of them don't know what is happening?"

"Horseshit! We're hundreds of miles away and *we* know! How do you not know when so many go missing?"

"People can justify anything once they're caught up in national goals. Many Italians accepted the racial laws against the Jews."

"Yes, but many more ignored them. Certainly in Soverato we never penalized the Jews."

"Maybe that's because we're far from the parades and promises of glory."

"Or maybe we're better people."

"Time will tell, Severio. We are about to be tested. You will be our guide through these dark days. Remember the proverb, 'In awful weather the true seaman arises.' I believe you are that seaman."

"I pray you are right."

After that conversation, Severio felt weighted down by events that he knew were beyond his control. But several weeks later, significant pledges of support offered new hope that somehow he would find a way to outsmart the Germans. His real challenge was to figure out a way to cope with the new commandant, Colonel Georg Richter, who had been personally selected by Himmler to rid Italy of all Jews.

Severio had been ordered to meet with the colonel in the morning. He welcomed the opportunity to get a bird's-eye view of his adversary.

Chapter Sixty-One

Soverato, German Headquarters, August 4, 1943

When Severio arrived at German headquarters he could not help but see the irony in the location. For at least two centuries the building had been a contemplative setting for monks. Now it was the center for barbarism and terror.

Once his credentials were examined, Severio was escorted to the first floor lobby. Most of the guards had a Nordic appearance, but he was surprised that one of the officers looked to be of Mediterranean stock. The handsome officer approached and introduced himself in flawless Italian.

"Good morning, Mr. Mayor. I am Lieutenant Franz Wolfe. I have been assigned to be the coordinator between your office and Colonel Richter."

"Lieutenant, your Italian is excellent. How did you acquire such facility with our language?"

"My Mother is Tuscan. She was my first teacher. Also I lived in Florence for the first nine years of my life."

"What are your expectations of me and my staff?"

"My expectation is that we will meet weekly to make all the necessary adjustments. I will be directly involved in assisting you in every aspect of the project. Colonel Richter has not yet specified his expectations, but that will occur before he leaves for Milan."

"I'm sure we can arrange regular meetings. I can assure you that we will keep you fully up to speed. I am anxious to meet Colonel Richter this morning."

Lieutenant Wolfe offered the mayor coffee and continued to provide more details about the upcoming meeting. "Colonel Richter does not speak Italian, so I will be the translator this morning and in all future meetings."

"Have you worked with this colonel before?"

"No. I just met him yesterday. We have had just a short time together."

"I don't mean to pry, but what kind of man is he?"

"I know from my superior officer in Florence that he is direct and insistent that results be achieved. He does not tolerate excuses and approaches all issues as if he were constructing detailed battle plans."

"Does he have any preconceived notions about Italy and our community?"

"I'm not sure what you mean."

"I'm asking what he thinks of his Italian allies."

"I hesitate to answer that because I only have second-hand information, but let me say he is not thrilled with the project being in Italian hands."

"Why is that?"

"I gather he has some very negative perceptions about the Italian performance in North Africa."

"Do you share those perceptions?"

"I think people often confuse appearances with the laws of nature. Perception is based on trivial contact or no contact at all. Italians are like any other people. Some are exceptionally organized and others are not. Any labeling of an entire population based on minimal experience is bound to be erroneous."

"I find your view somewhat startling, considering the reason you are here in Soverato."

Lieutenant Wolfe suddenly appeared uncomfortable with the conversation. "I'm not sure I follow you."

"The observation you made is exactly what is happening to the Jews. They're being arrested because of their race and culture."

"Mr. Mayor, I believe that this discussion, though interesting, is inappropriate. I am a soldier, not a philosopher, and I do not wish to discuss plans made by my superiors."

"Lieutenant, I am not seeking to discuss your role as a German officer but as a man who is the product of two cultures. I am an Italian. Who and what I am cannot be separated from my culture. Being a mayor is only a role and does not dictate my entire life."

As the lieutenant opened his mouth to respond, the door to the colonel's office opened. A short, squat man dressed in impeccable officer attired strutted out.

Lieutenant Wolfe saluted the officer. "Colonel Richter, this is Mayor Pittelli."

The colonel offered his hand and then motioned for the men to enter his office and be seated across from his desk. He perched upon a raised chair that allowed him to look down at his visitors.

Lieutenant Wolfe explained first in German and then in Italian that he would translate the interactions.

"Colonel Richter," Serverio said, "I would like to know how I can best serve your needs."

The colonel handed him a schedule indicating that the detention center must be completed by the first week in January.

Severio examined the schedule, frowning. "It may not be possible to be operational by that date."

Colonel Richter raised his voice. "Tell the mayor that we Germans have a precise schedule and that date will be met. There are no ambiguities in our language."

"Please understand, we are short of manpower and it has been impossible to secure construction materials."

"Tell the mayor to use women and children to fill in the gaps."

"Tell the colonel that we should use Germans. Lord knows

there are enough of them in Italy."

"Mayor Pittelli," Lieutenant Wolfe cautioned, "please be cautious in your response."

"Please exactly translate my words."

Colonel Richter grew impatient. He pounded the table and shouted, "I have had enough of this nonsense. Tell the mayor that I will no longer sit here and listen to his ranting in that infernal language."

After the lieutenant's translation, Severio reddened. "Translate this exactly as I say it. Charles the Fifth of Spain said, 'When I write poetry I write in French; when I speak to my mistress I speak Spanish; when I speak to God I speak Italian; and when I speak to my horse I speak German.'"

Lieutenant Wolfe shook his head. "You are playing with fire, Mayor Pitelli. There will be major consequences, not only for you but for others, if I translate this."

Controlling his anger, Severio nodded. "Tell him whatever he needs to hear."

Translating into German, Lieutenant Wolfe said, "The mayor understands the goals and will labor intensively to meet them."

"If this one-armed clown is an example of Italian leadership, I'm glad they're on the other side," Colonel Richter said. "Now dismiss him. From now on you will deal with him without me."

Again the lieutenant completely altered the response. "The colonel wishes to thank you for coming and he is sure that you will meet all his expectations."

Severio left the office with a new understanding of how difficult the next month would be.

Chapter Sixty-Two

Soverato, August 4, 1943

In the shadow of an ancient Roman pine tree there was a simple marble tombstone inscribed, "To our beloved Giancarlo, may he rest in peace." This memorial was merely a symbol. The remains of this twenty-seven-year-old citizen of Soverato were strewn over some battlefield in North Africa. Like so many young Italians, he had become cannon fodder and a victim of Il Duce's pact with the devil.

Rosella visited this site daily, bringing flowers and following the same rituals. She arranged the flowers in front of the tombstone and then proceeded to wipe clean the photograph of her brother on the tombstone. Giancarlo had been the youngest member of the Pastore family. Rosella was the eldest and thought of him more as a son than a brother. Their mother had died when he was only four years old, so his primary care had fallen to Rosella, who embraced the role.

The ancient tree was a special place for Rosella because it held memories of the many times she had taken Giancarlo there for picnics. The sound of the birds and the magnificent view of the sea reminded her of the little boy running through the fields and singing one of the songs he had learned in school. The pain of his loss never seemed to lessen. She had experienced the deaths of her parents, but they had not seared her soul like that of Giancarlo.

Before the war Rosella had been a cheerful person, noted for her friendliness and warm manner, but that person was gone. Once the emotional anchor for her family, she was now engulfed in sadness as she became possessed by fear. The death of her brother had created an overriding sense that her life was out of control. She had tried numerous times to shed this anxiety, but even the most basic activities required all her strength. In the evenings she would retire to her room after dinner.

After speaking gently to the memory of the brother she had loved so dearly, she rose and kissed the tombstone. She wiped away her tears and began to descend from the memorial site. She was not unaware that she had been a burden to her husband and on numerous occasions she had spent hours in positive self-talk, but she could not shake the foreboding sense of doom that engulfed her.

Severio had shown unlimited patience with her. She felt guilty for ignoring his needs. She knew that some men would have sought comfort elsewhere, but Severio was committed to her alone. Recently, though, even Severio seemed preoccupied and she worried that perhaps his patience was exhausted.

Chapter Sixty-Three

Soverato, that evening, August 4, 1943

The meeting with Colonel Richter had unnerved Severio. He realized just how precarious the situation was becoming. His whole world was in chaos and he had little time for his law practice. Before the war he would spend hours in research trying to find the best possible strategies for his clients. Then he would take a leisurely walk home through the main Piazza and be met by a loving wife and children. Rosella was so vibrant before the war. He could recall her melodious voice singing one of her favorite arias as he entered the house. There had been no songs in the Pittelli home since Giancarlo died. It seemed that Rosella was becoming more and more depressed. Somehow she continued to be a devoted mother, but the enthusiasm she had for life had vanished. On many occasions he had tried to rekindle her spirit, but lately he had no leftover energy to try.

At home, Severio sat at the dining room table going through the motions of eating, but his mind was miles away.

"Severio, you've barely touched your food. Is there something wrong with it?" Rosella asked, concern in her voice.

"No, it's fine."

"There must be something wrong because pasta carbonara is your favorite. Rachel made it especially for you."

Severio pushed away from the table and wiped his lips with a napkin. "It has nothing to do with the food. It's this damn war."

Rosella appeared confused. "What has it to do with you in Soverato?"

"It has everything to do with me. Soon it will be on our doorstep."

"How is that true? Italy is out of the war."

"That is true in one way, but not in another. The Germans are now totally in charge."

"Still, what does that have to do with you?"

Severio lit a cigarette. He had stopped smoking for two years, but with the constant tension he had fallen back into the old addiction. "Now they will be actively involved in Soverato, especially in regard to the Jewish community."

"But why is it your problem? What they do has nothing to do with you."

"Rosella, you don't understand. I am responsible for all of our citizens, especially for Rachel."

"Rachel is not our daughter. She's our cook."

"My God, Rosella, have you forgotten that her parents have been our friends for years?"

"That's true, but she is not family. If she presents a danger to our family, she must go."

"She is here because it was too dangerous for her in Rome."

"That was a fine arrangement when it didn't endanger us and our children, but things have changed."

Severio said forcefully, "It does not change the fact that I gave my word to protect her. I love her as though she were my daughter."

Rosella pushed back with equal force. "Have you forgotten that you have two daughters and a son of your own?"

"How can you question my love and dedication to our children? My family means more to me than life."

"Then prove it by having Rachel leave our home."

"I will not do that. It would put her in danger."

"I warn you, Severio, I will do anything to protect this family."

"Rosella, I'm shocked at you. Rachel has been a daughter to you also. If you cause harm to her, I will never forgive you."

Rosella stood up, walked to the door, and turned back. "I care about her, but blood is thicker than water. If it comes to a choice, I will choose blood."

"Please don't say a word to Rachel. She has enough to worry about."

"I will make no promises. Now I'm going to visit my sister. While I'm gone, you'd better think about what I've said." With that Rosella walked out of the house and slammed the door behind her.

Severio was lighting another cigarette when he heard a crash in the kitchen. He walked into that room and saw a broken pitcher on the floor. No Rachel. He climbed the stairs and knocked on her door. There was no answer, so he gently opened the door and found Rachel sitting on her bed with tears in her eyes.

"Rachel, what's wrong?"

She turned away and wiped her eyes. "Nothing is wrong. I'm just being foolish."

"Foolish about what?" he asked gently. "Did you hear something downstairs that upset you?"

"I wasn't trying to listen. I was in the kitchen getting a glass of milk. I heard what Rosella said about me."

"What exactly did you hear?"

"That the Germans are coming to Soverato and she wants me to leave. I would rather die than let them take me."

"Rosella is frightened and spoke out of fear. She loves you as I do. You know I will do anything to keep you safe. Please trust me, and for now, do not discuss this with Rosella."

Rachel began to sob. "I do trust you, but I don't think you or anyone can keep me safe. I'm so frightened that sometimes I think about killing myself."

"You must promise me that you will not harm yourself. If anything happened to you, I would never get over it."

"I'm so confused I cannot promise anything. If I have to leave here, where will I go?"

"I made a promise to your parents and I will keep it."

Severio went back downstairs, troubled in mind and spirit. He did not fully grasp the depth of his wife's fear until two days later. When he arrived home for dinner, he learned that Rosella had taken Rachel to the Benedictine Convent, asking Sister Mercedita to keep her safe until the danger passed. When she came back, she told Severio that she would not discuss the issue, and that if he brought Rachel back she would move out with the children and go to live with her sister.

Mulling over the situation, he realized that because of his position Rachel actually might be safer with the nuns. He would make it one of his primary objectives to keep close watch over her safety at the convent.

Chapter Sixty-Four

Rome, October 1943

The Jewish presence in Italy had deep roots. Despite years of exclusion and persecution, they had been able to retain their culture and thrive as viable members of Italian society. After the unification of Italy in the nineteenth century, their world in Rome offered complete citizenship with full rights. When the walls of their ghetto were torn down, the Jews were totally assimilated into Roman life. By the beginning of the twentieth century, the Jews were prospering on the site of the old ghetto and had been totally integrated into every aspect of Roman life. The assimilation had been so seamless that "the pope's Jews" became a symbolic name for Italian Jews.

In 1943 the community along the Tiber housed approximately 1,700 Jews, which swelled to 5,000 on Friday nights. The centerpiece of the community was the magnificent temple that had been constructed at the beginning of the twentieth century.

In the 1930s anti-Semitism grew gradually in Italy. Many Italians ignored the racial laws. When the Italian government began to collapse, the German presence became pervasive in Rome. The belief that the Jews could ride out the war safely in Rome became untenable.

German greed was alive and well. The Jews were informed that if they would provide 100 pounds of gold they would not be mistreated or deported. There were divergent views in the community on whether to pay this ransom, but finally a decision to raise the gold won out. The news was not a closely guarded secret, so the Vatican was well aware that this proposal had been made. Vatican officials offered to lend part of the money with a specific understanding that this was not to be a gift but a loan. The Jewish community graciously acknowledged the offer, but they raised the amount without the aid of the Vatican.

In fact, the proposal was a ruse. On October 10 the decision to raze the ghetto was made. Himmler ordered that the Roman Jews be rounded up, sent first to a detention center in Calabria, and then to Auschwitz where they would be killed. Bishop Huldol knew about this thinly disguised plan and informed the German bishops, saying, "We must intervene in this situation because if the Jews are taken I fear it will force the Vatican to speak out. I couldn't care less about these Jews, but this will have a negative effect on the work we are doing to strengthen the relationship between the Church and the state."

The German bishops disagreed with Huldol. They, by and large, sided with the German government, taking the position that the real enemy was Russia. They reminded Bishop Huldol that Germany was fighting an all-out war on Bolshevism, and Judaism was one of the support columns fortifying the philosophy opposed to Christ and His Church.

In the middle of the night on October 23, a fleet of German trucks rumbled past the Via Portia d'Ottavia and armed soldiers entered all the houses of the Jewish area, starting with those facing the Fontana delle Tartughe. Men, women, and children, some still half asleep, were carted into the trucks like laundry bags. The trucks then drove past the Vatican so that many of the soldiers who were new to Rome could see their first glimpse of Saint Peter's Basilica. The victims were held for two days in Rome before they were transported by cattle cars to Auschwitz.

Despite knowledge of this criminal act, the Vatican offered only an insipid comment about a series of arrests in the Jewish ghetto in the official Vatican newspaper a week later. The Germans had been correct in assuming there would be no public outcry even though this atrocity was committed in the very shadow of the Vatican.

The shepherd remained silent while the sheep were slaughtered by the wolves.

Chapter Sixty-Five

Soverato, October 25, 1943

For some men their home provided both sanctuary and sanity, but for Bishop Giacomo Bonelli his home was a dark place filled with hundreds of tomes on canon law. This was the area that invited no human contact, only the hard, cold guidance of those absolute rules and regulations that guard the orthodoxy of the Church.

In his home office, Bonelli could reflect on canonical critical issues without the distraction of pastoral duties. A brilliant canon lawyer, he rose rapidly to the episcopate, but he feared that his ascetic bearing and his discomfort in parochial settings had left him largely ignored by the past Holy Father. Parish life had no appeal for him and he avoided contact with the parishioners under his guidance except where his presence was essential, such as at confirmations. He had hoped that under the new pope he would be summoned to Rome and hence have a clear path to what he desired most, the red hat of a cardinal. He vowed that while he was bishop of Calabria he would prevent any political involvement on the part of priests and nuns. He had been warned by Bishop Huldol, a member of the German hierarchy, to forbid the clergy to involve themselves in any anti-Nazi activities and he thoroughly agreed.

The relations between Rome and the German government were tenuous at best and the incident in Rome in October had created further tensions. There were only a few formal protests about the treatment of the Jews. Bonelli had heard rumors that one of his priests in Soverato was arranging escape routes for Jewish refugees, so he decided he would confront the pastor personally. The bishop did not view himself as anti-Semitic although, like many in the past, he could not understand why the Jews had been so unwilling to accept Christ as their Messiah. Christ was the fulfillment of the prophets, but they ignored the obvious. "He came unto His own, and His own received Him not." Because the Jews consciously chose to reject Christ, they could not seek the aid of the Roman Church. It was the duty and responsibility of the Church to watch over and care for the baptized children who had accepted Him as their Lord and Savior.

Bishop Bonelli was not unsympathetic toward the Jewish plight in Europe, but he was adamant that the situation was not something that should directly concern the Church.

Monsignor Tomasso Donato was the complete antithesis of Bishop Bonelli. He was driven by two realities: his love for all people and his love for wonderful food. As the years passed, his body evolved into a rotund shape. The image of him waddling down the central aisle at Santa Maria's Church was treasured by every member of the Soverato community. Despite constant admonitions from his personal physician, the good monsignor made no attempt to lose weight and was counting on a positive genetic disposition. His parents, both slender, had lived long and healthy lives, so he dismissed the warnings and continued to search for the perfect cannoli.

Donato saw no distinction among people of different faiths and was comfortable in any environment. Dogma to him was mere suggestion, and his belief system was wrapped with an ever-expanding elastic band. Those who knew him casually might have thought he was just a jovial sort with minimal intellectual capacity, but nothing could be further from the truth. In seminary he had clearly been the most gifted student in his class. Initially bound for the Vatican or a post at the Gregorian University in Rome, he pleaded for a parochial assignment. Status held no appeal for him. He was actually embarrassed when the pope made him a monsignor. "Father" was the only title he ever took seriously.

As he entered the sacristy before celebrating Mass, he put on what appeared to be a brand-new pair of shoes. Actually the shoes were twenty-nine years old, but he wore them only while he said Mass. He had bought the shoes as a symbol to remind him each day that he was ordained for the service of others. The act of putting on the shoes was his way of preparing for what he was about to perform. He wanted the experience of celebrating the Eucharist to feel as if he was celebrating it for the first time. As he tied the laces, he uttered the same simple prayer of Saint Francis he had for twenty-nine years. "Lord, make me an instrument of your peace and love." The current situation in Europe greatly pained Donato, and lately he had added, "And please help me lessen the suffering of my Jewish brothers and sisters."

Monsignor Donato had many former classmates in Rome, so he was fully aware of what was happening to Jews all over Europe. After hearing the stories he feared that even in the remote village of Soverato, the Germans would hurt the Jews. Mayor Pittelli had recently briefed him about a planned new detention center and had determined that preemptive action was required. It was particularly painful to Donato that many of the murderers called themselves Christians. All of the mounting evidence made him reach out directly to the Jewish community, and he pledged to his friend of many years, Rabbi Luigi Contini, that every available Church resource would be available if the horror came to Soverato.

In the shadows of late afternoon, the chubby figure of Monsignor Donato entered the courtyard of the Benedictine convent. He had made an appointment to speak with the mother superior, Sister Mercedita, about his concerns.

He waited just a few minutes in the front parlor until Sister Mercedita entered the room and immediately asked for his blessing. He made the sign of the cross over her head. As they both sat down, he launched into his concerns.

During prior conversations, Sister Mercedita had told him about a series of ancient tunnels underneath the convent that could serve as potential hiding places. These ancient caves had been hewn from the clay hills centuries ago and currently were used as root cellars to store produce. Covered by antique walls, they had been adorned with colorful murals and could shelter up to one hundred people.

"Sister, I fear after what happened in Rome in October that no place in Italy is safe, especially since the mayor has been ordered to build a detention center."

"What does that mean?"

"It means they will transport the Jews out of Italy to the death camps I have heard my classmates talk about."

Sister Mercedita appeared surprised. "As a people, surely we will oppose this."

"After Mussolini's government collapsed, the Germans took full control of Italy. They will make no distinctions. They will take men, women, and children."

"That's horrible. We can hide some here, but do you think the Germans will honor the sanctity of the cloister?"

"The Germans honor nothing that stands in their way."

"Monsignor, this week we are to receive our annual visit from Bishop Bonelli. Should I make him aware of our plans?"

"Absolutely. I hope he will speak out against the German atrocities. Surely his office will have some influence."

"If ever there was a time when we need to pray, it is now. Please remember us in your prayers."

"And me in yours."

Monsignor Donato returned home to do what he could to ease the growing fears around him. He felt relief when it was time for Bishop Bonelli's annual visit.

Darkness slowly enveloped the town of Soverato as Bishop Bonelli's automobile entered the portico, passed slowly through the piazza, and parked on the side of Santa Maria's rectory. The chauffeur opened the back door, carried the bishop's luggage up the marble steps leading to the front door, and rung the door bell.

A few seconds later, Monsignor Donato opened the door with a broad smile. "Welcome, Your Excellency. I am thrilled that you found time to visit us." He kissed the bishop's ring.

Bishop Bonelli brusquely asked to be shown to his room so that he could freshen up before dinner.

Monsignor Donato took the bishop to the austere guest room in the rectory, knowing it was vastly different from the bishop's opulent apartment in Catanzaro. The furniture consisted of a simple pine bureau, a bed with a reading lamp, and a tiny washbasin. The shared lavatory was at the end of the hall.

Donato left him there, but he could not relax. He paced back and forth, waiting for the bishop to join him. He once again reviewed the menu with Angelina, the cook. He hoped the bishop shared his love for good food because the meal this evening consisted of five courses, each complemented by a local wine. The red Gattinara and Barollo were Christmas presents that he had saved for a special occasion like the visit of his bishop. He had resisted the temptation to sample them earlier. He opened the bottles to let them breathe and smiled at the wonderful bouquets that wafted through the simple refectory.

Eventually Bishop Bonelli entered the dining room and sat in the chair at the head of the table. Once he was settled, Angelina came into the room and poured some soup of the *papa*, the most famous of all Tuscan soups, into a bowl and placed it in front of him. Monsignor Donato filled the bishop's wine glass with ruby Gattinara, but the two men were unmatched bookends on the emotional scale. One was an eager, amiable host and the other was glacially remote, merely enduring a meal. The first course was eaten in total silence, causing discomfort to the normally talkative monsignor.

Though Donato was eager to chat, he thought it would be more prudent to allow the bishop to initiate conversation.

Bishop Bonelli finally said, "I understand from reading your dossier that you were an exceptional student in the seminary. I'm surprised that you were not sent on for further studies."

"I was supposed to go to the Dominican house of studies to pursue a doctorate in theology, but I requested a parochial assignment. Cardinal Agnelli intervened and had me assigned to this parish. I'm grateful to the cardinal because I've loved serving the people of this community."

"I am glad to know you are happy here, but I still find it difficult to understand why a priest with such academic acumen would prefer a parochial assignment to an ecclesiastical or teaching position."

Donato shrugged, unwilling to get into an argument about his preferences. "That simply goes to prove the difference in personalities."

As the meal progressed, Monsignor Donato observed that the bishop ate very little of each portion and never commented upon the meal. He fretted that perhaps he had chosen the wrong courses. Finally he could no longer be silent.

"I hope you are enjoying the meal, Your Excellency."

"It's fine."

Knowing that the bishop had visited the Benedictine convent, Donato decided that might be the perfect entrée to air his concerns.

"I know that you saw the Benedictine sisters today. Did you have a chance to speak privately with Sister Mercedita?"

Bishop Bonelli revealed some interest in his dinner companion. "I had an extended conversation with Sister Mercedita and an opportunity to address all of the sisters of the community."

"I'm sure Sister Mercedita was happy to have the benefit of your counsel."

The bishop responded coldly, "I don't believe Sister Mercedita relished the direct guidance I offered as her bishop and superior."

"'I'm not sure I understand, Your Excellency."

"I directly forbade her and the sisters to have any involvement in any social or political activities that could have a negative effect on the Church."

"What are you referring to?"

"I have it on good authority that the sisters have been harboring Jewish refugees."

"In my ongoing conversations with Sister Mercedita, we agreed to assist the mayor in providing whatever help we can to our Jewish brothers and sisters."

The bishop pointed his finger directly at the monsignor. "On whose authority have you done this?"

"I'm not sure you understand the gravity of the situation. The Germans are killing Jews all over Europe. Soon we may face the same horror in Soverato. The mayor has been ordered to build a detention center."

"And what has that to do with you and Sister Mercedita?"

"Your Excellency, innocent people are being exposed to unthinkable atrocities only because they are Jewish. I would ask that you personally protest these acts to the German high command in Calabria."

"My responsibility," the bishop said forcefully, "is to protect the Church. Whenever I see behavior that places the Church in a compromising position, I must intervene."

Monsignor Donato could no longer maintain a diplomatic pose. "But what is our role as Christians when we see such horrors?"

"I am not a coldhearted man, but these Jews are not our responsibility. You were ordained to work with the people of God, not to meddle in political matters."

"I must respectfully disagree. These are children of God and it is our responsibility to assist them."

"Monsignor, your responsibility is solely to provide sacramental guidance and grace for those who are members of the Body of Christ. Unfortunate as current circumstances may be, the Jews are not your parishioners and I forbid any further involvement on your part."

Donato struggled visibly but finally blurted out, "I am moved by the words of our Master Himself, who said, 'What you do for the least of my brethren you do for me.' When I see what is happening to the Jews, I know that we must act to save them."

"Do you have the effrontery to lecture me on Christ's words? We are not dealing with theological hair-splitting here. I am a direct descendent of Saint Peter and your priestly function can only come through me. Do you understand that you are required to obey me?"

"I believe that this is a matter of conscience and though it pains me greatly, I cannot follow your command."

"I am amazed that there is nothing in your dossier about your level of arrogance."

"You may think it is arrogance, but I believe it is the call to give Christian witness."

"Do you believe that you are above the guidance of your canonical superior?"

"In every other circumstance I would not hesitate to obey, but in this case if I were to do so, I would violate the expectations of our Lord. I do not understand your silence or the silence of the pope. Why does he not condemn these monsters from his balcony? Why has he not excommunicated those monsters who still call themselves Catholics?"

The bishop stood up, pointing his finger in a fury at Monsignor Donato. "You are hereby removed as pastor of this parish. When I return to Catanzaro, I will notify the Vatican of my action."

"Your Excellency, the only thing I ask for now is your personal blessing."

The bishop reluctantly made a hurried sign of the cross over Donato's head and strode angrily out of the dining room.

Monsignor Donato slowly sank into one of the chairs. He cried tears of anguish, not for himself but for all the innocents who were being hunted.

Chapter Sixty-Six

The woods near Dachau, November 2, 1943

Hans Keller was at peace with the thought that in the next hour he would be dead. He knew that the lorry was headed for some desolate spot in the woods where he and the others would be shot. He felt absolutely no fear and spent his last day on earth ministering to others. He was wiping the brow of one of the prisoners when he heard the drone of an engine. He realized a British fighter plane must have spotted the lorry and was headed for it.

As the driver attempted to pull into the woods, the armed guards jumped off the lorry and opened fire on the plane. It was no contest. The fighter plane returned fire and almost instantly killed all of the German guards. The truck remained miraculously intact.

Hans quickly climbed into the cab and drove the vehicle into the woods. He left the truck in the relative safety of the forest and walked to a nearby farm. Realizing he had nothing to lose, he approached a farmer who was busy loading bales of hay onto a wagon. Hans confessed that he was a prisoner from the concentration camp and that his comrades were seriously ill and needed assistance.

To his amazement, the farmer ushered him into the house and insisted that he change clothes and pretend he was the farmer's worker. Hans soon learned that the farmer was part of the local resistance. He had hidden Jews and Allied flyers in his barn over the past year.

Hans and the farmer traveled back to the lorry and drove all the priests to the farm. Once they were safely hidden in the basement, the farmer disposed of the lorry by driving it into a huge pond at the most remote part of his farm.

The next day it was obvious that none of the others had long to live. The farmer pledged that he would care for them and give them a decent burial when the time came. Judging from the tattooed numbers on Hans's arm, he presumed that Hans was a Jew and decided that the best way to secure his freedom was for him to meet with other resistance members who would lead him to Italy.

Once darkness descended over the land, two friends of the farmer led Hans through the woods to a small cottage where he spent the night. As the sun was rising the next morning, he was led to a vineyard and sequestered in the cellar behind a series of wine barrels. At midday another member of the group came to explain his options.

"You now bear a numbered tattoo that makes it not only dangerous for you but equally perilous for us. If you wish to attempt to reach Italy, I am afraid there will be a great price to pay."

"I am sorry, but I have no money."

"The price is not currency but pain. We need to remove that tattoo. The only way we can do it is to create a significant burn that will hide it. The cover story will be that you sustained the injury in an air raid."

"Do what you must do," Hans said.

At nightfall he was moved to a small village and led to the house of a local physician. He was encouraged to drink a large amount of schnapps in the next hour to deaden the pain. He was strapped to a table in the doctor's office. Most of his body was covered with some sort of rubber sheet with only his left forearm exposed. The doctor and two other men carried a large cauldron of boiling oil and poured it over his forearm. The pain was so intense that he immediately fainted.

When Hans woke up, he felt searing shocks of pain in his arm. He was given an injection of morphine. He was in and out of consciousness for the next three days. A week later, the doctor decided he was well enough to travel.

Accompanied by two of the men who had brought him there, Hans began a series of trips to various safe houses. Though the pain had lessened to some degree, he welcomed it as a reminder of all of the pain he had inflicted on the innocent.

Chapter Sixty-Seven

Philadelphia, December 16, 1943

After Stefano Pittelli left Kulpmont, his new grocery store became the place where he spent the greater part of his life. Seven days a week he labored in this tiny all-purpose center that had turned into the focal point of a mixed ethnic conclave in Philadelphia. The natural leadership qualities that made him the magnet for everyone in the mining community translated well into his current occupation. Stefano was at the center of everything that happened in his community. The store was more than a place to get bread and milk; for many it was a haven to visit with a sage who not only had the best sandwiches in town but also the best advice.

At six in the morning the sun was not yet breaking through the darkness as Stefano came down from his apartment above the store and gathered the Italian bread and newspapers that had been left on the front steps. As he walked through the aisles and placed the bread in bins, he jotted down the items that he would have to purchase the next day at the wholesale market. Once this was finished, he swept all of the aisles and filled the urns with the coffee that generated the wonderful aroma that penetrated the entire store.

By six thirty, the regulars began to trickle in for their usual daily needs, so Stefano occupied himself with preparing the meats and sandwiches. While customers and students waited to have their orders filled, he noticed a well-dressed man in a dark business suit he had never seen before. He knew everyone who frequented the store by name and only rarely did someone appear who was not in some way connected to his extensive social network.

When it was his turn, the stranger asked for an Italian sandwich filled with salami soprasatta and provolone cheese. While Stefano assembled the sandwich the stranger asked how late the store would be open. Stefano answered that it would close at exactly eight that night.

As the day went on, Stefano forgot the brief exchange, but as he was padlocking his front door that evening, he saw the man in the dark business suit standing in front of the store.

"Mr. Pittelli, may I have a word with you?" the stranger asked.

"Do I know you?" Stefano was surprised that the man knew his name.

The stranger took out his wallet and showed credentials that identified him as a United States Army officer.

"What do you want with me?"

The officer glanced behind him, and then looked back at Stefano. "Is there a place where we can speak in private?"

"I live upstairs and we can talk there." He opened the door to the apartment, so that the stranger could precede him.

As they ascended the stairs, Caterina called out, "Supper is ready."

"Someone is with me," Stefano said. "You and the children go ahead and eat without me. I'll join you later."

As the two men entered the parlor, Stefano said, "Please be seated."

They sat down across from each other.

"Mr. Pittelli, I am Colonel Arthur Russomano. There is a matter of extreme urgency that I need to discuss with you. You are probably surprised that I know who you are, but I know a great deal about you."

"Am I in some kind of trouble?"

"Not at all. Let me explain. We know that you were born in Calabria, Italy, and that your brother is the mayor of Soverato in

Calabria. He is involved in the Italian resistance movement and has on many occasions provided shelter and safe passage for American and British soldiers trying to escape the Nazis."

"Has Severio been harmed?" Stefano asked, feeling shocked that he had no knowledge of these activities.

"No, your brother is fine, but he is involved in a most important Allied mission. Currently there is a high-ranking German official who has renounced his affiliation with the Nazis. We believe he is hiding somewhere in Calabria. My department needs to provide assistance in securing this official's safety because we believe that he can offer significant strategic information about the inner plans of the Nazi government. We are attempting to help this person leave Italy and enter a free zone in Switzerland."

"What has this to do with me?" Stefano asked in confusion.

"Pardon me, but may I smoke?"

"You may, but how can an intelligent person like you smoke cigarettes?"

Colonel Russomano chuckled as he lit a Camel. "I see I am dealing with a man who does not mince words. Let me help you understand my interest in you. We need someone who is fluent in the language and who can gain access to your brother. That means someone he will trust and who his associates in Soverato will trust as well. We have determined, Mr. Pittelli, that the person we need is you."

Stefano almost fell off his chair. "Surely this is some kind of a joke. I have a family, a store to run. I can't just leave here and go into some crazy situation with Nazis and spies."

"I can understand that this is overwhelming, but we will arrange everything to enable you to make this trip and will provide someone to run the store in your absence."

"But how would this work? We are at war and I am an American citizen!"

"That is an excellent question, but we have already anticipated all of your questions."

For perhaps the first time in his life Stefano was speechless.

"Mr. Pittelli, I can understand that my being here is confusing and that it comes like a thunderbolt, but I know that you love this country. I would not be here if your assistance was not vital to the war effort. I also know you will need time to digest what I have told you, but it is critical that you tell absolutely no one about our conversation."

"Not even my wife? We have no secrets between us."

"You can tell her only that you are on a mission to Italy, but she must also be absolutely secret about your involvement. It is critical that any information pertaining to this mission be closely guarded. I would prefer that we discuss in detail what you can tell her if and when you accept this assignment."

"But how will my absence be explained to others?"

"You can tell them that an urgent family matter has occurred that needs your presence in Calabria."

"How much time can I have before I make a decision?"

"Would a day or two be all right?"

"Yes."

"Then I will come back on Thursday.'"

"Can you tell me the name of the person I am risking everything for?"

"Not at this time."

Stefano showed the colonel out and then went upstairs to consult his wife, hardly knowing what to think.

When the alarm went off the next Thursday, Stefano had been awake for hours. He had spent the past two days and nights going over and over all the reasons why this was sheer madness, but he could not cast aside his belief that this country had welcomed him and he had a duty to assist if his help was essential. He worried about his wife and children. Saying yes to the government's request put his loved ones at risk, not to mention the strong possibility that he was putting his own life in danger. After two days of balancing all the factors involved, by the time he opened the store in the morning, he had concluded that the pluses outweighed the minuses. He would go to Calabria, especially since he would see Severio after all the years they had spent apart.

Colonel Russomano arrived at approximately ten minutes after the lunch rush and was clearly pleased at Stefano's decision.

Over a giant sandwich he outlined the next steps of the process. "Tomorrow you will go to the FBI building on Chestnut Street at ten in the morning and meet with me and other members of the staff."

Once the colonel finished his preliminary instructions, Stefano could no longer resist asking, "Who is this person I am risking my life for?"

Colonel Russomano opened his briefcase, took out a file labeled "Top Secret" and glanced at it. "His name is Hans Keller. Actually, he is Father Hans Keller. He was stationed in the Vatican, but he was attached to a pro-Nazi bishop and was involved at the highest levels with the inner circles of the Nazi Party. He had direct access to everyone, including Hitler. We know that he was arrested as a traitor and sentenced to a concentration camp. We are unclear as to how he escaped, but through resistance information we are aware that he has been secretly transported from Germany to somewhere in Italy. Once secured, he will be debriefed and hopefully he will provide vital German information. He is fluent in English, French, and Italian as well as German and should have little difficulty passing as your business associate."

Colonel Russomano stood, shook Stefano's hand, and reached into his pocket, preparing to pay for the sandwich.

"The circumstances require that the sandwich be on the house." Stefano smiled, adding, "The free sandwich is a secret that you can share with no one, not even your wife."

Both men chuckled as the colonel exited the store.

Chestnut Street in Philadelphia was like a ghost town early on Sunday morning as Stefano reached the massive granite and marble edifice. He entered the elevator at four minutes to ten so that he would be at the office exactly at ten. As the clock in the city hall building chimed the hour he was met by an armed guard who asked him to be seated in the lobby. There was as yet no sign of Colonel Russomano, but eventually one of the doors opened and he appeared with his associates, all dressed in full service uniforms. The group walked to an elevator at the rear of the building that went directly to the nineteenth floor.

The irony of this entire scenario stunned Stefano as he realized he was entering a new phase of his occupational history: peasant, miner, grocer, and now international spy. As they exited the elevator, the colonel took a substantial set of keys out of his briefcase and located the one that opened a huge oak door leading into a spacious conference room.

The colonel gave Stefano a folder containing a series of documents explaining the details of his mission. Stefano sat and carefully read through the documents page by page. Colonel Russomano waited until Stefano had finished reading, and then he proceeded to make the formal introductions to the other officers at the table and begin his presentation.

When all of the details had been delineated, Stefano had significant concerns. "I understand everything that you have outlined this morning, but no plan is ever as simple as it looks. If for some reason I do not return, what happens to my wife and children?"

Without hesitation Colonel Russomano produced a document and handed it to Stefano. "You have in your hands a guaranteed policy issued by the government in the amount of $10,000. If the unthinkable happens, this amount will immediately be paid to your wife. There are no strings attached. This policy is issued to ensure your confidence that they will be safe and cared for financially."

Stefano was relieved, but he still had unresolved issues. "Does my brother know that I will be coming to see him and are you absolutely certain that he is all right?"

"He only knows that someone will contact him who will then escort Hans Keller out of Soverato. Our latest information acknowledges that your brother is well and has not been suspected of anti-Nazi activities."

"How will it work? Do I just show up at his home?"

"You will be escorted to a formal meeting at his office once your business dealings are finished and the person of interest is in the area."

"When will I leave for England?"

"In three days."

"Can you tell me how long I will be gone?"

"We believe that you will be home in approximately two weeks."

Stefano grimaced, but he said nothing.

The officers all stood and shook Stefano's hand, welcoming him aboard.

I will call you tomorrow to make the final arrangements," Colonel Russomano said.

On the morning Stefano was to leave Philadelphia, the weather turned bitterly cold. He realized that he was experiencing many of the same emotions as that morning so many years ago when he left Calabria for the voyage to a strange land. The first time he left his family was to ensure their survival. Again, in some sense, he was leaving so that others could survive.

After he closed his suitcase, he walked to the bedrooms of his three sleeping children and kissed their cheeks. In each room he knelt at the foot of their beds and prayed that the good Lord would watch over his family while he was away.

As he descended the staircase, he saw Caterina standing in the kitchen with a cup of coffee for him. She said nothing. Stefano drank his coffee, glanced at his watch, and knew it was time to go.

He went to the hall closet and took out his overcoat, scarf, and fedora. Caterina hugged him and adjusted his scarf. He quickly left the house. As he walked down the street, he turned back and smiled at her as she stood pressed against the dining room window.

The walk to the FBI building was quite a distance and the sidewalks were barely passable because the snow had hardened into sheets of ice. He paid them scant attention because his thoughts were already focused on the land he had left years ago.

The ride from downtown Philadelphia to the air force base took four hours. As soon as Stefano's car arrived, it received immediate clearance to proceed to hangar seventeen. Stefano had never been in a plane before and could only imagine how cold it would be at a high altitude. This concern was reinforced by the air force sergeant who brought him a parka, ski gloves, and a huge woolen blanket. Stefano learned that once they began their flight over the North Atlantic it could be well below zero on the plane.

After a half hour wait Stefano was escorted out to the runway and assisted into the four-engine prop plane. Once inside, the pilot informed him that they would fly to Gander, Newfoundland, where they would refuel. From there, they would fly straight to London.

Stefano shivered for most of the flight and was grateful that the copilot had a huge thermos of coffee that kept his hands as well as his throat warm. The air pockets way above the sea were reminiscent of the rolling ship that had brought him across the North Atlantic years ago.

After they touched down at the air base outside of London, Stefano was transported by an armed carrier to the docks where he was immediately taken to a British warship and escorted to the officers' quarters.

A tall officer in his forties smiled and said, "Welcome, Mr. Pittelli. I am Captain Myles Varley. I am a member of British Intelligence and have been briefed on your mission. I will attempt to bring you up to speed and inform you as to how the next week will play out."

"Thank you."

"You will be issued a valid Italian passport. In this briefcase is the passport for Hans Keller. To open the combination lock on the briefcase use the dates of your children's birthdays. Just the days. Not the years. We knew it would be easy to remember."

"Good idea."

"Father Keller's passport reads Franco Donatelli. He will have little difficulty passing as an Italian businessman because he is fluent in Italian. I suggest that you rest for now. Once we are near the Calabrian coast, I will come and assist you in climbing down the net. It is somewhat formidable the first time you do it. Once down, you will be picked up by a fishing boat and dropped near Catanzaro. On the last leg of your journey, you will be met by partisans who will drive you to a monastery in Baldolotto where you will spend the night. There you will be given instructions about your business meetings."

Stefano nodded, trying not to feel overwhelmed by so much information.

"Do you have any questions?"

"I'm sure I do, but at this moment I don't know what they are."

Captain Varley nodded. "We do our best, but be prepared to change plans if necessary."

"Hopefully all will go smoothly."

"Good luck."

Stefano's next leg of the journey went as planned. He climbed down the net from the warship, but it was no small feat. Finally he was aided onto the small fishing vessel. As the boat pulled away from the ship, he was instructed to go below and put on fisherman's clothing.

The trip from the warship to the coast of Calabria took less than an hour. At the pier, two small rowboats filled with armed men came to meet the boat. The men helped Stefano into the larger of the two rowboats. Once the vessel arrived at the furthest pier in the harbor, Stefano was assisted onto the wharf and instructed to wait for an automobile that would transport him to his overnight accommodations.

Chapter Sixty-Eight

Baldolotto, December 28, 1943

As Stefano watched, a tall, thin man with a mustache that curled up on both sides of his face motioned for the drivers to start their motors and go to the end of the pier. Stefano waited patiently. He had already learned that he was to anticipate nothing and be ready to follow instructions. The one comforting thought was that after all these years he was back on the soil of his beloved Calabria.

The door of the limousine swung open and the mustached man, who by this time Stefano presumed was a leader, addressed him in a friendly and reassuring manner.

"I am Giuseppe Spada. While you are here, I will be responsible for your safety. My instructions are that you will attend a series of business meetings over the next two days with merchants from Catanzaro. They are aware that this is part of a cover for you, but they know little else. We have learned the hard way that it is imperative that everyone know only what is essential to their performance. The Germans are ruthless. It is impossible not to tell them all that is known once they employ torture. Do you have any questions for me?"

"Yes. When will I be taken to meet the mayor in Soverato?"

"Sometime during the next two days after we receive notice that the person you are here to escort has arrived safely in Calabria. Now if there are no further questions, I suggest we go to your hotel so that you make an early night of it. You will need all your energy over the coming days." Giuseppe briskly shook Stefano's hand.

Stefano watched him disappear quietly in the still of the night, hoping everything went according to plan.

He rose the next morning and dressed like an Italian business executive carrying on the normal functions of his profession. He made his way to the refectory where he ate his breakfast and read the local newspaper.

In the corner of the refectory were Giuseppe Spada and the two men who had served as his guides. Giuseppe nodded and rose to greet him.

"Good morning. I trust that you slept well. Was everything to your liking?"

"Actually, I slept like a rock. The quiet of the monastery was conducive to a peaceful night. I live in a city where there is constant noise night and day. It's ironic that at a time of such great tension I'm in a place of prayer and peace."

"These are unpredictable times, my friend, and one learns to be ready for anything. If you keep your wits about you, this will turn out well. Yet be constantly aware that this town and the entire countryside are filled with Germans. A man never knows when he might be arrested and interrogated."

Despite this warning, Stefano felt a level of peace and confidence as he left the hotel and started to walk across the main piazza to his business meeting. He wondered how much this tiny village had been touched by the war, but this question was quickly answered as he passed a plaque containing the names of those already killed in the conflict. He felt a surge of anger against Mussolini for allowing these young men to become cannon fodder.

In the middle of the piazza a group of German soldiers were having coffee at the outdoor café. His guide, who was three steps behind him, whispered, "Act as if you have every right to be here."

Stefano placed his briefcase under his arm and walked with an air of calm authority, but his heart was pounding in alarm. When he reached the end of the piazza, he was met by a man who appeared to be a business associate. He warmly shook Stefano's hand and invited him into the building.

They entered a small room where Stefano was briefed on how he was to be involved in the business presentations. All of the businessmen understood that he was merely representing an Italian business for reasons known only to the partisans. Stefano was told that the participants would be supportive of his participation in the meetings. They left the room, walked to the end of a long hallway, and entered a conference room where there were three other seated businessmen.

After the preliminary introductions, coffee was served. No different from any other business meeting, the morning was filled with presentations and discussions. Despite his trepidations, Stefano played his part perfectly, injecting pertinent questions and observations throughout the meeting. To a casual observer there was nothing out of the ordinary.

At lunchtime, the businessmen left the conference room and walked down the street to the Ristorante Tritone. The proprietor checked his reservation book and escorted them to a corner table overlooking the garden. The café was filled with German officers. Since the Allied invasion in Sicily and Salerno, increasing numbers of German military were stationed in various parts of Calabria.

Studying the menu, Stefano was pleased to see so many dishes that once were part of his early childhood. After he made his choice, he turned slightly and noticed that one of the German officers at the table opposite them was staring at him. The few non-Germans outside of Stefano's group were not so formally dressed. Somehow this must have piqued the curiosity of the officer. Before they had a chance to order their meal, the officer approached the table.

"Good afternoon, gentlemen," the German said. "May I please see your passports?"

Stefano acted as if this was a routine request, reached into his suit jacket, and produced his passport.

The officer carefully examined the documents and handed all of them back except Stefano's passport.

"I see you are from Milano, Mr. Pittelli. What brings you to Calabria?"

Stefano made direct eye contact and calmly responded, "My business is in Milano, but I am originally from Calabria. I am here negotiating business contracts."

"What kind of business?"

"I am the president of Pittelli food products and my interest here is to secure annual supplies of olive oil and grain products."

The German officer appeared satisfied, but asked, "Where will you go from here?"

Stefano had not anticipated such a question and was not sure whether he should mention Soverato. "The next part of my trip will be in the Catanzaro area."

"Why didn't your business associates from Catanzaro meet you here?"

Though unnerved by this interrogation, Stefano said evenly, "My other business associates had prior commitments and could not meet here at this time."

The officer returned Stefano's passport. "I apologize for the interruption, gentlemen, and wish you *buon appetito.*"

When the waiter brought water, wine and a basket of bread, Stefano remained outwardly calm but his stomach was churning. He was fearful that if he reached for a piece of bread someone might see his trembling hand. After a few minutes he became more relaxed and began to eat his meal normally. He even managed to enjoy the delicious food.

The next day was a replica of the day before. Late in the afternoon Stefano learned that his passenger had safely arrived in the area. The mystery man had been escorted into a village near the monastery and would meet Stefano sometime tomorrow in Soverato.

Today Stefano was scheduled to meet with the mayor of Soverato to finalize the plan. He could hardly wait to see his brother again.

Severio had many dangerous issues to deal with, and today they were compounded by the fact that he had to orchestrate the escape of two men who were critical to the Allied war effort. He knew only that one of the men had been a member of the Nazi inner circle and the other was an American spy. This, coupled with the increasing pressure that the Germans were putting on him to complete the detention center in Soverato, weighed heavily on his mind and soul.

He arrived at his office at precisely eight in the morning and shuffled through a series of government reports. One communiqué could not be as easily dismissed as all those useless requests from Rome. It was a demand from Colonel Richter that the detention center be fully operational by the second week in January. If this date was not met there would be serious repercussions for him personally and for the citizens of Soverato as well.

Severio crumpled the report and threw it into the wastebasket. He wished that getting rid of Colonel Richter would be that easy, but he realized that he could no longer prevent the inevitable. He had fooled the Roman bureaucrats with a series of stalling maneuvers, but Richter was too cunning to be duped as easily. He was also aware that Richter was bringing in another Jew-hater by the name of Hanke who would report to him directly and neutralize Lieutenant Franz Wolfe, who had no stomach for building the center.

Severio started to pour a cup of coffee, but he was startled by a knock on his office door.

"Come in," he called.

The door opened and a figure entered.

Severio glanced up. "My God! Have I lost my mind?" He quickly embraced his brother. "Is it really you, Stefano?"

"Yes!"

They held each other for a long time, but they finally released each other as they wiped away the joyful tears of this reunion. They both began to speak at the same moment and then stopped, laughing together.

"You go first," Severio said. "Explain how you come to be here."

Stefano hugged his brother again, and then he quickly told his story.

Still in a state of disbelief, Severio said, "In my wildest dreams I could not have imagined that I would meet you here this morning. Where should we begin? Tell me about your life."

Ever the pragmatist, Stefano asked, "Shouldn't we discuss our mission first?"

Severio went to the sideboard and poured two cups of coffee. "That can wait. I'm not going to waste this opportunity."

For the next two hours, the brothers drank coffee and talked, bridging the many years that had passed.

Severio decided that the plan could include taking Stefano home for an early dinner because the meeting that evening would not take place until after seven. The train, which was almost always late, would arrive in Soverato about nine. He wanted Stefano to meet Rosella and their children.

Rosella was also shocked to see Stefano, but she quickly made him feel welcome at dinner. As the visit progressed, Severio noticed a positive change in her demeanor. Apparently Stefano's presence was having a beneficial effect on her. She had always known that Stefano's courageous act in going to America had enabled her to enjoy such a good life in Soverato.

Severio's heart was warmed at the smiling faces of his wife and brother. He thanked God for his dual blessings, for in one night he had found his brother and felt some hope for the health of his wife.

Chapter Sixty-Nine

Above Soverato, December 29, 1943

Hans Keller and his partisan escorts made their way slowly down the steep mountain terrain. Hans kept up despite his badly wounded arm and physical weakness. Every branch that brushed against his arm sent searing pain through his body, but he remained focused on the possibility that his cooperation with the Allies would do penance for the harm he had inflicted on others.

At the base of the mountain, the men entered a cottage owned by a local fisherman. Hans was issued business attire and informed of the evening's schedule. He would meet his escort, who would give him an Italian passport. Together, they would board a train. Now he was allowed to rest. After six thirty, they would wake him. He lay down on the straw mattress in the corner of the room, but he found it impossible to sleep.

Erich Hanke discovered that the train to Soverato was late. He now estimated that he would not arrive at the town until after nine that night. He wondered why Italians bothered to create train schedules. They ran their railroads as incompetently as the way they waged wars.

He agreed with Colonel Richter, his mentor, that the velvet glove approach was useless in Italy. Now that the spineless Italians had joined the Allies, Germans should ignore Italian sentiments. Hanke's presence in Soverato would allow Colonel Richter to meet Himmler's expectations regarding the Jews. The mayor and the ineffective Lieutenant Wolfe would be given a taste of Nazi *ordnung*, and it would be produce or be replaced. Under Hanke's efficient supervision, the detention center would be operational in early January.

Hanke felt pleased to remember that the Roman chapter of the Final Solution had gone off without a hitch. Not only had the roundup of Jews fed the egos of Hitler and Himmler, but Hanke and Richter had taken advantage of the opportunity to siphon off a large amount of gold. One of the benefits of his involvement in persecuting the Jews was that it was a grand opportunity for personal plunder. He had secretly arranged to have considerable sums of gold, currency, and art sent to a bank in Switzerland. Unlike Richter, he was not sure that Germany would win the war. No matter what the outcome, he would live in luxury for the rest of his life.

Stefano met the person he had come so far to help in the woods behind the Soverto train station. He handed Hans Keller a passport and a travel visa. Once onboard the train, they were to read business journals and never leave their compartment. Until they boarded, they were instructed by the partisans to remain hidden.

As the train approached Soverato, Erich Hanke took his valise down from the luggage rack and walked down the corridor to the lavatory where he washed his face and combed his hair before returning to his compartment. He welcomed the opportunity to spend a considerable time in the beach community. He relished the idea that once again he would be involved in activities that brought him great satisfaction. All those who opposed the Final Solution were powerless.

"Five minutes to Soverato," the conductor called, knocking on the compartment door.

Hanke sat down and gazed out the window at the moon shining on the Calabrian Sea. Crisp night air made visibility perfect. As the train slowed, he noticed a group of men coming from behind the station. What caught his attention was the tallest man in the group. He looked familiar. When the group walked under lantern light on the platform, Hanke hissed, "It can't be him. That traitor is rotting in Dachau!"

As the train stopped Hanke had an unobstructed view of the platform. No doubt now. He was clearly looking at Father Hans Keller. He felt renewed hatred wash through him as he quickly reviewed his options. *I could shoot him here, but that might put my life at risk. He may have accomplices. If I stay on the train I'll have more control in a small area. He might be part of some partisan group, so taking him alive to torture him later for information may be the best choice.* Decision made, Hanke locked his compartment and pulled down the shade on the door.

He waited impatiently for an appropriate time before he placed a silencer on the end of his Luger and opened his door. The train appeared to be relatively empty, so he would open only the doors where the shades were drawn. He knew that the doors would be unlocked because the conductor would not yet have had time to collect all the passenger tickets.

He opened the first door and saw an elderly couple. He politely excused his actions as selecting the wrong compartment. He continued down the passage checking compartments until he came to the last one. He felt a surge of excitement as he jerked open the door and stepped inside, Luger at the ready.

Hanke came face to face with Hans. "I knew it was you, Father Hans Keller. You always were too smart for your own good. Now you'll see who is really smart." He aimed his Luger at Hans, motioning with his other hand for the businessman to sit next to the traiter. "Hans, I never did like or trust you. Bet you wish you'd taken your priestly vows seriously. Now you're damned by both the Führer and the Catholic God."

Hans sighed, not surprised that he was betrayed on all fronts. The best he could do was try to protect Stefano Pittelli. Without thought, the Latin phrase he had said so many times to others came to him, *acta non verba*—deeds not words. Yes, he must act or all was lost.

"*Aegri somnia*," Hans said to distract Hanke.

"Don't spout that stupid Latin at me," Erich growled. "Speak German, as all the world will soon speak."

"A sick man's dreams," Hans translated. "You are a nightmare."

Hanke chuckled. "You are a dead man." He cocked his head toward the neatly dressed businessman. "I suppose he is helping you escape."

"No, I just met him. He doesn't understand German. I'm sure he is frightened. Let me speak to him in Italian."

"Stefano," Hans said in Italian, "act as if we are strangers and treat this German as carefully as you would a rabid dog."

"I don't know how you escaped Dachau, you faithless mongrel," Hanke growled. "But this time there will not be a second chance. If you move one muscle, I will kill both of you. You will follow my orders. We will get off at the next station. I will call Soverato and armed guards will take you back there."

Clearly terrified, Stefano spoke in rapid Italian, "What should we do?"

"What did he say?" Hanke angrily asked.

"He is totally confused and thinks this is a robbery. He's baffled, though, by the fact that you are a German soldier."

"Have him produce his passport."

In Italian, Hans said, "He wants to see your passport."

Stefano carefully presented the document.

Barely taking his eyes off his two captives, Hanke glanced at the passport and tossed it on the seat. "Looks in order." He focused on Hans again. "Why are you here and where are you going?"

"I don't know if you will believe me, but I had hoped to get to Switzerland and stay there until the war was over."

"Why did you betray our cause?"

"I was confused, especially after I killed the Lehmans at Wannsee. At the time I thought it was wrong to wage war against civilians, but now I believe what is being done to the Jews is for the benefit of all Germans. I will regret my betrayal forever."

"You have the tongue of a devil." Hanke appeared unconvinced. "How did you escape from Dachau?"

"Accident. I was in a transport attacked by British planes and all of the guards were killed. I walked away. A group of farmers hid me and eventually put me in touch with the underground. They had no idea who I was."

"Are you willing to provide the names and locations of these partisans that aided you?"

"Gladly. Even so, I know it cannot make up for what I've done."

A knock came on the compartment door, loud and insistent.

Hanke gave them a warning look to be quiet.

From outside the compartment, a voice announced. "Tickets, please."

Hanke concealed his Luger under his hat, but kept it aimed at Hans.

The conductor entered, appearing officious in attitude and uniform.

Hans and Stefano produced their tickets, which were summarily punched. The conductor turned to Hanke. "Ticket, please."

"My ticket is only valid to Soverato," Hanke said. "Tell this idiot Italian that I wish to buy a ticket to the next stop."

Hans made the request. "The price is two hundred lire."

Hanke reached into his pocket and took out a five hundred lire note while continuing to hide the Luger under his cap.

The conductor appeared annoyed by the slowness of the transaction, but he punched a ticket and reached into his pocket to make the necessary change. As he counted out the coins, he fumbled with them and two fell to the floor.

Hanke was taken off guard and glanced down at the coins on the floor.

The conductor pulled out a knife and plunged cold steel into the German's neck. Hanke struggled to raise his Luger and fire.

Hans knocked the weapon from his hand as the conductor plunged the knife into Hanke's heart. The German slumped forward in a pool of blood.

Stefano stared in horrified shock.

"You may call me Pietro. I was sent by Giuseppe Spada to make sure that your trip was uneventful," the conductor said. "I will take care of this dead swine. Remain calm and keep the cabin locked until I return. Do not open the door unless you hear four knocks."

Hans slumped back against the seat, staring at Hanke's body. They had broken bread and shared wine. They had worked closely together for Dr. Goebbels. How had it come to this? *Deo et regi fidelis*. Hans had been faithful to neither God nor the Führer. Hanke had been faithful to himself. They had both lost all.

At the sound of four knocks, Stefano opened the door. Accompanying Pietro were two of the partisans who had been Stefano's escorts in Baldolotto. They lifted Hanke and placed his body inside a large piece of canvas.

"There has been a change of plans," Pietro said. "You will disembark at the next stop." He quickly helped his comrades carry Hanke's body out the door.

Stefano turned to look at Hans. "This is all sheer madness. I am a grocer. Yet here I am up to my ears in spying and murder."

"Welcome to Nazi Europe," Hans said wearily.

"You are somehow important to the Allies. If it helps them, I guess it will be worth it." Stefano took out a white handkerchief and wiped the sweat off his forehead. "Do you think he really would have killed us?"

"Absolutely. Life means nothing to them."

Later, Stefano and Hans stood at the gate of the caboose next to the canvas that contained Hanke's body. When the train stopped, Pietro and the partisans picked up the canvas and they all disembarked about a half mile from the station. As they progressed away from the railroad tracks, they passed over a culvert that led to the sea. Pietro motioned the group to stop. The men wrapped chains around three large boulders and bound them to the canvas, then cast Hanke into the culvert.

"That Nazi pig will sleep with the fishes tonight," Pietro said.

The group walked in the clarity of the moon until they reached a tiny Calabrian fishing village. They waited in the dark while Pietro entered one of the cottages close to the piers. He was gone for a few minutes. When he returned, he carried clothes worn by the local fishermen.

"Put these on and give me your clothes and shoes," he said. "Also give me your passports. You no longer need them. We will burn them once you are inside the cottage."

The next night Hans and Stefano boarded a fishing boat that reeked of spoiled fish. The night was totally black due to a thick cloud cover and the sea was rough as they traveled against the incoming tide. The captain explained that they would be at the rendezvous in approximately two hours. As the cloud cover began to lift, a British warship with the letters "HMS" on the side came into view.

Onboard the ship, the smell of fish filled the tiny compartment as Stefano and Hans shed their fishermen's clothes and donned the apparel of sailors.

"What happened to your arm?" Stefano asked. "I don't intend to be nosy, but that is quite a burn."

"There's no such thing as nosy when a man has risked his life to save yours." Hans gently touched the red welt. "The partisans burned away the number that was tattooed on my arm at Dachau. We all knew that if I was stopped it was a dead giveaway."

"What is Dachau? Why brand you with a number?"

Hans stopped in shock. "I can hardly believe you don't know. Here, we have lived with this terrible knowledge for years."

"I've been in America."

"Dachau is a concentration camp where Germans keep prisoners, primarily Jews. I was in a block that housed priests and ministers. Our names were taken away and we were given numbers."

"Sounds terrible."

"Worse than you can imagine."

"You're German. Why were you sent there?"

"It's a long story."

Now fully dressed, Stefano sat down in a chair. "We have nothing but time on our hands. If you are willing to tell me, I'm interested in your story."

Hans hesitated, not relishing the idea of reliving his painful Nazi past. Yet Stefano had risked life and limb to help, so he was entitled to know the truth.

"I was born in a tiny village in Bavaria by the name of Passau," he began. "When I was nine years old my parents were killed in a train accident. My father, a brilliant architect, had a business partner. This kind man and his wife raised me as their own son. I also became an architect, but I grew bored with routine work."

"How could you be bored with such an exciting profession?"

"I was only doing preliminary drawings. It did not satisfy my needs. About that time I met Dr. Josef Goebbels."

"Isn't he a high-ranking Nazi?"

"Yes. He is the minister of propaganda for the Nazi Party. I was mesmerized by him and what he had to say. I was willing to do anything he asked of me. I studied hard and became a Catholic priest at his request."

"Aren't priests called by God, not the Nazis?"

"Not me. I became Hitler's priest so the Nazis could infiltrate the Vatican and affect its policies. I helped prevent the Church's interference in German politics."

"Were you a real priest?"

"That's open for discussion. I went to the seminary and was ordained in Saint Peter's Basilica. I was then assigned to a pro-Nazi bishop in the Vatican."

"How could you be a priest and a Nazi at the same time?"

"I realize this is difficult for you to believe, but at the time I fell in love with the vision of the new Germany. I was thrilled to be a part of it."

"It seems to me you were like the Italians who thought Mussolini was the answer to their prayers."

"I was so imbued with the role that I would have given my very life for the Führer."

"I cannot fathom such blind faith in a philosophy. I cannot give that kind of allegiance to any organization or government. For me, it is God and family. I love both of my countries, but there are limits."

"I respect you for that, but at the time there were no limits for me. I did things that cannot be changed or forgiven. When the war turned against Germany all of those who were most loyal pledged to give clear signs of our dedication to the Führer. Without hesitation I made that pledge, even though I had no idea what would be demanded of me." Hans began to weep.

"What did you do?" Stefano was torn between wanting to give comfort and feeling shock at the revelations.

"Di immortales virtutem approdare, non adhibere debent." Hans bowed his head.

"I don't understand your Latin," Stefano said.

"We may expect the gods to approve virtue, but not endow us with it."

"True enough."

"My assignment was to murder in cold blood the people who raised me."

"That's shocking! You didn't do it, did you?"

"To my utter shame, I did. And I deserve the pain that I live with every moment."

"May God forgive you," Stefano said.

"For I shall not," Hans concluded.

Chapter Seventy

London, January 7, 1944

The war had taken an exceptional toll on Captain Myles Varley. In the past two years his wife and two of his children were killed in London during one of the Nazi bomber air raids. He was riddled with guilt because he should have insisted that they leave the city and wait out the war in the Cotswolds with his sister. Coupled with this loss was the news that his brother had died at Dunkirk. His two surviving children now lived with his sister. His total dedication as head of the British counter-intelligence unit that was responsible for the coming invasion of Europe made it impossible for him to visit on any regular basis. The amount of surveillance of Nazi communications inside and outside of England consumed him. It also enabled him to confront his profound hatred of the Nazis.

Walking to the office in the rain, he thought that at some point in his life he would like live where the sun was a regular visitor. He and Evelyn had talked about spending their golden years in Greece or Italy, but the thought of being there without her was too painful to consider. As he arrived at the musty old building that contained stacks of classified information, he shed his raincoat, shook out his umbrella, and found the pot of coffee that was obviously left over from the night shift. After the first sip he thought that the brew would sober even the worst drunk in London.

Today was one of those rare opportunities to get a bird's-eye view of the inner workings of the Nazi machine. He was going to question a Nazi defector who had had exposure to every notable German leader, including Hitler. The defector had arrived aboard a British warship after being rescued from Calabria with the assistance of an American spy and local Italian partisans. As he reviewed the man's file he was struck by the fact that he was listed as a Catholic priest. It was strange that a Roman Catholic priest could provide strategic information. At this stage of the conflict, little shocked or surprised him, but this was different.

As usual, his biggest challenge was to suppress the revulsion he felt toward the brutal policies of the German government. He had been given multiple reports about the behavior of the SS in Poland and Russia. Having spent a considerable time at Oxford studying German music and art, he could not fathom how the German people could be involved in such atrocities.

Seated at his desk, he began to search for his glasses, which for the hundredth time he realized were on his head. He reopened the file on Hans Keller and jotted down the notes that would be his road map in the interrogation.

Hans Keller showered in the barracks, knowing that he was under constant surveillance. Now that they had a valuable informant, they wanted to ensure that there would be no suicide attempt. That possibility had long since passed. Hans was now committed to doing anything that would destroy his former masters. The past few days had somewhat alleviated the self-hatred he had experienced for months. Confessing his sins to someone he respected gave him a partial sense of peace that he had not experienced for months. This feeling was not a permanent reprieve from his guilt, but it helped to know that there were men like Stefano Pittelli all over the world, committed to ending the Nazi era.

After breakfast, he was issued a pin-striped suit, a white shirt, a conservative blue tie, and an ordinary fedora that made it easy for him to blend into any British business setting. He entered the back of the unmarked military vehicle. The ride to wherever he was going began with verdant farmland but shortly gave way to the rubble of streets that apparently had been recently bombed. There were a few ambulances carting out casualties of the raid. Hans once again felt the deep shame that came from killing civilians.

After a few attempts, the driver of the vehicle found a passable street, and then he drove down a long private driveway that led to a massive Victorian edifice almost completely covered with camouflaged nets and huge wooden images resembling trees. From the air it would resemble a park and would not be viewed as a strategic target. The driver parked the car, showed his credentials to the armed guards, and escorted Hans to the second floor, where he was asked to be seated while his escort and a guard sat and watched him.

After a moment, the phone on a nearby secretary's desk rang. She answered the call and motioned for Hans to follow the guard. He was led through a portico to a conference room. As he entered the room, a tall, handsome man dressed in civilian clothes greeted him.

"Good morning, Father Keller. I am Captain Myles Varley. Please be seated."

Hans was more than uncomfortable being addressed as Father.

Captain Varley initiated the conversation, offering Hans coffee. He explored Hans Keller's roots before he joined the Nazi Party. Varley made it clear that he wished to discuss only strategic perspectives and was not going to pursue any personal crimes. After a few moments of mild probing, Captain Varley came to the key question.

"Have you ever been privy to conversations or planning sessions that dealt with the Allied invasion of Europe?"

"I have had extensive conversations with Dr. Goebbels about the subject. Both Goebbels and Hitler are of the same opinion. They believe Normandy will be the place, despite the fact that an overwhelming number of generals on the staff believe it will be Calais. When last I heard, they were also unified in the belief that

Patton will head up the overall invasion. Hitler has ordered the beaches of Normandy fortified while German agents in England have been feeding information back to Berlin for the past eighteen months indicating that England is preparing to invade France sometime in early 1944."

"Is there any way that we could convey disinformation to, say, Dr. Goebbels that would shape Hitler's choice?"

Hans reflected for a few moments. "It would have to come from a true believer. If you can find someone close to Goebbels, it might work. Unfortunately the one closest to him was just killed by the partisans."

"Who was that?"

"His name was Erich Hanke, but he is no longer a possibility."

"What was he doing in Calabria?"

"I don't know, but the mayor of Calabria, a man by the name of Severio Pittelli, may be able to find out. If you're thinking of sending an Allied agent with misinformation, that person will certainly be disposed of after intense interrogation and torture."

"Father, you have been most helpful, but you realize that you will continue to be incarcerated because of security concerns."

"You really don't need to call me Father. Yes, I completely understand why I am being detained. If at any point I can be helpful, please call on me again."

Captain Varley rose from his chair. For the first time in countless interrogations, he shook the hand of the person interrogated. "You have been most helpful. Know that the end is coming for your former comrades."

Hans returned to the army barracks where he would spend the rest of the war in a solitude that would give him ample time to reflect on the misery his choices had caused others.

Chapter Seventy-One

Calabria, January 15, 1944

The past few months had been difficult for David Ferrara. The life of a partisan was far more strenuous than that of the ordinary foot soldier. Each day he had to forage for food, shelter, and ammunition, always aware that he was being hunted by a well-trained enemy. Fighting the Germans as a member of the Calabrian resistance, David had gone hungry, slept in the pouring rain, and been involved in frequent gun battles with German patrols. These hard realities were compounded by the knowledge that his fiancée's parents had been arrested in Rome and transported to Auschwitz. Though relatively safe because the Benedictine nuns in Soverato provided her sanctuary, Rachel had no idea of her parents' fate. He had not seen her for months, and often in the forest at night he would recall their lives before the war.

Three years ago life was simple for Rachel and David. Their parents had been neighbors and best friends for years Even though their marriage had been arranged, it was an anticipated joy for both of them. They had been playmates since infancy and their friendship had grown over the years into deep love. The war separated them when Rachel was sent to Soverato to live with the mayor's family. Her father, a prominent Roman merchant with extensive business acquaintances throughout Europe, realized that the persecution of the Jews would eventually reach Rome. His main factory was located in Rome, and it was not feasible for him to leave the city because he had extensive government contracts. He believed that Rachel would be safe in Soverato and appealed to his university friend, Severio Pittelli, to take her into his home. The Pittelli family lovingly welcomed Rachel, accepting her as a member of their family.

David could no longer stay away from Soverato. He needed to be with Rachel since he had received important news to share about her parents. They had both died in Auschwitz. He had asked permission from the partisan leader to be absent for a week while he visited her. Aware of what had happened to Rachel's parents, the leader had granted leave.

David traveled through the woods by day and only used the roads at night because there were fewer German patrols. The main roads were filled with checkpoints so he traveled exclusively through heavily tree-laden areas.

He knew that he had been identified in one of the raids on a German convoy the previous month. There was now a reward poster with his picture in most public buildings. Two of his compatriots had been captured in that incident and tortured. Before they were hanged, they had confessed and identified their comrades. David's passport was no longer of any use, so he had to constantly be on the move.

As he reached the top of the mountain overlooking Soverato, he reflected that today would be a day both of great joy and sorrow. It would be wonderful to see his beloved, but he would have to pierce her heart with the news about her parents. It was painful for him too, because he had loved them as though they were his own parents. He would feel the impact of their deaths every day, but if he and Rachel could wed this week, at least the pain would be shared. Mayor Pittelli and Rabbi Contini had arranged to officiate at their wedding once David arrived safely at the convent. David had conveyed a message through one of the partisans to the mayor that he would arrive at the convent late Wednesday night.

David could see the convent, but it was still too bright for him to gain access to the back gate. He hid in the olive grove above the ridge as darkness fell over the valley. As the moon began to replace the sun, the rays of both shone on the bell tower.

He could now enter the convent. He crawled on his stomach before sliding down a slight incline that led to the back gate. Scaling the gate, he hid in an alcove near the large wooden door. The only sound was the wind gently moving through the olive grove. He tapped three times on the door, giving a prearranged signal to the nuns.

After a few moments the door opened, and a nun motioned for him to enter. In silence she led him to a tiny room off the refectory and pointed toward a chair. He sat as she left the room and went through another doorway. This was the first time David had ever been in a religious house other than a synagogue. He looked around the room. A large crucifix hung on one wall above the portico and the rest of the walls were adorned with tapestries depicting Christian scenes. Though the scenes had no religious significance for David, he understood and respected the fact that they had meaning for those who were sheltering his beloved Rachel. He had the highest regard for this group of non-Jews who would risk the wrath of the Nazis to hide her and help him.

As he was examining the tapestries he heard footsteps. He turned and saw Rachel. He jumped up and ran to embrace her. The moment was so filled with emotion that neither could speak. They gripped each other with silent intensity.

Finally Rachel said, "David, I feared I would never see you again."

He held her hand and gently wiped the tears from her cheeks. "I told you I would come for you as soon as possible."

"I wanted to believe it, but in these times there is so little I can hold on to. I've been so worried about you and my parents."

The mention of her parents sent a chill down David's spine as he searched for a way to break the news. He could not yet shatter this reunion with the dreaded news and so he hesitated, trying to deal with the moment as if joy were the only emotion he was experiencing. But his face betrayed his anxiety.

"David, what is the matter? Why do you look like that?"

He realized there was no easy way to say what he must. "Rachel, I have lived for this day when I would see you again. Every day and every night I would dream about this moment. The thought of your love kept me alive despite the odds. You are everything to me, but—"

"But what? David, what is it?"

He took a deep breath. "Rachel, I have bad news."

"My parents?"

"The Germans rounded up the entire neighborhood in Rome and after a few days they were all shipped to Auschwitz. The report is that all of them were sent to gas chambers." He reached out to try to embrace her. "I am so sorry, my dear."

Rachel pushed him away, tears in her eyes. "Maybe they weren't captured. Maybe they're hiding like you. Don't say they're dead. You don't know for sure."

David gripped her hands tightly. "You may be right, my love. We cannot absolutely know."

"Hope. We must remain hopeful."

They sat down together, holding each other's hands.

When Sister Mercedita entered the room, she announced that Rabbi Contini and Mayor Pittelli had arrived. She took Rachel, who was in a trance-like state, and gently led her into the cloister.

Rachel was assisted by the nuns, who provided her with a white dress ordinarily worn by a postulant. It was adorned with flowers and lace for the occasion.

"You look beautiful," Sister Mercedita said, leaning forward. "The mayor told me what happened to your parents. My heart breaks for you. I will make this day as joyful as possible. Your parents are here in spirit, and all the love they feel for you is in this place today. No matter what, my child, love can never be blotted out by evil."

Downstairs, the mayor entered the convent, carrying a dark suit, tie, and shoes. "Hello, David. I brought you formal clothing and the rabbi has a yarmulke. We didn't think you would have the opportunity to find appropriate clothing for this occasion. How is Rachel?"

"Overwhelmed with grief and relying on hope that somehow her parents are hiding in Rome."

Severio frowned. "I have heard directly from her father's plant manager that they were captured along with 1,700 others and shipped to Auschwitz. However, it is probably wise at this time not to take all hope away from her. At some point she may be better able to face it."

"I agree. Today, even I cannot accept their deaths."

"I understand. There are many days when I still cannot believe that Giancarlo, my wife's brother, was killed in this stupid war. My wife may never fully accept the reality."

David shook his head in disgust and anger. "When will this awful killing stop?"

"Soon, I hope, because even in Soverato we are no longer safe. But enough of sad thoughts. I am here to celebrate the union of two wonderful people."

David changed his clothes. Although the suit was somewhat large, he felt like a different man when he gazed at himself in the mirror.

Severio agreed that he cut a *bella figura* as they walked upstairs to the large room where the ceremony would take place.

For years Rachel had entertained visions of this wondrous day, but without both families her joy was greatly diminished. One family was almost certainly dead and the other was hiding somewhere in the hill town of Tivoli. This was supposed to be a day of communal rejoicing, continuing centuries of Jewish celebration in the Roman quarter, but today the songs, dances, and attention to all the customs and rituals would be severely curtailed. Despite all the attempts of Sister Mercedita and the nuns, Rachel's heart was filled with anguish.

As the mayor walked her down the refectory's center aisle, David stood as her foundation of love. The rabbi embraced each of them, and then he began the ceremony, praising them for their willingness to pledge themselves to love in spite of all they had endured.

Rosella and Severio had arranged a small celebration following the service. The rabbi began the meal with a blessing and Severio offered a toast to the young couple, but because of the danger of discovery by the Nazis, the meal was brief.

Sister Mercedita led the newlyweds to the end of the cloister where there was a small, well-appointed apartment that was reserved for the bishop and visiting members of the sisterhood and clergy. Today the apartment was festively adorned with ribbons and wreaths. Sister Mercedita left the suite, uttering a prayer to the God of Abraham that he would watch over Rachel and David for the rest of the war.

Rachel immediately noticed that all of the earmarks of Christianity had been removed from the apartment and replaced by symbols of their faith. "David, even in this terrible time there are some who always give of themselves. I love these women. They have truly become my sisters."

She began to weep and rested her head on David's chest. He embraced her with such tenderness and strength that in spite of her pain she felt a moment of peace. She kissed David, first gently and then with increased passion.

Filled with years of waiting for this moment, they made love with a tenderness that helped ease the pain of the loss of those who had been ripped from their lives.

Chapter Seventy-Two

Soverato, February 26, 1944

The café at the end of Via Vittorio Emmanuele was for years the place where all the locals in Soverato would begin their day with a coffee, but lately the café was empty on most mornings due to the overwhelming German presence in the town. Members of the Gestapo and those remnant loyalists to fascism were relentless in examining documents with the hope of arresting a Jew or a partisan. This idyllic hamlet had gone into a period of hibernation after the Italian government collapsed. The racial laws had been ignored here, but now the townspeople were being pressured to identify all of their Jewish neighbors. The café had lost its social status, but it had acquired a new identification. Its basement was the secret meeting place of those attempting to gather without the scrutiny or interference of the Germans.

The backroom door was opened just enough so that the proprietor, Eduardo, could see the entire alleyway leading to the café. He was waiting for two guests who wished to be unobserved. They had arranged to meet in the wine cellar of the café at noon. Suddenly at the end of the alley he saw a familiar figure walking briskly toward the café dressed in the garb of a fisherman with his cap pulled almost entirely over his face.

Eduardo greeted him as he opened the door. "Good morning, Monsignor."

"Good morning, Eduardo. Weren't you fooled by my disguise?"

Eduardo chuckled. "With all due respect, Monsignor, I would recognize your walk anywhere, but I have to tell you that I was impressed by your speed."

"Fear is a great motivator, my friend. I was afraid that if I was stopped it would be curtains. All I know about fish is that it goes well with pasta."

"You should visit me more often. I rarely smile these days, let alone laugh."

The monsignor took off his cap and started down the spiral staircase.

"Make yourself comfortable. I will bring the rabbi when he arrives." Eduardo went to make coffee for the meeting.

At the end of the wine cellar was a room barely able to accommodate three people. It had a low ceiling and the aroma of wine barrels and stale bread.

The monsignor was barely seated when he heard the creak of the stairs. The apparition of the rabbi in peasant garb was almost as humorous as his own pretense to be a fisherman. He rose to embrace his longtime friend, saying, "We are both too old to impersonate people who actually work for a living."

As they sat, the monsignor began the conversation. "I know that the mayor has informed you that the Germans are putting pressure on him to finish the detention center."

The rabbi grimaced. "He has kept me abreast almost daily. He is having trouble stalling the inevitable."

"Why in heaven's name do they want a detention center here?"

"Because we're in a remote area and the transportation of Jews from here will be barely noticed in the rest of Italy."

The monsignor shook his head. "The people of this village will not stand by silently and let them cart away our neighbors."

The rabbi spread his hands in a gesture to indicate powerlessness. "They will be confronted with overwhelming odds and their fish hooks will be no match for German guns. In October in Rome in broad daylight they took 1,700 Jews and no one lifted a finger to stop them."

"Maybe they will not come here."

"They will come, Tomasso. Now is the time for us to act. Soon it will be too late to hide my congregants. There are Jewish communities all over Europe that could not believe it would happen to them and so many are dead today. One of my challenges is to explain to my people that they are in extreme danger."

"Is there any way I can help?"

"You have already helped in so many ways. Please know how much it means to me that you are here this morning."

The monsignor replied, "I am here because the God that we both love commands me to be here."

With tears in his eyes, the rabbi reached across the table and firmly grasped the hands of his colleague. "You have always been a dear friend."

"As have you. It doubly troubles me that some of those who persecute you call themselves Christians."

"That's nothing new. We have always been scapegoats for some Christians."

"But it's absurd! The Jews didn't kill Christ. The Romans did. My community has its roots in the Hebrew faith!"

The rabbi looked thoughtful. "Have you read the sermons preached by some of the Lutheran and Catholic bishops before the Nazis came to power? They labeled the Jews as evil creatures that should be burned at the stake. Martin Luther wanted all of us to be cast into the fires of hell. It may be late, but it looks as though he is getting his wish."

"I refuse to see that as anything but ignorant bigotry."

"I wish all the clergy in Europe were like you, along with all of the courageous nuns and priests who stand with us now."

"I tried to get the bishop of Calabria to speak out, but he refused and removed me from my parish. Yet I will not leave and I certainly will not abandon you. I'm no hero, but I cannot accept the official silence of my church."

"I wish the pope would speak out, but I am not sure the Nazis would be influenced by his appeal."

"I disagree. Many of the high-ranking Nazis were raised Catholic. The pope should publicly excommunicate them from the Church."

"Do you believe that would help?"

"I don't know, but God commands standing against evil without guarantees."

"If they drum you out, I'm sure we can find a spot in our community for you."

Both men laughed nervously.

Then the rabbi said, "All right. Now we need to establish a plan for the coming weeks."

"The Benedictine nuns can hide up to a hundred people. They have a series of caves and tunnels that are hidden very well. I have personal contacts in almost every monastery between here and Florence that can also provide temporary shelter. The biggest problem we face is obtaining passports and travel visas. The mayor is working on this."

"Many of my people may refuse to leave because they've lived in harmony here in Soverato, especially because this community has largely ignored the racial laws."

"The racial laws are ridiculous. We Italians have been conquered by every nation and tribe on earth. There is no such thing as pure Italian blood." The monsignor paused, "When will you tell your people to go into hiding?"

"As soon as the mayor tells me that the center is almost complete. Even then I will need your help in telling us exactly where and how many can be sheltered."

"I will immediately ascertain the places and numbers. One of my nephews works for the government in Catanzaro, but he is also a member of the resistance. He will provide me with the information we need."

"I bow to your judgment."

Both men stood and again embraced each other.

"You are a singular blessing.'"

"So are you. I pray that we can save everyone in our community."

Chapter Seventy-Three

Soverato, March 2, 1944

Georg Richter was suspicious by nature and trusted no one, with the exception of his fellow loyalist, Erich Hanke. Even in military school he had maintained a distance from all the officer candidates and had never shared any of his private thoughts. Loyalty to the cause and his Führer was so high on his priority list that he had turned in his own father to the Gestapo for making anti-Nazi remarks at a union meeting. He did not feel the slightest twinge of guilt when his father was arrested and sent to Mauthausen concentration camp, where he contracted typhus and died.

This same level of fanaticism was a requirement of all who served under him. Personal involvement in the killing of civilians in Poland and Russia may have caused guilt or shame in some men, but for Hanke these activities were sport.

The assignment in Italy was complicated by a host of issues. Richter needed an aide who would follow without question the orders that had been given by Himmler. After his performance in the Jewish ghetto of Rome, Captain Hanke was exactly the man who would light the fire under all those in Soverato who had hindered the construction of the detention center. The only problem was that Hanke was supposed to be in Soverato three days ago. Somewhere along the way from Rome he had disappeared. It seemed that everyone in the area was vanishing, particularly a large number of local Jews.

Colonel Richter had reached the point where he could no longer tolerate the incompetence of the local mayor, who had no concept of German *ordnung*. Mayor Pettelli's lack of focus and adherence to strict objectives was compounded by the behavior of Richter's adjutant, Lieutenant Wolfe, who, he suspected, was in collusion with the mayor. Before departing for Milan where he would be for three weeks, it was imperative that Richter have a discussion with Lieutenant Wolfe. He called the lieutenant and arranged to have a morning meeting before he left.

Franz Wolfe despised Richter. In the past week he had seriously considered requesting a transfer, but his intense loyalty to Field Marshal Schutzen prevented him from doing so. He believed Schutzen had selected him for this assignment because he understood that Wolfe would strictly follow a code of honorable behavior toward civilians. He also feared the coming of another inveterate believer, Erich Hanke.

Franz was the only link of decency in the chain of command. If he left, the mayor and the entire community would be at even greater risk. Mayor Pittelli was an honorable man assigned an odious task that threatened to compromise his moral code. Time was running out. Danger to the community was imminent. Richter would no longer listen to his counsel, so Franz believed public reprisals were just around the corner.

Wolfe realized that this morning's meeting would not be a briefing session but a series of ultimatums. He had read the report of the Jewish arrests in Rome and knew that Richter and Hanke were the architects of that outrage. Without any public outcry, Richter would be free to replicate the process all over Italy. Himmler's seal of approval had trumped the field marshal's influence. Sparing a miracle, all hell would soon break loose on every Jew in Italy.

As Franz entered the colonel's office, Richter barely looked up at him. Richter immediately launched into a diatribe about Italian incompetence and began to berate Franz for his inability to produce the required results.

"I am grossly disappointed in the state of affairs in Soverato," Colonel Richter said. "That poor excuse of a mayor has performed pitifully. I will no longer tolerate his insubordination."

"Mayor Pittelli has faced one impediment after another that has made the schedule unworkable."

"Lieutenant, you have been here too long. You have been assimilated into the Italian culture and have forgotten the concept of German discipline."

"I am a good German and—"

"Because you are apparently a pet of the field marshal I have tolerated your excuses, but I will not fail in this assignment. I have Himmler's total support. The goal is a Jew-free Italy and that is what I will deliver."

"Colonel, this assignment cannot take place in a vacuum. There are valid objections that must be confronted."

Richter screamed, "Nonsense! No more excuses! You are hereby given a direct order. Meet the schedule. If a week before I return you are behind schedule, you will publicly execute the mayor in the main piazza. Every day after that you are to hang ten men, women, and children until the center is complete."

"Surely you cannot be serious."

"The fact that you are a favorite of Schutzen will not prevent you from carrying out this order."

"Do you realize how the Italians will react to this?"

"I could care less."

"You will drive many into the partisan ranks."

Richter smirked. "I have been at the Russian front fighting against barbarians. Do you think that a weak-kneed group of Italians will frighten me? Are you clear about my order?"

Franz remained silent.

"I am giving you a direct order. Is that clear?"

"It is clear, Colonel." Franz knew that further conversation was useless. He had to find another way to minimize the human damage that was about to occur in this village.

"Good. Now get out of my office. I have much to do before I leave for Milan."

Chapter Seventy-Four

Soverato, March 8, 1944

The sounds of the bustling street beneath the window of Lieutenant Franz Wolfe's apartment slowly built to a level that made continued sleep impossible. It was nearly time for him to report to the detention center and leave the only place in Soverato where he could hide from the growing concerns of his duty.

The Nazi doctrine had become a cancer that infected both the victors and the subjects of their brutality. Initially the new Germany had been such a pure concept that he was willing to sacrifice even his life for so lofty a goal. He could now see that he had ignored the many contradictions that were obvious to anyone who searched with a critical eye. But like many, he had gone along on the crest of the wave of blind enthusiasm. He had fooled himself into believing that basic human rights would only be temporarily suspended and would be reinstated as the new Germany progressed.

The actual combat part of his military career was harrowing, but it never required being complicit in harming innocent civilians. He had fought against soldiers and had killed human beings, but they were combatants out to kill him, not civilians. Now he was caught in a world of cognitive dissonance. What he believed was diametrically opposed to the requirements of his assigned work.

How could he implement orders that demanded the murders of women and children? What would his mother say if she knew he was involved in building a way station from which civilians would be sent to gas chambers?

He opened the wardrobe in his bedroom and stared for a few moments at his uniform. He wished that he didn't have to wear it on the street because despite his fluent Italian it made him the target of hate for every citizen in Soverato. Each morning he noticed the cessation of conversation as he entered the café for his coffee. The hope of anonymity faded as soon as the other patrons saw the swastika. The opportunity to explore the Italy of his youth was impossible. He was part of an occupying force that had destroyed the local way of life and was now transforming this idyllic beach community into a hub of horror.

The situation was compounded by Colonel Richter, who had no use for Italians and whose bigoted bile prevented him from seeing the beauty of the culture. Unlike the colonel, Franz knew Italians were not cowards, but many questioned their relationship with Germany. Richter saw this as weakness, but Franz understood the strength of anyone who refused to be part of the German tidal wave.

In the café, Franz felt unwilling to tolerate the silence of the local customers, so he quickly finished his coffee quickly and walked to the detention center. His options at this time were limited and none were without significant price tags. He could request a battlefront assignment, but he knew he would be replaced by someone Richter would choose and that would mean immediate reprisals and executions in Soverato. Mayor Pittelli, whom he had come to admire and respect, would surely be replaced and probably hanged if Richter had his way. Wolfe had surmised that the mayor was involved in secret partisan work that would be halted if he left his current post. Another officer that replaced him would probably be more aligned with Richter's hatred of the Jews. Remaining in Soverato presented an array of moral issues as well. It seemed that there was no viable option. Richter would soon return. Franz didn't know how he could continue to stall the project.

As he entered the center, he was surprised that the mayor was already at his desk.

"Good morning, Franz. How are you this morning?"

"I've been better."

Severio looked surprised. Up to now Franz had not shared any of his thoughts or feelings. He left his desk and walked slowly to the area where the coffeepot was warming. He poured himself an espresso and held out a cup, clearly inviting Franz to join him. Franz nodded and both men sat at a tiny round table.

"Too much wine and late-night dining?" Severio asked.

Franz shook his head. "I wish that was the reason; that would pass in a day."

"Does it have anything to do with the detention center?"

"It has everything to do with it."

"Working beside you these months I believe that your heart is not in this work."

"Franz smiled wryly. "That, my friend, is a gross understatement."

"I cannot believe that even though you and Richter wear the same uniform you have anything in common. What are you struggling with?"

Knowing that Severio's line of questioning might cost the Italian considerably, perhaps even his life, Franz answered, "I loathe what I am being asked to do. This detention center is only a ruse. All who come through here will face certain death."

"Do you not believe, as Richter does, that regardless of age or gender the Jews are enemies of the state?"

"Richter is a horrible excuse for a human being and I share nothing with him. His lust for Jewish blood is psychotic. There is nothing he would not do to please Hitler and Himmler, including killing you and your family."

"Will you finish the center?"

"If I don't, you and a series of civilians will be publicly murdered until it is completed. It must be finished before Richter returns from Milan."

"In the meantime I must find ways to protect all of my citizens."

"That will be most difficult because on his return he will want the names of all the Jews in Soverato and the neighboring communities. He is bringing a captain here by the name of Erich Hanke who was in charge of liquidating the Roman Jewish ghetto. Hanke will report directly to Richter and is as much a Jew-hater as Richter."

"Do you have any suggestions for how I can protect my citizens?"

"They must act now. If it is possible, they must get passports and travel visas. Switzerland is their only hope. If they don't have valid papers, I urge them to immediately secure hiding places."

"I can provide temporary hiding places, but the German documentation is another problem. What would we need to successfully forge the paperwork?"

"It would be essential to have an authentic government seal and some actual passports and travel visas. The Gestapo is superb at recognizing poor forgeries."

"And how could we get them?"

Franz smiled. "I could have you shot for posing that question. Are you asking me to secure them for you?"

Well beyond caution, Severio said, "Yes, I am. I may be going out on a limb, but I have great trust in you, Franz. You are as unhappy with the detention center as I am."

"Maybe so, but I'm not sure I have the level of courage that cooperation with you requires. I've faced death before, but if Richter finds out he will torture me."

"I have no desire to be a hero, but I must do this. Will you join me?"

Franz paused briefly. "Can you provide a superb forger?"

Severio smiled. "It just so happens that I have one in my family."

Chapter Seventy-Five

Benedictine Convent, Soverato, March 11, 1944

Kneeling, Sister Mercedita prayed for guidance and strength. She was about to send four sisters to Lugano with the intention of providing cover for Rachel. Mayor Pittelli had informed her that the German officer in Soverato had been involved in killing Jewish refugees and the cloister would be no guarantee of safety. Rachel had been coached in the fundamentals of Catholicism, but she had no in-depth knowledge of the religion. In order to compensate for this, Sister Mercedita thought that rather than traveling alone, Rachel would blend in as just another nun as part of a group.

The plan was to take the early train to Rome and stay at the motherhouse of the Sisters of the Sacred Heart, which was located in the center of Rome above the Spanish steps. The second part of the journey would take place the next day. They would arrive at the Swiss border late in the evening. Once processed through the border, the nuns would be met by sisters from the Benedictine convent of Santa Maria della Neve in Lugano. Once safe, Rachel would remain at the convent until David was free to join her.

The morning of the trip, Rachel rose early and was assisted in dressing in a full nun's habit so that she would look exactly like the other sisters. Once completely dressed, she was shown how to place her hands under the garment in the traditional way nuns varied themselves. She had spent the last week practicing this and many other gestures. She had rehearsed her prayers with the nuns during the day and had memorized Catholic doctrine at night, all the while ever grateful for the kindness and concern shown to her by the sisters. Sister Mercedita and the other nuns had a deep respect for Judaism and every tutorial was ended with a prayer to the God of Abraham.

Breakfast in the refectory was always eaten in silence while one of the nuns read from either the Bible or one of the fathers of the Church, but this morning things were different. The nuns were allowed to speak to Rachel and had time to bid her farewell and Godspeed. The sisters formed a line in the hallway as Rachel left the refectory.

Severio and Rosella Pittelli stood at the end of the line. Since Stefano's visit, Rosella had felt great remorse over her earlier behavior. She needed to express her contrition for forcing Rachel to leave her home.

When Rachel stood in front of her, Rosella began to weep. "Rachel, please forgive me. My fears after Giancarlo's death took over my life. I had no right to send you away. I am so sorry."

"I understand. Truly I do. You and Severio will always have a special place in my heart." Rachel embraced Rosella. "Take care."

Sister Mercedita was patiently waiting in the hallway. When the chimes of the clock sounded, she said, "It's time to go."

Rachel and the four nuns went to the front gate and entered the waiting automobile while the drivers placed their luggage on the overhead racks. It was difficult for Rachel to leave the sanctuary of the convent for this unknown destination. It would also be much further away from her beloved David. She prayed that her arrival in Lugano would be the first step toward their reunion.

The platform at the train station was relatively empty. As usual, the train was late. The brilliant sun was already scalding the landscape, so the nuns entered the tiny station building. They began to say the rosary. Rachel had been well schooled in this practice and easily followed the ritual. Finally the train arrived. To their relief, it was filled primarily with families traveling to the eternal city. Not a single German soldier was apparent. So far the first leg of the trip to freedom had gone perfectly.

When the train arrived at the Stazione Ferrovia in the center of Rome, the scene was chaotic. The cacophony of the voices of thousands of travelers made it impossible to hear anything intelligible. Holding hands, the nuns made their way through this frenetic mob to the front of the station where they observed two men with signs welcoming them to the city. The mother superior in Rome had arranged transportation directly to the motherhouse.

The ride to the convent was eerie for Rachel. This had been her home for years. Now it was the place where her parents had been arrested and transported to the death camp. She had so loved Rome, but now as she looked out her window she saw only the dreaded symbol of the swastika. It was ubiquitous, as were the German soldiers walking in the street. She closed her eyes and tried to recall this city as it once was.

The convent of the Sacred Heart was situated in one of the premier locations in the city. From the front terrace, it was possible to see not only Saint Peter's but also the great synagogue of Rome. The synagogue had been a wonderful focal part of Rachel's life as a child. She began to weep as she thought about her parents and their last days near the Tiber.

When she arrived at her bedroom, it was quite late and she was exhausted. She realized the next day would be even more taxing. Sleep came easily to her as she dreamed of happier times when she and her parents would walk the streets of Rome. One of her favorite spots was not far from the convent in front of the Borghese that overlooked the Piazza del Popolo. Her father had taken her there many times. After stopping for a soft drink, they would wend their way back to the Jewish area and meet her mother for dinner near the Portico. The memory of those days soothed her. For a short time she once again felt as if she was in the presence of her parents.

The chapel bell roused Rachel from sleep. Sister Evangeline and Sister Margarita came to assist her in dressing. There would be time for breakfast and even a few moments to sit in the courtyard before leaving for the train station.

At two thirty, the mother superior advised the nuns that it was time to leave. They arrived at the station fifteen minutes before departure. Because the train originated in Rome it was on time. As they boarded, one of the conductors approached them and tipped his hat. He led them to an empty compartment.

"Sisters, this compartment is one class above your tickets, but it is unoccupied so I will make sure you have complete privacy."

"Thank you," Sister Evangeline said.

"In these days it pays to do a favor for God. Say a prayer for me and also for Italy."

"We will," Sister Evangeline said.

As Rachel sat down with the nuns in the comfortable compartment, she tried not to think about all the German soldiers she had seen on the train. "I will feel safer if we all stay together and only leave when it is essential to use the lavatory."

"That is a good idea," Sister Evangeline agreed. "We will do exactly that."

Rachel did her best to relax, but she remained tense as the train sped toward a safe destination.

When they were an hour from Lugano, the compartment door opened and a German officer entered. "Good evening. I am sorry to trouble you, but I would like to see your papers."

Rachel felt her heart speed up, but she remained outwardly calm.

The nuns reached beneath their habits and produced their passports. The officer examined each one. At first it appeared that this was merely a formality, but then he reopened the compartment door and motioned toward an armed guard.

"Please keep these holy women company while I have individual chats with them in my compartment." He turned to the nuns, and said, "I was raised Catholic and went to a Catholic gymnasium and university. Like you, my dear sisters, I have extensive knowledge of the Roman Church. It will be my pleasure to have in-depth conversations with you about your faith."

Rachel was terrified. Though she had spent several weeks learning a great deal, she would be no match for someone who had an in-depth knowledge of the Church.

"I doubt this German guard speaks Italian. Tell the officer that four of us are teachers and Rachel is our cook," Sister Evangeline said in Italian as she left the compartment.

After twenty minutes, Sister Evangeline returned. She was followed by Sister Margarita, whose time away from the compartment was about the same. When she came back, it was Rachel's turn.

As she entered the officer's compartment, she remembered to keep her trembling hands tucked inside the habit.

"Please be seated. I am Captain Karl Schoenfelder."

"I am Sister Rachel."

"How long have you been in the convent?"

"I've been a member of the community of Santa Anna for seven years."

"And your family, do they live in Soverato?"

"My parents are dead, but they lived most of their lives in Rome."

"Next to Berlin, Rome is my favorite city in Europe," Captain Schoenfelder said. "Where did they live in Rome?"

"In a lovely section near the Borghese."

"I am not familiar with that area. Is it a place that a tourist would know?"

"It's above the Piazza del Popolo."

"Why did you become a nun?" Captain Schoenfelder's asked, voice harsher.

"I felt that God was calling me."

"So you thought God wanted you to become a teacher?"

"Oh, heavens, no. I'm not that smart. I'm a cook in the convent."

"Sister, could you please tell me the sequence of the liturgical calendar."

Panic gripped Rachel. She had no idea what the answer was. "I know the answer, but when I get nervous I forget easily. That is why I could never be a teacher."

"I understand. Why don't you tell me the origin of the Gregorian chant and how the hours are chanted in meditative religious orders."

Rachel decided to avoid the question by asking one of her own. "Why are you asking me these questions? I am not a teacher. I am a cook."

"Sister, I am starting to believe that you are not a nun. Perhaps you are an enemy of the state and maybe even a Jew."

Close to fainting, Rachel sat speechless.

Captain Schoenfelder rose, removed his Luger from its holster, and opened the compartment door. He motioned for one of the armed guards to watch over Rachel while he proceeded to the other compartment.

Entering, he glared at the nuns. "I ought to arrest all of you for meddling in German affairs that have nothing to do with you. Aiding anyone in an escape attempt is a crime punishable by death. I should have the four of you shot as an example. I will notify the Gestapo in Soverato of your activities. Do you understand me?"

"What will you do with our sister?" Sister Evangeline asked.

"She will be transported back to Soverato for questioning."

Captain Schoenfelder left the compartment and returned to where Rachel was being guarded. At the next station, she was removed from the train and escorted back to Soverato.

The following six days were filled with systematic physical and psychological torture. She was deprived of sleep, stripped naked, and confined to a freezing damp room in the basement of the German prison. Despite the lack of sleep and the brutal physical torture, she refused to give up the names of anyone who had aided her. The torture escalated. She was repeatedly raped by four of the attending soldiers and warned that she would be made available to the entire barracks when they tired of her.

Nearly insane from the pain, she could no longer hold out and confessed that she had been aided by the nuns in both cities and Mayor Severio Pittelli. Even though they had broken her, she never gave up the name of her beloved David.

She was confined to the dungeon while the Gestapo awaited word from Colonel Richter regarding his disposition of the case.

Chapter Seventy-Six

Woods near Soverato, late March 1944

David stared out the broken window of the abandoned cottage buried deep in the woods near Baldolotto. He had just received the news about Rachael's capture. Sister Mercedita had gotten word to him through the mayor's contacts that she had been captured near Lugano and returned to the German prison in Soverato. He knew the barracks were housed in the center of an old prison on the outskirts of Soverato and would be filled with German soldiers retreating from the Allied advance in the Salerno region.

David understood only too well what the Germans did to their prisoners. Some of his comrades had been captured in Catanzaro the past month. They were tortured for days before the Germans hanged them on piano wire in the main piazza. The thought of Rachel at the mercy of the Gestapo was more than he could bear. His initial impulse was to storm the barracks at Soverato, but that would be headstrong and futile. His group of partisans was primarily interested in acts of sabotage, so the rescue of a single woman would never make even the bottom of the priority list.

The experiences of this past year had changed David from a serene, pensive intellectual into a dedicated assassin. Still, he was uncertain whether he could sustain one more significant loss in his life. He had slit men's throats, blown up trains, and kidnapped high-ranking German officers, but none of that had caused him to suppress the love and dedication he felt toward his loved ones. If he lost Rachel, he didn't know if life would have any meaning for him. He could not eat or sleep for worry.

Engulfed in thought, David did not notice that someone was standing behind him. A few coughs made him turn to find Matteo, his dearest friend and comrade.

"I just heard about Rachel," Matteo said. "Whatever you're planning to do, I want to help. I have lost my parents and brother to these bastards."

"Thank you." David was deeply touched. Any rescue attempt would pose almost certain death for all involved. He reached out to shake Matteo's hand, but Matteo grabbed him and held him with such intensity that the tears that had been blocked flowed against the gentle giant's chest.

"I understand, David," Matteo said, with a gentle pat on the back. "We will find a way."

"I must save her."

"We will. Without your knowledge, I concocted a plan that I hope will lead to Rachel's escape. I know a partisan who grew up in the Tyrol area, but he was educated in Germany and is fluent in the language. The essence of my plan is to secure false transit visas and present a document ordering Rachel to be transferred to Catanzaro. In the past week seven German soldiers have been ambushed by partisans outside of Baldolotto's high command. The easiest part of the plan is securing German uniforms. After that, pray for luck."

David immediately hugged his friend. "I will never forget this, Matteo. When can we make the attempt?"

"I got these architectural drawings from the mayor. They show the egress and access. No doubt, it holds high risk, but I believe we can do it."

"For me there is no risk because life without Rachel would not be worth living. But, Matteo, I fear for your safety."

Matteo shrugged. "I always wanted to be an actor; this will give me a chance to play a part on a bigger screen. The only negative aspect is wearing a German uniform. I'll have to hold my nose while I get dressed."

David smiled. "Do you speak any German?"

"Actually I do. *Kusse mein tuchas in der Rhein.*"

"What the hell does that mean?"

"Kiss my ass in the Rhein."

David laughed for the first time in days. "I'm sure your fluency will really make a difference." He grew serious. "What do we do next?"

"Follow me."

David and Matteo left the upstairs of the cottage to look for Antonio, the German-speaking partisan who had agreed to be the official interpreter. David knew the plan would rise or fall on Antonio's ability to fool the German officers in Soverato.

When the three partisans were ready to rescue Rachel, they drove into the prison courtyard. German soldiers were busy loading trucks that appeared to hold building materials. Two armed sentries stopped the vehicle containing David, Matteo, and Antonio. As the guard asked for documents, Matteo rolled down the window.

Seated in the back of the automobile, Antonio opened the door on the left side, got out of the car and in impeccable German addressed the sentry in a very harsh voice. "Is it the custom of a German soldier to be so sloppily dressed? Are you not aware that you represent the Führer?"

The sentry, whose uniform was open at the top, attempted to close a button, dropping the papers Matteo had given him.

Antonio continued to berate the soldier. "Do I have to wait all day while you get properly dressed? What is your name?"

In a trembling voice, the man replied, "Corporal Dettmer."

"Well, Corporal Dettmer, if I ever see you again in this fashion I will personally send you to the Russian front. Now open the gate."

Antonio reentered the vehicle while the flustered corporal opened the gate.

"Well done, Herr Antonio. You acted just like one of the swine," Matteo said.

"That was the easy part."

Matteo parked the car, and the three men quickly entered the building where they were met by a German sergeant who reviewed their papers. They were ushered into the main office, and the sergeant introduced them to the officer on duty. After examining their documents, he led them to the basement where all prisoners were kept.

Fearing that if Rachel saw him she would give away the plan, David hung back in the hallway.

"Open cell door number seven," the officer commanded.

The prison guard opened the door, stepped into the cell and said, "Get up, you bitch, and get dressed. You are going to Catanzaro."

David squelched his rage as Rachel stumbled out of the cell. He was horrified at her condition. Her face was so swollen that her eyes were totally closed. Her entire body was bruised and her scalp was covered with patches of dried blood.

Antonio grabbed Rachel's arm and said in brusque German, "You will come with us and tell us everything you know about the partisans in this area."

As they ascended the stairway, the German officer attempted to engage Matteo in conversation. "Where are you from in Germany?"

Matteo ignored him, keeping all of them walking at a fast pace.

"Answer me," the officer commanded.

Matteo ignored him again.

"Stop!" the officer shouted, reaching for his Luger.

Without hesitation, Antonio reached out, grabbed the officer by the neck and snapped it as if it were a twig. One of the soldiers in the corridor blew his whistle. Matteo turned and fired, but the sound of the whistle had already reached the first floor. Three armed guards descended the stairs, firing as they approached the group. All of the guards were killed in the skirmish.

Matteo clutched his chest, mortally wounded. David tried to lift him, but Matteo refused his aid. "You must leave now."

Torn, David hesitated, but Matteo pushed him forward. "Please, live for me."

David clasped Rachel's hand. "You're safe now." He felt her tremble as he led her forward.

Apparently the sounds of gunfire had not been heard by the guards in the courtyard. The thick walls of the basement had muted them. They walked through the prison corridors with an air of normality. The appearance was that of the simple transfer of a prisoner.

Once outside the prison, David gently helped Rachel into their automobile. As Antonio drove past the sentry point without incident, Rachel said, "I thought you were a dream."

"I will always be here for you."

Chapter Seventy-Seven

Soverato, April 3, 1944

Things had been going well for Sergeant Oberkfell since his assignment to the detention center in Soverato. First he was included in the process of determining the validity of official documents by Lieutenant Wolfe. This morning he was notified that because Wolfe was out of town for two days, Colonel Richter had a very important task for him to perform. As he entered the corridor leading to the colonel's office, he did a quick self-inspection to make sure that his uniform was neatly tucked and his shoes gleamed. It was common knowledge that the colonel was a stickler for rules and he wanted to make a good impression. He knocked lightly on the colonel's door.

"Come in, Sergeant."

"Good morning. Heil Hitler."

"Heil Hitler!" Colonel Richter said. "Please be seated. Before we begin this morning, I would like to offer you some coffee and genuine German strudel. I received it last night from one of my comrades who passed through on his way to Rome."

"Thank you, Colonel. That's very kind of you."

"Sergeant, it has come to my attention that persons have recently been captured by the Gestapo despite the fact that they had perfect passports and travel visas. They were captured for other mistakes they made, but these authentic documents have become of great concern to me and the high command. I am going to need your direct assistance in this matter."

"I am privileged to be of help."

"Help me understand what happened at the meeting between you and Lieutenant Wolfe."

"Well, sir, at the detention center in the locked document room we examined authentic documents so that we would know how to spot counterfeit ones held by enemies of the state."

"Who has the key to the document center?"

"To my understanding, there are only two keys. You have one and I have the other."

"Do we have an exact inventory of what is contained in the document room?"

"Yes, sir. There is a series of seals and all of the passports and travel visas are numbered."

"When was the last time you took an accurate accounting of the entire room?"

"Six weeks ago."

"Sergeant, I am going to rely on your absolute discretion to take that inventory and to tell absolutely no one—and I mean no one—about this assignment. Do you understand?"

"Absolutely, Colonel Richter. I will begin the work immediately. It should be finished by morning."

"Thank you, Sergeant Oberkfell. You have been most helpful."

"You are welcome. Heil Hitler."

"Heil Hitler!"

Colonel Richter had always known that Lieutenant Wolfe was resistant to the detention center, but now he would receive concrete proof that would enable him to root out all opposition and finish the center at the same time. If any seals or documents were missing, he would have the leverage to deal with Wolfe and Pittelli. He smiled and pressed his hands together, anticipating the series of chess moves he would make after the sergeant's report. Wolfe and

Pittelli had no idea who they were dealing with, but they would soon find out.

Sergeant Oberkfell was frantic as he searched the document room over and over. He could not fathom how one of the seals and three official documents were missing. His instinct told him that perhaps he should speak to Lieutenant Wolfe to see if he had any idea, but he resisted because he had been pledged to absolute secrecy. He decided he would tell only the colonel about his findings.

Colonel Richter thanked the sergeant for his information and again exacted a promise of absolute secrecy. He was now able to implement the plan he had devised the previous night. He took a piece of official letter paper out of his desk and composed a personal invitation.

Dear Dr. and Mrs. Wolfe,
It gives me great pleasure to invite you to attend a surprise dinner honoring your son next week. I have arranged for army personnel to drive you here, and my office will arrange your accommodations. Again, I would like to remind you that this is a surprise. I know your son will be thrilled to see you.

Sincerely,
Colonel Georg Richter

Rising early had been Richter's custom since childhood, but this morning he was awake even earlier than usual. Sleep was not interrupted by anything that troubled his spirit, but rather by the joyful anticipation of his meeting with Lieutenant Wolfe. Weeks of annoyance and anger were now to cease as he compiled the list of obstacles that soon would be eliminated. Wolfe, Pittelli, and a host of minor players thought they could sabotage his plans. With their feeble attempts they had been lulled into the belief that they could block the building of the center.

Now Richter had the evidence to deal with all of them, and this pocket of resistance would soon be blotted from the face of the earth. The detention center would be a masterful achievement that would enable him to achieve Himmler's goal of a Jew-free Italy. The Jews would be transported seamlessly to Auschwitz.

Richter would receive the Berlin staff position he deserved. In many respects, the final triumph in Soverato would be more satisfying than the annihilation of the Roman ghetto. There had been no real resistance in Rome; it had been merely a question of logistics. In this tiny hamlet there had been intrigue, sabotage, betrayal, and a group of meddling neophytes who challenged his ability to overcome their collusion.

Like a child who cannot wait for Christmas morning, he glanced at his watch every five minutes as he warmed his hands by the fire and dreamed of his place at the inner circle in Berlin.

Lieutenant Franz Wolfe had apprehensions about his meeting with Colonel Richter even though the center was nearly finished. The structure was intact and certainly there could be some minor glitches, but the time of subverting Richter's will had passed. The good news was that while Richter was away Franz and Severio had developed serious plans for a mass escape and the opportunity to save more refugees and Jews. He had never underestimated Colonel Richter, but he was also well aware that he and the other conspirators had caught a break with Hanke's absence. The mayor had told him that Hanke had been killed by the partisans. Their plans would have been seriously hampered had Hanke been present in Soverato.

Lieutenant Wolfe arrived at the colonel's office precisely at eight in the morning. He saluted the colonel. The salute was not returned. The colonel motioned for him to be seated. Lieutenant Wolfe had the same reaction he had had in combat just before the shelling began; there was an eerie silence in the room and the tension was palpable.

Colonel Richter sat for a few moments just staring at him from behind his desk. Finally he said, "Lieutenant, there have been some extraordinary events that have occurred in my absence that require me to determine whether these events are somehow linked."

"Sir, what events are you referring to?"

The colonel took a pad from his desk and began to create what appeared to be a road map. "Let me begin with a Jewish woman by the name of Rachel Lamendola. She was captured near the Swiss border attempting to escape. She was impersonating a Catholic nun and had what appeared to be a valid passport and travel documents. Do you know this woman?"

"Sir, I do not." The chess game had begun and he must carefully anticipate the next move.

"She lived with the mayor and she was helped to escape from the Gestapo headquarters in Soverato two days ago. Three guards were murdered in the escape. Did you know about this?"

"I heard about the escape, but I have no knowledge of who she was."

"Did you have any civilian reprisals for these murders?"

"No, Colonel Richter. I did not think it was under my jurisdiction."

"I know that Mayor Pittelli had her placed in a Benedictine convent. Do you believe he was behind the escape?"

"I would seriously doubt that. He is not a violent man."

The colonel continued to sketch his map. "The next interesting piece of my puzzle is that Captain Erich Hanke boarded a train from Rome to Soverato. He never arrived here. Now one could make the supposition that he is AWOL, but I know this man and he relished being my direct assistant in Soverato so that is not plausible. Do you have any suspicion as to what happened to Captain Hanke?"

It appeared to Wolfe that the colonel was ready to confront him but was enjoying the situation too much to precipitate confrontation just yet. "I have no idea where he is. Why would you even ask me that question?"

"Patience, Lieutenant Wolfe. All of your questions will be duly answered." Again Richter wrote on his pad. "Next there is the question of the vanishing Jews of Soverato. Yesterday I assigned guards from the barracks to pick up four Jewish families for questioning, but these families have mysteriously disappeared and no one knows where they are. Can you imagine where they are?"

"I have no idea."

"The next part of all of these seemingly unconnected events is that documents and seals are missing from the records office. Do you have any knowledge of this?"

"Why would I?"

"Sergeant Oberkfell informed me that you requested a series of travel documents and visas. Why did you need them?"

"I needed them so that I could spot forgeries. Seeing original documents enabled me to do my duty."

"Why didn't you notify me about your interest in that type of work?" Ritcher probed.

"I thought you were only interested in capturing and housing Jews in our area."

"Do you think I'm a fool, Lieutenant Wolfe?"

"Certainly not, but I have trouble following your logic." Wolfe was poised for Richter to make his final move.

"You have never shown any enthusiasm for our mission, Lieutenant Wolfe, and I believe you have failed in your work."

"My record is unblemished. There is nothing to indicate that I have failed."

"Your record prior to Soverato is unblemished, it's true, but I believe you are in league with this incompetent mayor."

"You have no evidence to support this."

"I have all the evidence that I need."

"And what precisely is your evidence?"

"You have been involved directly with providing documentation to unauthorized persons." Richter pointed a finger at Wolfe.

"You have no proof of that. The only thing you can convict me of is that I have raised legitimate concerns about innocent civilians."

"Innocent civilians? As a soldier you are required to rid Italy of the Jewish plague."

Wolfe knew the game was up. "Real soldiers do not harm innocent civilians. There can never be any justification for this, no matter what glorious goals are put forth."

"And is your vision superior to that of the Führer?"

"I was so devoted to the Führer that I would have given every drop of my blood for the fatherland. However, I did not realize that the price for his utopia would be the suspension of humanity's most basic laws of decency."

"You are on dangerous ground, Lieutenant Wolfe."

"We are both on dangerous moral ground if we do not see what we are involved in."

"Are you directly refusing to participate in plans that have come directly from Himmler?"

"I am questioning the value of these plans because they are in conflict with the military code of honor."

"You are a solder and bound to obey the commands and orders of your superiors."

"But what must I do if the orders are immoral?"

"Morality is not for you to decide."

"I believe that it is something that I must decide."

"Are you willing to suffer the consequences of such behavior?"

"You do not frighten me. I refuse to be any further part of your madness."

"You may assume the role of hero or perhaps even martyr, but I am a master chess player. I knew days ago that you were a traitor. I read your dossier and found the address of your parents in Passau. They are now en route and will be here late tomorrow afternoon under armed guards. They believe they are coming to Soverato for a surprise dinner in your honor. Before they arrive you will have a choice to make. Give me the names and locations of all the Jews in hiding, as well as all the conspirators, or watch your parents be tortured and hanged. Checkmate, Lieutenant Wolfe. Be back here tomorrow at noon to tell me your decision."

"Is there no end to your madness?"

"It is you that is mad. Why give up everything worthwhile for a group of strangers? Will your noble ideas help you with the choices I have given you? Now get out of my sight before I change my mind and shoot you."

Lieutenant Wolfe left the German headquarters knowing that he and his cohorts were in an impossible situation. He had known in his heart that there would be consequences for his actions, but this was viler than he had ever imagined. As he struggled to regain composure, he realized that he needed to inform those who would immediately be impacted. He headed for Mayor Pittelli's office.

He opened the door and before either Salvatore or Severio could greet him, he blurted out, "Colonel Richter knows everything!"

"How the hell did he find out?" Severio asked.

"It's a long story, but part of it is that your cook was captured and confessed."

"Oh my God—Rachel! What have they done to her?"

"That is the only piece of good news. Partisans rescued her. I believe she is safe. Richter will make examples of us to show his complete authority. He will begin with you, Severio, and your family."

"So you really think he will publicly execute me?"

"Not just you, but your wife and children."

"That fucking bastard!" Salvatore said. "We have to kill him."

Wolfe shook his head. "Killing him would only make it worse. The high command would order reprisals and hundreds would be murdered to avenge his death."

Severio nodded in agreement. "Does he know that you gave us the documents?"

"He does. He set the perfect trap for me. He sent for my parents. They will arrive tomorrow afternoon. They believe there is to be a ceremony to honor me, but he will use them to get us all. He gave me two choices. Turn over all involved and the locations of all Jews in hiding, or watch my parents hang. I must give him my answer at noon tomorrow."

"Why didn't he demand the choice immediately?"

"He wants me to suffer all night with the choices."

"Richter must be killed." Salvatore paced the room.

"We still have some time," Severio said. "Let us agree to do nothing foolish and to meet here tonight at midnight."

"I'll be here," Franz Wolfe said.

Severio put his hand on Wolfe's shoulder. "Franz, somehow there will be a way."

Wolfe left, shaking his head.

Severio pursued one dead end after another with Salvatore. After three hours, Severio's face suddenly lit up.

"Salvatore, is your cousin the physician a fascist?"

"Of course not. What the hell has my cousin to do with this?"

"What are his politics?"

"Same as mine. He thinks all politicians are full of shit. Forget my cousin. Let's focus on what we're going to do."

"Call your cousin and have him meet us here. Tell him it's a matter of life and death."

Chapter Seventy-Eight

Soverato, Colonel Richter's office the next day

Today was going to be a red-letter day in the career of Colonel Georg Richter. He had proved his mettle on the battlefields of Poland and Russia, but now he could add master detective and sleuth to his achievements. In a few moments Lieutenant Wolfe, the smug aristocrat, would come into his office and beg for mercy. After Richter remained resolute, the lieutenant would provide all of the information necessary to break the organization that had the audacity to oppose the will of the German government. Once this was achieved, Wolfe would probably believe that Richter would spare him and his parents, but the true joy would come when Richter informed the lieutenant that his parents would join Wolfe's friends on the gallows. Lieutenant Franz Wolfe's fate would be prolonged torture.

Richter looked at his watch and happily observed that it was almost noon. He poured a cup of coffee, the third of the morning. He walked behind his desk, set down his cup, and assumed the solemn face of judge and executioner.

Lieutenant Franz Wolfe entered the room with a calm demeanor. "Before I give you my choice, I want to ask you a question."

"What is your question?"

Wolfe walked to one corner of the room where a large map of Europe hung on the wall. He pointed at the map, and then he stepped back to Richter's desk. "Please show me so that I can understand Germany's great destiny. What do you envision that map will look like in two years?"

Richter appeared surprised and pleased by the question. He stood up, turned his back on Wolfe and walked toward the map. He picked up a pointer.

Lieutenant Wolfe took advantage of the diversion he had created to pull a vial out of his pocket and pour a clear liquid into the colonel's cup of coffee.

"Hitler's vision is my vision. I see a Germany that totally dominates Europe." Richter pointed to various places on the map. "There will be German troops in every one of these countries. The economies will thrive due to German superiority. In each of these lands there will be no trace of the Jewish race. The map will be labeled the Golden Era of German History. Nothing can stop the Third Reich."

"That is what I thought you would see," Wolfe said.

"Exactly." Richter set down the pointer, returned to his desk, and began to drink his coffee.

"So, Colonel Richter, you envision what the Führer promised the German people?"

"Lieutenant, I see unique structures created by German architects like Dr. Speer that dominate every city in Europe. Cultural and business centers that are founded on the genius of the German government will be the norm. I see an end to the stranglehold of all organized religion. There will be the finest universities that will develop curricula that laud the wonder of the Third Reich. The entire world will know how our Fatherland rose from the ignominy of Versailles to the land where the Führer is revered as prophet and war king. A land where the weak perish and the strong enjoy the spoils of war for a thousand years. Do you once again see what I see?"

Wolfe stood in front of the colonel's desk. "I see a different scenario. Every major German city will be obliterated by bombings. The German people will rise up and overcome their Nazi masters. I see a world where those who were murdered are remembered. I see a sentence of infamy for Hitler and all the monsters that followed him. I see humankind never again allowing a race to be murdered for bogus racial purity."

With the veins bulging in his neck, Richter shouted, "You are a coward and a traitor!"

"And you are a monster so filled with hate that you do not deserve to breathe the same air as those you persecute."

"Turncoat! I'll take special pleasure in torturing you and your family."

"Enough. You presented me with two choices. The first was to reveal the names of the local Jews and all who aided them. The second was to refuse the first and know that my parents would die. Two impossible choices. Each is so horrible that your sadistic mind would rejoice in either of them. Checkmate. As a master chess player, I assume that is what you thought."

"True!"

"Your move to end the game was premature. Your lack of imagination precluded another possibility. The choice I make is that *you* will die instead of the Jews or my parents."

Richter laughed. "If you kill me, there will be reprisals and hundreds will die. I, on the other hand, would receive an honored soldier's burial with all appropriate pomp. In death, I would still be victorious."

"I don't think you understand, Colonel Richter. No one is going to kill you. The choice will be all yours. You are going to kill yourself."

"That is preposterous. I would not kill myself even if you tortured me."

"That will not be necessary; you are going to kill yourself with your own Luger. You see, you have received a drug in your coffee that in a few instants will paralyze you. Once this occurs, I will take your gun, put it into your hand, raise it to your temple and assist your finger in pulling the trigger."

"Ridiculous. I feel fine." Colonel Richter attempted to pull out his revolver, but he no longer had the necessary coordination.

Wolfe stripped away Richter's Luger.

"The guard outside the door will hear and know what you have done," Colonel Richter said in a weak voice, collapsing into his chair.

"There is no guard. This morning I gave him detailed instructions regarding a shipment of construction materials that were to be checked. He has been reassigned to your beloved detention center and will be gone for hours. I had a chat with him. I asked him if you had been behaving strangely lately. I strongly hinted that I was concerned about your mental health."

Richter weakly clawed at his collar, breath rasping in this throat. "Don't do this. There is still time."

"On the contrary. There is very little time. First I would like to read the names of some of those so-called weak individuals who defeated you." Wolfe pulled a list from his jacket and read, "Rabbi Contini, Mayor Pittelli, Salvatore Salvato, and Rachel Ferrara." The list went on.

As Franz Wolfe read the names, he placed the Luger in Richter's hand and raised it to his head. He squeezed the trigger. The revolver fired. Richter slumped to the floor.

"You will murder no more Jews."

Lieutenant Franz Wolfe left the room, walked through the front entrance, and crossed the piazza.

Later that day, Wolfe joined Mayor Pittelli, who sat in the sunshine reading the paper as if he had not a care in the world. Franz ordered an espresso and turned to the mayor with a huge grin on his face.

"You would not believe that anyone would take his life on such a glorious day, but someone we know did. Colonel Georg Richter is dead. I will report the suicide to my superior in Florence."

"Will he accept the death as a suicide?"

When the waiter brought the espresso, Wolfe gulped it down. "That's the beauty of this. I am very close to Richter's superior officer. He will accept my version. I'll embellish the colonel's behavior and make it more than believable."

"I wonder if they'll send us another such officer."

"Perhaps. It is possible they will elevate me to the position."

"Could we be so fortunate?"

"Maybe. Even so, there will still be danger."

"True. Yet every day that we can postpone the horror lives will be saved."

Wolfe nodded. "Sometimes I cannot believe that I am immersed in this drama."

"You are involved because in your soul there is a sense of right and wrong. If we live through this, we will never regret what we've done."

Wolfe shook Severio's hand. "Today is not a day for espresso." He hailed the waiter. "Champagne!"

As they toasted all who helped in the demise of Colonel Richter, Severio appeared concerned. "What will become of the detention center?"

Franz Wolfe smiled wryly. "The Lord often works in mysterious ways. Sometimes buildings catch fire and burn to the ground. Many times it is the fault of electrical wires. If that should happen, I would expect you to stamp 'urgent' on the rebuilding process."

Severio smiled, nodding. "I'll keep that stamp ready."

They raised their champagne glasses and drank to their future.

Author's Note

On a beautiful morning in Rome, I drank coffee at the Piazza Nova and spent hours reading in the shadow of one of the most beautiful fountains in Europe. As I perused the *Herald Tribune*, which kept me in touch with the States, I was entranced by the Fountain of the Four Great Rivers. The magical sound of the water and the beauty of the statues gave life to the fountain. I felt lucky to be in this magnificent city as a student priest and to have the opportunity to roam through the annals of history.

With all of Rome's varied treasures, I had to resist the temptation to see it as a tourist. It is a city of living moments that leap out from doorways, fountains, and cobblestone streets. The voices of the Forum can still almost be heard as the sun glances off the Palatine Hill. Rome touches hearts and souls, especially mine. I could even imagine having lived there in another life. With all these poetic ruminations rushing through my veins, I finished my last drop of coffee. I still could not summon up the desire to leave this wonderful piazza. I ordered another cup.

There was no immediate need for me to race back to the Graduate House of Theological Studies, so I went for a promenade toward Saint Peter's Square. Along the way I met a group of American tourists and offered my services as a tour guide who would escort them through Saint Peter's. I enjoyed hearing the familiar accents of New York, New Jersey, and the East Coast, which immediately took me back to the land of my birth.

After an hour of pointing out what I knew, I bade them farewell and made my way back to the college. I was in my room for about ten minutes when the switchboard rang and told me that I had a call from the States. I was pleasantly surprised, but I couldn't imagine who would be calling me.

When I was connected by the operator, I could tell by the tone of Tom Daly's voice that something was wrong. My first thoughts went to my parents, but in that case, why wasn't my brother or sister calling? Tom didn't mince words. "Sal, I have terrible news. Jack Murphy was killed in an accident last night."

Shocked to the core, I blanked out on the rest of the conversation and merely muttered that I would take the next plane home. Jack was a fellow priest. We had been stationed together in Westfield, New Jersey, for the last three years. He was my best friend. I could not imagine him dead at the age of twenty-nine.

The plane ride was interminable, as were the memories of Jack. His innocent face could charm the devil out of his socks. He was a choir boy who always had the twinkle of mayhem in his Irish smile. Once when we were in New York wearing lay clothing so we could better blend into the crowd, he took me to Asti's Restaurant where they sang Italian opera because he knew how much I loved opera. Arriving at the restaurant, we saw a long line of people waiting to get in. Jack told me to wait while he went into the restaurant. In the blink of an eye, he returned and informed me that I was now Dr. Tagliareni, the great Italian heart surgeon from Rome.

We were led to the head of the line by Mr. Asti and escorted to a ringside table. Stunned by Jack's crazy behavior, I whispered to him, "What the hell do I do if someone has a heart problem here?" With a twinkle in his eyes, he said, "Just start banging on their chest." That was Jack, a life force that captivated everyone who was privileged to know him. Now he was dead. I was devastated by the loss, not only for myself but for all the other people in his life.

I resumed smoking cigarettes and chain-smoked the entire flight. Arriving at Kennedy Airport, I was greeted by close friends. Reality hit me hard. My emotional pain began to intensify. I learned that Jack had visited my mother the evening he died because he was coming to see me in Rome two weeks later and she had a package for him to deliver to me. She had asked him to stay for dinner, but he had plans to dine with a colleague, Bill Kelly, and told her that he would take a rain check. After dinner, Jack and Bill left the restaurant in a blinding storm. Jack missed a turn and wound up in the wrong lane. A mile down the road, at the peak of an incline, he hit a car head-on. He and the driver of the other car were killed instantly. Bill was asleep on impact and only slightly injured.

Listening to the details made Jack's death even more real to me. As I approached the rectory where my friend's body was to be viewed, I felt sick. I stumbled into the parlor and knelt by his casket. Tears flowed. This wonderful man who had brought so much light to others was now gone from our midst and the pain was beyond belief. His wonderful family was there to comfort, as Jack would have done. It was easy to understand the source of his kindness and love.

The next three days I preached sermons about my friend. Little did I know that though I was in agony, this would be the easy part. The real anguish would come with the loneliness that gripped me when I returned to Europe. The loss was so final. It remains with me to this day because of who he was and the joy and meaning his friendship had for me.

Jack's death shook the roots of all my beliefs of immortality that are the province of the young. We are on a road that isn't supposed to turn toward death and illness, at least not until we pass the demarcation of middle age. It was difficult to comprehend that Jack, a person so alive with all of the energy and dynamism of youth, had ceased to be. The pain was searing and kept floating to the surface through a familiar song, a favorite place, or the mention of his name. There were no insulated places where the pain did not seep.

In Rome, I was immersed in overwhelming sadness. How could such a vital life be obliterated? Depressed and feeling alone, I reread *Man's Search for Meaning,* the account of the Holocaust through the eyes of Dr. Viktor Frankl, the Jewish psychiatrist. Each page seemed directed to my feelings. I knew that, somehow, this book would be the beginning of my healing.

Dr. Frankl was teaching at the University of Vienna, not so far away. I decided that I would try to make the opportunity to study with him. I called the university and asked to be connected with Dr. Frankl's office. To my amazement, Dr. Frankl answered the phone. After a few moments of conversation, he invited me to visit him at the university.

I found it easy to fly to Vienna on the following Tuesday. The plane ride was smooth, but my stomach was in knots at the thought of being in the presence of someone whose work and life I had come to admire so greatly. I practiced my responses to the questions that I thought he would ask, but they seemed stilted and plastic. No amount of practice was going to make me comfortable with the actual meeting.

The cab ride seemed too brief. By the time I ascended the steps of the university, I was soaked with sweat. My rational side asked, "Why are you letting this get to you? You've met dozens of renowned people before. This is not your first excursion into the world of the famous." This momentary respite was drowned in my gastric juices and the urge to bolt and run. My brain attempted to halt the panic with the plausible question, "What's the worst thing that can happen?" Instead of creating calm this pushed my anxiety into high gear.

The secretary ushered me into a small waiting room. After a short time, she asked me to walk up a flight of stairs where Dr. Frankl would meet me. Fortunately, I had passed the panic stage and had somehow attained a state of assurance that all would be fine. As I reached the top of the stairwell, there stood a short man with a gleaming head of snow-white hair. Dr. Frankl seemed engrossed in what he was reading and did not notice me standing there. I stood silently and waited to be recognized. Finally he noticed me. I was struck by his chiseled features and electric blue eyes. He warmly shook my hand as he welcomed me to Vienna. Bolting at a pace I could hardly keep up with, he led me to a small lecture room where we chatted for the next two hours.

I became Dr. Viktor Frankl's student, and he radically changed my life. The Holocaust, which I had always regarded as a tragic episode, transformed into personal reality in our many conversations. Never preaching or ranting with the righteous vengeance of one who had lost so much, he often stopped in the middle of a conversation that had no connection to his incarceration to tell a story as though it had happened yesterday. The horrible but distant statistics, categorized in columns of numbers, became people with names, faces, and stories. These were sisters, mothers, fathers, friends, old, and young. No longer were they numbers in history class or newsreel moments that flashed on the screen and then faded away.

The horror became more intense when it had reference points to my life. Although no one can fully understand the Holocaust, I began to see it in the light of my own human experience. These moments at dinner, during class, while walking through the city with him, or speaking with other Holocaust victims, opened a wellspring of insight that was powerful and clear, even without smooth edges and final conclusions.

Through Dr. Viktor Frankl's eyes and the experiences of other survivors, I witnessed the stories of the atrocities. I understood that it could have happened to me and my loved ones. I imagined holding the hands of my infant children, waiting to be slaughtered, or watching my parents be herded into a cattle car bound for the crematoria. His words and the stories of so many others who contacted him daily had a lasting impact on my consciousness and spirit. They made the events tangible and were bridges to those horrendous times. No one could ever understand or explain the evil that they had experienced firsthand, but their pain had a lasting impact on me.

Time does not diminish the acts of cruelty that are the hallmarks of the Holocaust. It is not the passage of time that heals the wounds of these horrors. To continuously honor the victims and recount the stories is not the maudlin search for vengeance. It is the obligation to keep alive that portion of those who suffered by personalizing their lives. These were not merely numbers that can be aggregated into collective tragedy. These were singular persons with the human needs and drives that we all possess. They were neighbors, friends, members of their communities, parents, children, elders. Life was stripped away from them without cause.

Now I live with **Dr. Viktor Frankl's** stories in my mind and soul. In memory of all those who died and all those who at great risk stood up for the Jews, I have finally shared some of these stories in hopes of raising the reality that there were people all along the spectrum of this enormous atrocity. There were those who relished the horrors, those who courageously overtly and covertly opposed the policies of their governments, and those who around the world—the majority of people—stood in silence and washed their hands of culpability.

Hitler's Priest is one story within the larger story of the Holocaust. I focus on two families that lived through this period, basing most events on reality, to keep vigil against the forces of evil that created the Holocaust. I will always be grateful to those who shared their pain and memories with me.

About the Author

Salvatore Tagliareni is a story teller, writer, business consultant, art dealer, and former catholic priest. For over twenty-five years he has successfully engaged private and public companies in their search for outstanding performance. A gifted speaker, he is blessed with a great sense of humor and can invigorate an audience with his insights on life and leadership. He was profoundly influenced by his relationship with Dr. Viktor Frankl, the author of *Man's Search for Meaning*. The desire to humanize the memory of those that perished in the Holocaust is imbedded in his spirit.

An accomplished strategic thinker, he is also captivated by the search for wonderful food and wine. His ultimate goal is to find the perfect cannoli.